BUT *THOSE* WEAPONS ARE NOT PERMITTED . . .

Kana began to climb. His nails tore and broke and his uniform was plastered with dust and clay, but he wormed his way up into the embrace of a thorny bush.

"Terra?" He kept his voice low. But at the answer to his question he pushed forward recklessly. That moan could only have been born of real suffering.

His forward spring brought him to the very edge of the thicket facing west. Collapsed half over a fallen tree, veiled from the Llor riders by only a thin screen of brush, was a limp body.

Kana hardly dared to touch the body when he saw the extent of the burns which had charred away most of the green-gray tunic. Flamer wound! He turned the heavy head to the light. The flamer had not touched the face and though it was contorted and twisted in agony, Kana knew who it was he supported in his arms.

"Deke! What—what have they done!"

The dark eyes struggled to focus. It was as if Deke Mills came haltingly back from a long distance, driven by some overwhelming sense of duty.

"All—dead— Hart Device— Tell Hansu—Hart Device— Galactic—agent—hiding— Burned us down." Some spark of strength steadied his voice. "Tried—tried to get Yorke to renegade too. When he said no—flamed us from behind. All dead—thought me dead too. Crawled—crawled—hours and hours crawled. They had flamers— Tell Hansu—flamers—"

"There's a Galactic Agent with them and they have C.C. arms," Kana repeated with cold steadiness.

"Tell Hansu—C.C. behind it—wipe us out if they can. Mustn't be cut off here. Back to ships—report— From behind—no chance—" Mills' whisper thinned and then died. . . .

BAEN BOOKS BY ANDRE NORTON

Time Traders
Time Traders II
Star Soldiers
Warlock
Janus

STAR SOLDIERS

ANDRE NORTON

STAR SOLDIERS

This is a work of fiction. All the characters and events portrayed in this book are fictional, and any resemblance to real people or incidents is purely coincidental.

A Baen Books Original Omnibus

Baen Publishing Enterprises
P.O. Box 1403
Riverdale, NY 10471
www.baen.com

ISBN: 0-7434-3554-0

Cover art by Stephen Hickman

First paperback printing, August 2002
Second paperback printing, November 2002

Cataloging-in-Publication Number 2001025926

Distributed by Simon & Schuster
1230 Avenue of the Americas
New York, NY 10020

Typeset by Brilliant Press
Printed in the United States of America

Contents

STAR GUARD

Introduction:
The Mercenaries

When the dominant species of a minor nine-planet system revolving about a yellow sun known as "Sol"—situated close to the fringe of the Galaxy—gained knowledge of space flight and came out into our lanes of travel there arose a problem which Central Control had to solve, and speedily. These "men," as they called themselves, combined curiosity, daring, and technical skill with a basic will-to-compete against other races and species, an in-born thrust to conflict. Their answer to any problem was aggressive. Had this "will-to-battle" not been recognized at once for what it was and channeled into proper outlet, infinitesimal as their numbers were among us, we have been told that their influence might have torn asunder the peace of the stellar lanes and plunged whole sectors into war.

But the proper steps were taken at once and the Terrans were assigned a role which not only suited their nature but also provided a safety valve for all other belligerents among the systems which make up our great confederacy. Having been studied and carefully evaluated by Central Control psycho-techneers the Terrans were appointed to act as the mercenaries of the Galaxy—until such a time as these too independent and aggressive creatures would develop for themselves some less dangerous calling.

Thus there came into being the "Hordes" and "Legions" we find mentioned again and again in the various solar histories of the period. These organizations, manned by either "Archs" or "Mechs," carried on a formalized warfare for any planetary ruler who desired to enhance his prestige by employing them to fight his battles.

The Archs who comprised the Hordes were limited to service upon primitive worlds, being equipped with hand weapons and fighting in personal combat. The Mechs of the Legions followed technical warfare, indulging in it, however, more as a game in which it was necessary to make one's opponent concede victory, often without actual battle.

When still in the newly hatched stage "men" were selected to be either "Archs" or "Mechs" by rigid aptitude tests. After a period of intensive schooling in their trade they signed on for "enlistments" under field commanders. A portion of each payment made to the individual Horde or Legion commander by his employer was returned to their home world, Terra, as a tax. In other words, this system exported fighting men and the materials for war and became merchants of battle. Within a generation they accepted their role among us, apparently without question.

Three hundred years later (all students turn, please, to folio six, column two—the date of "3956 A.D." is a reckoning peculiar to Terra, we use it in your source material for this section because all reading will be based upon certain accounts written by the Terrans themselves) a minor Horde was employed by a rebellious native ruler on Fronn. While so engaged this organization uncovered a situation which changed history for their species, and perhaps for the Galaxy as well. Whether this change will operate for the general good for us all remains to be seen.

(From a lecture in "Galactic History XX" delivered by Hist-Techneer Zorzi at the Galactic University of Zacan—Subject of the lecture: Minor Systems' Contribution to Historic Changes—presented first on Zol-Day, 4130 A.D.—Terran reckoning.)

1

Swordsman,
Third Class

Because he had never been in Prime before, Kana Karr, Arch Swordsman, Third Class, would have liked nothing better than to brace his lanky length against the wall of the airport and stare up at those towers thrusting into the steely blue of the morning sky. But to do that was to betray himself as a greenie, so he had to be satisfied with glances skyward taking in as much of the awesome sight as he could without becoming conspicuous. More than ever he resented the fate which had delivered him at Combatant Headquarters a whole month later than his recruit class, so that he would probably be the only newcomer among those awaiting assignment in the Hiring Hall.

Actually to be at Prime itself was exciting. This was the goal toward which ten years of intensive training had pointed him. He put down his war bag and rubbed his damp hands surreptitiously against his tight breeches; though it was a crisp early spring day he was sweating. The stiff collar of his new green-gray tunic sawed at his throat and the cheek wings of his dress helmet chafed his jaws. All his accouterments weighed more than they ever had before.

He was acutely conscious of the bare state of the belts crossing his shoulders, of the fact that his helmet was still crestless. The men who had shared the shuttle with him, scintillated with the gemmed loot of scores of successful missions, veterans every one of them.

Well—to achieve that status was only a matter of time, he repeated silently once more. Every one of these emblazoned figures now passing had stood there once, just as bare of insignia, probably just as uncertain inside as he now was—

Kana's attention was caught by another color, blazingly alive among the familiar waves of green-gray and silver. As his lips made a narrow line, his blue eyes, so startlingly vivid in his dark face, chilled.

A surface mobile had drawn up before the entrance of the very building to which he had been directed. And climbing out of it was a squat man swathed in a brilliant scarlet cloak, behind him two others in black and white. As if their arrival had been signaled, the Terran Combatants on the steps melted to right and left, making a wide path to the door.

But that was not in honor, Kana Karr reminded himself fiercely. Terrans on their home planet paid no deference to Galactic Agents, except in a style so exaggerated as to underline their dislike. There would surely come a time when—

His fists balled as he watched the red cloak and his guardian Galactic Patrolmen vanish inside the Hiring

Hall. Kana had never had direct contact with an Agent. The X-Tees, the non-human Extra-Terrestrials, who had been his instructors after he had proved capable of absorbing X-Tee and Alien Liaison training, were a different class altogether. Perhaps because they were non-human he had never really ranked them among those rulers of Central Control who had generations earlier so blithely termed the inhabitants of Sol's system "barbarians," not eligible for Galactic citizenship except within the narrow limits they defined.

He was conscious that not all his fellows were as resentful of that as he was. Most of his classmates, for example, had been content enough to accept the future so arbitrarily decided for them. Outright rebellion meant the labor camps and no chance to ever go into space. Only a Combatant on military duty had the privilege of visiting the stars. And when Kana had learned that early in his career, he had set himself to acquire the shell of a model Arch, discovering in X-Tee training enough solace to aid his control of the seething hatred for the fact that he was not allowed to range the stars as he willed.

The sharp note of a military whistle proclaiming the hour brought him back to earth and to the problem at hand. He shouldered his war bag and climbed the steps up which the Agent had gone a few moments before. He left his bag in the lockers by the door and took his place in the line of men winding into the inner hall.

The Mechs in their blue-gray coveralls and bubble helmets outnumbered the Archs in his particular section of that creeping line. And the few Archs near him were veterans. Consequently even when surrounded by his kind Kana felt as isolated here as he had in the street.

"They're trying to keep the lid on—but Falfa refused

that assignment for his Legion." The Mech to his left, a man in his thirties with ten enlistment notches on his blade-of-honor, made no effort to keep his voice down.

"He'll face a board for refusing," returned his companion dubiously. "After all there's such a thing as a run of hard luck—"

"Hard luck? Two different Legions don't return from the same job and you talk about luck! I'd say that some investigating was called for. D'you know how many Legions have been written off the rolls in the past five years—twenty! Does that sound like bad luck?"

Kana almost echoed the other listener's gasp. Twenty Legions lost in battle over a period of five years—that *was* pushing the luck theory too far. If the modern, expertly armed Legions which operated only on civilized planets had been so decimated, what of the Hordes that served on barbarian worlds? Had their "luck" been equally bad? No wonder there had been a lot of undercover talk lately, comment that the price Central Control set on space—the price that Terra had paid for almost three hundred years—was too high.

The man before him moved suddenly and Kana hurried to close the gap between them. They were at the enlistment barrier. Kana pulled at the lock on his armlet to have it ready to hand to the Swordtan on duty there. That strip of flexible metal, fed into the record block, would automatically flash on the assignment rolls all the necessary information concerning one Kana Karr, Australian-Malay-Hawaiian, age eighteen and four months, training: basic with X-Tee specialization, previous service: none. And once that went into Hiring there was no turning back. The Swordtan took the band, allowed it to rest on the block for an instant, and handed it back with the lackluster boredom of one condemned to a routine job.

Within there were plenty of empty seats—Mechs to the left, Archs to the right. Kana slipped into the nearest seat and dared to stare about him. Facing the tiers of seats was the assignment board, already blinking orange signals and, although he knew his number could not possibly come up yet, he felt he must watch that steady stream of calls. Most seemed to be for the Mechs—sometimes four and five arose together and went through the door at the far end.

The Archs—Kana leaned forward in his seat to count the men on his side. At least twenty Swordsmen First Class, with even two Swordtans among them, were there. And fifty or more Second Class rankers. But—his eyes sought for other crestless helmets—he was the only Third Class man present. The recruits who had preceded him out of Training must have been hired before he came. Wait—red light—

Two S-2 men got up, settled their tunics with a twitch and adjusted their belts. But before they moved into the aisle there was an interruption. The board flashed white and then off entirely as a small party of men tramped down to ascend two steps to the announcement platform.

A Combatant, lacking the crossed shoulder belts of a field man, but with four stars shining on the breast of his tunic, stepped out to face the murmuring Swordsmen and Mechneers. He was flanked by the red-cloaked Galactic Agent and the latter's Patrolmen. Kana identified the three swiftly—humanoid. The Agent was a Sarmak native, the Patrolmen from Nyorai—the length of their slender legs unmistakable.

"Combatants!" the Terran officer's parade ground trained voice snapped out, to be followed by instant silence. "Certain recent events have made it necessary to make this announcement. We have made a full investigation—with the able assistance of Central

Control facilities—into the trouble on Nevers. It is now certified that our defeat there was the result of local circumstances. The rumors concerning this episode are not to be repeated by any of the Corps—under the rule of loyalty—general code."

What in Terra! Kana's amazement might not be openly registered on the masklike face presented him by the blood of his Malay grandfather, but his mind raced. To make such a statement as that was simply asking for trouble—didn't the officer realize that? The Galactic Agent's frown proved that *he* wasn't pleased. Trouble on Nevers—this was the first he'd heard of it. But he'd wager half his first enlistment pay that within ten minutes every man in this hall would be trying to find out what were the rumors being so vigorously denied. It would spread like oil slick on a river.

The Agent stepped out; he appeared to be arguing with the officer. But here he could only advise—he could not give direct orders. And it was too late to stop the damage now anyway. If he had made this move to allay fear, the Combatant officer had only given it fresh life.

With a decided shake of his head the officer started back down the aisle, the three others having, perforce, to follow him. Once more the lights flickered on the board. But the hum of talk rose to a gale of sound as soon as the door closed behind the quartet.

Kana's attention went back to the board just in time. Three more veterans had arisen on his own side of the hall, and, trailing their numbers, came the familiar combination he had answered to for the past ten years, almost more his name than the one his mixed island ancestry had given him.

Once through the other door he slackened pace, keeping modestly behind the rankers who had answered the same call. Third Class was Third Class and ranked nobody or nothing—except a cadet still in training. He was the lowest of the low and dared not presume to tread upon the heels of the man who had just stepped onto that lift.

The other was an Afro-Arab by his features—with maybe a dash of European blood bequeathed by one of the handful of refugees fleeing south during the nuclear wars. He was very tall, and the beardless, dark skin of his face was seamed with an old scar. But the loot of many campaigns blazed from his helmet and belts and—Kana squinted against the light to be sure—there were at least half a dozen major notches on his rank sword, although he could not be very far into his thirties.

They lined up in an upper hallway, the Archs who had responded to that last call. And the veterans presented a brilliant array. Both Arch and Mech who served in the field off Terra were accustomed to carry their personal savings on their bodies. A successful mission meant another jewel added to the belt, or inset in the helmet. A lean season and that could be sold for credits to tide its owner over. It was a simple form of security which served on any planet in the Galaxy.

It was two minutes after twelve before Kana came inside the assignment officer's cubby. He was a badge Swordtan, with a plasta-flesh hand which explained his present inactive status. Kana snapped to attention.

"Kana Karr, Swordsman, Third Class, first enlistment, sir," he identified himself.

"No experience"—the plasta-flesh fingers beat an impatient tattoo on the desk top—"but you have X-Tee training. How far did you go?"

"Fourth level, Alien contact, sir." Kana was a fraction proud of that. He had been the only one in his training group to reach that level.

"Fourth level," the Swordtan repeated. From the tone he was not impressed at all. "Well, that's something.

We're hiring for Yorke Horde. Police action on the planet Fronn. Usual rates. You embark for Secundus Base tonight, transship from there to Fronn. Voyage about a month. Term of enlistment—duration of action. You may refuse—this is a first choice." He repeated the last official formula with the weary voice of one who has said it many times before.

He was allowed two refusals, Kana knew, but to exercise that privilege without good reason gave one a black mark. And police action—while it covered a multitude of different forms of service—was usually an excellent way to get experience.

"I accept assignment, sir!" He pulled off his armlet for the second time and watched the Swordtan insert it in the block before him, pressing the keys which would enter on that band the terms of his first tour of duty. When he checked out at the end of the enlistment, a star would signify satisfactory service.

"Ship raises from Dock Five at seventeen hours. Dismissed!"

Kana saluted and left. He was hungry. The transients' mess was open and being a combatant in service he was entitled to order more than just basic rations. But a dislike of spending pay he had not yet earned kept him to the plain fare he was allowed as long as he wore the Arch tunic. He lingered over the food, listening to the scraps of shop talk and rumor flying back and forth across the tables. As he had suspected the announcement made in the hiring hall had given birth to some pretty wild stories.

"Lost fifty legions in five years—" proclaimed one Mechtan. "They don't tell us the truth any more. I've heard that Longmead and Groth refused assignments—"

"The High Brass is getting rattled," commented a Swordtan. "Did you see old Poalkan giving us the fishy eye? He'd like to bring the Patrol in and mop up. Tell you what we ought to do—planet for some quiet in-fighting at a place I could name. That might help—"

There was a moment of silence. The speaker did not need to name his goal. All mankind's festering resentment against Central Control lay behind that outburst.

Kana could stall no longer. He left the hum of the mess hall. Yorke Horde was a small outfit. Fitch Yorke, its Blademaster, was young. He'd only had a command for about four years. But sometimes under young commanders you had better advancement. Fronn—that was a world unknown to Kana. But the answer to his ignorance was easy to find. He made his way through the corridors to a quiet room with a row of booths lining one wall. At the back of the chamber was a control board with banks of buttons. He pressed the proper combination of those and waited for the record-pak.

The roll of wire was a very thin one. Not much known of Fronn. He ducked into the nearest booth, inserted the wire in the machine there, and put aside his helmet to adjust the impression band on his temples. A second later he drifted off to sleep, the information in the pak being fed to his memory cells.

It was a quarter of an hour later when he roused. So that was Fronn—not a particularly inviting world. And the pak had only sketched in meager details. But he now possessed all the knowledge the archives listed.

Kana sighed ruefully—that climate meant a tour in the pressure chamber during the voyage. The assignment officer had not mentioned that. Pressure chamber and water acclimation both. Serve him right for not asking more questions before he signed. He only hoped that he wasn't going to be sick for the whole trip.

When he went up to return the pak he met a Mechneer standing by the selector—an impatient Mech whistling tunelessly between his teeth, playing with the buckle of his blaster belt. He was only slightly older than Kana but he carried himself with the arrogant assurance of a man who had made at least two missions, an arrogance few real veterans displayed.

Kana glanced back at the booths. He had been the only occupant, so what was the Mech waiting there for? He dropped the pak on the return belt, but, as he reached the door, its polished surface reflected a strange sight. The Mech had scooped up the pak on Fronn before it vanished into the bin.

Fronn was a primitive world, a class five planet. Any Combatant force employed there must be, by Central Control regulations, an Arch Horde, trained and conditioned for so-called hand-to-hand fighting, their most modern weapon a stat-rifle. No mechanized unit would be sent to Fronn where their blasters, crawlers, spouters would be outlawed. So why should a Mech be interested in learning about that world?

Idle curiosity about planets on which one could not serve was not indulged among Combatants. It was about all one could do to absorb the information one could actually use.

Now Kana wished that he had had a closer look at the thin face which had been so shadowed by the bubble helmet. Puzzled and somewhat disturbed he went on to the commissary to lay in the personal supplies his new knowledge of Fronn suggested it wise to buy.

Wistfully he regarded and then refused a sleeping bag of Uzakian spider silk lined with worstle temperature moss. And the gauntlets of karab skin which the supply corpsman tried to sell him were as quickly pushed aside. Such luxuries were for the veteran with enough treasure riding his belt to afford a buying spree. Kana must thriftily settle for a second-hand Cambra bag—a short jacket of sasti hide, fur-lined and with a parka hood and gloves attached, and some odd medicament and toilet articles, in all a very modest outfit which could easily be added to the contents of his war bag. And when he settled the bill he still had left four credits of his muster allowance.

The corpsman deftly rolled his purchases into a bundle. "Looks like you're heading to some cold place, fella," he commented.

"To Fronn."

The man grinned. "Never heard of the place. Back of nowhere—sounds like to me. Look out they don't stick a spear in you from behind some bush. Those nowhere guys play rough. But then you guys do too, don't you?" He stared knowingly at Kana's Arch uniform. "Yessir, kinda rough, slugging it out the way you do. Me, I'd rather have me a blaster and be a Mech—"

"Then you'd face another fighter with a blaster of his own," Kana pointed out as he reached for the bundle.

"Have it your own way, fella." The corpsman lost interest as a bejeweled veteran approached.

Kana recognized in the newcomer the man who had preceded him to the assignment officer's cubby. Was he, too, bound for Yorke Horde and Fronn? When the spider silk sleeping bag was slapped down on the counter for his inspection, and other supplies similar to Kana's modest selection piled on it, he was reasonably sure that guess was correct.

At sixteen and a half hours the recruit stood beside his bag in the waiting section of Dock Five. So far he was alone save for the corpsmen who had business there and two spacer crewmen lounging at the far end. To have arrived so early was the badge of a greenie, but he was too excited under his impassive exterior to sit and wait elsewhere. It was twenty to seventeen before his future teammates began to straggle in. And ten minutes later they were swung up on the carry platform to the hatch of the troopship. Checking his armlet against the muster roll, the ship's officer waved Kana on. Within five minutes he entered a cabin for two, wondering which of the bunks was his to strap down on.

"Well"—a voice behind him exploded in a boom—"either get in or get out! This is no time to sleep on watch, recruit! Haven't you ever spaced before?"

Kana crowded back against the wall, snatching his bag away from the boots of the newcomer.

"Up there!" With an impatient snort his cabin mate pitched the younger man's bag up on the top bunk.

Kana swung up and investigated. Sure enough, a small knob twisted, and a section of the wall opened to display a recess which would accommodate his belongings. The rich note of a gong interrupted his exploration. At that signal the veteran loosened his belts and his helmet, putting them aside. And Kana hurriedly followed suit. One bong—first warning—

He stretched out on the bunk and fumbled for the straps which must be buckled. Under the weight of his body the foam pad spread a little. He knew that he could take acceleration—that was one of the first tests given a recruit in training. And he had been on field maneuvers on Mars and the Moon—but this was his first venture into deep space. Kana smoothed his tunic across his middle and waited for the third warning to announce the actual blastoff.

It had been a long time since Terrans had first reached toward other worlds. Three hundred years since the first recorded pioneer flight into the Galaxy. And even before that there were legends of other ships fleeing the nuclear wars and the ages of political and social confusion which followed. They must have been either very desperate or very brave, those first explorers—sending their ships out into the unknown while they were wrapped in cold sleep with one chance in perhaps a thousand of waking as their craft approached another planet. With the use of Galactic overdrive such drastic chances were no longer necessary. But had his kind paid too high a price for their swifter passage from star to star?

Though a Combatant did not openly question the dictates of authority or the status quo, Kana knew that he was by no means alone in his discontent with Terra's role. What would have happened to his species if, when they had made that first historic flight, they had not met with the established, superior force of Central Control? According to their Galactic masters the potentials of the Terran mind, body and temperament fitted them for only one role in the careful pattern of space. Born with an innate will to struggle, they were ordered to supply mercenaries for the other planets. Because the C.C. psycho-techneers believed that they were best suited to combat, their planet and system had been arbitrarily geared to war. And Terrans accepted the situation because of a promise C.C. had made—a promise the fulfillment of which seemed farther in the future every year—that when they were ready for a more equal citizenship it would be granted them.

But what if Central Control had not existed? Would the Agents' repeated argument have proved true? Would the Terrans, unchecked, have pulled planet after planet into a ruthless struggle for power? Kana was sure that was a lie. But now if a Terran wanted the stars, if the desire for new and strange knowledge burned in him—he could buy it only by putting on the Combatant's sword.

A giant hand squeezed Kana's rib case against laboring lungs. He forgot everything in a fight for breath. They had blasted off.

2

First Testing

Kana must have blacked out, for when he was again aware of his surroundings he saw that his cabin mate was maneuvering across their quarters, getting his "space legs" in the weak gravity maintained in the living sections of the ship. Lacking his helmet, his tunic open halfway down his broad chest, the veteran had lost some of his awe-inspiring aura. He might now be one of the hard-visaged instructors Kana had known for more than half his short life.

Space tan on a naturally dark skin made him almost black. His coarse hair had been shaved and trimmed into the ridge scalp lock favored by most Terrans. He moved with a tell-tale feline litheness and Kana decided that he would not care to match swords with him in any point-free contest. Now he turned suddenly as if sensing Kana's appraising stare.

"Your first enlistment?" he snapped.

Kana wormed free of the straps which imprisoned him and dangled his feet over the edge of the bunk before he replied.

"Yes, sir. I'm just up from Training—"

"Lord, they send 'em out young these days," commented the other. "Name and rank—"

"Kana Karr, sir, Swordsman, Third Class."

"I'm Trig Hansu." There was no reason for him to proclaim his rank, the double star of a Swordtan was plain on his tunic. "You signed for Yorke?"

"Yes, sir."

"Believe in beginning the hard way, eh?" Hansu jerked a jump seat from its wall hollow and sat down. "Fronn's no garden spot."

"It's a start, sir," Kana returned a bit stiffly and slipped down to the deck without losing a one-hand hold on the bunk.

Hansu grinned sardonically. "Well, we're all heroes when we're first out of Training. Yorke's a trail hitter and a jumper. You have to be con to keep up in one of his teams."

Kana had a defense ready for that. "The assignment officer asked for a recruit, sir."

"Which can mean several things, youngster, none of them complimentary. S-Threes come cheaper on the payroll than Ones or Twos—for example. Far be it from me to disillusion the young. There's mess call. Coming?"

Kana was glad that the veteran had given him that invitation, for the small mess hall was crowded with what seemed to his bedazzled eyes nothing but high ranks. There was gravity enough so that one could sit in a civilized fashion and eat—but Kana's stomach did not enjoy the process any. And soon such sensations would be worse, he thought grimly, when he had to go through pressure conditioning before landing on

Fronn. He regarded the noisy crowd about him with a growing depression.

A Horde was divided into teams and teams into doubles. If a man didn't find a double on his own but was arbitrarily paired by his commander with a stranger, some of the few pleasures and comforts of Combat field service were automatically endangered. Your double fought, played, and lived by your side. Often your life depended upon his skill and courage—just as his might upon yours. Doubles served years of enlistments together, moving in a firmly cemented partnership from one Horde or Legion to another.

And who in this glittering gang would choose to double with a greenie? The situation would probably end by his being assigned to a veteran who would resent his inexperience and provide him with the makings of a tough jump right from the start. Waugh—he *was* getting space blues tonight! Time to change think-tracks for sure.

But that subtle unease which haunted him all that long and eventful day lingered, coming to a head in a strange and horrifying dream in which he ran breathlessly across a shadow landscape trying to avoid the red ray of a Mech blaster. He awoke with a choked gasp and lay sweating in the darkened cabin. Hunted by a Mech—but Mechs did not fight against Archs. Only— it was some time before he was able to sleep again.

The beams of the ship's artificial day brought him to life much later. Hansu was gone, the contents of his war bag spilled out on his empty bunk. A wicked needle knife, its sheath polished smooth by long wear against the bare skin of its owner's inner arm, caught Kana's eye. Its unadorned hilt was designed for service. And its presence among the gear meant that Kana was now sharing the quarters of a man practiced in the deadliest form of Combatant in-fighting. The recruit longed to pick it up, test its perfect balance and spring for himself. But he knew better than to touch another's personal weapons without the express permission of the owner. To his fellows that act was a direct insult which could lead only to a "meeting" from which one of them might never return. Kana had heard enough tall tales from the instructors at Training to make him familiar with the barracks code.

He was a late arrival at mess and ate with apologetic speed under the impatient eye of the stewards. Afterwards he went on to the small lounge deck where the Combatants sprawled at leisure. There was a card game in progress, and the usual circle of intent players about a Yano board. But Trig Hansu was a member of neither group. Instead he sat cross-legged on a mat pad, a portable reader before him, watching the projection of a pak.

Curious, Kana edged between the gamesters to see the tiny screen. He caught sight of a fraction of landscape, dark, gloomy, across which burden-bearing creatures moved from left to right. Hansu spoke without turning his head.

"If you're so curious, greenie, squat."

Feeling as hot as a thruster tube Kana would have melted away but Hansu pushed the machine to the right in real invitation.

"Our future." He jerked a thumb at the unwinding scene as the recruit dropped to his knees to watch. "That's a pak view of Fronn."

The marchers on the Fronnian plain were quadrupeds, their stilt legs seemingly only skin drawn tightly over bone. Packs rested on either side of their ridged spines and knobby growths fringed their ungainly necks and made horn excrescences on their skulls.

"Caravan of guen," Kana identified. "That must be the west coastal plains."

Hansu pressed a stud on the base of the reader and the screen blanked out. "You asked for indoctrination on Fronn?"

"From the archives, sir."

"The enthusiasms of the young have their points. And you're just out of Training. Specialization—knife—rifle—?"

"Basic in everything, sir. But specialization in X-Tee—Alien Liaison mostly—"

"Hmm. That would explain your being here." Hansu's comment seemed obscure. "X-Tee—I wonder what they spring on you in that nowadays. What about—" He swung sharply into a series of questions, delivered rapid fire, which were certainly very close in their searching value to what Kana had faced back in Training before he had been granted his mark of proficiency. When he had answered them to the best of his ability—having to say frankly, far too many times, "I don't know"—he saw Hansu nod.

"You'll do. Once you get a lot of that theory knocked out of your head, and let experience teach you what you should really know about this game, you'll be worth at least half your pay to a Blademaster."

"You said that X-Tee specialization explained my assignment, sir—?"

But the veteran appeared to have lost interest in the conversation. The Yano game broke up in a noisy if good-natured argument, and Hansu was tapped on the shoulder by one of his own rank and urged into the group reforming for a second round.

And because he had not answered that question Kana began to note more carefully the caliber of the men about him. These were not only veterans, but long-service men with a high percentage of stars. The scraps of conversation he overheard mentioned famed commanders, Hordes with long lists of successful engagements. Yet Fitch Yorke was a comparative new-comer, with no fame to pull in such men. Wouldn't it have been more normal for them to refuse enlistment under him? Why the concentration of experience and skill in an obscure Horde on an unknown planet? Kana was certain that Hansu, for one, was an outstanding X-Tee expert—

But during the next few days he saw little of the veteran, and the landing on Secundus after the bore-dom of the trip could not come soon enough.

The temporary quarters assigned to Yorke's men was a long hall, one end of which was a mess station while the other was tiered with bunks. With a hundred men dragging in supplies and personal equipment, greet-ing old comrades, sharing Horde rumor and Combat news, the room was a hurricane of noise and confu-sion. Kana, not knowing just where to go, followed Hansu down the length of the room. But when the Swordtan turned to join a glittering circle of his peers, the recruit was left to hunt a dim corner suitable to his inexperience and general greenness.

There was not much choice. The S-Threes congre-gated in the least desirable section by the door. And with a sense of relief Kana noted several whose uni-forms were as bare of ornament as was his own. He tramped over and claimed a top bunk by tossing his war bag up on its pad.

"D'you see who just mustered in?" one of his neigh-bors demanded of the young man beside him. "Trig Hansu—!"

A low whistle of astonishment became words. "But he's top brass! What's he doing in this outfit? He could claim shares with Zagren Osmin or Franlan. Yorke should be flattered to get the time of day from him."

"Yeah? Well, I've heard he's strange in some ways. He'll cut a top outfit any time to get off the regular

travel lanes and visit a new world. He's space whirly
over exploring. Could have had a Horde of his own
long ago if he hadn't always been jumping off into the
black. And, besides, brother, haven't you noticed something else about this particular crowd? Yorke's snaffled
himself more than one big name in this pull-out.
Hello—" He noticed Kana's bag and now he turned
smartly to survey its owner.

"So—something new here. A nice greenie out to
make his fortune or die on the field of glory. What's
your name and condition, greenie?"

There was no bite of sarcasm in that demand and
the speaker did not outrank Kana very far in either
years or service.

"Kana Karr, S-Three—"

"Mic Hamet, S-Three—that clay-clawer resting his
sore feet over there is Rey Nalassie, also of our lowly
rank. First assignment?"

Kana nodded. Mic Hamet's dark red hair was
roached in the scalp ridge, but his unusually fair skin
was reddened rather than tanned by exposure and there
was a spattering of freckles across his somewhat flat
nose. His friend uncoiled long legs and rose to a
gangling six-foot-two, his lantern-jawed face solemn,
though his sleepy gray eyes displayed humor and
interest.

"They scraped us out of a rotation depot. We had
bad luck a while back. Rey got bit by a bug during our
last stretch and we had to default out of Oosterbeg's
Horde four months short. So we were flat enough in
the purse to sign on here when the assign officer
looked at us as if we were slightly better than muck
worms."

"You doubled yet, Karr?" asked Nalassie in a husky
voice.

"No, I was delayed in leaving Training. And all the

fellows who shipped out of Prime with me were vets—"

Mic lost his half grin. "That's tough luck. Most of us Threes are paired already and you wouldn't want to double with either Krosof or the rest—"

"Heard tell that if you come in solo, Yorke puts you with a vet," Rey volunteered. "Got a theory youth should be tamed by age—or something of the sort."

"And that's worse than tough," broke in his partner. "You shouldn't team up with anyone until you know him. I'd play it single as long as I could, if I were you, Karr. You might be lucky enough to find some good fella who's lost his partner. Stick with us until you do double if you want to—"

"And a very good way to stay out of trouble with the jeweled ones"—Rey nodded toward the rankers' side of the hall—"is to get out of here." He put on his helmet and buckled the chin strap. "They aren't going to muster until morning, we can still have a night on the town. And, fella, you haven't seen excitement until you've seen the leave section of Secundus."

Kana was enthusiastic until he thought of the leanness of his purse. Four credits wouldn't even pay for a meal in a base town—he was sure of that. But, as he shook his head, Mic's fingers closed on his arm.

"No quibbling, fella. We'll be a long time in the back country and we aren't comfortable, shipping out with credits sticking to our fingers. We'll stand you—then when you get your first star, you can repay in kind— that's fair enough. Now, quick about it, before someone gets the idea of putting the younger generation to labor for the good of their souls!"

Beyond the walls of the Combat area a typical leave town had grown up. Taverns, cafes, gambling establishments catered for all ranks and purses, from Blademasters and Mechmasters to recruits. It was certainly no place to visit with only four credits, Kana thought again as he blinked at the light of the gaudy signs lining the street before them.

And, to his discomfort, the ideas of his guides were not modest. They steered him by the cafes he would have chosen and dragged him through a wide door where Terran gold-leaf was overlaid with the sea-green shimmer of Trafian scale lac. Their boots pressed flat the four-inch pile of carpets which could only have been woven on Caq, and the walls were cloaked with the tapestries of Sansifar. Kana balked.

"This is strictly a glitter boy's shop," he protested. But Mic's hold on him did not relax and Rey chuckled.

"No rank off field," Mic reminded him sardonically. "S-Threes and Blademasters—we're all the same in our skins. Only civilians worry about artificial distinctions—"

"Sure. In Combat you go where you please. And we please to come here." Rey sniffed the scented air which stirred the shining arras, shaking the figures on them to quivering life. "By the Forked Tail of Blamand, what I wouldn't give to be in on the sacking of this! And here comes mine host's assistant."

The figure loping toward them was one of the skeleton-lean, big-headed natives of Lupa. He greeted them with a professional smile, disclosing the double row of fangs which tended to make Terrans slightly nervous, and inquired their pleasure in a series of ear-taxing growls.

"Nothing big," Mic returned. "We have muster tomorrow. Suppose you let us trot around by ourselves, Feenhalt. We won't get into trouble—"

The Lupan's pointed grin widened as he waved them on. When they passed through a slit in the curtain to the next room Kana commented:

"I take it you're known here?"

"Yes. We got Feenhalt out of a hole once. He isn't a bad old Lupan. Now—let's mess."

They escorted Kana through a series of rooms, each exotic in its furnishings, each bizarrely different, until they came to a chamber which brought a surprised exclamation out of him. For they might have stepped into a section of jungle. Gigantic fern-trees forested the walls and looped long fronds over their heads, but did not exclude a golden light which revealed cushioned benches and curving tables. Among the greenery swooped and fluttered streaks of flaming color which could only be the legendary Krotands of Cephas' inner sea islands. Kana, meeting such travelers' tales in truth, bemusedly allowed his companions to push him down on a bench.

"Krotands? But how—?"

Mic's knuckles rapped and drew a metallic answer from the bole of the fern tree immediately behind them. Kana reached out to find that his fingers slid over a solid surface instead of rough bark. They were in a clever illusion.

"All done with mirrors," Mic assured him solemnly. "Not that it isn't one of the best bits of projecting Slanal ever designed. Feenhalt's got the business head—but it's his boss who thought up this sort of thing. Ha—food."

Plates arose out of the table top. Warily Kana tasted and then settled down to hearty stoking.

"It'll be a long time before we get another feed like this," Rey observed. "I heard Fronn's no pleasure planet."

"Cold to our notion—and the native culture is feudal," Kana supplied.

" 'Police action,' " mused Mic. "Police action doesn't match a feudal government. What is the set-up—kings? Emperors?"

"Kings—they call them 'Gatanus'—ruling small

nations. But their heirship is reckoned through the female line. A Gatanu is succeeded by his eldest sister's son, not his own. He is considered closer kin to his mother and sisters than to his father or brothers."

"You must have studied up on this—"

"I used a record pak at Prime."

Rey looked pleased. "You're going to be an asset. Mic, we've got to keep our paws on this one."

Mic swallowed a heroic bite. "We sure have. Somehow I am visited by a feeling that this jump is not going to be foam-pad riding, and the more we know, the better for us."

Kana glanced from one to the other, catching the shadow glimpse of trouble. "What's up?"

Mic shook his head and Rey shrugged. "Blasted if we know. But—well, when you've trotted around the back of beyond and poked into places where a 'man' is a mighty weird animal, you get a feeling about things. And we have a feeling about this—"

"Yorke?"

The morale of any Horde depended upon the character of its Blademaster. If Yorke could not inspire confidence in those who followed him—

Mic frowned. "No, it's not Fitch Yorke. By all accounts he's a master to latch to. There have been a lot of the glitter boys beside Hansu to sign up for this jump—you can always tell by that how a Blademaster stacks. It's a feeling—you get it sometimes—a sort of crawling—inside you—"

"Somebody kicking at your grave mark," Rey contributed.

Mic's big mouth twisted in a grin aimed at himself. "Regular mist wizards, aren't we? Step right up—read your future for a credit! Fronn isn't going to be any worse than a lot of other places I know. Through? Then let's show our greenie Feenhalt's private rake-off. Only time the old Lupan showed any imagination—And, flame bats, does it ever pay off!"

Feenhalt's flight of imagination turned out to be a gambling device which enthralled a large selection of Combatants. A pool sunk in the floor of a room was partitioned into sections around a central arena. In each of the small water-filled pens sported a fish about five inches long, two-thirds of that length was mouth lined with needle teeth. Each fish bore a small colored tag imbedded in its tail fin and swam about its prison in ferocious fury. The players gathered about the pool studying the captives. When two or more had chosen their champions, credit chips were inserted in the slots on the rim and the pen doors opened, freeing the fish to move into the arena. What followed was a wild orgy of battle until only one warrior remained alive. Whereupon the bettor who had selected that fish collected from those who had sponsored the dead.

No more attractive game could have been devised to snare credits from the Combatants. Kana measured the twisting finny fighters carefully, at last choosing a duelist with an excellent jaw spread and a green tail disc. He bought a credit chip from the house banker and knelt to insert the releasing coin in the lock of the pen.

A meaty, hair-matted hand splayed against his shoulder and Kana only caught himself from landing in the pool with a back-wrenching twist.

"Outta th' way, little boy. This here's for men—"

"Just what—!" Kana's words ended in a cough as Mic's fist landed between his shoulders and someone else jerked him away from the man who had taken his place and his fish. The fellow grinned up at him maliciously. Then, as if he expected no more trouble, he turned back to encourage the fighter released by the recruit's chip.

All the good humor was gone from Mic's face and even Rey's dancing eyes were sober as they moved Kana away, holding him motionless between them in an "unarmed in-fighting" grip against which he knew better than to struggle.

"We blast—now—" Mic informed him.

"Just what"—he began again—"do you think—"

"Fella, you might have dug your own grave there. That was Bogate—Zapan Bogate. He has twenty duel notches on his sword—eats greenies for breakfast when he can get them." Mic's words were light but his voice deadly serious.

"Do you think I'm afraid—" Kana smarted.

"Listen, fella, there's a big difference between being prudent and alive, and kicking a Zartian sand mouse in the teeth. You don't last long after the latter heroic deed. You can't be given a yellow stripe for ducking a run-in with Bogate—you're just intelligent. Someday one of the big boys—Hansu or Deke Mills or somebody like that—is going to get annoyed with Bogate. Then—man, oh, man—you'll be able to sell standing room at the fracas to half the forces and be a billion-credit man! Bogate is sudden and painful death on two crooked feet."

"Besides being about the best scout who ever sniffed a trail," cut in Rey. "Bogate at play and Bogate in the field are two different characters. The Blademasters tolerate the one on account of the other."

Kana recognized truth when he heard it. To return and tackle Bogate was stupid. But he still protested until they were interrupted by Hansu. The veteran, followed by two base policemen, bore down upon them.

"Yorke men?" he asked.

"Yes, sir."

"Report to Barracks—on the quick. Blast-off has

been moved up—" He was already past them to round up more of the Horde.

The three started back to the Combat area at a trot.

"Now what?" Rey wanted to know. "Last I heard we launched at noon tomorrow. Why all the hurry? We haven't even had muster line yet."

"I told you," grunted Mic, "that there was a smell about this—not perfume either. Octopods! That dinner we downed—and pressure chamber conditioning coming up! We're going to be might sorry we ate, mighty sorry."

With this dire prophecy still ringing in his ears Kana collected his war bag from the bunk he had not had a chance to occupy and took his place with Mic and Rey on the hoist platform to be slung on board the transport. Counted off by fours Kana found himself sharing a pressure chamber with his two new acquaintances and a supply man—the latter obviously bored by his juvenile company. They stripped to their shorts, submitted to shots from the medico. And then there was nothing left to do but strap down on the bunks and endure the ensuing discomfort.

The next few days were anything but pleasant. Slowly their bodies were forced to adapt to Fronn, since the planet was *not* going to adapt to them. It was a painful process. But when they landed on that chill world they were ready for action.

Kana still lacked a double. He clung to Mic and Rey as they had advised, but he knew that sooner or later that threesome must be broken and he would be assigned a partner. He was shy of the veterans, and the three or four other S-Threes who were not yet paired for muster-line were not the type he desired to know better. Most of them were older men with experience who were incorrigible enough to remain permanently in the lowest ranks. Good in the

field, they were troublemakers in barracks and had
shifted from one Horde to another at the end of each
enlistment with the relieved sighs of those who had
just served wafting them on their separate ways. Kana
continued to hope that he would not draw one of
them as a double.

The Terrans' first sight of Fronn was disappointing.
They planeted at dusk, and, since Fronn was moonless, marched through darkness to the squat, rough-
hewn stone building which was to serve them as
temporary barracks. There were no fittings at all in the
long room and the three sat on their war bags, wondering whether to unroll sleeping bags or wait for
further instructions.

Rey's long nose wrinkled in disgust as he moved his
boots from a suspicious stain on the dirty floor. "I'd
say we got this place second hand—"

"Second hand?" Mic asked. "Closer fifth. And most
of the others before us were animals. This is a Fronnian
cow barn if my nose doesn't deceive me."

The call Kana had been dreading came at last,
doubles were to register at the table a Swordtan had
set up at the far end of the room. Rey and Mic, after
a word of encouragement, got in line.

Kana hesitated, not knowing just what to do, when
the harsh rasp of a new voice startled him. Zapan
Bogate and another of the same type had fallen into
line near him. A third of their pattern stood beside
Bogate grinning.

"Jus' a greenie—don't know what to do next. Poor
little lost greenie. You, Sim, go and take him by the
hand. He needs his nurse—"

Kana tensed. With Bogate's encouragement Sim
shuffled forward, his brutal face twisted in a wry gri-
mace he might have intended as a smile.

"Poor little greenie," Bogate repeated, his voice rising

so that half the line were turning to see the sport. "Sim's gonna look after him, ain't you, Sim?"

"Sure am, Zap. Come along, greenie—" His hairy paw caught Kana's sleeve.

What followed was mostly sheer reflex action on the recruit's part. The disgust which that touch aroused in him triggered his move. His hand chopped down across the other's wrist, striking the hand from its hold. As Sim goggled, Bogate stepped out of line, his small eyes gleaming with sadistic joy.

"Seems like the greenie don't favor you, Sim. Whatta we do to greenies who don't know what's good for them?"

Kana thought he was alert but Sim surprised him. He had not expected the hulking bully to follow code custom. Sim's slap across his face had power enough to swing him half around, blinking back tears of pain. As he regained his balance Kana's mind was working feverishly. Barracks duel—just the sort of encounter these bullies wanted—legal enough so no watching Combatant would dare to interfere.

He had a single advantage. They would expect him to choose the usual weapons—swords with shielded points. Thanks to his study of the record-pak on Terra he had an answer which would give him a chance to escape a nasty mauling.

He and Sim were now surrounded by a circle of expectant spectators. Kana tasted the sweet flatness of blood from the lip the other's slap had scraped against his teeth.

"Meet?" Automatically he asked the proper question.

"Meet."

"Give me your sword, Sim. I'll cap it for you," Bogate ordered genially.

"Not so fast." Kana was glad that his voice sounded so even and unhurried. "I didn't say swords—"

Bogate's grin faded, his eyes narrowed. "Yeah? Guns is out—not on active service, greenie."

"I choose bat sticks," returned Kana.

A moment of utter and uncomprehending silence was his first answer.

3

Forward March

Those Archs who had been longer on Fronn began to understand, though Sim apparently did not. As he glanced to Bogate asking for direction, Hansu elbowed his way into the center of the circle. Behind him was another man, much younger, but bearing himself with the same unself-conscious authority.

"You heard him," Hansu said to Sim. "He's chosen bat sticks. And you'll meet here and now. We want this over before we march out."

Sim was still bemused and, seeing that, Kana began to hope. Blunted swords were one thing—a man could be maimed or even killed when he faced an expert in such warfare. But armed with one of those wands made of a highly poisonous wood which left seared welts on human skin—the whips used by Fronnian caravan men to subdue the recalcitrant guen—he had a chance, and maybe more than just an even one.

Kana unbuckled his helmet strap and found Mic's hand ready to receive the headgear as he discarded it. Rey edged up to help him unfasten his cross belts.

"Know what you're doing, fella?" he asked in a half whisper as Kana shed his tunic.

"Better than Sim does, I think," Kana returned, peeling off his shirt.

His first little spark of hope was growing into steady confidence. Sim was still confused and Bogate's grin had been wiped from his ugly face. The young man who had followed Hansu disappeared. But before Kana had time to shiver in the chill of the unheated building he was back, carrying in gloved hands two of the bright crimson bat sticks. Seeing what he held, those who knew Fronn gave him quick room.

Kana drew on a gauntlet and gripped the nearest stick. They were of equal weight and reach. And, as the circle of spectators moved out to give them room, the recruit believed that Sim's battered face now registered a certain uneasiness.

They came on guard at command, using the canes as they would the heavier and more familiar steel. But where a duelist must fear only the blunted point of the sword, here the slightest touch would bring pain. Their boots made faint whispering sounds as they circled, the sticks meeting with a thud as they thrust and parried.

Kana, after the third pass, knew that he was facing a master swordsman, but he also guessed that the relative lightness of this strange weapon was bothering Sim and that his opponent was not quite sure of himself or aware of the potentialities of the cane he wielded.

There was a single stroke which would put an end to the duel. Kana wondered if Sim realized that. A raking sweep across arm muscles—the resulting pain would make that limb useless for minutes. He concentrated on achieving that, his world narrowed to the cane he was using and the swaying, dodging body before him. Sim had abandoned the more obvious attacks and was settling down to a semi-defensive action, apparently content to leave experimentation to Kana, thereby displaying more shrewdness than Kana had credited to him. With none of his confidence shaken, but more warily, Kana circled—using the traditional thrusts and parries which were a beginner's. Sim must be drawn into the open in the belief that he faced a novice.

Something struck him in the short ribs and glanced along his flesh. It brought with it a blaze of agony almost as bad as a blaster burn. Kana set his teeth as, encouraged by that scoring, Sim's defense changed to an attack the recruit found hard to meet. He was forced back, giving ground willingly enough with a single aim in mind—to reach that point on the muscled arm before him.

Sim's cane got home again, up the angle of Kana's jaw. The younger man shook his head dazedly, but a leap back bought him a moment in which to pull himself together. That sharp retreat must have given Sim the idea that his opponent's nerve was breaking, for now he bored in with a wild whirlwind of blows. There came the moment Kana had waited for, his cane drew a torturing line across Sim's sword arm just below the shoulder. And, more unprepared than Kana had been, the older man cried out, clawing at the red welt, his cane rolling across the floor to strike against Kana's boot. The recruit brought his stick up in formal salute.

"Satisfied?" He asked the traditional question.

Sim was speechless with pain as he nodded, though the hatred in his small eyes fought with the agony of his hurt. Since he could no longer hold his weapon he must concede, but he was far from satisfied.

Kana became aware of the buzz of talk about them. Snatches of conversation informed him that these connoisseurs were discussing his exploit from every possible angle. He dropped his cane to the floor and raised his hand to the burn on his jaw.

"Don't touch that, you young fool!" snapped the voice of authority. The young man who had provided the canes pushed Kana's hand away and began dabbing delicately at the welt with a yellow grease. As it spread across the reddened skin Kana felt a coolness draw out the fire. He stood patiently while they doctored the slash on his side and then shrugged into the shirt Mic brought him.

"All right, all right!" Hansu's deep growl cut through and across the din. "The show's over—"

But as the others shuffled back into line the Swordtan stood between Kana and Sim, eyeing them both with a steel-based coldness. "For brawling in barracks," he announced, "three days' field pay fine! And if either of you have any clever ideas about trying it again—you'll deal with me!"

Kana, unable to don his helmet because of his jaw, gave ready agreement to keep the peace, and Sim's mumble was also accepted.

"You—Lozt, go in with Daw." Hansu jerked a thumb to the end of the line. And Sim, nursing his limp arm, obediently passed Bogate to take the indicated place beside a dark, wiry veteran. Kana remained where he was.

"I'll answer for this one," the younger veteran spoke up and Kana sensed that this had been decided between his two superiors. Still uninformed as to who his partner was, he followed along.

"Mills and Karr," Hansu set them down together on

the muster roll as members of the team he himself commanded.

"Mills"—there was something familiar in that name. Kana went back to claim his bag trying to recall where he had heard it before and ran into a highly excited Mic and an equally amazed Rey.

"Let me touch you," Mic greeted him. "Maybe some of that luck will rub off. I can sure use it!"

"You must have been born with a sword in your hand and a star in your mouth!" contributed Rey. "How do you rate Deke Mills for a double, greenie?"

Deke Mills! Again that name almost rang a gong, but still he couldn't remember.

"Great Blades!" Mic's eyes and mouth were circles of astonishment. "I don't believe he knows what has happened to him! Somebody ought to teach greenies the facts of life before they ship them out into the cruel, cold world. Deke Mills, fella, is a star-double-star. He's nudging people like Hansu for top honors. Space, he could have his pick of doubles out of the whole Horde! He might have partnered Hansu if Yorke hadn't insisted that Trig command a team."

Kana swallowed. "But why—" His mouth was suddenly dry.

"Not for your pretty blue eyes anyway," Mic told him. "He was unattached and so were you. Yorke's rule is a vet with a greenie where there's last minute choosing to be done. You're lucky in that you were at the right place at the right time. Lucky, you're dripping with the stuff!"

"I'd rather stay with you two." Kana spoke the truth. To double with a notable such as Deke Mills was the last thing he wished. He would do everything wrong, and all his mistakes would be magnified in such exalted company. At that moment he would almost rather have walked beside Sim.

"Cheer up." Mic grinned. "We're in the same team. And Mills is acting as one of Hansu's aides—you may not see too much of him after all."

"Better cut along," warned Rey. "There's Mills by the door. Don't keep him waiting."

Kana scooped up his bag, wincing as he moved his head. Yes, the young veteran stood by the door talking to a handful of rankers. Kana hurried, beginning to wish that he had used his privilege and refused this assignment.

It was close to midnight, ship time, when he joined Mills. Outside there were rays of a dull bluish light, weak and dim to Terran eyes. Kana gathered that instead of remaining in the odorous barn for the night the Combatants were moving out of the Fronnian town to the camp site the first comers had established.

The street was roughly paved and drawn up there was a line of light, two-wheeled carts. Each was pulled by a gu—most of which were bubbling ill temperedly— granted plenty of room by the alien soldiers. As Kana followed Mills' example and tossed his bag into the leading cart he passed close to the first Fronnian he had seen in the flesh.

This was a Llor, one of the dominant race on the continental land masses. Humanoid in general appearance the native stood a good seven feet. In a climate where the Terrans were glad to wear double-lined winter clothing, the Llor was bare to the waist. But nature had provided him with a coat of thick curly hair, close in texture to the wool of a sheep, from which came a pungent, oily odor only apparent to those from off world. This hairy covering was thinner on the face—an odd face to non-Llor eyes for the nose was bridgeless and represented by a single nostril slit, while the eyes bulged from their round sockets in a singularly disconcerting stare. The mouth was small and round, and if the Llor possessed any teeth they were not visible. His only garment, save for a harness which supported a sword and a hand gun, was a short kilt made of strips of tanned hide, each hardly wider than a thread of fringe. Boots with pointed toes, the tips of which were capped with wicked metal spikes, were laced to his knees.

As the Combatants loaded their baggage aboard the cart the Llor lounged at ease, chewing on a section of purple-blue cane and spitting noisily at intervals. When the bags of six men had been piled on the vehicle he tended, he straightened, prodded the snarling gu with a bat stick and the cart creaked on, the Terrans falling in behind.

Blue lamps fastened to the blank, windowless walls of the structures they passed afforded enough light to march along the street, but the footing was rough.

"This is Tharc, capital city of Skura's province." Mills' voice rose over the clatter made by the metal wheels of the cart. "Skura's Chortha of the Western Lands. And he aims on being Gatanu—that's why we're here."

"Assignment officer said this was to be police action," Kana returned.

Maybe this was the trouble Mic had sensed back at Secundus. There was a wide difference between policing a turbulent border for a rightful ruler and supporting a rebel chieftain in a bid for a throne.

"Since Skura claims to be the rightful heir, this could be loosely termed police action—"

But Kana thought he detected a dry note in Mills' voice. Had he made a bad error already in uttering a statement which could be taken as a criticism of Yorke's hiring orders?

"Gatanu Plota's sisters were twins. There is some dispute as to who was the elder. Each had a son—so now there's a disagreement over the proper heir. Plota is dying of the shaking sickness—they give him three months more at the most. Skura's party is out of favor at court and Skura was sent here last calm season. He's more an exile than a Chortha. But he made a treaty with Intergalactic Trading for some mining rights and collected enough ready cash to deal with Yorke. The I.T. has been trying to get a foothold here for a long time—the local trade is an iron-tight monopoly of a sort. So they were only too glad to underwrite Skura's bid for the throne. Oh, it's a gamble all right, but if Skura becomes Gatanu he'll pay double what Yorke could collect elsewhere for the same length of service."

"Whom do we fight?"

"S'Tork, the other nephew. He's less of a fire-eater than Skura and has the more conservative nobles and most of the Wind Priests behind him. But he's no fighting man and has no following of troops. Here an army is built around the household warriors of the nobles. And if a lord is not personally popular enough to attract unattached warriors, well, he hasn't an army. Very simple. Skura thinks that with the Horde under his flag it may not even come to battle—that he will be able to bluff the opposition right off the field—"

The pavement ended abruptly at the walls of Tharc and the wagon trundled on into the ankle-deep dust of a road which was hardly more than a caravan track. They passed under the fangs of a portcullis, out of Skura's capital and into the open country.

A line of guen waited with their merchant owners for open passage into Tharc. Kana noted that these travelers were somewhat shorter than the giant Llor soldiers. Also they were completely muffled in thick hooded robes and stood apart, as silent and feature-less as ghosts, to let the Terrans past.

The Horde camp was a mile beyond, the yellow camp lights making a welcome break in the darkness of the moonless night. Under their glow Kana found the tent assigned him, unrolled his bag, and crawled in for a few hours' rest.

There followed a week of intensive drill to shake down the newly assembled Horde into fighting trim— during which Kana was either too occupied with field problems, or too bone tired physically to speculate about his surroundings and the future. But some ten days later they lined up in marching order in the grim gray pre-dawn which on Fronn seemed chillier and more foreboding than the same hour on Terra. The Horde were to move east, toward the distant range of mountains which divided this western province from the rich central plains which the ambitious Skura already thought of as his own.

Kana had to admit that the rebellious Chortha was a perfect example of semi-barbarian war leader. Followed by a troop of fast-riding cavalry, mounted on the hard-to-control male guen, he had pounded through the Combatant camp area on numerous occasions. His popularity with his own people was wide and each day witnessed the arrival of more nobles and their personal retinues to swell the ranks of the native army encamped beyond. Daily, also, the caravans of draft guen wound in to dump supplies or reload material to be transported on to the mountains.

This morning Kana was on point marching duty with Rey, as one such assembly of hooded, muffled drivers and complaining animals shuffled by, raising a thick dust. Once the supply train was on its way, the Horde would swing out too, not on the same trail but across country— with the point men the only contact with the road.

Kana burrowed his chin into the soft lining of his high jacket collar, glad that he had selected one with the fur-lined hood which covered head and ears. The cold of the Fronnian dawn was cruel.

"There goes the last one—" Rey's words came in a puff of milky air as he raised his signal gun and fired a bright red burst into the dark sky.

With rifles resting in the crooks of their arms, the two Terrans fell into the springy, ground-covering stride of Combatants on march along the edge of the road. Within seconds they caught up to the rearmost gu and were rapidly overtaking the head of the caravan when Kana's attention centered upon one of the robed drivers. He had never seen any of the traders without their figure-concealing garments, but he knew that they were a different race from the hairy Llor who ruled the land.

The Llor cultivated the ground, lived in cities under a loosely feudal government, and were fighters. But these traders, who held a monopoly on both transportation and barter of goods, were another breed. A race nurtured on far sea islands, great mariners and travelers—far roving, but making no permanent settlements on land, they were named Venturi and kept entirely to themselves on the mainland, conducting business only through one of their number in each group who was elected to what they apparently considered the unenviable post of liaison man. The Venturi remained therefore anonymous and ghostly creatures as far as the Terrans were concerned, featureless in their hoods, one exactly like another as to height and gliding walk. Only now—here was one who was different. Where his fellows glided as if they progressed on skates, this one strode. He was not leading a gu either—but journeyed, with empty hands, a little to the right of the regular procession.

Kana's eyes narrowed as he slowed step to keep behind the stranger. It was almost as if this robed wayfarer were not actually one of the Venturi at all. Then Rey drew even with the hooded stray and abruptly the other's pace altered to the gait of his

companions. Kana hurried to catch up with Nalassie.
They reached the top of a rise. A thicket lay below.
The two Swordsmen had either to take to the road to
pass it or make a wide detour north. Kana murmured,
hardly above a whisper:

"North!"

Rey looked surprised but asked no question. Instead
he obediently set a course which would put the thicket
between them and the caravan.

"There's a stranger among the Venturi," Kana
explained.

Rey slung his rifle and squatted down on the moist
turf, detaching a scout's speecher from his belt. "I'll
report."

Kana kept on at a steady trot, determined to catch
up with the supply train and watch the suspect. He
was counting the hooded figures to be sure his man
was still among them when Rey joined him.

"Llor cavalry heading toward this road a mile on.
If there's anything wrong, they'll handle it. We're to
keep out of trouble with the Venturi."

They followed along with the caravan. It was full
day now and the sun streaked the sky with yellow.
Ahead mounted men milled around some disturbance
in the center of the road.

Kana and Rey quickened pace to see what was the
matter. A gu was down in the dust, kicking and bar-
ing its formidable fangs at the Llor troopers who were
holding consultation over it.

The caravan halted, allowing the Venturi leader to
advance alone. He was met halfway by the commander
of the troop and, after some moments' talk, he returned
to his party for a second conference which led to a
second merchant going on to the stricken gu. The Llor
spread out, leaving only their officers by the animal.
Some, Kana noted, drifted back so that they were now

on a line with the supply train. It must be that they were engaged in some stratagem—as if they dared not become openly involved in the accusation or search of the Venturi party.

Their trap was sprung with a sudden shout from one of the troopers. He had dismounted and now his gu jerked its head loose from his grip on the reins and, blowing a green foam from its mouth and nostrils, dashed straight for the beasts of the caravan, its rider running with it, making futile grabs for the reins.

Before the oncoming fury of the maddened cavalry mount the heavier-burdened guen went wild, pulling free from their leading cords, or dragging the Venturi with them. One of the hooded figures, without any gu, took to his heels and fled in a pounding run straight for the point where Kana and Rey stood watching. Kana was tempted to tackle the fugitive, but the orders had been clear—this job was to be left to the Llor.

The troopers who were along that side of the road fanned out and rode to surround the fleeing trader. One of them whirled over his head a loop of shining stuff which curled through the air to ring the runner. He changed step, stumbled when trying to check his speed, and went down with a crashing force. Some of the Llor dismounted and walked toward the captive confidently, as if they expected no further resistance.

But the man on the ground writhed to a sitting position. And a second later a bolt of red fire struck down the nearest trooper. With a shriek of agony the Llor plunged across the loose soil.

"Flamer!" Rey yelled.

Both Terran rifles centered and two shots cracked almost as one. The trapped man jerked and fell back to earth with a heavy limpness which told them no more bullets were needed.

A Llor wearing the half circle of an under officer

was on the scene, using the butt of his riding bat to roll over a hand weapon of dull metal—one which had no business on Fronn. With that out of reach of the dead hand two of the troopers stripped off the Venturi robe. A Llor lay there, there was no mistaking the curled pelt and the pop eyes of the masquerader.

"This—" the Llor officer touched the flamer with his bat. "Do you know of this?" he spoke slowly in Space Trade Talk.

"It is a firearm—very bad," Kana answered. "We do not use them."

The officer nodded. "Then where get?" he wanted to know, reasonably enough.

Kana shrugged. "This one—he is not of yours?"

The commander of the troop pushed through the ring of his men and bent to stare at the slack face of the native. Then with his own hand he tore away the belt of the fringed kilt. Reversed, the buckle bore an orange-red arrow-shaped mark.

"News-seeker of S'Tork," he identified. Then, lapsing into the native tongue, he gave a series of orders which set the troopers to rolling the body into a torn robe and lashing it on the back of a protesting gu.

To the Terrans' surprise nothing was said to the Venturi. The road was cleared and the supply train plodded on, not one of its guardians turning to look at the group about the spy. The flamer remained in the dust until the commander approached the Combatants and indicated it with the spurred toe of his boot.

"You take—"

It was more an order than a request. But Kana wanted nothing more than to do just that. This was a problem which must be taken straight to Yorke. What was the latest and most deadly weapon of the Galactic Patrol doing on Fronn in the hands of an enemy spy?

4

Classic Move To Disaster

On the top of the upturned provision box which served the Blademaster for a table lay the evidence. Fitch Yorke sat on a bed roll, his head and shoulder resting against the knotty trunk of a wind-twisted tree, his blond hair bright against the dark purple-blue of the bole as he chewed reflectively on a stick and regarded the flamer with a brooding frown. But Skura was not inclined to take the matter so quietly.

The Llor rebel leader strode back and forth across the blue clay soil, crushing the calm season ridges in it with grinding boot soles, as if he nursed some spite against the land itself.

"What say you now?" he demanded. "This is not yours. But it is off world. So—then from where?"

"I want to know that also, Highness. This is against

our law. But you did not find it in our hands—it was brought by a news-seeker of the enemy."

The "Yaaah" that burst from his woolly throat was more the roar of a hungry feline than an assent. "Evil from S'Tork—could else be expected? Against this— what good are swords—rifles? Are even the weapons of your so-fine Swordsmen strong when they face a fire that cooks and kills? We do not fight with flame. When I take much treasure to Secundus and ask who will give me aid in battle, I am told ask this or that fighting lord—but not such a one, or such a one—for on Fronn only certain ones may fight. So I give up the treasure and you come. Now—S'Tork numbers among his warriors those who have fire weapons! This is not clean dealing, Terran. And we Llor do not welcome double tongues—"

Skura paused before the flamer and Yorke. "Also"— the woolly head swung around and the pop eyes raked across Kana and Rey—"when the news-seeker was in our hands and could be questioned—what chances? Terran bullets send him speechless into the final shadows. Did you not want him to answer us, Blademaster?"

Yorke did not accept the challenge. "These"—he pointed to the flamer—"are very deadly, Highness. Had not my men killed, none of yours might have lived. I regret that we could not question that spy. Now we can only get our answers from S'Tork's camp—"

"Steps have been taken along that trail. If that refuse from the craw of a byll has indeed such arms we shall know it." Without another word Skura mounted his gu and pounded out of the Terran camp, with his personal guard left several lengths behind as usual, kicking at their mounts with the spur tips of their boots.

When Skura vanished in a cloud of blue dust Hansu and Mills materialized out of the background and Yorke lost his languid pose.

"Well?" One eyebrow slanted inquiringly toward the Blademaster's hairline.

"Better have it out now, rather than later," Hansu returned. "Somebody must be working out of season and with real backing. That's Galactic Patrol stuff—"

"Who?" Yorke spit out a bit of twig.

"Some Mech down on his luck," suggested Mills, "or—"

"Or somebody out to do a little empire building on his own," Hansu concluded for him. "We won't know until Skura's spies can report back."

"Arms and men—or just arms? That can be pretty important." Yorke got to his feet. "Either way—it's a mess."

Hansu shrugged. "Just arms and *we* have a better chance."

"You think this could be a show-down? Well—could be, could be. But if they think they have us rigged for a smash they'd better revise their plans." The Blademaster did not appear disturbed. "We might even get an answer to the old question too. What if Arch were matched against Mech? On a world such as this the nature of the country would be on our side. A light, highly mobile force against a mechanized division. Strike and away before the heavier body can move—" He looked almost eager to begin such an experiment.

"All right." Hansu picked up the flamer, and his soberness was in contrast to the other's momentary enthusiasm. "Maybe we can have a chance to prove how good we are. But no one can read the future. And this gun gets decommissioned right now!"

Yorke walked away and then Hansu held his own court of inquiry. Painstakingly Rey and Kana were taken over the events of the past few hours from Kana's noting of the hooded spy to his death.

"Next time see if you can nick a man in a less vital

spot," was the Swordtan's comment when they had finished. "I'd give a month's pay to have a few words with that one. Dismissed."

The flamer disappeared and there were no more references to it during the next few days. The Horde was in the foothills of the mountains, winding along paths worn by the clawed feet of the guen. Giant rock ledges layered black and white added to the gloom of the passage. The air, which was rarefied even on the plains, grew more tenuous. And, in spite of their conditioning on the trip to Fronn, the Combatants were left gasping after each stiff climb. Overhead the sky in daytime held a yellowish tinge and an icy wind licked at them from the snow fields of the peaks.

Seven Fronnian days' travel brought them over the hump and to the down slopes leading to the rich eastern section of the continent. Between the heights and the sea lay only these plains—unless one ventured north to meet another arm of the mountain range.

There had been a few skirmishes with royal outposts. But the three pass forts commanding their road had been abandoned before the rebels reached them, a circumstance which did not relieve Terran minds. Long years of battle training had taught them to be highly suspicious of anything easy. And added to this worry were the rumors that they might just be heading into a trap. The one encounter with the spy had been built into a brush with a group of armed Mechs. And even wilder stories were beginning to make the rounds of the night camps. While Yorke and his officers presented an impassive front, the Combatants kept apart from their native allies—and the service took on the aspect of an engagement from which the off-world fighters would be only too glad to withdraw.

One mid-day Kana accompanied Deke Mills in a tedious climb to the crest of a pinnacle which would afford them a clear view of the road ahead. As Mills adjusted the screw on his far vision lenses, Kana cupped his gloved hands about his eyes and tried his unaided sight. There was a glint below which could only be light striking metal—and it moved.

"They're waiting for us down there," Mills agreed. "Two—three royal standards. Three companies at least. There go Skura's mounted scouts. Wait—they're waving a flag! Parley?"

Kana could just make out those dots drifting down the mountain road to clot in a black blot.

"Yorke should know about this. Tell him they've signaled for a parley and it looks as if Skura is going to oblige—"

Kana slid down to locate the Blademaster at the foot of the pinnacle, occupied with a native map, his three Swordtans in consultation. At the news of the parley Yorke mounted the riding gu Skura had given him and rode off after the native van while Kana climbed back to Mills.

"Look!" The young veteran thrust the glasses into Kana's hands. "Over there—to the left. What do you make of that?"

Kana looked. There was a small body of the Llor rebels riding forward to meet a handful of royalists. But another group had dismounted and were making their way undercover to half circle the conference spot.

"An ambush? But they're meeting under a parley flag!"

"Just so." Deke Mills' voice was dry.

For a long moment there was little action below. The conferring leaders, mounted on guen, remained under the wind-whipped parley standard. Then the hidden rebels struck. The group of officers became a melee of fighting Llor and guen. Rebels dragged unsuspecting royalists from their mounts, leaving some limp upon the ground and pulling others with them back into the shelter of the rocks. As the angry enemy tried to follow, those in ambush covered the kidnappers with a wave of fire from their air rifles until the royalists were forced to retire in confusion. And the parley streamer beat the air over ground occupied only by the dead. The surprise had been as successful as it was treacherous.

The two Terrans, shocked by this drastic betrayal of a code which had been ingrained in them from their earliest days of training, climbed down to join their fellows.

"Something up?" Mic, quick to sense their tension, asked as they scrambled by him.

Kana nodded but Mills did not pause to explain. What that act of violence might mean to the Combatants no one could guess. It might even lead to a complete repudiation of their contract with Skura and their speedy return to Secundus.

Quick as they were about returning to the command post they arrived only seconds before Yorke. The Blademaster's face was an emotionless mask, but the set of his mouth, the gleam in his eyes, showed his worry.

Mills made his report and when he had finished Yorke laughed, though the sound held no mirth. "Yes"—his voice cut across the silence of the group—"it is true. Hansu, Bloor"—he jerked a beckoning finger at the two senior officers—"come along. This is the time for us to talk too. And"—his eyes swept the circle of Swordsmen—"you, you and you—" Kana realized with a start as Mills prodded him in the ribs that he was one the Blademaster had selected, together with Deke and Bogate. A pace or two behind the officers they trotted downhill.

Deke unslung his rifle, a gesture the other two copied. Accurate as the air rifles of the Llor were, the men who used them had neither the skill nor the startling marksmanship of the Terrans. If Yorke needed any show of force to back his meeting with Skura he was going to have it.

They found the rebel leader in a rocky defile where the caravan trail of the mountains widened into a respectable road. Llor mounted and on foot provided an audience for the scene in the center of that dusty track. Three royalist officers, bloody from minor wounds, their arms strapped behind them, were lined up before Skura who was haranguing them in the native language. He paused as the Terrans pushed through the ring of his men. It was impossible for any Combatant to read expression on the furred face of the rebel leader, but it was plain that Skura did not relish the arrival of Yorke.

Together the three Swordsmen planted themselves and their rifles in open view. It might be possible that they would be called upon to use those arms.

Yorke edged his gu on until he was abreast of Skura. The Llor about the leaders pulled back. They had seen too many examples of Terran shooting to wish to provide targets.

"Highness, what have I seen—this is not the proper way of war—" Yorke's voice was not pitched for speechmaking but it carried well.

"I am Gatanu, the Gatanu makes war as he pleases," Skura returned. "These serve S'Tork. Men of mine have they killed, so—"

His hand moved in a swift gesture. Steel flashed in the air and the three royalists fell forward as their dark blood splattered as far as Skura's boots.

Yorke's mouth was a single hard line. "That was ill done, Highness. From evil springs evil."

"So? On your world you do as custom rules. Customs are different here, off-worlder!"

The Llor leader was within his rights. And Yorke could make no answer. One of the rules of the Combat forces was not to question any native dealings with each other according to the established customs of the alien world. Perhaps on Fronn the desecration of a parley flag was accepted as a regular move in war time. But Kana heard Bogate mutter:

"No luck outta this—no luck for us when there's blood on a truce flag."

The Blademaster turned and rode away and in a compact group the Terrans fell back to their own force. But added to their constant suspicion was now another disturbing thought. War as they knew it was governed by certain unbreakable rules. Should these few laws to which they had always sworn allegiance be broken, what might be the end?

There was a council of war to which a representative from each team was summoned, while the remainder of the Combatants stood to their arms and prepared for trouble, suspecting attack now not only from the royalists but from their so-called allies as well.

By dawn the decision was made. Since Skura had quoted custom their contract held and under it they must go into battle with the rebels. The royalists had been beaten out of the foothills and the rebel forces were spreading out in long pinchers. Skura had some companies of infantry but guen cavalry was his preferred arm and his few regiments of foot moved as light wings to the heavier Terran Horde. According to his intelligence the royal army opposing them was small. The majority of the great lords of the plains had not yet chosen sides. A quick victory over this force—it was really only the household troops S'Tork had managed to marshal against them—would bring the nobles to declare for the rebels and the whole of the plains would fall to Skura with only a few isolated mopping-up expeditions to be sent against lords stubbornly holding for his cousin.

The shrill fluting of the Llor war trumpets sounded across the rolling country. And the rebels appeared confident of the outcome of the battle as small detachments of foot trotted up to join the wings of the Terran company, and troops of cavalry rode on to establish contact with the enemy.

The Horde stripped for action. Gone were the ornaments and the attention-catching trappings. They were in a uniform green-gray battle dress which blended with the patches of bare soil as they took cover.

Kana stretched his legs along a slight hollow and rested the barrel of his rifle on a conveniently crooked limb of the runty bush which gave him cover. Overhead a flock of flying creatures zigzagged and screeched their fear and anger at this invasion of their private world.

The plan of battle was simple, but one classic in Llor tradition. The pincher claws of the cavalry would attempt to encircle the enemy and herd them in toward the center where they must face the devastating fire of the Archs. And since S'Tork's inferior force had been unwise enough to offer battle the rebels saw no reason why the maneuver should fail, for the only answer to it was retreat.

Kana looked around as Mills crawled up to join him. The veteran surveyed the recruit's choice of position critically before he gave unspoken approval by settling down to pick his own loop-hole in the cloaking foliage. Under the blast of the trumpets there was a low rumble of sound, the deep-throated shouting of the Llor battle slogans. Mills grinned at Kana.

"The flag's up—here we go!"

Their view of the battle was necessarily limited. And

for what seemed like a very long period of time only
the distant growl gave any indication that a struggle
was in progress. Then came a burst of riders out of
a small coppice. They milled about, apparently uncertain. But the color of their trappings was not to be
mistaken. These were royalists who had been hunted
into the waiting jaws of the trap in which the Terrans
were the teeth.

Another group came out of the wood, and in this
several mounts ran free and wild, dodging the men who
strove to catch their reins. A dismounted Llor ran
lightly from cover and behind him hobbled another,
using a lance as a crutch. The hesitating troop which
had preceded these strays broke in two. One, the
smaller portion, dressed ranks, drew swords and rode
back into the trees; the other, keeping very little order,
came on down the valley. Kana picked his target before
the fellow came into reasonable range. Here there were
no war trumpets, no battle songs, but the hidden line
of the sharpshooters tensed. And, as the party of fugitives passed that outcrop of rock which gave the
Combatants a range marker, a withering blast of fire
tore them out of their saddles, sending the guen mad
with fear. One or two broken figures crawled along the
ground, but not a rider passed that rock.

Kana could not close his eyes, though his insides
twisted. This proved to be very different from firing
at humanoid robots set to dash and dodge across a
carefully marked rifle range—which had been his only
test of marksmanship before. A second ago he had fired
at a good target—that was all the squeeze of the trigger
had meant to him then. The Llor he had centered his
sights upon had had no identity as a living creature.
But—! He gagged and fought against a rising push of
nausea. He was given little time to examine his
muddled emotion for a second wave of royalists had

been beaten out of the woods. This time they were
mingled with their pursuers, whirling in a mounted
dance of death with a detachment of the rebels who
hacked them downslope to the lines of the dead the
Terrans had shot. But the enemy were giving a good
account of themselves, there were almost as many
empty saddles among the rebel band.

"Skura!"

Kana had not needed Mills' identification. The rebel
chieftain was unmistakable as he beat and slashed his
way to the leader of the loyalist troop. That officer,
as imposing physically as the would-be Gatanu,
accepted battle with the same eagerness. And, while
their followers struggled around them, the two leaders settled down to expert saber work. The royalist was
bleeding from a slash high on one shoulder but it did
not impair his efficient swordplay. As yet Skura was
untouched.

The ring of tempered metal upon metal carried to
the Terrans, but they continued to hold their fire.
There was too much chance of shooting the wrong man
in the melee. The gu ridden by the royalist attempted
to use its teeth on Skura's mount. And in one such
lunge it jerked its rider out of position. Skura's blade
bit deep into the other's forearm and the royalist's
sword fell from helpless fingers. Skura had just raised
his blade to deliver the death stroke when he himself
crumpled, collapsing over his gu's head into the dust.

Perhaps only the Terrans saw that pencil of flame
spray from the wood to strike down the rebel leader
in the moment of his triumph. The Llor who, seconds
before, had been locked in a death struggle were
shocked into quiet, all staring at Skura. Then, with a
wild wail of horror and despair, his followers attacked,
killing ruthlessly. Two royalists escaped into the woods.
The rest were dead.

"That was a flamer!" Kana's voice was swallowed up in the cries of the Llor.

They had gathered up the Chortha's body and were tying it in the saddle. Then they rode north. Mills got to one knee to watch them go.

"That's the end of the war," he remarked.

As if his observation were a signal, the piercing whistle of recall brought the Combatants out of line, withdrawing to secondary positions. Alert and ready the Terrans waited out the afternoon. But what Mills had said at the moment of Skura's fall proved to be true. The death of the rebel chieftain demoralized his followers, the war was at an end and the Llor avoided the off-world men. The Combatants suspected that minor rebels were trying to make deals. And at that moment the future of the Horde was bleak. However, when such defeats had occurred before in Combatant history, the Horde or Legion retained by the defeated leader had always been given free access to its transport ships and allowed safe conduct off the planet.

Soldiers are largely conservative, ruled by custom, and since custom was now on their side and they were freed from an entanglement most of them had come to regard as risky, there was a feeling of relaxation, of "Well, the worst is now over," in the Horde camp that night. They kept a patrol about the environs of their position, and there was no slacking on guard. But the death of Skura, who had left no heir to rally his men, absolved them from their pledged support. And now, with something of a holiday lightheartedness, they looked forward to a speedy return to Tharc where the transports waited.

The only gloomy reaction to the events of the afternoon was the realization that the shortness of the campaign would mean only basic pay. But Kana and some others sensed that the future might not be so bright.

The recruit noted that Yorke, the three Swordtans, and some veterans, including Mills, did not drag out their bed rolls that night. And when he was roused for second guardpost duty in the very early morning he saw the light still shining in the small tent where the officers had gathered.

Skura had been killed with a flamer—which meant that at least one more illegal weapon was in the hands of the enemy. Who had brought the arms to Fronn and why? Kana puzzled over that as he took his post. The chill black of the Fronnian night was alive with sounds which might or might not signal danger. But a circle of guard lamps set at intervals around the camp made a barrier of light.

Flying things attracted there and blinded by the radiance beat around the lamps, making a funnel of winged bodies down to the very lens. Hunting these bemused tidbits came larger creatures, some on four legs and some on two, others skimming on wings themselves. This was rich feasting and not a few vicious quarrels ensued.

Suddenly the low-hanging branches of a bush were pushed aside and a man stepped out into the full beam of the light, halting as if he wanted to be recognized. And the newcomer was no Fronnian.

Kana's rifle went up until its sights covered that swaggering design of crossed rockets on the breast of the stranger's tunic. A Mech—in full uniform! Kana whistled for the guard and snapped:

"Stand where you are—hands up!"

The other laughed. "Not planning to do anything else. I've a message for Yorke."

5

Morning After

A slap across his sleeping bag shocked Kana into groggy wakefulness some hours later. Mills towered over him.

"Hit dirt," the veteran commanded brusquely. "We're pulling out."

Pulling out they were and with unusual speed. Kana had barely time to throw his bag on a cart already moving. And he was still rubbing the smart of sleep out of his eyes as he fell in with his team. They were marching in "hostile country" order he noticed—scouts out on the wings. And Terran drivers, not Llor, prodded the baggage guen into action. In fact in all that winding column there was not a native Fronnian to be seen. Nor were they headed back into the mountains toward Tharc, but instead following a trail which led away at right angles, north along the foothills.

The new road dwindled into the faintest of tracks within a mile or so. From the exasperated comments voiced about him Kana gathered that none of the lower rank Combatants knew where they were headed or why. And more than once he caught muffled suggestions about the mysterious troubles which had recently overwhelmed other Hordes and Legions light years from home. In spite of their usual fatalism, the morale of the mercenaries might be seriously affected if the situation continued.

Perhaps this new move was the result of that visit the Mech had paid their camp in the early morning. But the confidence the Terrans had shown after Skura was slain was fast changing to a growing uneasiness.

After a space the trace they followed grew so narrow that it seemed they must abandon the carts. Two of the scouts came in to report, a native with them, a Llor of the petty officer class, wearing a stained bandage about his head, one arm in a grimy sling. Rumor rippled down the ranks.

"There's a big river ahead—and no bridge—"

Before that news had reached the tail of the last team the call to general council was whistled. Yorke's voice, clippy and tinny, came through the speakers.

"Men, the situation is not promising. We were informed that S'Tork has enlisted the services of Mech renegades—how many we do not yet know. We have not been offered safe conduct, and we cannot return to Tharc without it. Until we can make a treaty and enforce the recognition of our position under general Combat usage, we must mark time. We shall send a message to Secundus—"

"And who's going to grow a space drive and fly it there through space?" Kana heard someone ask grimly in a half whisper.

"We have information," Yorke was continuing, "that there is another mountain gap to the north which we may cross if we cannot come to terms—we are now heading toward that. In the meantime we must do nothing to arouse the enmity of the royalists, give them any reason for declaring that we fought on after the death of Skura. Under no provocation, no matter how severe, is any Swordsman to use his weapon against a Llor—until this order is countermanded. We shall continue in 'hostile country, plan three' until further notice. Change the loads on the large carts to backpacks for the guen. Only the three small handcarts can be used from this point on. We shall establish a night camp beside the river—"

The use of resisting guen for pack animals was not easy. And it was nearly twilight before the detachment of which Kana was one, pulling and batting their snarling beasts down to the lighted area of the camp the van had set up, gained the river. The site of the Terran position was on a bluff above the dark, oily water which washed the clay bank with unwholesome ripples. And an almost vertical descent plunged into a powerful current. They need not fear a surprise attack from that direction.

Kana strode along the bank, looking at the flood. From the white foam collars wreathing the rocks there he judged that the current was too swift to grant them an easy crossing. As his eyes trailed bubbles downstream he saw dancing dots of light moving through the blackness of the night, coalescing on the same bank farther east. Another camp? Then the Horde's line of march must have been paralleled by a detachment of Llor.

Luckily the Horde carried their own rations. Natives who themselves depended upon the natural produce of their land could not readily gauge the superior mobility of an army for whom the supply problem consisted of a relatively small amount of condensed food tablets and other concentrated rations, weeks' needs being carried easily in an individual's own belt pouch. The ancient "scorched-earth" policy would not be effective against Terrans—unless they could be kept from their base for a period comprising months.

"Dumb woolly heads!" As Kana dropped down by Mills and Mic he heard Sim's thick voice rumble, "What do they think they can do—"

"It's not what the fur faces are gonna do." That was Bogate. "Skura wasn't killed by no fur face. I was there. I tell you, fellas, he got burned right through the middle—neat and clean! Me, I'm a Swordsman, and a ten-year man, and I know better'n to spit in the face of a flamer!"

"Flamer?" questioned someone. "But if they have flamers they'd have cut us to pieces back there. And we were winning until Skura took it."

"Lissen." Bogate's voice overbore the other's. "I saw what I saw! That was a Mech that was marched in to see Yorke last night. And he wasn't no observer either! What if S'Tork has a whole renegade Legion hid back there?"

"You're talking feathers and fluff!" challenged one of his companions. "A whole Legion turned bad—why, they couldn't have set course for here without Prime knowing it!"

Bogate's sardonic bark of laughter cut that down. "There's a million-trillion ways you can beat the High Brass back at base—and you know it. Just because it ain't never been done before, is no sign that some smart guy can't pull it off. Lookit here, a Mechmaster what wanted to, could grab hisself off a world like this—set up as Control Commissioner or something. Ain't that right, Mills?"

Deke Mills slapped away one of the flyers drawn by the lamps. "Entirely true, Bogate. And you're also right in that exactly that is what may be happening now.

If so"—he paused and then continued—"if so we must be prepared to fight our way off-world."

Several voices protested and then sank to silence under Bogate's growl.

"Ain't you bumble-wits got it into your heads yet that when a fella breaks the top laws he ain't gonna let tongues wag if he can help it? We go back to Secundus and shoot off our mouths about flamers and Mechs here and the mop-up crew is gonna head straight to Fronn to see what's what. Think, can't you. Who's liable to have flamers—what kinda support these here renegade Mechs got?"

The sudden tense silence which answered him was that of men who were beginning to think and didn't like it.

Due to Hansu's use of Mills as his aide, Kana's acquaintance with his double was not a deep one. He messed with and shared the quarters of Rey and Mic, meeting with Mills only when duty brought them together. But now he ventured to ask his quiet companion a question.

"This could reach clear to Prime, couldn't it?"

Mills did not turn his head. But a second later he snapped:

"Explain that!"

Kana described the actions of the Mech in the information library, retailing his belief that the man was waiting for the pak on Fronn.

"No Legion badge on his helmet?"

"No, sir. I thought he might have just signed up. But why—" He fell silent but his thoughts were very busy.

How could any Mech be recruited for illegal service on Prime? S'Tork *must* be backed by more than a mere handful of renegades!

"Yes—why and how." Mills' whisper added to his formless apprehension. "This is a case of going into

battle blindfolded." The veteran got to his feet and
Kana trailed him.

They were, the younger Swordsman discovered,
making a circuit of the camp, passing from post to post.
When they reached the east Mills gave the password
and stepped beyond the brilliance of the lamps into
the night. As their eyes adjusted Kana located the
bluish haze of the Llor encampment. Contrary to their
usual custom the Fronnian forces were keeping their
torches ablaze. But they had not advanced any toward
the Terran site.

A single moment of study was enough to satisfy
Mills. He tramped south, stopping now and then to
study the darkness. Farther off was another barrier of
lights across the road over which they had just come.
The Llor had cut off any possible retreat.

To the west stood the mountain wall. There were
no gleams of blue on the heights. The Terran camp
was not yet ringed in—or did the Llor believe that the
mountains themselves were barrier enough? They might
consider that they had the off-world army pinned down
with the mountains and the river and the two bodies
of their own troops.

Mills reached the last post, but he did not turn back
into camp. "Hansu tells me," he began abruptly, "that
you're an AL man. What do you make of the Llor—of
this situation? Surely they must know they haven't
bottled us up. We could blow them out of our way
whenever we wanted to show strength. They have something in reserve—they must have!"

"You can never tell about a feudal civilization with
alien natives. Skura was inclined to overestimate his
own powers. This is the first time a Combat force has
been on Fronn." Kana shrugged. "You know that X-Tee,
Alien Liaison, is pure guesswork at times. We can't get
inside the skull of a creature whose whole mental

processes may be different. The Llor, it's my guess, are either just what they outwardly appear to be—simple barbarians—or else—"

"Or else," Mills caught him up, "something so tortuously complicated that we shall never be able to cope with them. Or they may have expert advice and assistance—"

"From a Mech Legion?"

"I don't see how they could have that! The transportation problem to Fronn alone—! Why, no troopship can clear for anywhere in the Galaxy without a sealed route-tape to its known destination. And yet that Mech on Prime was taking indoctrination for this planet—Prime! Right where the least rumor of such a move should damn it from the start. And suppose a Legion, or a part of a Legion *has* turned rotten—why select Fronn for their operations? What does a frontier world possess that would make such a risk within the bounds of profit?"

"What sort of mineral rights did Skura sell Interplanetary to raise the pay for Yorke, sir?"

Deke Mills squared around to face Kana, amazement in his eyes. Almost, the younger Swordsman thought, as if a gu had addressed him in good Basic.

"Out of the mouths of greenies," he said. "Mineral rights, trading rights, and maybe a good chance for a double cross all around with the Terrans to blame everything on! Lord of Space! That could be the answer to a lot of questions. Mechs could be smuggled in on trade ships—flamers provided—everything! But"—he stared thoughtfully at Kana—"you keep your mouth shut on that bright idea, understand? We already have enough rumors flying around now without adding one so logical it can be believed."

"Then you think we've more than renegades against us, sir?"

"Alien reasoning—how do we know how their minds

work? The C.C. doesn't understand, doesn't want to. They've never even tried to know what makes us tick. We're the slightly comical, childish mercenaries—with minds that don't match their pattern charts. So they fit us into the general scheme of things and try to forget us. And because we have functioned in that niche, they've stopped worrying about us. Their idea of a Terran has become so much of a set figure that they do not see us as we are at all, but as they think we are—two very different things. You know"—Mills paused for a moment as if a new thought had struck him—"that in a way gives us a protective covering. We've learned things which would surprise the Galactic Agents. So these Trade boys—non-Terran, of course— Terra cannot trade—figure out a neat, strictly illegal scheme—and they don't stop to think of our part in it at all. We're just pieces to be shoved around on a game board. But what will happen if *we* begin to make moves on our own? We should try just that—"

Kana tensed. Was Mills choosing to pass along real information? Did the Terrans have some way of fighting back against the protective parentalism of C.C. which might even now keep them earthbound? The odd sixth sense which was part of the make-up of any A.L. man quivered into life. He thought of questions—ten—twenty of them—he wanted to ask. But there was no time, for in the camp Swordsmen were moving among the tents and saddled guen stood in the light marking Yorke's headquarters.

"Do we march?" Kana hurried to catch up with Mills.

Before the Blademaster's tent were the three Swordtans and a group of under officers. It was plain there was an argument in progress and at last Yorke turned impatiently from Hansu and reached for the reins of his gu.

"Until I return you're in command," he said.

A party of three Llor, high-ranking nobles by their war harness, were waiting, the lamps painting their furred faces with a slightly sinister shadow. The other two Swordtans mounted, but the Llor leader was in no hurry to leave. He gestured at Hansu and asked a question. Yorke answered, and still the Llor did not move. Yorke's gaze fastened on Mills. He beckoned the young veteran forward. Hansu nodded and snapped the Swordtan's insignia from his helmet, passing it to Deke.

"You're my deputy. The Llor demand that all our High Brass attend. And they've seen you at our conferences in the past so you can pass as an officer. But—" perhaps Kana was the only one who saw that the fingers which passed the badge from one man to another closed bruisingly tight on Mills' hand— "watch out." Mills mounted a gu and the small cavalcade swept off. Their progress across country was marked by the blue of the Fronnian torches as they sped eastward to the camp of the royalists downriver.

Hansu wasted no time after Yorke left. Working by quiet orders passed from man to man, the Combatants went into action. The tents were left standing. But all other gear was sorted and skeleton packs of one change of clothing, blankets and cold-weather wear, were assembled by each man. Medical kits were passed out, along with rations and spare ammunition. Then the men turned in, half a team at a time, for a few hours' sleep. When Kana roused in the early morning the camp presented the appearance of having been sacked by the enemy.

Everywhere the war bags of the Swordsmen gaped, their less useful contents spilled. The force was now prepared to move fast and keep moving. Hansu must expect trouble.

With the rising sun the Terrans could see the hide

tents of the royalists on the river bank to the east, and sight the clustered standards of the troops which had followed them through the foothills. The lamps on the barrier were switched off but not dismounted from their bases. For if the Horde had to travel light, these, too, must be left behind.

Hansu had stationed men along the river. Their principal occupation, as Kana observed from an eastern sentry post, was to toss in bits of wood fastened to cords in order to study the current. After about an hour of this they straggled back to report. But Kana knew that to cross the stream here, especially if they were forced into that act under fire, was suicide.

It should not come to that. The Llor had asked to treat. Yorke would return with the safe conduct and the Horde would march back to Tharc. If the Llor followed the rules of Combat that was all they could do—*If*.

Llor rode leisurely down the mountain road, holding their guen to an ambling pace. All wore the royalists' badges, though, as they made a detour about the Terran camp, Kana was not the only one to suspect that the majority had not been on that side of the conflict three days before. They were armed but their weapons were sheathed and slung. And they appeared content to ride slowly to the river, shouting remarks which no Combatant deceived himself into believing were complimentary.

"That woolly-face with the blue sash—" Mic squatted beside Kana in the outpost—"I could make him change his mind about stupid Terrans—with just one squeeze of the trigger—"

The Llor belted with the blue sash was gesturing, gestures which were rankly insulting on any planet. He was escorted by a choice group of friends whose howls of delight led him on to bigger and worse efforts. Mic's sights covered in turn several important points of the comedian's anatomy as he sighted for the shot he could not make.

"Aren't you here ahead of time?" asked Kana.

"Oh, I'm not your relief. We're to double up on the posts from now on, Hansu's orders. There's a nasty smell rising, and it isn't all from wool either. Yorke's been gone almost ten hours. It doesn't take that long to sign a retreat treaty. You bring your pack with you?"

Kana kicked the roll by his feet. "Sure. But Hansu won't march until he hears from Yorke—"

"I don't think so. Now—just what is that?"

The sun of Fronn was pale and feeble compared to the Sol which warmed Terra, but it did give light and now behind the milling Llor, from the edge of a small thicket on the river bank, those pale rays were reflected by some bright surface directly toward the Terran lines in a regular rhythm.

Three letters of their own native tongue, a cry for aid so old that its origin was long ago lost in the mists of Terra's war-torn past—a signal only one of their own kind would send! Kana laid down his rifle.

"Take over!" He moved before Mic could stop him. His hours of duty at this post had not been wasted. There was a way, if not an easy one, to get down to that coppice without venturing into the open now patrolled by the Llor.

Kana lowered himself over the edge of the cliff, kicking for holds with the toes of his battle boots. Fly-fashion he was able to crawl down to the few inches of beach. There was about a foot of sand and gravel between the base of the cliff and the rushing water. With his back to the wall, hidden from anyone above unless he leaned far enough over to sight him, Kana fought his way by inches along the stream. Once or twice the lapping water curled about his toes and he dug his fingers into the soil at his back for a hold. The worst was losing his sense of direction, for he had to stop every few feet and look up for the trees which were his goal.

How long that crab's journey took he could not have testified, but it seemed to him that he had been at it for at least an hour when the sight of black-green foliage set him turning to face the cliff. A bundle of roots protruded from the bank within reach and he began to climb. Dried clay powdered his face and he wiped his eyes with one hand while he held on with the other. His nails tore and broke and his uniform was plastered with dust and clay, but he wormed his way up into the embrace of a thorny bush.

"Terra?" He kept his voice low. But at the answer to his question he pushed forward recklessly. That moan could only have been born of real suffering.

His forward spring brought him to the very edge of the thicket facing west. Collapsed half over a fallen tree, veiled from the Llor riders by only a thin screen of brush, was a limp body.

Kana hardly dared to touch the body when he saw the extent of the burns which had charred away most of the green-gray tunic. Flamer wound! He shrank from causing the torture he knew his grip must bring as with infinite horror he raised the other. The blackened, seared body writhed out of his hold and a moan sounded the wounded man's pain. Gritting his teeth, Kana took hold for the second time and fought the other's feeble attempts to pull free. At last he turned the heavy head to the light. The flamer had not touched the face and though it was contorted and twisted with agony, Kana knew who it was he supported in his arms.

"Deke! What—what have they done!"

6

If The Faith
Be Broke—

The dark eyes struggled to focus. It was as if Deke Mills came haltingly back from a long distance, driven by some overwhelming sense of duty.

"All—dead—Hart Device—Tell Hansu—Hart Device—"

Kana nodded. "I should tell Hansu that Hart Device is responsible?"

Deke's eyes gave assent. "No—not alone. Galactic—agent—hiding—Burned us down." Some spark of strength steadied his voice. "Tried—tried to get Yorke to renegade too. When he said no—flamed us from behind. All dead—thought me dead too. Agent came—looked. I saw him clear—agent—tell Hansu—C.C. backing Device. Crawled—crawled—hours and hours

crawled. They had just flamers—no big stuff. Tell
Hansu—flamers—"

"There's a Galactic Agent with them and they have
C.C. arms," Kana repeated with cold steadiness.

For a long moment Mills lay quiet in his hold,
summoning up strength.

"Tell Hansu—C.C. behind it—wipe us out if they
can. Mustn't be cut off here. Back to ships—report—
Combat—report—"

One of the charred stumps of hands stirred, pawed
at Kana's sleeve.

"I'll tell him, Deke," he hastened to promise.

"From behind—no chance—Hart Device—" Mills'
whisper thinned and then died. Then he said quite
clearly and coherently:

"Give Grace, Comrade—!"

Kana swallowed, his mouth dry. For an instant he
was back again in the chapel on Terra, half the Galaxy away from this Fronnian wood. He had been drilled
in the Ritual, he knew what had to be done. But
somehow, in spite of all the solemn instructions, he had
never really expected to be called upon to give the Last
Grace—

Deke's pain-filled eyes held his. His duty done, he
was waiting for the release from the world of agony
which held him. Mills knew what his wounds meant.
Nothing could be done for him even by the Medicos
on Secundus. And he could not be transported there.
Slowly, trying not to add to Mills' pain, Kana lowered
the other to earth and opened his own tunic to reach
the slender knife all Combatants wore on their breasts.
This was the "Grace" of the fighting man—to be carried with him awake or sleeping all his life—to be used
for one purpose only.

Kana drew the steel into the light. He raised the
plain cross hilt to his lips and said the proper words,

hearing his own voice as if it belonged to a stranger, knowing that Deke's twisted lips were trying to shape the same plea.

"—so do I send thee home, brother-in-arms!" Kana ended, he could not delay any longer.

The knife slipped into the place instruction had taught him to seek. Then he was alone—left to slip that wet blade back in its sheath. It could not be cleaned except in the earth of Terra. There was one thing more—the husk which had been Deke Mills must not be left for the Llor and it was beyond his power to carry the body back to camp.

From his belt Kana unhooked a cartridge. With great care he unscrewed its cap and placed it on the body. Then he threw himself back toward the cliff. The blast came in a sheet of flame before he was quite over the bank. When that fire died Deke Mills would never be found.

Kana inched his way upstream at the fastest pace he could manage, trying to keep his mind blank of all but Mills' message to Hansu. With Yorke and the other Swordtans murdered, Trig Hansu now commanded the Horde.

He found the end of a rope dangling over the bluff below the sentry post and with its aid got up to the camp. At the top he found not only Mic but Hansu waiting for him. Downriver a pillar of black smoke penciled into the sky and the Llor were gathering at the edge of the wood. Kana made his terse report.

"They flamed Yorke and the rest from behind when Yorke would not agree to join them. A C.C. Agent watched the whole thing secretly. Hart Device leads the Mechs. Deke was mortally wounded but crawled—as far as the wood over there. He said he saw C.C. flamers but none of their big stuff—thought that they were out to get us all."

Hansu's expression did not change at the name of the renegade Mechmaster or at the mention of the Agent. And almost before Kana finished speaking he was giving orders to the handful of veterans nearby.

"Dolph, you take over Team One, Horvath, Team Two. Prepare to move out. And send Bogate here."

Hansu asked one more question of Kana in a low voice:

"Mills?"

Kana found no words to answer that. He drew out the Grace Knife to display its stains. Behind him, through his sick misery, he heard Mic's breath catch. But Hansu made no comment. And he asked nothing more.

It was Mic who helped Kana sling his rifle and shoulder his pack, guiding him back to the busy camp. The gear they had discarded the night before was being built, under Bogate's orders, into a wall of supplies stretching from one lamp line to another. Except for the men working to erect that barrier the Combatants were lining up to the west, facing the mountains.

"Done, sir!" Bogate saluted Hansu. Five of the Terrans were stationed at intervals along the discarded baggage, and each cradled in his hand one of the fire cartridges.

"Ready with those beasts?" demanded Hansu.

The squad which had herded the pack guen to the far side of the camp shouted an affirmative.

"Men"—Hansu wheeled to face the teams—"you all know what has happened. If the faith be broke, then so is the contract which bound us. Yorke and the others were murdered, shot down from behind by flamers. Mills lived long enough to warn us. You know that it is not superior numbers, or strength of arms, that wins a war. The side which goes in with the will to victory has the advantage. When we march out of here we have to cross a hostile planet. Every native may be ranged against us. But unless we can reach Tharc we have very little chance. Remember this—our lives are at stake, yes. But the Combatant whose single aim is to keep alive usually dies in the first charge. To die is our common lot, no man escapes that. But if we die in the tradition of the Hordes—that is a good ending for any of us.

"They believe that they have us walled in, that we cannot break out of their cage of mountains, river and troops. But we shall show them that they dare not underestimate a Swordsman. With this fire to cover our tracks we shall head west—into the mountains. Before the death of Skura they told us that the mountains were to be feared, that the natives there have never submitted to the Gatanu's rule and are dangerous. If that is so we may find allies—at least we shall be headed in the right direction. Whoever wants to keep alive must aim at victory. It is the winners who kill and the losers who are killed!"

The Horde greeted that statement with a cheer as Hansu signaled the men by the barrier. Squalling guen were sent running wild toward the Llor who milled around beyond the boundaries of the camp. And the Fronnian troopers were forced to scatter before the loose animals, trying to head them away from their own lines. But the guen, with the diabolical tempers of their kind, attacked the cavalry mounts whenever they came in contact.

Falling into "hostile country" order the Horde moved out. Puffs of flame blossomed along the wall of abandoned supplies, providing a thick smoke to hide their going. And the heat of the fire would keep back the Llor for some time.

The Terran line of march followed the river where there was little cover. And within half a mile the stream sank deeper as outcrops of black and white rock grew more frequent. Kana took his turn at hauling the small carts which transported such of the general supplies as they had to have. There were two of these and the material they carried might mean the difference between life and death for the men they rolled among.

It was close to twilight when Kana released his hold to a relief and, rubbing his rope-chafed hands, fell back into line. So far Hansu had given no orders to camp. They ate as they marched, hard rations, and sipped the water from their canteens. There had been no signs of pursuit. But the Blademaster evidently intended to put as many miles between them and their last camp as was humanly possible.

The river stopped them for the second time. Sunk now in a deep gorge, it sliced across their route. They would either have to cross or turn back. In the last dwindling light of day they made camp, taking advantage of the rough ground to conceal their bed rolls. It was then that Kana was summoned to report to Hansu.

"You were down to the stream edge back there. Current bad?"

"Slick and fast, sir. And I think deep too. It must be even deeper here."

"Hmm—" Hansu dropped to his knees and wriggled forward to the rim of the drop. He brought out a pocket flash and lowered it by a cord into the depths, revealing the surface of the cliff as it descended.

The river had cut that gorge, and at times it must have been a wider and stronger stream, for it left in its passage a series of ledges—a giant's staircase, marking the stages of its sinking. Not very wide and unfortunately far apart—they were still ledges and so promised a means of winning down to the water. The light oscillated above the racing flood and the vicious fangs of boulders made up rapids which choked half its bed. Landslides had partially dammed the stream, leaving a residue in stones too big for the water to tear away. To try to swim that would be asking for a smashed and broken body. And the light's rays were too limited to show what awaited on the other side. Hansu coiled the rope, loop by loop, bringing up the light.

"We'll have to wait for daylight," he said impatiently. "A Galactic Agent—you are sure Mills said that?"

Kana could only repeat what he had been told. Then he added: "The Llor are confident, sir—a lot too confident. Wouldn't they have to be pretty sure of their backing before they turned on us?"

Hansu made a sound which had little in common with real laughter. "Oh, yes, we have reputations. But then they must have advisers to whom such reputations are merely amusing. The Llor are fighting men and if the advantages appear to lie on their side, they are going to do just as they please. Skura murdered his enemies even under the parley flag, this will be more of the same. Maybe it's all an old Fronnian custom. However"—his lips drew back in what was close to a lion's snarl—"they had better not make too many bright plans for the future—even acting under C.C. advice!"

"What do you know about the Cos?" the Blademaster demanded a minute later, snapping Kana out of some dark thoughts.

"They are mountain natives, aren't they, sir? There wasn't much about them in the pak on Fronn. I got the impression that they're not of the same race as the Llor and that they are deadly enemies of the plains dwellers. But they aren't Venturi either."

"They're a pygmy race—at least the Llor consider them so. And they *are* deadly—to anyone who tries to invade their territory. Use poison darts and mantraps.

But whether we're headed into Cos country now, I don't know. And their quarrel may be only with the Llor—there's always that hope. Anyway, we have no choice but to advance. And now you're going to work, Karr."

"Yes, sir?"

"You're attached as Alien Liaison man from now on. Figure out what you need for a 'first contact pack' and get it together tonight. We'll have no time in the morning and you must have the kit ready to use. Bogate!"

The veteran, a black blot in the deepening night, moved up.

"You take scout tomorrow. Karr here will be the AL man for your party."

"Yes, sir." There was no indication that Zapan Bogate had ever seen Kana before. "How many men?"

"Not more than ten. Wide scout—hostile country. I want a con job all the way—"

"Yes, sir! Con it is!"

The feeble illumination in the camp came from hand flashes muffled in spider silk. But it was enough to guide Kana to his place with Mic and Rey. He hunched down, drawing his one blanket about his shoulders, and tried to think coherently. As AL man with the advance scouts tomorrow he would have to have some kind of a trade kit—trade was always the easiest form of contact with unknown tribes. But he knew so little about the Cos—pygmies, perpetual enemies of the Llor, addicted to poison darts and mantraps to keep their mountain territory sacrosanct. The common offerings—food—adornment. This problem should have been foreseen before they burned the excess baggage. If the Combatants had obeyed orders they had already stripped themselves of the very things he would need.

Food— Almost all aliens had an innate curiosity

about off-world food, especially if they lived in a rugged country on a near-starvation diet. And of all Terran foods there was one in particular which the Combatants always carried with them, one grown only on their native world, which most extraterrestrial life relished. Intersystem Traders had been trying to export it for years. But the Terrans had ruled it a military supply and so controlled its production—keeping it for the troops and a few of their favored alien friends. As a bargaining point it had been too precious to destroy back at the last camp. Their ration of it must be lashed on one of the carts he had helped to drag. He should ask the Medico for a supply.

Ornaments—the veterans had stripped their wealth from the dress uniforms. Each man would carry his own in a waist treasure belt. Kana must beg for the showiest pieces. Well, no time to lose. Neither Mic nor Rey owned anything worthwhile. But there was the whole camp to canvass.

Kana dropped his blanket wearily and started off on his task, his first quarry being the Medico. Crawfur heard his plea and then detached one of the small boxes from the nearest cart. Kana signed for a packet as big as his hand—a packet which would have brought the equivalent of a deputy-control officer's pay for half a year had it been offered for sale in the black markets on half a dozen different planets.

And on hearing of the other need Crawfur unhooked one of the pockets of his own belt and contributed to the cause a Ciranian "sunstone" which drew light from a muffled lamp to make a warm pool of fire in the donor's hand.

"Might as well take this. My neck's worth more than that. Don't hesitate to ask—we all know what we may be up against. Tal, Kankon, Ponay." He roused his assistants and explained.

When Kana left the group he had the packet of sugar, the sunstone, a chain of Terran gold about a foot long, a ring made in the form of a Zacathan water snake, and a tiny orb of crystal in which swam a weird replica of a Poltorian lobster fish. He returned to his own place half an hour later the breast of his tunic bulging with glittering treasure, rings on every finger and arm bands braceleting his arms. The loot was sorted out under a lamp. This and this and this were eye-catching "come-on" pieces to be displayed as a lure. But this and that and that should be reserved as personal gifts to win the favor of chieftains or war leaders. He made up three packets according to their future use and put them away before he curled up and tried to sleep. Without the bright rim of the lamps about the campsite the heavy dark of the Fronnian night walled them in—they might be within a giant box trap, the lid slammed down upon them.

Kana could see those icy sparks of light which were the stars—suns which warmed strange worlds. And somewhere, overshadowed by the brilliance of so many others, Sol had its place, while around its yellow glory wound in their orbits the worlds he knew best.

Green earth. Out here there were other green worlds, as well as blue, red, white, violet, yellow—but none of them wore just the same tint of green as that which covered Terra's hills. Terra—man's home. Mankind had come late into space, and had been pushed to one side of the game Central Control managed. But there were many worlds where native life had never reached intelligence. What if man had been allowed to spread to those—to colonize? What if the very ancient legends of his race were true and there had been earlier trips into deep space from which the voyagers had never returned? Were there worlds where once Terran colonies had taken root? Where he could find his own distant kin free of the Central Control yoke, men who had won the stars by their own efforts?

He drifted into sleep thinking of that. But then he was crouched in a Fronnian thicket, a bloody knife in his hand—

"—up!" Kana rolled over. The dawn was gray and above him Bogate, rifle slung over his shoulder, marching supplies in place, stood, his thumbs hooked in his waist belt, his helmet gleaming in the growing light.

Kana rolled his own kit together hurriedly. The AL packets he crowded into the front of his tunic where he could reach them easily.

"Moving out now?"

"Shortly. Draw your rations and fall in."

Hansu and a picked party equipped with ropes were already busy at the rim of the canyon. Three men had worked their way, ledge by ledge, to the sliver of beach far below. There they took turns, one roped to another, wading and swimming out into the flood, wedging native lances and driftwood between the boulders, trying to make a barrier which might save a man, swept from his feet, from being washed away. It was plain that Hansu was determined to get them across the river.

The pioneers below had fought their way less than half the distance across when Kana, together with Bogate's scouts, started down. They fastened rifles, packs, and other supplies into waterproof coverings which were lowered on a makeshift platform faster than they climbed. Kana was dangling on a rope between two ledges when a shout which was half scream tore at his ears and nerves. He did not turn his head—he dared not. A moment later the rope a few feet to his right, taut seconds before with the weight of the scout who had crawled over the rim beside him, slapped the rock loosely—that weight gone.

Even when his boots rested on the next ledge Kana did not look down. He rested, spread-eagled against the wall, his fingers gritting on the rock, the sweat dripping from his chin.

Three ledges more and he reached the shingle. The men who had preceded him were still gazing downstream, a bewildered horror in their eyes. But there was no time to mourn as there had been none to save. Bogate slid down the last length of rope and was shouting orders:

"Get your gear, you Lothurian leaf eaters! We cross over and then we go up—and we do it in space time!"

They did it—if not in space time—with the loss of another man, sucked under by the current and smashed against a rock, then by some freak of the flood flung contemptuously back at them limp and broken. But roped, sometimes thrown off their feet and carried downstream, fighting from one boulder to the next, they got across. Another of their company, nursing an arm snapped like a twig during his final two-foot fight for the shore, remained there to watch the guide ropes they had left for those following.

Up the cliff they crept from handhold to handhold, shaking with effort, their fingers slippery with sweat, their hearts and lungs laboring. Salt stung in their eyes and the rawness of their hands, but they climbed.

Kana concentrated on the foot of earth immediately before his eyes, and then on the next higher and the next. This had gone on for hours—would go on and on without end.

Then a hand closed about the wrist he had extended for a fresh hold. He was lifted with a yank which brought him sliding on his face across the lip of the wall to lie panting in tearing gasps, too bone weary to reach for the canteen of water his mouth and throat craved.

He sat up as Bogate came along. There was a coil of rope about his waist—that must be knotted to other lengths, the whole dropped to form a ladder for the Horde.

Kana drank and was able to scramble to his feet when their rifles and packs were hoisted. Nor was he the last to fall in as Bogate gave the signal to move on—into the dark future of the mountains.

7

The Badlands

As they left the river the rest of the scouts fanned out. Only Kana continued with Bogate. He was a supernumerary in this operation, his duties beginning if and when they found traces of intelligent life. To his surprise, instead of ignoring his presence entirely, Bogate waited for him to catch up, asking:

"Just what do we look for?"

"Hansu thinks we may find Cos—they're a pygmy race supposed to inhabit these mountains—hate the Llor and are highly dangerous—use poison darts and build mantraps."

Bogate's reply to the sketchy information was a grunt. The wind was rising in gusts which whistled eerily between the heights, propelling the migrating puff-balls—circular masses of spiky vines which traveled so until they found water where they could root for a season. Of a sickly, bleached, yellow-green, they were armed with six-inch thorns and the Terrans granted them the right of way. This was the start of the Fronnian windy season. And to fight across the ranges during that period was to front dangers no Llor would willingly face.

A weird moaning rose to a shriek among the rocks far above them as the wind was forced through crevices and cracks. But for the most part the scouts were sheltered from the full blast by the ridges.

Here the soil was a mixture of gravel and clay, liberally salted with the rocky debris of slides. Each side canyon or gully had to be blazed with a fluorescent brand so that the Horde would keep to the main trail. They detoured around boulders taller than a man until Kana began to wonder why such a large number of landslides should occur in the length of a single dried watercourse. Suddenly the answer to that lay before his eyes and it was grim.

Sun flashes reflected from something half buried in the soil. He knelt to scrape away the earth. A Llor sword protruded from under a rock. And its haft was still encircled by the finger bones of a skeleton hand!

"Smashed flat—like a bug!" was Bogate's comment. The veteran's eyes narrowed as he looked along the way they had come and then on up the slit at the dusky shapes of the mountains. He had been too well trained by warfare on half a hundred planets not to mistake clues.

"Rolled rocks and caught 'em. Neat. This Cos work?"

"Might be," Kana assented. "But it was a long time ago—" He was interrupted by a shout which sent Bogate sprinting ahead.

The narrow canyon they had chosen to follow widened out into an arena—an arena where a deadly game had once been played and lost. Bones brittle with years carpeted the arid floor. And Llor skulls, very human looking, mingled with the narrow, fanged ones of guen, were easy to identify in the general litter, but not one skeleton was unbroken or entire. Kana picked up a rib, the bone light in his fingers. He had been right—those deep indentations could only be the marks of crushing molars. First there had been a killing and then—a feasting! He pitched the bone away.

Keeping aloof from the mass of ghastly relics the Terrans walked around the wall of the valley. There were no weapons in that gray waste, no remains of Llor war harness. Even the trappings of the guen were missing. The dead had been stripped completely. And since they lay unburied, the massacre must have gone unavenged.

"How long ago, d'you think?" Bogate's throaty bellow was subdued.

"Maybe ten years, maybe a hundred," Kana returned. "You'd have to know Fronnian climate to be sure."

"They got caught bunched," Bogate observed. "Larsen," he snapped at the nearest scout, "climb up and use the lenses—cover us from above from now on. I'll take point on the other wall. The rest of you—go slow. Soong, report back on the speecher. We haven't seen nothin' livin' so far. But we don't want *our* fellas caught like this!"

At a snail's pace they progressed to the far end of the valley of death, threading the narrow opening there as if they feared any second to hear the roar of an avalanche. But Kana, taking notice of the barren countryside, thought that the Cos would not ordinarily inhabit that section. The slaughter behind them might be the sign of some war—if Cos *had* caused that havoc. The tooth marks on the rib continued to haunt him. Some primitive peoples ate enemy dead, believing that the virtue of a brave foe could be so absorbed by his slayer. But surely those scars on the bone had never been left by the molars of a humanoid race!

There were other meat eaters in plenty on Fronn. The ttsor, large felines, the hork, a bird or highly evolved insect (the record-pak had not been certain) a smaller species of which was tamed and used by the nobles of the land for hunting, much as the ancient lords of his own world had once flown their falcons for sport. Then there were the deeter, whose exact nature was uncertain for they were nocturnal and dug pits to trap their prey. But those mysterious creatures inhabited the swamp jungles of the southern continent. Which left—the byll! But he had thought that those highly dangerous, huge, flightless birds were only to be found on the plains where their speed in the chase earned them their food. More dangerous than the ttsor—who did not willingly attack—the bylls were twelve feet of bone, muscle, wicked temper, and vicious appetite.

This mountain country was bare of vegetation except for a few clumps of knife-edged grass, withered and sear from the long dryness of the calm season. On the plains this grass was ruthlessly burnt off by the Llor, but in these mountain gullies it flourished in ragged patches to slash the skin of the unwary.

The scouts took hourly breaks, ate ration tablets, drank sparingly from their canteens and pushed on. The country about them looked as rugged as a lunar landscape in their own system, lacking all life. It was when the dried stream bed they followed branched into two that Bogate called a halt. Both of the new canyons looked equally promising, though one angled south and the other north. The Terrans, shivering a little in the bite of the wind from the snow peaks, were undecided.

Bogate consulted his watch and then compared its reading with the length of the shadows beyond the rocks.

"Quarter of an hour. We split—return here at the

end of that time. You"—he indicated four of the scouts—"come with me. Larsen, you take the rest south."

Kana scrambled up the wall of the northern fork, lenses slung around his neck. Zapan Bogate was in the lead and had gained on his companions. The man immediately below Kana was having heavy going. Slides blocked his assigned route and he had to make frequent detours.

It was by sheer chance that Kana caught that flicker of movement behind Wu Soong. A rock shadow bulged oddly. He swung his rifle and shouted a warning. Soong threw himself flat behind a rock and so saved his life. For the ugly death which had been stalking him struck—empty air.

Kana fired, hoping to hit some vital spot in that darting red body. But the thing moved with unholy speed, its long scaly neck twisting with reptilian sinuosity. He was almost certain he had hit it at least twice but its frenzied darts at the rock where Soong had gone to earth did not slow. No longer silent, it shrieked its furious rage with a siren blast which tore their ears.

A burst of white fire enveloped the byll. When that cleared the giant bird lay on the ground, headless but still struggling to move its shattered legs.

"Bogate," Kana shouted down, "those things sometimes hunt in packs—"

"Yeah? Fire the recall, Harv," he ordered one of the awe-stricken men. "That ought to bring Larsen. We'll stick together. If there's any more of them, stalkin' us in crowds, we're gonna be ready for 'em. And not all scattered out so close to dark."

Soong made a wide circle around the body of the byll to join the others as Bogate gave Kana an order.

"You keep an eye out—cover us back to the forks."

From then on they investigated every shadow, every

crevice in the canyon walls. It was with a sigh of relief Kana saw them back to the fork where Larsen and his men waited. Bogate put them all to work at once, rolling up good-sized boulders, erecting a breastwork which should stop any byll's charge.

"Those things hunt at night?" he wanted to know.

"I don't know. By rights that one shouldn't have been back here in the mountains at all. They're meat eaters and their regular territory is the central plains."

"Meaning that if they do come here, it's because they *can* hunt?"

Kana could only nod in agreement. As arid as the country seemed to be, it must harbor life—enough life to attract the bylls.

Since a fire was out of the question—they dared show no lights—the scouts huddled together behind the wall of their temporary fort. The mountains cut off the light of the sinking sun. In the gloom Kana found himself listening—for what he did not know.

The wind rose again to swoop and wail. But through their hours of travel the Terrans had become so accustomed to its moans that they no longer heeded it. In one of the infrequent intervals of quiet, when the mountain blasts died, Kana listened again. Had he heard—? But nothing stirred beyond the wall.

They slept in fitful snatches, two of their number on watch in turn. Kana was dreaming when an elbow in his ribs brought him into full wakefulness and Soong's sibilant whisper warmed his ear.

"Look!"

Up and far ahead was a wink of light—a light which flickered to prove that it was no star. And to its left—another! Kana used the lenses. Those were fires right enough—beacons! In all he counted five. And beacons on those heights could only mean that someone was alert to the Terran invasion of this mountain territory.

Not the royalists—the flames were not the blue of Llor torches. As he watched one winked and disappeared, then it blinked out again—off and on—in a pattern. There was no mistaking the meaning of that—signals! Would that exchange of information lead to such a one-sided battle as had taken place in the arena they had crossed that day?

"Signals!" Bogate was awake and watching also. "They must have spotted us!"

Kana heard rather than saw the veteran scramble over the wall. A moment later a growl from the dark relayed the other's displeasure. Kana climbed the barrier to look back along the route they had come. He saw then what had brought that grunt out of Bogate. High on the cliffs which walled the canyon was a speck of light. But they had no more than sighted it than it disappeared, not to be seen again. An answer to the signal ahead?

The veteran cleared his throat with a rasp. "Maybe that was 'orders received.' " He parroted the official phrase. "Soong, use the speecher. Tell Hansu about those signals—"

"Well," he added a few moments later, "the show must be over for tonight—"

He was right, three of the fires ahead were gone, and the two remaining seemed to be dying. Kana shivered as icy fingers of wind pried within his coat. Were they going to walk into trouble?

"Camp answered," Soong reported out of the dark. "They saw a fire a little ahead of them, but not the others. Told 'em about the byll, too. They're at this end of the bone valley."

"Good enough. Turn in. We'll go on tomorrow."

In the morning Bogate chose the southern fork of the old river for exploration. Since Tharc lay to the south, it was logical to head in that direction. Whether the presence of byll in the other valley influenced his decision, or the fact that the fires they had watched had been to the north were points he did not discuss with the rest of the scouts.

Their new path was clearer of rock slides than any they had found so far and within a half mile Kana noticed an upward slope. They were climbing at last, instead of burrowing at the bottom of rock-walled slashes.

But they had not been an hour on their way before they came upon their first trace of the mountaineers. Luckily their experience with the byll had made them overly cautious and they were constantly alert to any faint indication of the abnormal. Larsen, who was in the lead, stopped abruptly at the edge of a wide, smooth expanse of sand. When Bogate came up the scout pointed to a curious depression in the center of the strip.

Kana, recalling one of Hansu's warnings about the Cos, spoke first:

"Might be a trap—"

Bogate looked from the recruit to the depression. Then he walked away to choose a stone, under the weight of which he staggered, waddling up to plop his burden onto that smooth surface.

There was a crack. Sand and stone together rushed down into a gaping hole. Kana inched up to look. What he saw made his insides twist as his imagination leaped into action. It was a trap, all right, a vicious, deadly trap. And the captive who fell into it would die a lingering death on the spikes artfully planted below.

The Terrans exchanged few words as they crept around the edge of the pit. On the other side Soong reported on the speecher, informing the Horde of this new risk.

From then on their progress slowed to a crawl. Not only must they watch for bylls, but every smooth patch of ground underfoot became suspect. They tested three more such stretches by Bogate's method, to have the last open again into darkness, this time a darkness from which such a frightful stench arose that they made no attempt to examine it closer.

"Do we now journey straight to someone's front door?" Soong shifted the weight of the speecher from one hip to the other.

"If we do—he's the sort who doesn't welcome visitors." Kana's attention was divided between the cliffs which walled in the stream bed and its flooring—death might come suddenly from either direction. And *he* was the AL man—the one supposed to contact the opposition. But none of the training he had known prepared him for a situation such as this—bare mountains which showed no signs of life—and these unmanned defenses against invaders. You couldn't contact an enemy who wasn't there. The Cos—if Cos they were—plainly pinned their faith on the devices of the weak or few in number—devices which would kill at a distance without involving too closely those who used them. If he could only bring about a meeting, convey to the mountaineers the idea that the Horde, winding its way into their jealously guarded territory, had no quarrel with them—on the contrary was now arrayed against their own ancient enemy, the Llor.

He was reasonably sure that any Cos spying on them would be stationed on the heights. And when the scouts took their break at the end of an hour's advance, he approached Bogate with a plan of his own. The veteran surveyed the tops of the cliffs uneasily.

"I dunno—" He hesitated. "Yeah, if they're spyin' they're up there—I'll grant you that. But they may be miles away—and we can't lie around waitin' for you to prowl, huntin' for somethin' which maybe ain't there. We'll see later—"

Kana had to content himself with that half promise. But the country offered an argument on his behalf
not many minutes later. They rounded a curve and
found themselves fronted with a wall of rock down
which the vanished river must once have crashed in
spectacular falls. Bogate waved to Kana.

"Well, here's a place where somebody's gotta climb.
Suppose you do it and see what you find. Take Soong
with you."

They shucked off their packs, taking only their rifles,
and began the ascent—not up the water-worn face of
the falls but along the relatively rough cliff to the left.
After he finished this enlistment, Kana thought as he
crept fly-wise from handhold to handhold, he would
be qualified for service with a crack mountaineering
Horde.

When they reached the top they faced west again.
Here once more was the bed of the stream, but it was
narrower than in the canyon below. And not too far
ahead the somberness of the rock was broken by
patches of yellow-green vegetation which promised
moisture.

"There is something—" Soong pivoted slowly, studying the landscape.

Kana sensed what bothered his companion. He, too,
felt as if they were under observation. Together they
surveyed every foot of the rocky terrain. Nothing moved
and the wind tore at them, whirling dust devils before
it over the edge of the falls. They were alone in a dead
world—and yet something watched! Kana knew it by
a twitching between his shoulder blades, a cold crawling
which roughened his skin with nervous tension. They
were being watched—with a detached, non-human
curiosity.

"Where is it?" Soong's voice came plaintively
between the howls of the wind.

Kana knelt in the sand and brought out his number one package for trade contact. He selected a bare stretch of stone and laid out upon it the pieces he believed flashy enough to catch the eye and pin the attention of any native. Then he pulled Soong with him to the far left, picking out concealment well above the stream bed.

As the minutes passed Kana began to wonder if his nerves had misled him. The gold chain, the handful of bright stones drew the weak sunlight to make a flashing pool of fire which would have attracted the attention of any watcher, would have brought him out of cover had he been of any race the Terrans knew.

"Lord of Space!" Soong's voice hissed between his teeth.

Something had moved at last. A shadow floated with liquid, feline grace between two rocks and stood above the trade station. Kana's breath caught. A ttsor! That greenish fur—treasured by the Llor for mantles of state—could not be mistaken. The round skull with its large brain case, the fringed ears— A tail, able to grasp and hold, whipped around and selected the gold chain from the display, holding it up before the large yellow eyes. The ttsor sniffed at the rest of the collection, using the giant thumb claw of one paw to spread then around, and dropped the chain. It was not interested in what had no food value.

Kana's hand shot out to depress the barrel of Soong's rifle.

"It won't attack—don't shoot!"

The ttsor stiffened, its body tense, its head pointed upstream. Then in an eye wink it was gone and they saw it speeding away, up out of the river bed to the heights.

A sound reached them above the moan of the wind—a muffled roar Kana could not identify. He

looked upstream. Then he whirled and grabbed for
Soong, dragging him back from the lower part of the
valley which was now a deadly trap. Together they ran
for the cliff. Kana saw the white faces of those below
turned up to him. Soong fired into the air—the three
spaced warning signals—and Kana waved his arms
trying to urge the others back against the canyon walls.
His message must have made sense for they scattered
and ran—some to one side and a few to the other. How
many made it he did not have a chance to see before
the black wall of water poured over the lip of the falls
to hide the scene in a wild welter of spray.

The flood arose to lap at Kana's boots, lashed at him
with spray. Shoulder to shoulder with Soong he wedged
himself between anchoring rocks. Again the unseen
mountaineers had used nature to defend their country, had turned loose this flood to rid their land of
invaders. Soong was busy with the speecher trying to
warn the Horde marching along the path of disaster.

8

Death By
The Water—
Death By Fire

Out of the foam below broke the head and shoulders of a man fighting his way to safety, tugging a weaker struggler behind. They groped to the air and clung, braced against boulders, as the waters dashed over them. And across the canyon Kana thought he saw another dark figure reach safety. Did only three survive?

With Soong he angled down the wall and helped drag Bogate and the half-conscious Larsen out of the grip of the flood. Shivering, the four wedged themselves on a narrow ledge, only a foot or so above the stream which showed no signs of shrinking. Bogate shook his head, as if to clear away some mist as tangible as the spray still drenching them.

"Somebody musta pulled a cork," Larsen commented between coughs.

"D'you see anything up there?" Bogate wanted to know.

"Just a ttsor. It gave us warning of the flood. If it hadn't been for that, we'd have been caught—"

"And so would we." Larsen pulled at the sodden collar of his coat. "This is a booby trap to end 'em all. What about the boys downstream?"

"Sent 'em a message," Soong answered. "Whether they got it in time—" There was no need for him to complete that sentence.

A faint hail came from across the canyon and they sighted a waving arm. Bogate carefully levered himself to his feet.

"Hooooah!" His bull roar rang out.

There was a welcome answer, three of them. But there was no way to cross the turbulent river and join forces. So they began to travel back toward the forks in two parties, the water between. Kana and Soong still had their rifles but their packs were gone. The chill air stiffened the wet clothing on the Combatants' shivering bodies. At the sinking of the sun they crouched in a hollow between two pinnacles of rock where the worst of the wind blasts were fended off, and so spent the night. Once a mournful, lowering call echoed down from the peaks. Kana took it for the hunting cry of a ttsor. But the presence of that lion-like creature here argued that, for all its apparent barrenness, there was life to be found in the badlands. For the ttsors ate not only meat but fruit and grains—perhaps here they raided the mountainside villages of the Cos.

If the Combatants slept that night it was under the drug of sheer exhaustion. And when Kana roused with the coming of light his legs and arms were so painfully cramped that he had to pinch and beat life back into his numb limbs. But across the canyon one of the other refugees waved a salute from a headland.

They began again that creeping journey along the jagged teeth of the heights. Below the river still spun, flicking around the old slides. And, even as Kana watched, a section of the cliff wall, undermined, gave way—tossing rocks and clay out into the current. So warned, they back-tracked from the rim. But here, for every mile of progress east, they traveled almost as much over or around obstacles, skirting side chasms, flanking butts and peaks. It was snail journeying and their hands left smears of blood on the stone. Even the incredibly tough Ciranian reptile hide of their boots showed scars and scratches.

And a fear which none mentioned rode them. That morning when Soong had tried to reach the Horde with the speecher he had raised no answer. At every rest interval while they panted in the thin air, he bent over the obstinate machine, fingering the keys with relentless energy, but never getting a faint click in reply.

Kana thought he knew what had happened, his imagination painting a very stark picture. The Horde had come up the river bed—to meet head on that flood, speeding even more as the ground sloped. The Terran force must have been caught, to be swept away to as final an end as the older Llor army had met in the valley of bones!

So vivid was this picture that, as they approached the fork, Kana lagged behind, unwilling to look for the debris of such destruction. But Soong's shout of discovery drew him against his will.

One of the light carts was jammed into the rocks just below them, twisted almost out of shape. Bogate's wide shoulders sagged as he hunched perilously over to view the wreckage. As they stared at the evidence which blighted their hopes, a wild shout drew their attention across to where those on the other side of the river were excitedly pointing behind them at the other fork. Bogate straightened, his lusty strength coming back.

"Maybe some of 'em made it!"

Two of the scouts on the other side had disappeared, but the third continued to wave.

"The problem of getting across remains," Larsen pointed out. "We can't swim that—"

"We got across the other river, didn't we?" Soong demanded. "What we did once we can do again."

They could do anything now! The knowledge that some of the Horde must have escaped was a stimulant which sent them to perch on stones just above water level while Bogate lowered one of the rifles, stock first, to test the pull of the river, only to have it almost ripped out of his grasp.

Across the water a knot of men appeared, among them Hansu. They were burdened with coils of rope and split into two groups, leaving one directly across from the marooned scouts. The Blademaster and the others went upstream, uncoiling rope as they clambered above the water line.

Here the gap, through which the water must enter the wider bed, was deeper and narrower than at any other point along its sweep from the falls. Hansu's men fastened the rope end to an unwieldy bundle and tossed it into the flood. Soong and Bogate, rifles ready, lay belly down on the rocks. The bundle flashed downstream and they plunged their rifles in to capture it. There was a breathless instant when it seemed that it might escape—then all four of them had it and the rope end it brought them was safely in their hands, linking them to the party across the river.

To fight through those few feet of water was a

nightmare of effort. In his turn Kana brought up against a half-sunken rock with force enough to make his head swim with pain. Then hands reached out to drag him in. Coughing up brackish water, he lay on a spit of gravel until they pulled him to his feet. The rest of the trip to the other valley was a mechanical obeying of orders, of being led. And he did not really rouse until he found himself lying on his back, a pack under his head, while Mic and Rey stripped off his soaked clothing and rubbed him down with a blanket.

Mic scowled. "What'd you do up there—blow a dam?"

"Sprung a trap—I think," Kana sputtered the words over a cup of hot brew Rey thrust upon him. There was a fire blazing not too far away and the glow of warmth within and without his shivering body was pure luxury.

"So. Well, we have one of the trappers—"

Kana's eyes followed Mic's finger. Across the fire squatted a figure neither Llor nor Terran. About four feet tall, the creature was almost completely covered with a thick growth of gray-white hair. About its loins was a brief kilt of supple ttsor fur and it wore a thong necklet from which depended several thumb claws of the same felines. Even more expressionless than the less woolly Llor, the prisoner stared unblinkingly into the fire and paid little or no attention to his surroundings.

"Cos?"

"We think so. We caught him feeding a signal fire up on the cliffs night before last. But so far we haven't been able to get anything out of him. He doesn't answer to trade talk, and even Hansu's Llor can't bring an answer out of him. We pull him along, he sits when we stop—he won't eat—"

As he talked Mic opened his pack and pulled out

spare clothing while Rey contributed more. Kana gratefully donned the donations, watching his own clothes steam before the fire.

"Good thing our warning reached you in time—"

Mic did not quite meet his eyes. "The flood caught five of the men—a cart got hung up on a rock and they were working to free it. Then we lost three crossing the first river and a couple when the fur faces jumped us later—"

"The Llor followed you?"

"Part way. They faded out when we reached the bone valley. I suppose that gave them an idea of what they could expect. Anyway they chased us in and there's no going back that way—unless we want to fight the whole nation. The rebels are all loyal royalists now and only too ready to attack the nasty Terran invaders—" There was a bitter undertone to that.

"What's it like up ahead?" Rey wanted to know.

Swiftly Kana outlined what he had seen. As he spoke their faces grew bleak. But before he had finished Hansu strode up to the fire.

"See any Cos signs above the falls before that water came?" the Blademaster demanded.

"No, sir. We saw nothing but a ttsor and it gave us the alarm. I'd laid out a trade packet on a rock because we felt as if we were being watched. The ttsor came down to look it over and then—"

But Hansu was staring across the flames at the captive Cos. "All we need to know is locked up in that round skull over there—if we could just pry it out. But he won't eat our food, he won't talk. And we can't keep him until he starves. Then they would have good reason to strike back at us."

The Blademaster went around to stand beside the prisoner. But the white-wooled pygmy never changed position nor gave any indication that he was aware of the Terran commander. Hansu went down on one knee, slowly repeating some words in the sing-song speech of the Llor. The Cos did not even blink. Kana reached for the trade packets he had carried so long, made a hasty selection, and passed on a small package of sugar and a stone-set wrist band.

Hansu held the gemmed circlet into the light before the sullen captive, turning it so that the stones flashed. The offering might have been totally invisible as far as the Cos was concerned. Nor when the sugar cake was held within sniffing distance did he make any move to investigate. To him the Terrans and their gifts did not exist.

"He's a stone wall and we're up against him," Hansu said. "We can only—"

"Let him go, sir, and hope for the best?" Kana's X-Tee training suggested that.

"Yes." Hansu stood up and then pulled the Cos to his feet. Compelling the captive by his great strength, the Blademaster marched the pygmy to the edge of the Terran camp and a good hundred yards beyond. There he released the mountaineer's arm and stepped away.

For a long space the Cos remained exactly where he had been left—he did not even turn his head to see if they were watching him. Then, with a skittering movement, the speed of which left the Combatants agape, he was gone, vanishing at the far side of the canyon. Somewhere a stone rattled, but they saw nothing of the trail he took.

The Horde camped there for that night and, though they watched the mountains ahead and the cliffs walling them in, there were no more signal fires.

"Maybe," Mic suggested hopefully, "uncorking that river was their biggest gun. When they saw that it didn't work, they went into hiding, to let us gallop by—"

"We don't know how their minds work," Kana warned. "To some species—take ours for example—a failure such as that is merely a spur to try again. To another type it would signify that their Gods, or Fate, or whatever Power they believe in, is opposed and they should forget the whole project. The future may depend upon that Cos we freed and the report he makes. But we shall have to be prepared for anything."

Soon after the march began the next morning they passed the site where the byll had been killed. The carcass had been torn apart and largely devoured by unseen scavengers in the night. But the severed head, with its toothed bill gaping, was a grim warning. One of the duties of the flankers was to keep close watch against sneak attacks from the carnivorous birds.

Close to mid-day they came upon a pool fed by water seeping through the left canyon wall, perhaps from the river flowing down the other fork. Here they filled their canteens after purifying the liquid and washed some of the dust from their hands and faces. This grit, borne by the wind, was in their mouths as they ate, inflamed their eyes, and sifted down between clothing and skin to prove a minor torture.

Alert to the danger which might come from above, the scouts reported a second major attack before it got underway. The Cos, relying upon methods which had served them well in the past, sent boulders crashing down. But none of the rough missiles killed, for those who attempted to so bombard the winding snake of the Horde's advance were picked off by sharpshooting flankers and woolly bodies crashed along with the rocks while others fled. Ahead, on a mesa-like formation, was a rude fortification which so commanded their line of march that the Terrans dared not try to pass.

This time the Cos made no attempt to hide their presence. With the coming of evening beacons blazed

in the fort—forming a barrier of light about it much
as the camp lamps of the Combatants had done for
them on the plains. There could be no storming this
from below. Facing the Horde the rise to the mesa top
was steep and an ominous row of boulders ready for
use fringed the rim. Hansu whistled for a gathering.

"We have to take that fort," he began baldly. "And
there's only one way in—from the top." He took off
his helmet and threw into it black and white pebbles.
"Lot-choice—"

Lot-choice it was. Kana grabbed a pebble with the
rest, holding it concealed in his hand until the word
of command. In that moment he found that the stone
he held was black, as was Rey's—while Mic, to his
disappointment, had a white one.

Hansu gave a detailed inspection to the band who
were to make the climb. The volunteers stripped themselves of all trappings except one belt. Their rifles were
slung over their shoulders and each man wore his
sword-knife and carried five of the explosive fire
cartridges.

They used the deep shadows at the floor of the
canyon to cloak their withdrawal from the main command, back-tracking on their path of the afternoon to
a point where the flankers had reported the cliffs scal-
able. There, utilizing the last scrap of twilight before
the night clamped down, they started up. And, once on
top, the fort lights not only provided them with a guide
but a certain amount of illumination. Their advance was
a slow creep. To run into a Cos sentry would be fatal.
As a warning of that the Terrans had their sense of
smell—luckily the wind blew toward them. The oily body
odor of the Llor, distinguishable at several feet by off-
world noses, was multiplied fourfold in that given off
by the Cos. The mountaineers could literally be smelled
out of ambush, a betrayal of which they were unaware.

The ominous reek filled Kana's nostrils. He drew his
legs under him and reached out to tap Rey's shoulder,
knowing that that silent warning would be passed down
the crawling Terran line. A Cos was ahead, slightly to
the left. With his head raised to follow the scent, Kana
wriggled on. He felt Rey's fingers on his ankle as the
other joined him. The Cos must be located and elimi-
nated, efficiently and without giving any warning to the
fort.

Kana lined up a neighboring pinnacle with the lights
of the fort. His nose told him that the Cos must be
there, and it was a logical position from which to watch
not only the cliff but the Horde below.

Then he saw what he was searching for—a blob of
black outlined against the fort beacons, the hunched
head and shoulders of the mountaineer sentry. Kana
tensed for a spring as he unhooked the carrying strap
of his rifle. With that timing and precision in attack
he had been drilled in for most of his life, he uncoiled
in a leap, bringing the strap about the woolly throat
of the sentry. A single jerk in the proper direction and
the Cos went limp. Kana eased the body to the ground
with shaking hands. The trick had worked—just as the
instructors had assured them that it would. But
between trying it on a dummy and on a living, breathing creature there was a vast gulf of sensation. He
pulled the strap away with a twitch and rubbed his
hands along his thighs, trying to free his flesh from the
feel of greasy wool.

"All right?"

"Yes," he answered Rey and took the rifle the other
offered him, making a business of re-attaching the
strap.

There were no more sentries sighted. And at last
the Terran force gained the point they wished—to the
west and above the fort.

The center building of that eagles' nest was familiar in shape, though in bad repair. When the Cos had taken over this stronghold they used for its core an earlier fortification or outpost erected by the Llor. The handful of brush and stone huts grouped around the half-ruined watchtower and the wall of loose stones were their own additions—neither displaying any great skill in military engineering.

From below sounded the shrilling of Terran battle whistles. And by the fires of the Cos they could see the white forms of the mountaineers manning the wall, levering into place their rocky ammunition, ready to roll it down to meet any frontal attack. Kana snapped open one of the fire cartridges and pitched it at the nearest brush-roofed hut.

To the yellow flames of the Cos beacons were added the bursting stars of the Terran fire balls, flaring up to turn the hut into an inferno. The startled Cos, caught between the Horde below and this new menace, ran back and forth. And that moment of indecision finished them, though the end did not come from the Terran attackers but from within their own stronghold.

Out of the fires a black shadow came to life, sweeping straight up into the night. It hovered over the fort and red death rained from it. Cos, their wool afire, plunged blind and screaming over the drop or ran to meet death head on. But the strange flying thing spiraled skyward, flitting over the valley to lay more bombs in the ranks of the Horde.

The Terrans on the heights tried to catch the swooping wing in the sights of their rifles, firing in wild fury at its outline. Under their concentrated blast the wing staggered, tried to level off, and then hurtled on into the night, leaving a scarlet path of destruction which not only engulfed the fortress of the Cos but the Horde pocketed below.

9

Show Our Teeth
And Hope

At dawn the Terran force held the fort, but the price had been high. A quarter of the Horde had either died quickly in the bombing raid of the unknown aircraft or were granted grace for hideous wounds during the hours which followed. So the victory bore more the shade of a defeat.

"Where did the Cos get that wing?" Mic, his left arm a roll of shielding plasta-flesh to his shoulder, was not the only one to ask that.

The alien machine was proof that there must have been strangers hidden in the Cos stronghold, either inciting the mountaineers against the Terrans, or as spectators. Combatants inspected the ruins of the fort while parts of it still blazed, searching for evidence of the origin of the flyers, but the flames had left them no readable clues.

"That wing never got away unharmed," Rey reiterated to any who would listen. "It must have crashed—it was sideslipping when it went out of sight!"

"Where there's one of those," Mic returned, "there're probably more. Space demons! With those they can fly over and dust us whenever they want to! But why haven't they done that before?"

Kana put a pack behind Mic's good shoulder and settled his back against that support. "Lack of supplies may be the answer. Probably they haven't enough machines to chase us. We forced that one into the open by firing the fort huts. And I think Rey's right, it crashed on ahead. Anyway—from here on we don't have to march down the middle of a canyon, providing them with a perfect target."

For that was the Terrans' greatest discovery—the well-defined road running along the cliff straight west from the Cos fort. And Hansu was determined to get his mangled command up out of what might prove to be a deathtrap. The Combatants licked their wounds and explored the fort, sending scouts out along the road, well into the second day. The number of Cos bodies found within the enclosure was fewer than they expected and there were no Aliens among them.

"An expendable rearguard," Hansu deduced.

In the end the corpses of the enemy were carried to the small central area of the fort and given the same burial granted the Terran dead—total destruction in the flames. Beneath ground level, in a chamber hollowed from the rock of the mountain, they found a cistern of water and a line of bins filled with grain and dried fruits. The grain could not be eaten by Terrans, Medico Crawfur announced, but the fruit was not harmful and they chewed its leathery substance as a welcome variation to ration tablets.

On the third day they reorganized and combined the

shrunken teams and took up the march in good order. But there was no longer any talk about a quick return to Secundus. By unspoken consent discussion of the future was limited to that day's journey and vague speculation concerning the next.

"Just show our teeth and hope—" was the way Mic put it as he started out between Kana and Rey. "If we could only get out of this blasted tangle of rocks!"

But there was no end to the rocks as the trail from the fort climbed higher. Taking his turn Kana became one of the scouts ranging ahead. They were working their way up the slope of a peak which had once been volcanic. And now patches of snow laced the ground. Kana chanced upon a break in the wall of that cone, a place where they might normally expect opposition. But the pass was undefended. And accompanied by Soong he halted to look down into a hollow, the deepest part of which lay at least a Terran mile below. Cupped there was a lake and the yellow-green of Fronnian flora patterned small, regular fields, while a village of stone-walled, domed huts clustered by the water. Nothing moved in those fields, no smoke hung above the village. It might have been deserted an hour—or a century—before.

The scouts spread out, making their way down the side of the bowl—alert and ready. But all they flushed out of the tall grass was a khat, one of the stupid rodents that furnished the main meat supply of Fronn. Crossing small fields carpeted with the stiff stubble of grain, they came to the lake.

Soong pointed to the shore line where deep marks were scored in the mud.

"Boats— And not too long ago."

"Can't see any. Maybe they went that way—"

A long finger of water angled south toward the wall of the crater. Whether it washed the outer wall of the cone they could not be sure. But no boats were to be seen. And further exploration proved that, except for a khat or two, and four small guen penned in a corral, the valley was empty.

So the Horde came down in peace. The finger of lake draining south was discovered to enter a break in the wall and from signs the Terrans were inclined to believe that the inhabitants of the valley had fled in that direction.

But the most exciting discovery was made just beyond the village—a mass of wreckage—the flying wing! No evidence of the other-world origin of the pilot remained. But the machine was not Terran Mech—as they had suspected all along.

Their nearest to an expert on machines, El Kosti, spent several hours pulling at the jumble of wires and metal with a company of Combatants to lend assistance.

"This came from Ciran," he reported to Hansu. "But there are modifications I can't identify. I'd say it might originally have been a trade scout—though I couldn't swear to it. But it is not Terran stuff."

Back again to the thought that there was some cloudy conspiracy—that C.C. was moving against them. Why? Because they were Terran mercenaries? Kana wondered about that. Was Yorke's Horde with its quantity of trained veterans marked down in someone's book as being expendable—to be wiped out so that its loss would cause trouble back home? Was pressure thus being brought to bear to force mankind out of space? He watched Hansu taking careful visa shots of the wreck as Kosti pointed out those portions of the machine which most clearly indicated its probable origin. The Blademaster was collecting evidence—but would he ever be allowed to present it to the authorities? Did he honestly believe that any of them would reach Secundus—let alone stand in

Prime's hall of justice to testify to this act of treachery?

Hut by hut they searched the village. Only trash remained in the rooms, along with pieces of furniture too large or heavy for refugees to move. Three explorer ration paks were discovered in the refuse, proving that at least one other-world visitor had been there recently. But these were standard paks which revealed nothing about the one who had used them—he could have been from one of twenty different planets.

Without boats or the means of making a raft the Terrans could not use the water exit from the crater valley. But there was a second road leading on southwest and they took it. From that day on the march became a nightmare. The windy season was on them and the storms brought swirling clouds of snow to hide the trail. Some of the men were lost in a single hour's march, dropping out of line never to be sighted again, in spite of the efforts to keep the lines moving and intact. Some frankly gave up, and could not be beaten to their feet after a rest, drifting into that fatal sleep which meant death. Had they not been mercenary trained, bred to withstand severe physical strain from their childhood, perhaps none of them would have won through. As it was they lost fifty men before they came to the western slopes of the range. Now the mere fact that they were going down again, with the plains of Tharc before them, gave them a renewal of spirit and kept them going on stumbling feet.

At least they had to fight only one thing at a time. Since the battle at the fort they had not sighted the Cos. The mountaineers must have gone into hiding during the storms.

On the fifth day after they left the crater valley, Kana was weaving weakly as he set one foot carefully before the other. He made his way down a ravine and crossed bare ground, glad to miss the crunch of snow. The walls of the tiny valley cut off the worst of the wind and he leaned against the bank to catch his breath. A trickle of water flowed past him southwest.

"Down!" He said the word aloud, savoring it, enjoying its meaning. Now the mountains lay behind, the plains were open to them.

But not yet were they out of the broken "badlands" which encumbered this side of the range also. In the wilderness of mesas and knife-edged valleys there were the colored splotches of vegetation, growing quickly on the moisture fed by the winds. But there was no discernible sign of a road or of any other evidence of civilization. They could only continue to march south, heading for the level land enclosing Tharc.

Kana stumbled along beside the thread of stream, following the defile simply because he could not now summon the strength necessary to climb out of the ravine. Plants uncurled leaves to the sun. A spray of tiny green blossoms, hung on delicate, lacy stems, bowed to meet the water.

"Yaah—!"

Kana came around in a half crouch, his rifle ready, to see Soong pick himself out of the stream, swearing at the greasy mud. Looking up at Kana his round ivory face split into a wide grin.

"We have come out of winter into spring. Now I think we shall live."

"For a while," Kana conceded thoughtfully. He was tired, so tired he wanted to drop down on the earth where he stood and rest—forever.

"Yes, we live. And perhaps that shall disappoint some. Ho, now a river—in truth a river!"

Soong was right. The tricklet spilled out to join a river. Here the flood ran clear so that the Terrans could see the flat stones and gravel which floored its bottom.

And the watery reach lacked the fury of the mountain courses they had met.

"Not deep—this one we can wade. Fortune displays a smiling face at last!" Soong squatted down and ventured to test the temperature of the fluid with a forefinger, withdrawing it quickly. "Born in snow, yes. We shall have very cold feet—"

They walked along the bank for a distance. Out of the withered drifts of last season's grass a khat exploded with a muffled snuffle of panic. It skidded to the edge of the water, slipped on clay and, wildly kicking, plunged over. Its struggles continued in the water, keeping it afloat.

From the opposite bank shot a vee of ripples heading for that point of disturbance. The khat shrieked, a cry of agony almost human with pain and terror. Blood rilled out to stain the water and other lines of ripples converged toward it.

The Combatants stood aghast at the sight. But the struggle ceased seconds after it had begun. On the stones at the bottom lay clean-picked bones.

Lazily, glutted, three small forms floated. They were six-limbed, frog-headed creatures, but their jaws were the jaws of rapacious carnivores, and their four eyes, set in a double row above those vicious jaws, were black beads of ferocious, intelligent hunger.

Kana moistened his lips. "Tif."

"What—?" Soong shied a stone at the small monsters. They glided off a foot or two, but they did not return to the opposite bank. Instead they lingered just out of range, their attention fixed on the Terrans—waiting—watching—

"Bad news," Kana answered Soong's half question. "You saw what happened to that khat. Well, that will happen to any living thing that tries to cross water where tif live."

"But there're only three and none of them are more than a foot long—"

"Three of them we can see. And where there're three—there're more. They travel in schools. Three in sight may well mean three hundred in cover, ready to attack when there's meat enough!"

No, there was no way of judging how many of the frog-devils infested the river. And there was no practical way of getting across a stream so guarded. If the record-pak on Prime had not been so limited in its information! Or if the Terrans only had friendly natives to provide them with advice.

The limpid water seemed very peaceful, but as the Combatants moved downstream the tif swam effortlessly to parallel their path. Now and then the little monsters were joined by others of their species, come from the shadows below the banks, who paddled out to confer with the three in mid-stream, eye the Terrans for themselves, as if estimating their bulk, before retreating again to their hidden dens.

"Spreading the word—meat on the hoof—" Kana stopped.

The shallow river had widened as they followed it south, and now it was islanded with dry-topped rocks forming an irregular path. The Terran scout studied these—stepping stones? Could some sort of net be rigged above and below to keep off the tif? A few of the men might be able to cross here, leaping from rock to rock. But the whole Horde, burdened with disabled and wounded, could not do it. The problem would have to be turned over to that handful of experts in survival Hansu had gathered on his staff—veterans who pooled knowledge gained on a hundred different worlds to keep them and their comrades alive on this one.

But suddenly the breeze brought a familiar reek to

his nostrils. He had not scented that since the night at the Cos fort. Kana threw himself down behind a bush and Soong landed beside him a moment later.

Almost directly across the river a tall Llor rode out on a sand spit. He carried no lance but balanced an air rifle across his saddle, thus proclaiming his rank as a regular of the royalist guard, rather than a warrior-follower of some provincial noble. The trooper dismounted to approach the water gingerly, inspecting the ripples before he struck down into them with the butt of his weapon. Plainly he was aware of the tif.

But safe on the sand he sat cross-legged, taking out a length of purple cane to chew while he waited. The Terrans flattened themselves every time the Llor's glance swung carelessly across their too-thin cover. There was no hope of withdrawing unseen now.

The Llor spat pieces of pulped cane into the water and once or twice threw stones at the clustering tif. More and more ripples headed for that tongue of gravel as beneath the surface the small masters of the river gathered. Now and then the Llor watched them and gave birth to that snorting sound which served his race for laughter. But, Kana noted, he was careful to stay away from the water.

A mewling cry brought the trooper to his feet. Out of the woods came a party of riders. The one in the van wore a short scarlet cloak lined with ttsor fur and carried before him on a perch attached to his saddle a trained hork—thus identifying himself as a member of the Gatanu's own household. But among the other riders was the hooded, robed figure of a Ventur.

The noble did not dismount, but his guard did, pulling the trader with them. For, astonishingly enough, the Ventur was a prisoner, his hands lashed at his back. The Llor held a conference with their scout, their leader going so far as to ride out on the spit to peer curiously into the water, while the guards urged their captive to the bank.

Then, to the horror of the watching Terrans, they calmly picked up the smaller trader and flung him into the stream where the water was now whipped to a foam by the swarming tif.

Kana's first avenging shot snapped the noble out of his saddle—to plunge into the river headfirst. Methodically the Terrans fired in volleys, picking off the murderers on the far bank. Five of the party were down before the other three fled for the protection of the trees. But none of the fugitives reached that grove.

There was a continued flurry in the water where the tif greeted this rare abundance of meat. Kana dared not look at the place where the helpless Ventur had fallen. Death in battle was commonplace—he had been trained to believe that it would be his own end. But the callous cruelty he had just witnessed was to him a terrifying thing.

"By Klem and Kol'." Soong twitched at his sleeve and pointed to the river.

Something struggled there, flopping about—hampered by sodden robe and bound hands. And in an ever-widening circle about the Ventur floated tif, limp and belly up. Kana leaped to the top of the nearest rock and then to the next. A stripped Llor skull snarled up at him as he jumped the water gap which cradled it. The Ventur was on his feet, winding toward the sand spit where a moment later Kana and Soong joined him. Kana drew his knife.

"I cut those—" he said in the trade tongue, motioning to the hide thongs which bound the other's arms.

The Ventur retreated a step. His struggle to gain the shore had not dislodged his masking hood. Unable to read anything from the gray expanse, broken only by the eye-holes, Kana did not follow him.

"Friend—" Kana used that word with all the emphasis he could give it. He pointed to what was left of the Llor noble. "Enemy of us—enemy of you—"

The Ventur might be considering that point. Suddenly he wheeled and backed toward the Terrans, extending his bound wrists as far as he could. Kana sawed through the wet thongs.

His hands free, the Ventur caught the dangling reins of the noble's mount. An unusually well-trained and therefore highly valued animal, it had not bolted with the rest. The Ventur mounted somewhat awkwardly. His hooded head turned from the river to the bodies of the Llor on its banks and the skeletons in the water where the tif, replete, still floated, their menacing eyes on the prey they could not reach.

One hand groped beneath the robe and came out with a small damp bag. A finger which was closer to a green-gray claw indicated the lazily swimming death and then the inert bodies of the tif which had threatened *it*. It motioned as if sowing something from the bag on the stream. When Kana nodded, the bag was tossed to him and the Ventur kicked the gu into a racking gallop back into the woods.

"Is that something to knock out the tif?" Soong questioned. "Do you suppose they knew he had it when they threw him in?"

"I don't think so, or they would have taken it from him. Maybe its effects are permanent—those floating over there haven't come to—"

The tif which had attacked the Ventur to their own undoing still drifted belly-up, their wicked mouths open. And Kana noticed that their active fellows avoided them. The bag in his hand might grant the Horde a safe crossing.

And so it did. The gritty white powder it contained, strewn on the water upstream, kept off the tif until the Terran force was across. Whether the poison had a permanent effect the Combatants never learned, but as the rearguard trailed through the shallows tif bodies bumped the stepping stones and washed ashore on the spit.

Hansu identified the insignia of the Llor dead as that of the Household Corps. But he was more interested in the trouble between the Ventur and the guardsmen. The great deference paid the hooded ones on the march of Skura's troops east had underlined the belief that then the Llor wanted in no way to antagonize their silent transport specialists. Yet now a Llor noble had calmly ordered one of the Venturi thrown to a horrible death. Somehow the balance of power must have shifted amazingly during the days when the Horde had been fighting across the mountains—shifted to embolden the Llor to show an arrogant contempt for those they had respected for generations. Events certainly suggested that the Llor now had backing so strong that they believed they could make themselves the undisputed rulers of all Fronn. And was that support more than a renegade Mech Legion?

As the Combatants marched on, through valleys which spread out to the level lands of the plains, their alert uneasiness increased. Here the armored, moving fortresses of the Mechs could operate to the greatest advantage. Scouts spent hours each day watching the sky as well as the country before them for signs of aircraft. But since the clash with the party of Llor at the tif river they sighted no enemy. This land appeared to be left to the ttsor, the byll, and the wild khat upon which the two preyed.

On the second day after the Terrans had crossed the river their scouts sighted a village. It was a small frontier settlement, semifortified, ringed with corrals. Here the wild guen of these northern plains were rounded up once a year, sorted, and the duo-yearlings sold after a minimum of training. The pens were full now and a mounted force could move faster. Hansu decided it was wise to turn cavalry and the Combatants altered their line of march, heading for the town.

10

To The Sea

As the Horde spread out in a half-arc across the eastern approach to the town, the first signs of life, other than the restless guen in the corrals, showed in a band of Llor, some riding, some trudging humbly on foot, headed from the domed houses toward the Terran lines. The foremost rider waved over his head a hastily constructed parley flag.

Remembering the fate of Yorke and his officers, neither Hansu nor any other of the Combatants moved from the cover they had taken on the first sight of the Llor. Apparently disconcerted by meeting with only empty landscape the Llor leader reined in his gu and sat, waving the flag at the brush and trees, his followers clustered timidly about him—trying to face in all directions at once.

"Lords—War Lords of Terra—" called the leader, addressing the empty air. And his words lengthened oddly until "Terra" might well have been "terror."

Without rising to view Hansu answered:

"What would you, Corban?" giving the other the honorary title of a headman of a city.

"What would *you*, Lords of Terra?" countered the Llor. He handed the flag to one of his companions and sat, his hands on his thighs, facing in the direction of the Blademaster's voice. "Do you bring us war?"

"We war only when it is offered us. Where open hands hold no swords, we show palms in return. We but wish to travel the road to our homes."

The Llor swung out of his saddle and started to the Terran lines. One of his followers attempted to detain him, only to be pushed aside as the Fronnian, his hands held ostentatiously before him, advanced.

"My hands are open, Lord. I close no road to you."

Hansu arose to meet him, holding his own palms up.

"What would you then, Corban?"

"Word that my village will not be trodden into the earth, nor the blood of my people shaken wet from your swords, War Lord."

"Has not the war banner been raised against us?" countered the Blademaster.

"Lord, what have little men to do with the fine words of Gatanus and nobles? He who sits on the hork-winged bench means little to us—there are always those to gather taxes in his name, whatever it may be. We wish only to live and depart not into the Dark Mists before our time. And stern things have been said of you off-world ones—that you fight with fire those who deny you what you would take. Therefore come I to treat with you for the life of my village. Grain is yours, and the fruits of our fields—and whatever else you wish. Guen also—if it be your will to strip our pens of the newly caught wild ones. Only take your fill and go!"

"Then what if the Gatanu's men come and say unto you, 'You have fed the enemy and given him guen to ride upon. You are one with him'?"

The Corban shook his head. "How can they in truth say that? For you are an army of men trained in strange and horrible forms of warfare. Nay, all of Fronn knows that nothing can stand against the might of your sword-arms. For you fight not only blade to blade after our custom, but with fire which sears from a great distance and with death rained from the air. Some of you crawl in mighty fortresses of metal, lying snug within their bellies as they creep across the ground and crush your enemies under their weight! These things are widely known. So the Gatanu's men cannot believe that a village guard would dare deny you anything you desired. Therefore, I entreat you, Lord, take what you will and go—leaving us our lives!"

"You have seen the Terran fortresses which creep, the machines which fly through the air?"

"Not with my eyes, Lord. For I am an outland man—though Corban of men who do not flinch from hunting the ttsor on foot, nor from snaring the guen of the dales. But in the south all men have seen these wonders and the word has spread to our ears."

"These are then to be found about Tharc?"

"Yes, Lord, there are many of your wonderful machines there now. You wish to join them? It is well. But I entreat you—take what you want and go."

Hansu dropped his empty hands. "Good enough. We shall not invade your village, Corban. Send us supplies and one hundred guen—those broken to saddle use. And we shall not be deceived if you give us wild ones, but if you do we shall come and choose for ourselves."

The Corban raised his hands to his breast and then forehead in the salute a vassal renders his lord. it shall be even as you say. We shall bring you a conqueror's share and thank you for your mercy."

The Llor party went back to the village and Hansu addressed the shrunken Horde.

"—that's the picture. From this fellow's description there must be a full Mech Legion at Tharc. They have heavy stuff as well as wings with them."

"What about Truce Law?" called a voice from the ranks.

"Let's face it. Truce Law was broken when they flamed Yorke and the rest. Mech renegades aren't alone in this—they couldn't have brought in heavy stuff without help—a lot of it. And now they believe they can settle us whenever they wish. I don't care how much backing they have—they don't dare let any news of this get back to Prime. So their first move will be to shut us away from the ships at Tharc."

Shut off from Tharc—bottled up on Fronn—unable to get away. Kana watched the uncertainty mirrored on the faces of those about him begin to change to something else—a grim determination. Generations ago the weaklings, the irresolute, had been weeded and bred out of the Combatant strain. The mercenaries were, by the very nature of their trade, fatalists. Few lived to retire, or even to go into semi-service at the base. And they had followed many lost causes to the end. But this was a new experience. The code which to them was a creed, an unshakeable belief, had been flouted. And for that someone was going to pay!

"We'll get 'em—" The words were drowned out in a growl of assent.

But Hansu's gesture silenced that. "We're not alone," he reminded them. "Once Combat Law is broken here, what will happen? Others will begin to set Mech against Arch."

He did not need to continue. They knew what that

would mean—vicious civil war on half a thousand
planets, one Terran force pitted against another, bleeding their own world white—

"That has to be stopped here and now. One message to Combat Center and it will be!"

"We can't face up to big stuff in the field!" someone shouted.

"We won't try to. But we've got to get a messenger to Secundus or Prime. And the rest of us must hole
up and wait for Combat to move."

"Stay in the mountains?" There was no enthusiasm
in that question. They had had enough of Fronn's
mountains.

Hansu shook his head. "We have an alternative. First
we must learn more about what is going on. Now—set
hostile country camp. Swordtans, scouts, report to me."

They went to the duties in which they had been
drilled. Kana joined the others at the cart where Hansu
waited for them. The commander had spread out a
much-creased sheet of skin and was frowning at the
blue lines which crossed and re-crossed its surface.

"Bogate"—he turned to the head scout—"when that
Corban comes out with supplies, round him up and
bring him here. These guen hunters must know the
land for miles, know it intimately. We want all the
information about it we can pry out of them. Mechs
can't operate in rough territory—so we've got to keep
to broken wilderness."

"But all around Tharc is open plain," one of the
Swordtans objected.

"We have no intention of going to Tharc. They'll be
watching for us to try that."

"The only space port—"

Hansu corrected him instantly. "The only *military*
space port is at Tharc. You are forgetting the Venturi!"

Kana's lips shaped a soundless whistle. The

Blademaster was right. The Venturi! As hereditary traders of Fronn they had some centers of their own on the mainland. And not too far from the western sea was a small off-world space landing used by the few alien traders who had managed to establish contact with the Venturi for a limited exchange of goods—mostly exotic novelties the Fronnian merchants were suspected of reselling at fabulous profit. To reach there—to take control of one of the trading ships—that offered a better chance than to try to blast their way into the toothed trap which was now Tharc.

"There is a space port near the Venturi holdings at Po'ult," Hansu was explaining. "There is no regular schedule of ships, but off-world traders do come. And we may have luck in making a deal for shelter with the Venturi. If we head straight west we should strike the sea not far from Po'ult."

The Corban was only too willing to provide any assistance which would insure getting these dangerous Terrans out of his territory. Kneeling with two of his best guen hunters over the map Hansu had produced, he asked one question which the Blademaster had to parry adroitly.

"But why, Lord, must you seek out a path through this wilderness? To the south the road is wide and smooth and there your brothers await you."

"It is our wish to visit the Venturi of the coast—and not to come upon them by a well-marked road—"

The Llor's tiny circle of a mouth moved in the Fronnian equivalent of a smile.

"Ha. Then it is true—that which has been whispered from mouth to ear—that the day of reckoning with *those* is coming? No longer shall the hooded ones keep the trails, nor be the only buyers and sellers to carry goods from one village to the next! That is good to hear, Lord. Eat up the Venturi forts along the coast if you will—and all the Llor shall speak kindly of you to the Ruler of the Winds. For when those fall, then there shall be rich spoil for all."

Eagerly he consulted the map. "Now here is a path—it lies among the western mountains and there may be Cos. But to *you* what are Cos—you may brush them out of your way as we brush the fas-fas beetles from our floors. And this path will lead you directly to the sea above Po'ult. May your hunting there prosper, War Lord!"

"Indeed may it," piously returned Hansu. And he moved his fingers in the Three Signs of those air, fire, and water spirits who must be consulted on Fronn before any major undertaking.

The Corban warmed still more and became their champion with the guen herders, personally inspecting the stock his fellow citizens had run out from the village corrals, and rejecting ten animals, much to the bafflement of his men who were prepared to make a handsome profit from the ignorance of off-world men, for Hansu insisted on paying for the animals. That night he gave a feast, using a month's supplies with the abandon of a Chortha of a province. To the future conquerors of the Venturi he would deny nothing. And a handpicked corps of guides, selected from the most hardy and far roving of the guen hunters, was detailed to accompany the Horde to the foothills of the western mountains.

That was a day and a half journey—mounted—and Hansu pushed them to the utmost, driven himself by the desire to get out of the dangerous level country before they were sighted by a Mech patrol.

On the morning of the third day when they were well on the mountain trail they found the Llor guides gone. Distant behind them was the smudge of smoke in the sky and bits of charred grass drifted down. The

hunters had lighted a plains fire to drive the wild guen
into a netting place. Hansu watched that haze with
satisfaction. It would effectively cover their trail, which
was perhaps why the Llor hunters had lit it.

Now began the old nightmare of climbing, climbing and being ever alert for an attack. Though the
hunters had insisted that this route lay on the edge of
Cos-held country and that the mountaineers had very
seldom troubled the caravans which used it, they could
not be sure of a peaceful penetration. And the Llor
had been unable to answer Hansu's questions as to
whether the Venturi caravanmen had some pact with
the Cos which insured that safety. However, the Terrans
had no alternative but to advance.

The trail was marked with those narrow stone pillars erected by the Venturi, the pictographs on them
untranslatable. And it was made for the use of guen.

That night they went without fire, camped in small
groups, strung out with sentries between. But the hours
of darkness were not broken by alarms and they sighted
no beacons on the heights.

Kana had tramped behind Hansu for most of that
day, and now, his blanket pulled about him for warmth,
he crouched by an outcrop trying to snatch some sleep
while the Blademaster sat cross-legged a yard away and
listened to the reports of scouts.

"—no deal with these Mechs?"

"Not a chance." Hansu's voice brought him fully
awake. "Mills said that Hart Device was in command."

"Device! I still think Deke musta been wrong.
Device wouldn't go outlaw—"

"That's just the point, Bogate. If Device is the
commander at Tharc—and I see no reason not to trust
information Mills died to bring us—then this is no
matter of a Mech Legion gone outlaw. Hart Device is
a new leader—just as Yorke was. His Legion is small

but tough, well equipped, and Hart has the reputation of delivering. I'd be willing to lay half a year's pay that he has a large percentage of vets—just as we have. I wonder—" His voice trailed off.

But Kana, tired as he was, caught that hint. A Legion, a Horde, both consisting of well-trained men, locked in a death struggle. No matter which won in the end, the death toll would be high. So many veterans removed from action. It was beginning to add up to an ugly sum.

"If the Code's broke"—Zapan Bogate's rumbling whisper had thoughtful undertones—"hell's to pay! Why—Archs won't have a chance!"

"Not at the old game, no. But that is no reason why we can't start a new one."

"But—we're Combat men, Hansu—"

"Sure. Only there's no rule about who or what we have to fight." There was an absent note in the Blademaster's voice as if he were thinking aloud.

"Anyways, now we got just one job." Bogate heaved himself up. "To get outta these blasted hills and see the Venturi. We gonna try to take 'em, sir?"

"Not if we can help it. They may welcome us with open arms if what that Corban hinted is true and the Llor have turned against them. Their territory is too rough for the Mechs. This Po'ult of theirs is built on an island off the coast—sheer rock straight up from the sea. They have their own ways of getting ashore and you can't bring up heavy stuff to batter it."

"Good place for us to hole up—if they'll let us."

"That's what we'll have to arrange, Bogate. If we can make them see we have a common enemy, maybe they'll make it a common war. Take scouts out in the morning as usual."

"Yes, sir."

At dawn the trek began again. Snow lay in patches

along the trail, and the patches became solid sheets, drifting across the track, drifts through which men on foot beat a way for the slender-legged guen. But in that struggle they lost animals, for the wild, newly captured mounts were not tough enough for a battle such as this. The second cart became a casualty—and with it one of the medical corpsmen who did not have a chance to relinquish his drag rope as it slithered over the edge of a drop and plunged to a slope far below.

"Alert!" The war whistle shrieked the message along, to set numb hands unslinging rifles, freeing sword-knives. That was the only warning they had before the battle of the pass began. But now they were not tangling with Cos but with a party of Llor in flight, desperate to win through, back to the plains and safety. And because of their desperation they came on without caution, trying to hack their way through the Horde.

The struggle was a short one, the rear guard of the Horde never firing a shot. But it was bloody. For the Llor died to a man and they had been so reckless in their attack that they cut down in their insane scramble men who would not normally have been drawn into a hand-to-hand combat.

The Terrans, already spent with their struggle through the snow to these heights, licked their wounds that night and camped, sick with weariness, on the edge of the battlefield. Wind-driven snow covered the fallen and the Combatants who could keep their feet moved among the wounded striving to ward off frozen death.

"Raiding party being chased home—" The sear breeze pulled the words from between Mic's chapped lips. "Maybe we're marching straight into a fire someone else started. Hope the Venturi won't think we're more of the same—"

Rey rubbed one cheek with a handful of snow. "Never a dull moment." He wheezed and then coughed until his whole rangy body shook. "Next time we have a premonition about any enlistment—me, I'm going to believe it! What a paradise replacement barracks was—why did I ever leave Secundus?"

Kana beat gloved hands together. Secundus seemed very far and long ago. Had he *ever* eaten in a room where flame birds flitted on the walls? Or was that a dream and this present nightmare stark reality?

"We'll just plow on and on through this"—Mic kicked a pile of snow—"until it is deep enough to bury us. Then next season they'll find us all nice and stiff and export us as 'native art'—"

"Were these Llor running from a brush with the Venturi?" Rey wondered. "I thought they were afraid of them. Remember all that trouble about the spy just out of Tharc? We weren't to touch the traders. And even when they found their man the Llor didn't say anything to the caravan people."

"The Llor believe now that they are going to take over Fronn," Kana said. "They must have hated the Venturi for a long time and see a good chance to get back at them now. You scouting tomorrow, Rey?"

"I am—for my sins. And you?"

"Likewise."

Mic nursed his healing arm. "They're sure whittling us down to size, these mountains. Have bad luck every time we climb. Fifty lost back there—twenty here—and more wounded—"

"Not as bad as when the wing bombed us," Rey reminded him. "As long as we can fight back—"

"Yes, I know. But see you come back from scout, you long-legged byll!"

"You know"—Rey stopped rubbing the snow down his jaw line—"that's an idea. If a fella could get him say ten-twenty of those birds and train 'em—as the fur faces trained their horks. They don't make any noise before they jump, do they?" He turned to consult Kana as an authority. "No? Well, put 'em on the enemy's track and let 'em go. Better than a Mech crusher in country such as this."

"And just who is going to catch and train them?" Mic was beginning, when another Arch appeared out of the dark.

"Karr?"

"Here!"

"Report to Blademaster."

Kana groped his way to where Hansu had holed up between two overhanging slabs of rock forming a half-cave. The faint blue of a captured Llor torch gave a ghostly, morbid hue to the faces of those clustered about it. And one of them had no face at all—only the blank mask of a hooded Ventur.

"Karr, sit down." Kana folded up just inside as the Blademaster turned back to the hooded one.

"Will this man do?"

The muffled head moved, but no word was spoken for a long moment as Kana shifted under the gaze of eyes hidden behind round holes. Then the trader made an assenting gesture which was more a quick jerk than a Terran nod.

"This Ventur was a prisoner of that troop of Llor," Hansu explained. "He's going back to his people and you're the AL man who'll accompany him to make contact. We want a base—a chance to hide out until we can notify Secundus. Use your judgment, Karr. You are the only AL trained man we have left. Make the best deal you can with them. Impress upon them that we're as much against the Llor now as they are—tell their leaders what that Corban said to us."

"Yes, sir."

Hansu looked at his watch. "Take rations and extra ammunition. We have no idea how far we now are from Po'ult—the map isn't accurate. And"—he hesitated, his eyes boring into Kana's— "just remember—we have to have that base!"

"Yes, sir."

11

Truce Of Wind

The trail ran along a broad ledge from which the snow had been scoured by the night winds. Below was the dull, dark green of twisted trees and a gray expanse laced with white where tempest-driven waves beat upon the water-worn rocks of the western seashore.

Kana's pace slowed as he looked out over that heaving floor of water. Winged creatures wheeled, dipped, and screamed over the narrow strand, seeking out tidbits thrown up by the flow. But, save for them, he might have been viewing an empty world.

No sun shone today and under the pewter clouds the land stretching down to the sea was grim and forbidding.

"We—go—"

Kana started. In all the five hours that they had been traveling together those were the first words the Ventur had spoken. Now the trader hovered impatiently at the far end of the ledge, waiting to climb down to sea level. Traces on the path marked the retreat of the Llor twenty-odd hours before. But there were no signs of any Venturi pursuers.

They had seen no one so far though they had passed numerous sites intended by nature for easy defense. One might well believe that the traders had no wish to protect their territory.

Now the Combatant toiled down the slope to come out upon a well-marked, smoothly surfaced road along the coast. And within a few minutes they did face a Ventur sentry.

The hooded one who kept watch there conferred with the guide while Kana allowed them the privacy these strange people appeared to desire. He did not join them until the wave of a gloved hand brought him to the small building. Out of this the two traders pushed the first mechanical vehicle the Arch had yet seen on Fronn. It was scarcely more than a platform of metal, possessing three wheels, one at each corner of its wedge shape, and no visible motor. The Venturi guide seated himself on the narrow point and motioned Kana to take his place on the wider section behind. Hardly had the Terran pulled his legs under him than they took off—not at the skimming speed a land jopper would have displayed on his native world—but faster than a marching stride.

As they whisked along he saw no indication of any military patrol. It was as if the Venturi, having driven the Llor into the mountains, no longer worried about an attack, which argued an amazing self-confidence with strength to back it.

The road curved and curled, following the natural contours of the shoreline. They came around one such curve to front the Venturi port.

Here the sea bit into the land in a great semicircle

of a bay, a natural harbor into which the traders had built a series of wharves. Inshore clustered window-less, high-walled buildings with the look of warehouses and trading depots. It was as they approached these that Kana saw the first signs of the recent battle. But all the Venturi in sight were going about their busi-ness with no hurry or confusion. From the odd ships at the wharves—their superstructures completely cov-ered to give them the look of giant turtles—poured a steady stream of goods— Or did it?

The vehicle stopped and Kana got off. No—those ships were being loaded, not unloaded! The flat cars were transporting goods to the sea, not away from it. It was apparent that the traders were stripping the depot—it had all the signs of an orderly evacuation.

"Come—"

Again his Venturi companion hurried him on. They slipped through a maze of lanes between the build-ings, hugging the walls at times to avoid swiftly mov-ing cars piled with bundles and bales. And at last they came to a smaller structure so close to the sea that the waters dashed up on its outer wall.

The day without was dull and gray but it was even darker inside the building. Kana blinked, then his wrist was grasped and he was pulled on to the far end of a corridor. As the Ventur stopped before what seemed to be a solid wall, that expanse parted, allowing a greenish light to shine out.

Kana stared about him with a frankness he did not try to disguise. The walls of this room arched over him to meet in a cone's point. Thick pads provided seats for the three Venturi who sat behind low tables. One wall—that to his left—had been covered with a tangle of apparatus which several of the hooded ones were methodically dismantling and packing away in cases. At the entrance of the Terran these stopped their work and slipped out, leaving the Combatant to face the other three.

They had been at work, too, sorting piles of thin sheets of some opaque substance, selecting a few to be encased in a metal chest, tossing others into discard on the floor. Their records, Kana guessed.

The trader who had brought him from the mountains delivered a report. And it was an almost soundless process, as if the Venturi did not communicate by voice alone. When he had done, all the hooded heads swung in Kana's direction. He hesitated, not knowing whether he should speak first. So much depended upon making the right impression. If he could only see their faces—

"You are from off-world?"

It took him a second to decide which one of those baffling masks had addressed him. He thought it was the middle one and replied accordingly.

"I am of Terra—of the Combatants of Terra."

"Why are you here?"

"Skura of the Llor brought us to fight for him. Skura was killed. Now we wish to return to our own world."

"The Llor war—" Was it only his imagination or was there a chill in that voice?

"We no longer fight for the Llor—we fight against them. For they would slay us."

"What seek you of us here?"

"A place to stay until we can find an off-world ship."

"At Tharc are such ships to be found."

"At Tharc are also our enemies. They will not allow us to gain those ships."

"But those at Tharc are also of Terra. Do you war with your own kind?"

"They are evildoers who have broken our laws. They would keep the knowledge of their evil from our

Masters-of-Trade. If we can return with the evidence against them, they shall be punished."

"At Tharc only are such ships," repeated the Ventur stubbornly.

"We have heard that near Po'ult is a place where the starships of off-world traders come," Kana countered with growing desperation. Hansu should have come himself to argue this. He was making no impression at all.

"Traders do not transport men of war—traders do not fight."

"But we met Llor in the mountains fleeing from a battle with traders—traders they no longer welcome in the plains. No, Master-of-Trade—the hour is coming when even you may be forced to bare sword and use rifle in your own defense. We spoke with a Llor Corban who foretold the sacking of your mainland holdings—of a new day coming to Fronn when the Venturi would not rule the caravan routes. Those who would press this change upon you are prepared to do it with the sword. And they are also *our* enemies. We are fighting men, trained to battle from our earliest years. Those whom our swords serve sleep easy at night. And it seems that you will have need of allies, Master, if rumor speaks true."

The hooded figure changed position slightly, almost as if he had answered that with a shrug.

"We be of the sea. And the Llor are not of the sea. If we keep to our own place, what need have we of swords? And soon enough the dwellers on land will come to know their mistake."

"If you dealt only with Llor, perhaps that would be true. But the Llor have these others to aid them. The renegade Terrans they company do not fight as we do, rifle to rifle, sword to sword. Rather do they have mighty machines to obey their will and they hunt from the sky, raining fire upon those they would destroy. With passage through the air the sea is no barrier. Tell me, Master, are there not off-world men who would be glad if your hold upon the trade of Fronn ceased to be? Such men will give support in war to those who serve them best."

When they did not have a ready answer to that a tiny spark of hope came to Kana. If the Venturi were deserting their shore bases, preparing to withdraw to their island fortresses for an indefinite length of time, then the Horde might reach the sea coast only to discover themselves in another trap. His chance—their only chance—was to win at least grudging support from these traders before they departed.

"These things of which you speak have already been told to us. The sky machines have been sighted. So you think they would follow us—even into the outer ocean where no Llor dares to drive a ship?"

"I believe this, Master-of-Trade, that peace has departed from Fronn and that the time has come when all upon its surface will be compelled to choose whether they shall follow this war leader or that. It was against the law that these sky fighters and moving fortresses were brought here. And when men go outside the law—a law which has might to back it—they do so weighing risk against return—as you in trade weigh risk against profit. They play now to rule this world. And if they win—what will they care for the Venturi? You shall be eaten up and your trade kingdom shall be as if it never was!"

The middle Ventur arose, his robes making a faint whispering as he moved, for they were of a finer material than the drab coverings of the caravan men.

"We are not of those who make treaties or deal with rulers," he stated firmly, "but the words you have spoken shall be carried to our elders on Po'ult. And to this much shall we agree—you may bring your people to this—the Landing of Po'ult—and they may abide here through the great storms—until our elders come to a decision, for we shall be gone from here this day. This is spoken by Falt'u'th, so be it recorded.

A murmur from the others gave assent. The guide who had brought Kana waved him to withdraw. He brought his hand up in salute and the Venturi leader nodded. As the Terran left the room the men who had been dismantling the machine on the wall hurried past him to resume their work.

Venturi hospitality was not expansive. Kana was transported from the Landing of Po'ult at once. As the wedge car ascended the slope behind the settlement he noticed one of the turtle ships drawing away from the dock. As it neared the middle of the bay it slowly submerged until only a conning tower was left above water, and with that cutting the waves it headed to the open sea.

Kana and the Ventur reached the guard post at dusk and the Terran was thankful to note that the trader intended to spend the night there. The Combatant was shown into a windowless inner room, one wall of which gave off a faint greenish gleam, provided with a mat which could be either seat or bed, and left to himself. He ate his rations and curled up on the pad, aching with weariness.

The next morning it was made clear to him that the Venturi regarded this outpost as the boundary of their concern with him and from that point he was to proceed alone. But now the pale sun was banishing the gloom of the day before and, as he swung along at the ground-eating pace of the marching Arch, his confidence in the future grew. After all—even if the traders had not opened Po'ult, they were allowing the Terrans the use of their port on the coast. And it was situated not far from the landing field Hansu had spoken of—they had only to await the coming of an off-world trading ship.

Kana's hopeful outlook continued to grow as he climbed the pass, and it colored the report he was able to make to Hansu before noon.

"They gave you no idea as to when they would let us know their decision?" The Blademaster pinned him down.

"No, sir. They were stripping the Landing, withdrawing to their sea strongholds. Seemed to think that they could outsit the trouble—"

"I have yet to see a neutral win anything—especially when the enemy wants something he has. But we can't quarrel with even half luck—we'll settle for the use of their port buildings now."

When the van of the Horde reached the outer guard post they found it deserted, the building empty, the sentry and the wedge car gone. And as they marched on down to the Landing nothing moved in the narrow lanes between the warehouses. The turtle ships had vanished—a last conning tower slicing the waves could just be seen far out on the bay. But not a Ventur, not a scrap of their goods was left in the silent and empty port.

Hansu posted sentries, though he allowed that the sturdiness of the thick walls would be ample protection against the most that even a Mech force could throw against them. The Blademaster took up quarters in the house backing upon the sea where Kana had met with the Venturi leaders. The apparatus was gone from the wall of the room, leaving holes and dangling brackets, but the small tables were still bolted to the floor and a seat pad had been left behind.

For the first time since they had left Tharc the Combatants were under roofs. And none too soon, for the rising wind of the night brought with it the banners of a storm.

The thick walls kept out most of the howl of the wind. But one could lay a hand against their surfaces and feel the vibration of such tempests as the Terrans had not known before. They need fear no attack while this held.

Curiosity led them to explore their new quarters, finding a few discarded articles, the use of half of which they could not deduce. Kana, with Mic and Rey, armed with Terran night torches, dared a trap door they discovered in a far hallway and descended a steep flight of steps whose risers had not been fashioned for off-world feet. They ended in a cellar, half natural sea cave, in which a water-filled slip ran part way up, slopping back and forth with the force of the wind-driven sea without.

Flicking his light across the water Kana sighted a line fastened inconspicuously to a hook embedded in the floor, pulled taut below the surface. Something heavy must be tethered there!

He gave it a questioning tug. There was an object on the other end all right. The three of them dragged it together, bracing their feet and trying to free what lay below with a series of sharp jerks. Seconds later they pulled up the slimy incline a strange craft. It was rounded, contained, like the turtle ships—more so, for it lacked the conning tower.

"A bomb?" ventured Mic.

"No, not when it's anchored that way." Kana moved around the end. "One man escape ship maybe."

"They went off and forgot it—?"

"No," Kana denied again. "It was hidden—so I'd say we still have a visitor."

"Left behind to watch us—" Mic's eyes roved about the rough walls. "Perhaps he's to set some traps, too."

"I don't think that the Venturi have the trap-type mind," Kana defended the traders. "I'd say we were left an observer—maybe even a contact with Po'ult, if we handle it right. However, perhaps it would be better if we kept a watch on this." He kicked the ship with the toe of his boot. Whoever traveled in that would have cramped quarters indeed. A Terran could not fit in it at all, not even when flat and unmoving.

They reported the find to Hansu and the ship was transported to an upper hall. A searching exploration was made of all the Landing buildings without any concrete results.

The storm had not blown out by morning. Instead it increased and it became almost impossible, because of the wind and driven spray, to win from one building to another. But this would continue to keep off attack—which almost balanced the Arch disappointment at being unable to search for the space port Hansu was sure must be close at hand.

Kosti examined the escape ship with care and solved the riddle of its opening, displaying to his crowding comrades the narrow padded slit within, which would cradle the body of the navigator.

"What kinda man would fit in there?" demanded Sim.

"Perhaps not a 'man' at all," Kosti returned.

"Huh?"

"Well, none of us have seen a Venturi without one of those muffling robes. How do we know if they are like the Llor—or us? This could be comfortable for a non-human."

Kana eyed the slit speculatively. It was too narrow for the length if it were fashioned to accommodate a humanoid. It suggested an extremely thin, sinuous creature. He did not feel any prick of man's age-old distaste for the reptilian—any reminder of the barrier between warm-blooded and cold-blooded life which had once held on his home world. Racial mixtures after planet-wide wars, mutant births after the nuclear conflicts, had broken down the old intolerance against the "different." And out in space thousands of intelligent life forms, encased in almost as many shapes and bodies, had given "shape prejudice" its final blow. The furred Llor and Cos were "man"-shaped, but it might be that they shared Fronn with another race, evolved from scaled clans.

Why not snake or lizard? There were races whose far ancestors had been feline, and others who had, dim ages ago, sacrificed the wings of birds to develop intelligence and civilization—and yet the Yabanu and the Trystian were now equal partners in the space lanes. As for reptiles—what of the lizard Zacathans, whose superior learning had confounded half the universe and yet who were a most peace-loving and law-abiding collection of scholars?

Kana, remembering the Zacathans he had known and admired, viewed that padded cushion with no aversion, only curiosity. What did it matter if a body was covered with wool, or with scales, or with soft flesh which had to be protected by clothing? The Venturi he had met had not been in any way terrifying or obnoxious creatures—once one became used to their constant concealment of their faces and forms. Now he wanted to know what they were really like—and why they shrouded themselves so carefully.

But the owner of the escape ship, if he were concealed somewhere within the Landing, made no move to declare his presence. And the storm continued. On the morning of the second day Hansu fought his way across a short strip of court to a nearby building and returned, being once hurled against a wall with a force which almost lost him his footing. Kana, waiting, grabbed for the Blademaster's coat and dragged him inside. The commander gasped painfully before he could speak.

"We can't face this. It is the West Wind Drive!"

Kana recalled the record-pak. The West Wind Drive, that paralyzing push of Fronn's terrible windy season when all life went to cover and death itself rode the blasts. There would be no hope of surviving even a short journey in the open. Anything caught outside the shelter of the Landing would be whirled off and battered flat. Their luck had held—bringing them out of the mountains behind the strong walls of the port just in time.

"No spacer would try to land now," Kana pointed out. "They would be warned."

Hansu nodded. But it was plain that his inability to do something about the situation was an added irritant.

"I wish I could meet the Ventur." He gazed down the hall as if he could summon the hidden one out by the force of his will. "We must be ready to move the minute this clears."

Their future was still a race for time. If the Blademaster could get a messenger aboard a spacer before Hart Device located them and brought up his wings—they would win. And—did the Venturi hold the deciding cards in this game?

12

On To Po'ult

The inactivity caused by the storms began to bore the Combatants. At first they had been content to sleep much of the time, rebuilding the stores of energy worn out by the trek across the mountains. But now they roamed restlessly through the buildings, making reckless sorties from one to another during what they believed were lulls, or allowing their irritation to show in sudden snarling quarrels. But Hansu was prepared to meet this. There were drills in unarmed combat and scouting as well as follow-the-leader hunts in which a handful of veterans hid and the younger members of the teams traced them in silent pursuit.

Since the storm established a perpetual gray dusk one could no longer distinguish day from night. It might have been noon or well into evening when Kana climbed one of the perilously steep flights of narrow stairs to almost roof level of a warehouse. His eyes had long since adjusted to the pallid green light given off by the walls and he moved softly, intent upon reaching the small platform just under the curve of the domed roof. From there he would be able to see into the large storage space which occupied the center section of the building. He was a hound and Sim was hare today. It had become a matter of pride for the recruit to locate this one veteran, even if he must devote every moment until the sleep period to the problem.

As Kana climbed, the light faded. He put out a hand to touch the steps as a guide. But he was still at least three from the top when he stopped and shrank against the wall. He sensed that he was not alone.

From below he had estimated that the platform was about five feet square. There was a trap door above it which must give upon the roof—and in this wind nothing could perch outside for an instant. The roof!

Kana's shoulder rubbed the wall as he forced his memory to reconstruct the outline of this warehouse building as he had seen it from the headquarters two hours before. It was like all the rest, a rounded dome which offered small resistance to the wind. The roof—

He took the remaining steps cautiously. Then he stretched to his full height, raising his arms above his head until his fingers were on the surface above him. But what he expected he did not find.

Twice during these scout games he had climbed to these vantage points in warehouses and both times he had discovered that the roof vibrated faintly, a trembling born of the blasts beating across it. But here it was quiet, as if insulated against the outer world. And he still believed that he was not alone.

With his finger tips he explored the ceiling, locating the small trap door which should give on the roof. As his hands fingered its hinges he realized that here was a difference. There was no fastening on this side. The latch which kept the door from swinging down must be on the other side!

Kana slipped his torch from his belt and snapped it on at the lowest power, no longer caring if Sim sighted him. The platform was covered by that gritty dust which constantly sifted through the air during the storms. His boots had left plain tracks in it. But there were other marks too, though these were shapeless scuffs which could not have been left by a Terran unless he had purposely tried to conceal his spoor. And directly under the trap door were other marks he could not identify.

He beamed the torch up at the door. It was firmly set; he could hardly see the lines marking the square. The two hinges glistened. Kana investigated delicately. Grease—some sort of grease so recently applied that it was liquid instead of viscid and its strange odor was sharp as he brought his smeared finger to his nose. Someone was using this door. But to go outside—that was impossible!

Kana aimed the beam at the ceiling, beginning his examination farther out than the platform. After a careful study he was certain that there was a space overhead between the ceiling he saw and the outer dome of the building. The curve was curtailed, the angle between the side wall and the dome sharper than it should be. But what a perfect hiding place! No Terran would attempt to explore the roofs in the storm. He was prepared to take Knife-Oath that he had discovered the hiding place of the Venturi spy! Hansu need only station a guard here and—

A whisper of sound, so faint it barely reached his ears, made him snap off the torch and back against the wall to the left of the stairs. Some of the green radiance seeped up, but the light was so faint he could

not really see. He must depend upon his ears—his
nose.

For now he was aware of an odor. Below, where the
bales of trade goods had once been stored, smells
fought with one another and the general aroma was
often sickening to a Terran. But this was different,
faintly spicy and fresh—transporting him for an instant
to the gambling establishment on Secundus. There was
nothing unpleasant about it and it was growing stronger.

Next came a soft plop and Kana froze, hardly daring to breathe. Something, his ears told him, had fallen
from the trap door to the platform. He swung his torch
before him as if it were a flamer.

Other sounds reached him—movements he was not
sure of.

He pressed the stud of the torch, setting the power
at full. And it flashed on, pinning in its thick beam the
creature who had just stepped from the last loop in
a rope ladder to the floor. It made one grab for the
rope and then froze, erect and quiet, accepting the fact
that escape was now impossible.

The cushioned bed in the escape ship had been a
clue right enough, but reality out-stripped imagination.
If this were a Ventur—and Kana had no reason to
doubt that—the second major race of Fronn had little
or nothing in common with the Llor physically.

Its extreme slenderness gave it the appearance of
greater height than it really possessed, for it was shorter
than he. Its arms fitted to the barrel of the trunk
without any width of shoulder and the pouchy neck
was only a shade under the girth of the chest. The legs
were long and as thin as a gu's ending in flat, webbed
feet, and there were two sets of upper limbs, all
equipped with six-fingered hands.

But the head was the least humanoid, four eyes set
in pairs on either side, a wide mouth which now gaped

in surprise, no visible chin—Kana started as with horror he realized where he had seen the like before—in miniature. This was a tif—a tif turned land dweller with only its size and greater brain case to distinguish it from the ferocious hunters of the river.

As Kana remembered the tif he knew the cold chill of fear—until he met those eyes blinking in the torture of his light. The black beads of hate, promising all manner of evil to come, which had watched him from the stream were not here. These larger orbs were golden, intelligent, mildly peaceful. And the Arch guessed that the Ventur was as alarmed as he—tif the other might look, but tif in nature he was not.

None of those four hands had gone to the knife which was sheathed on the Ventur's hip. A shiver crossed the green-gray skin beneath the scanty tunic which covered it to mid-thigh. Abruptly Kana switched off the torch.

And then it was his turn to blink as a green beam, far under the power of his own, struck him, flitting from head to boots and back again.

"One only?" The question out of the dark did not sound as if it had come from between those wide loose lips, out of the wattled throat.

"Just one."

The light went to his hands and then to his sword-knife at his belt. It centered there for a moment as if the Ventur was studying the weapon—as if that undrawn blade answered some private question for the other.

"You will come?" The green light pinpointed the dangling ladder.

Kana did not hesitate. He thrust his own torch back in its loop and stepped forward.

He made the short climb up the rope and wedged his shoulders through the trap door. It was a tight fit.

Above was a pocket-sized room. A spongy pad covered a third of the space and he sat down on one end of it as his host emerged from the floor and made some adjustment which brought more light from the walls. There was, in addition to the pad, a flat box and a neat pile of containers. By the end of the cushion was a small brazier emitting coils of spicy, scented smoke. The quarters might be cramped, but the hidy-hole was provided with Venturi comforts. And now the frog-man seated himself on the other end of the pad, pushing aside his folded robe.

"You have watched us?" Kana asked.

"I have watched you." The ungainly head, its four golden eyes fixed on the Terran, gave a twitch of agreement.

"For the Masters-of-Trade?"

"For the nation," the other corrected swiftly. "You are traders in death. Such bargains may be evil—"

"You are a speaker-for-many?"

"I train to be a speaker-for-many. I am but one of limited years and small wisdom. You are a lord over many swords?"

It was Kana's turn to deny honors. "I, too, am but a learner of this trade. This is my first battle journey."

"Tell me, why do you creep through these buildings spying upon one another?" the Ventur asked, a note of real puzzlement in his voice.

"We train ourselves—that we may come upon the enemy secretly. It is a practice of our art."

The four eyes continued to regard him unblinkingly. "And the Llor is now this enemy you would creep upon unseen. But why—did not the Llor summon you to Fronn in their service? Why should you now turn against them?"

"We were brought to serve the Chortha Skura. He made a bargain with our Masters-of-Trade. But he was killed in the first battle. According to custom we then ceased from battle and asked to be returned to our own place. But the Llor invited our Masters to hold a meeting over this matter, and when they were gathered together the Llor killed them treacherously. It was then that we discovered that they had with them certain outlaws of our own kind whose desire was to hunt us all down lest we return to our Masters-of-Trade and report the truth of what was done.

"Now our enemies hold Tharc where our spaceships land. We came to Po'ult hoping to find a trading spacer that would carry a messenger off-world for us—"

"But those which land here are not ships of war."

"It does not matter whether they are or not. They are not so small that they have not space for one or two men besides their crew. And once our Masters-of-Trade know what has happened they will send ships to take us off."

"Then you do not wish to stay on Fronn? With such arts of war as you know you might win the leadership of this world."

"We are of Terra. To us that is the world to call home. All we wish is to leave Fronn in peace."

The Ventur leaned forward to draw in deep breaths of the smoke arising from the brazier. Then, without a word, he opened a round box and brought out two small basins or handleless cups. They were fashioned in the form of spiraled shells of a delicate blue-green across which moved amethyst shadows. Into each of these he measured a minute portion of golden liquid poured from a small flagon as beautifully made as the cups. Then he held out one to Kana while he lifted the other, chanting some words in his own tongue.

Kana accepted the cup gingerly. He could not refuse to drink—it was offered with too much ceremony, though what effect the native liquor might have on a

Terran stomach and head worried him, even as the stuff slid smoothly over his tongue and he swallowed. There was no sensation of heat such as Terran strong drink brought—only a coolness, a tingling which spread outward to the tips of his fingers and the surface of his skin. He set down the empty cup. Now what he sensed was mingled in some odd way with the scent from the brazier and the green radiance of the walls, as if taste, touch, smell and sight were suddenly one, all the keener and sharper for that uniting.

The Ventur shrugged his robe into place about his shoulders.

"We go now to your Master-of-Swords—"

Did he heard those words with his ears, mused Kana, or did they ring in his mind only? He stood up, this strange clarity of the senses persisting, and watched the frog-man drop the rope into the darkness below the trap door. On the platform the Ventur paused to adjust his hood, hiding his strange face.

"He's in the other building," Kana warned, remembering the storm.

"Yes—" The robed shadow glided noiselessly along, almost entirely invisible to anyone who did not know where he was. Kana knew that that must have protected him as he spied upon the Combatants.

They covered the few feet between the door of the warehouse and the recessed entrance of headquarters clinging to one another and both Kana's coat and the skirts of the other's robe were soaked with sea spray as they won to their goal.

Not only were his senses more acute, Kana decided, but his reactions were swifter. He was conscious of so much he had not noted before—that there were subtle differences in the shades of green light from room to room—that sounds hitherto drowned out by the muffled roar of the wind were perceptible.

"What's that—!" A Swordsman coming down the hall halted at the sight of the Ventur.

"Messenger to Hansu," Kana explained, hurrying his companion on to meet the Blademaster.

Hansu and two of the Swordtans glanced up frowning at the interruption. But they were alert at the sight of the trader.

"Where did you—?" the Blademaster began and then addressed the silent Ventur. "What is it that you wish?"

"It is rather what you wish, Master-of-Swords," the other returned. "You desire a meeting with our Masters-of-Trade. But I have not the right to answer in their name. This one of you"—the cowled head gave a half turn to indicate Kana—"has made clear to me why you are here and what you wish. Grant me"—he mentioned a space of Fronnian time—"and I shall have an answer for you."

Hansu did not hesitate. "Done! But how can you communicate with your people? In the storm—"

Kana received a vivid impression of the Ventur's amusement. "Do you then have no means among you of talking across distances, Terran? We have been rated a backward people by off-world races, but we have not displayed all our knowledge and resources before them. Come with me if you wish and see. There is no trickery in what I would do, only the use of things built by intelligent beings for their safety and comfort."

So it was that Kana and Hansu returned to that hidden room to watch the Ventur, his hampering robe discarded, open a thin box and display a silver mirror disc and a row of small levers. These he raised or lowered in a pattern, with infinite care, as if he worked out a complicated combination.

The mirror misted and at the coming of that film the Ventur moved quickly to snatch up a slender rod. With the pointed tip of that he traced a series of waving lines. They faded from the disc and there was a moment of waiting until the mist reappeared and a second collection of lines were inscribed. Four times that happened and then the trader put aside his pen.

"There is a matter of time now," he informed the Combatants. "We must wait until the Masters reply. I only report, it is for them to give orders."

Hansu grunted. There were cruel lines of weariness about the Blademaster's mouth, a cloud of fatigue in his eyes. Hansu was a man worn close to the edge of endurance. And what ate into him was not only the future of the Horde—but something even more important. He was fighting for more than their escape from Fronn—for a goal which might be of far greater importance than the lives of all the Archs on this world.

The Ventur inhaled the brazier smoke, but his golden eyes watched the Terrans.

"Master," he said to the Blademaster, "this much I can tell you—there has not been any off-world ship land here for ten tens of clors—"

Kana tried to translate the time measure. Close to four months' ship time! His mouth set hard.

"And that is not as it was in the past?"

"It is not," the Blademaster was answered. "We do not care for off-world trade, so its lack did not disturb us. But now—perhaps you can read another meaning into this. Also, what can you do if the trade ship comes not? Your enemies hold the port at Tharc."

"One thing at a time. Let me speak to your Masters and then we shall see—"

A tinkle of sound came from the box. The Ventur looked at the mirror. Although the Terrans could make nothing of what he saw there he spoke in a moment or two.

"The Masters summon you to Po'ult to speak with them in private council. And because you have met with treachery on Fronn, there shall be those of master rank who shall sit among your men as hostages while you are gone. To this do you agree?"

"I agree. But when do I go?"

"The first fury of the storm will ebb tonight. They will send a ship in, but you must be ready to return with it at once, for this lull will not last long."

"Am I to go alone?"

"Take one man if you wish. May I suggest this one." A claw finger pointed at Kana. "He speaks the trade tongue well."

Hansu did not object. "Let it be so."

The lull came as the Ventur had foretold. And the two Terrans went with the trader down the sea-slimed steps to the dock. Kana saw the vee of spray cutting down the bay, heralding the approach of a Venturi vessel. It arose from the water and came in to the pier with perfection of handling. Then a hatch in the conning tower opened and four robed figures disembarked. Three glided up to the Terrans, the other remained by the ship.

"This Master Roo'uf, Under-Master Rs'ad, and Under-Master Rr'ol—they shall stay with your men."

Hansu escorted the Venturi back to introduce them to his Swordtans. Then, with Kana at his heels, he climbed the ladder leading to the hatch. Within was a second ladder dropping into green dimness and the Combatants descended while strange odors and stranger noises closed about them as they went. The Venturi spy touched Kana's sleeve and drew him to the left.

"It is the thought of the master of this ship that you would be interested in watching from the lookout as we travel— This way."

They squeezed along a passage which was almost too narrow to accommodate Terrans and found themselves in a circular space where a wide seat pad ran three-quarters of the way around, broken only by the door through which they had entered. Directly facing them was a section of what appeared to be transparent glass. And beyond that they could see the clustered buildings of the Landing.

A Ventur without a robe was seated on the pad watching the scene intently. He gave them only a casual gesture of greeting before the dock began to recede and the whole shore line whipped to the right as the ship turned. The voyage to Po'ult had begun.

13

Life Or Death Trade

Po'ult rose out of the sea abruptly—the toothed rock walls of the island's rim lifting vertically from the sea without any softening fringe of beach. And on the crest of those walls were no signs of buildings.

Having afforded its passengers a single good look at the island the ship submerged until even the conning tower was under water. The Terrans were led down close to the keel, to wedge themselves into a smaller craft with two of the Venturi. Vibration sang in the walls of that tiny boat but there was no other indication that they had left the parent vessel.

Kana tensed. The sensation of being confined far below the surface of the sea oppressed him. But their voyage did not last long and when the hatch was raised they were in an underground port, a large-scale copy of the subcellar landing place back on the continent. They saw but little of the Venturi city, being taken

161

along passages chiseled through the native rock to a
room near the top of the cliff, one side of which was
transparent. Their guide withdrew and Kana went over
to that window, craving the feeling of freedom it gave.

"Volcano crater," Hansu observed.

The center of the island was a cup, its walls terraced
and planted, a grove of trees extending into a miniature woodland in the depth of the hollow. But there
were no signs of buildings.

"But where—"

The Blademaster looked beyond the peaceful carpet of vegetation to the crater walls.

"We're in their city now," he explained. "They've
hollowed out the cliffs—"

In a moment Kana saw the evidences of that—the
regular openings in the rock which must equal such
windows as the one before which he now stood.

"What a scheme!" he marveled. "Even a bomber
would have a hard time putting this out of commission—
unless it dropped hot stuff—"

At the corner of the Blademaster's jaw a tiny muscle
pulled tight.

"When the law is broken once, it can be easily
fractured again."

"Use hot stuff?" Kana's horrified amazement was
genuine. He could accept the enmity of the Mechs,
even the struggle for power backed in some mysterious way by Central Control Agents, but the thought
of turning to nuclear weapons against—! Terra had
learned too bitter a lesson in the Big Blow-up and the
wars which followed. Those had occurred a thousand
years ago but they had scarred the memories of his
species for all time. He could not conceive of a Terran
using nukes—it was so unnatural that it made his head
reel.

"We've had evidence enough that this is not just a

Mech plot," Hansu pointed out relentlessly. "We may be conditioned against hot stuff because of our past history—but others aren't. And we daren't overlook any possibility—"

That was an axiom of the corps he should have remembered. Never overlook any possibility, be prepared for any change in prospects—in the balance of force against force.

"War Lord"—one of the frog people had come up silently behind them—"the Masters would speak with you."

No hospitality had been offered them before that meeting, Kana noted, disturbed, no gesture made which could be termed friendly. He fell a step behind the Blademaster and stood at attention as they entered a room where four Venturi, their robes laid aside, awaited them.

The soft fabric of their short tunics was a somber blue-purple and there were gems set in their belts and in the broad bracelets they wore encircling all four upper limbs. At some distance squatted a fifth, writing pen in one hand and a block of the mirror stuff on the floor before him.

A single seat pad was placed facing the court and Hansu took his seat there, Kana standing behind him.

"We have been informed of what you wish." The Ventur whose tunic boasted a symbol stitched upon its breast opened the meeting without ceremony. "You wish a place of refuge for your men until you can make contact with your superiors off-world. Why should we be interested in what happens to interlopers, introduced on Fronn through no fault of ours? And since you are now being hunted by the Llor and these new allies of theirs, it might mean that in giving you sanctuary we would bring upon us the wrath of those at Tharc."

"Does not a state of war already exist between you

and Tharc?" countered Hansu. "When we crossed the mountains we were met by a party of Llor driven off from an attack on the Landing. From them we rescued one of your men."

The frog-man's broad face displayed no emotion the Terrans could read.

"The Venturi do not war, they trade. And when it is not time to trade, when the world is disturbed, we withdraw until the mainland is sane again. So has it been in the past and that system has always worked to our advantage."

"But before did the Llor ever ally with those who could bring war through the air? Perhaps Po'ult cannot be captured from the sea—but what if you are attacked from above, Master of Many Ships?"

"*You* have no machine which can ride the wind, are these others then more powerful than you?"

"They are ones who have been trained in a different mode of making war. And it is against our custom for them to use that warfare upon such a world as Fronn. With the weapons they have they can make themselves master of this whole planet if they wish. Do you think that your withdrawal will avail you if that is their plan? One by one they shall search out your island strongholds and rain destruction upon you from the air. They may even bring to subdue you the burning death—which is a weapon forbidden to all living creatures—a weapon so terrible that its use once wrecked my own world and sent my race back to barbarism for centuries. For"—Hansu repeated the warning he had voiced to Kana earlier—"when the law is once broken, it is easily fractured again. These renegades have broken our law by coming to Fronn, and from that they may go on to worse things—"

"If you do not fight as do these others, then why or how could you be of service to us?"

"Just this—" Hansu held himself stiffly erect, braced as if facing an enemy charge. "The news of what has occurred here must be carried to our first rank Masters. Only they have the power to deal with these outlaws. And that message must be carried by one to whom they will listen. Give my men refuge and I, myself, will take the message off-world. And I promise you that when I am heard by our inner Council there shall be a reckoning and Fronn shall be cleansed. So that here off-world men shall be forbidden to land—as has happened on other planets—and you shall be left to manage your affairs as you wish. Do you not know that there are those who do not wish to see the trade of Fronn only Venturi trade? They would help the Llor to break you as they would a rotten stick for a night campfire—for the Llor are ignorant of the mysteries of your craft and those from off-world would speedily take it all into their own hands—to hold forever! You have never welcomed the alien traders and they would be free of your restrictions."

Was the Blademaster making an impression? Kana could not tell. And his hopes sank when the spokesman of the Masters answered:

"You say much which we must consider in council. Be thou becalmed in our waters this night—"

That last had the flavor of some formula of hospitality. And the Terrans discovered that it meant escort to a room overlooking the valley where two of the treasured smoke braziers filled the air with spicy scent. One of the Masters came in, followed by a lesser trader bearing a tray on which were set out three cups and a ewer. The Master poured out a small measure of the same liquid Kana had been given in the hidden room, and proffered the cups to the Combatants with his own hands. Again Kana sipped the icy stuff and felt it seep through him, bringing once more the heightened senses, the alertness of mind and body. The ceremonial drink was borne away and small tables set up on which were laid a series of dishes, none containing more than a mouthful or so of that particular viand.

"These foods have been exported off-world," the Master assured them. "They can be safely eaten by those of your species."

The Terrans ate, thankful for the change from rations, finding the subtle flavors intriguing. The Venturi were artists in food, striving for strange effects—substances were hot and cold at the same time, a sharp sour was followed by a bland sweet, the whole blending into a feeling of gastronomic content such as Kana, for one, had never before experienced.

"Your city is well concealed." Hansu gestured toward the bucolic scene in the crater valley.

"The plan was not intended to conceal," corrected the Master. "When our far-off ancestors first crawled from water to land they lived in caves within the cliffs of these sea islands. So, instead of building in the open, our race built within the land—for it is our nature to wish our living space to be enclosed and close to water. As our intelligence and civilization grew our cities became such as Po'ult. We are uncomfortable on the dry plains of the large continents—each of us must serve his apprenticeship there as a duty but he is joyful when he may return to his home island. Are you of a race which lives in the open as do the Llor?"

Hansu nodded, and began to describe Terra, her blue skies, green hills, and open, changeable seas.

"Tell me, since you appear to be one who thinks upon matters beyond his duties for the day, why do you sell your skill to war? You are not barbarian as are the Llor, who are a young race. You must come of an old people, perhaps older than we. Why have you not realized that what you do is a waste, a negation of growth and good?"

"We are born with a will to struggle, a desire to match our strength against that of others. Among our kind when that inner urge is stilled the tribe or nation which has lost it declines. We broke into outer space—and that was a struggle and goal which absorbed us for centuries—we were eager for the stars. But we discovered that space was not ours—that there we were deemed as young and barbaric as the Llor. There were many races and species before us and they had fashioned a code of law and order to control newcomers. Those who exercised that control judged us and ruled that we were, because of our temperaments, unfit for space except within the boundaries they set. Since it was in our nature to fight, we were to provide the mercenaries for other planets. We were geared to that service, a small piece fitted into *their* pattern. And so it is with us—the price we must pay for the stars since there is this guard upon the stellar lanes."

"To me that does not sound like an equal bargain," commented their host. "And when any bargain is uneven, there comes a day when it will be declared no bargain and he who has been defrauded will go elsewhere to trade. Does the time come when you of Terra will go elsewhere?"

"Perhaps. And what happens here on Fronn may decide that."

"May your trading be even, the profit good!"

"May your ships ever return filled from far voyaging." Hansu made the proper answer as the Master left them.

The Combatants were not summoned to attend the Masters again that day. Soon the storm closed in for a second prolonged buffeting and the window through which they watched the crater was obscured most of the time by foam and flying debris caught up by the gusts.

"D'you think we have a chance?" Kana ventured to interrupt the silence as Hansu stared into the wildness without.

"At least they're now giving us the attention due honored guests. When they fed us they acknowledged equality. And when you win one point you have advanced that far. But their logic is not ours. We cannot deduce what they are going to do by what we would do in their place. You, as an AL man, should know that. This *is* your first enlistment?"

"Yes, sir."

"Why did you try for AL rating?"

"I liked the basic course, sir. There was a Zacathan instructor—he made me think a lot. And the way his mind worked fascinated me. Through him I met other X-Tees. So I signed for specialization testing and I passed the prelim. It isn't too popular a course—too many extra hours. But—well, sir—it never really seemed like work to me. And visiting around in the X-Tee quarters was more interesting than taking town leave—at least I liked it better though we weren't encouraged to—"

"Make off-world friends, no. Just to learn the minimum enabling us to get around on other planets—*I* know!"

"Deke said something like that once, sir," mused Kana. "That Central Control had a mental picture of us and it was so well established that they didn't see the real Terrans at all—"

"Mills knew what he was talking about. We're breaking law and custom right now—daring to treat with these Venturi on our own. And it's about time we did more of this."

When Kana curled up on the pads for sleep he left

the Blademaster still brooding by the window. Outside
the night was a black whirlwind but here the roar was
the faintest of murmurs.

In the morning they were shown a bathing place
with a pool of sea water deep enough for swimming.
And afterward they dined again lavishly. Their visit with
the council did not come until mid-morning.

"We have considered this problem," the foremost
Master began when the Blademaster had taken his seat,
"and your argument has within it many points with which
we must agree. However, the future is always chance.
We cannot transport your men here, our economy is a
tight one, our space limited—we could not house such
a number of off-world beings for an indefinite period.
We cannot, in fact, use sea transport at all, except for
short intervals, until the peak storms of this season are
over. But then, neither can your enemy move against
you. Therefore you have about ten dytils in which to
study the situation and make your plans. At the end of
that time, if you can see a chance to get off-world with
your message, we agree to transport your men, not here
to Po'ult, but to a larger island south of here, farther
asea, on which we pasture our caravan guen during the
stormy season. We will undertake, moreover, to supply
your men with food and instructions in the art of netting such sea creatures as they may safely devour."

"And in return you ask of us?"

"And in return we ask your word that you will speak
with your Masters so that off-world men be forbidden
to land on Fronn to fight our battles. And that those
who may come be granted that right only after the
Venturi has had their application and know the purpose for which they wish to visit us. We do not wish
Fronn to become tributary to another world, or be
possessed by some trading combine of distant stars."

"To this I agree, not only as a bargain, but because

it is what I believe myself," Hansu retorted. "We return now to the Landing?"

"Within two light periods of this dytil there will be a second lull. Then you shall return, and with you one of our Those-who-talk-for-many to be a link with us across the distance. Fair winds and a good profit to you, Lord of Many Swords."

"And to you, Master of Ten Thousand Ships, a smooth sea."

The lull which gave opportunity for their return to the Landing came at last and was longer than the previous one. In fact, the calm continued so long after their arrival on the main continent that, had it not been for the advice of the Venturi communications expert, the Terrans might have made the mistake of trying to reach the space field. But his warning kept them close to the buildings and the predictions he made were fulfilled when a scream arose out of the dark, whistling above the thud of waves on the shore—the opening cry of a new storm.

"We have received no off-world signals from any starship." The Ventur sipped at a drink made from Terran ration pellets dissolved in water. "It is the belief of the Masters that none may planet here again. Why should they? If Tharc is now open to their use and the Llor encourage them to think that in the future they shall not have to deal with us—why then should they come here?"

"True enough." Hansu swallowed the warm broth.

"And if there is no chance of finding a ship here, you will make other plans?"

"We may have to go to Tharc."

The frog-man had no eyebrows to raise, but he did radiate polite incredulity. Only courtesy kept him from asking how that was to be done. But Hansu did not volunteer any explanation.

The storm did not last as long as the previous one and Kana knew that the series of such strong blows was now on the wane. It was noon on the following day when the Ventur announced that it was safe to go into the open. The Combatants were eager to get out, to draw the chill fresh salt air into their lungs and poke about in the curious rubbish the winds had piled against corners of the warehouse courts.

A shout from the farthest-ranging exploring party brought all those within earshot. Jammed at a crazy angle between outlying buildings, where none of the Horde had been stationed, was the mashed wreckage of a machine—looking as if some giant had caught it up and wrung it around as a man might a wet under-tunic.

"A crawler—that's a crawler!" the awed voice of its discoverer repeated. And, while no one disputed him, they could hardly believe the evidence of their own eyes.

A crawler—not as large as a land fortress certainly, but in its way as formidable a piece of mechanized war machinery—to be so mangled and tossed here as if it were constructed of straw.

The outer hatch was open, forced straight up by the impact, and now Kosti climbed up the battered metal shell to look in. When he pulled out of the hole his face was greenish beneath its tan and he swallowed convulsively.

"She—she had a full crew on board—" he reported. Thereafter no one was in any hurry to join him at his vantage point.

"How many?" Hansu appeared below and started to climb.

Unwillingly Kosti peered into the wrecked crawler for the second time. His lips moved as he counted.

"—four—five—six. Six, sir."

Hansu called down over his shoulder, "Larsen, Bogate, Vedic, lend a hand. We want them out."

Reluctantly the men he had summoned scaled the mound of the tipped crawler as the Blademaster lowered himself into the machine. Even when they had the grisly job complete and the six bodies were laid out in the nearest shelter Hansu did not seem satisfied.

Five were Mechs and the Blademaster carefully studied their service armlets. But the sixth, though he wore the uniform of a veteran Mechmaster, was alien. And Hansu stood staring down at his crumpled form for a long minute after he arose from searching the torn and stained clothing.

"Sarm," he said so low that if Kana had not been at his elbow he would not have caught the word at all. "Sarm!"

And his bald astonishment at that identification would have been the reaction of any Terran. Of all the Galactic races the Sarm from Sarmak would be the least likely to associate with the mercenaries they held in the deepest contempt as barbarians. They were not openly rude about it as were the Ageratans or the Dzaraneans, they merely ignored Combatants. Yet here was a Sarm, in a Mech uniform, perhaps in command of a Mech crawler—

"Sir—"

Hansu was shaken out of his trance by the urgent summons from Kosti now hanging half out of the plundered machine. "What—?"

"Cargo aboard her, sir. Looks like arms—"

The dead Sarmakan was left to himself as not only the Blademaster but every man within hearing hurried back to the side of the wreck. Larsen appeared in the hatch, handing through a box which Kosti lowered to the pavement. They clustered in a circle while Hansu squatted down to break the sealing with his sword-knife.

Inside, rolled in oiled fabric, was a series of bundles. And the Blademaster lost no time in freeing the first of its wrappings. As the last strip of stuff dropped away he held, plain to their recognition, a flamer of Galactic design.

"How many more boxes inside?" he asked Kosti in a flat voice.

"Three, sir."

Hansu arose. There was a bleak look on his face. But a grim determination overrode other emotion.

"Any way of telling where this thing was when the storm hit?" he asked Kosti. "Do these operate on route tapes the way a ship does?"

"I don't think so, sir. It has manual controls. But I can check—" He edged back into the crawler.

"Pretty far from Tharc, sir." Larsen broke the quiet. "And a scout wouldn't be hauling cargo—"

"Just so." But Hansu had already turned to the Ventur who witnessed the whole scene curiously from the doorway of the warehouse. "You're sure no spacer planeted near here?"

"None at the place we have used. Our mirrors of seeing would have told us—"

"And there is no other landing space within a day's travel? This crawler was carrying cargo. It would not have been carrying arms away from Tharc—not in the windy season. But it might have been trying to reach there from a ship which planeted elsewhere."

The Ventur's nod agreed to the logic in that. "This is a heavy and well-built machine. Those within it, if they did not know the full fury of our winds, might believe themselves safe in its belly. It is true that so they might try to travel to Tharc. But it is equally true that those in Tharc—where the Llor know well the strength of the winds and would warn them—would not venture forth. Let me signal the Masters. It may well be that a ship has made a landing elsewhere."

He vanished into the building. And a few moments later Kosti brought discouraging news from the machine.

"They were on manuals when they smashed up, sir. No tapes. But I don't think she was scouting. The heavy guns were all still under wraps—two of them in storage cradles. She might just have come off a ship and they were driving her in."

"Why not land at Tharc?" Hansu mused. He brought his balled fist down on the edge of the broken caterpillar tread by his shoulder. "I want every bit of her cargo, everything on the bodies of her crew, anything which may give us a clue, brought over to headquarters. And I want it done now!"

14

The Hidden Ship

Though they found indications to prove that the crawler had been part of the cargo of a ship and recently landed to proceed under its own power—perhaps to Tharc—there was no clue as to where that ship had planeted. And in the end it was again the Venturi who were able to supply the missing piece of the puzzle.

The trader's communication expert threaded his way through the group of veterans to Hansu. He wasted no time in getting to the point of the news he had received from his superiors.

"There is an off-world ship grounded six gormels to the south—"

Kana was attempting to translate "gormels" into good Terran miles and making heavy weather of it, when the Ventur continued:

"It is set among the rocks on the coast so it is safe from the winds."

"How large a ship?" Hansu shot back.

The Ventur gave the odd movement of his upper pair of arms which was his species' equivalent of a shrug. "We are not trained in recognizing the capacity of your ships, Lord. And if it had not been that near there we have a small post—" He hesitated before hurrying on, and Kana suspected that that post he mentioned was more a spy than a trader's station. "But this ship is smaller than that which used to planet near here, and it landed secretly during the first storm lull—"

"Fifty miles—" Hansu proved quicker at translation. "The ground between us?"

Again the Ventur shrugged. "Most is waste land. And there will be more heavy blows."

"But a small party could cross overland?" persisted the Blademaster. "Or would your people provide transportation by sea?"

The answer to the last question came first in a vigorous negative. Some trick of the currents offshore along that section of coast forbade landing except in the dead serenity of the calm season. As to crossing overland, the Ventur had no opinion, though he was courteous enough not to speak his truthful estimate of the state of mind of creatures attempting that feat now.

However he agreed to draw up a schedule of the storms and lulls which could be expected during the next three or four days. And Hansu had a second message relayed to the Masters at Po'ult.

The reply came that in the next lull the transports would put in, take on board the majority of the Horde, and leave a small party to make their way to the hidden space ship. It was a desperate plan, but not as desperate as the one they had faced earlier, the necessity for going to Tharc.

The Ventur liaison officer reported for a last check, comparing his set of maps with Hansu's rudely drawn sketch of the coastline and pointing out where the ship must now be.

"The Masters send their wishes for your success," he concluded. "Do you go tonight?"

"Not until the Horde has sailed," Hansu replied absently. His gaze roved over the men assembled in the room. Not all the Combatants could crowd in to hear this final decision—there were the sick and wounded. But who out of that company were going on the venture south? Kana knew that that was at the fore of every mind there.

He did his own secret choosing. Kosti, the small, lean man, had to go. Alone of the Horde he had knowledge of mechanics—had the know-how to take a ship—if they were lucky enough to steal it—into space. And Hansu—Kana was certain that the Blademaster intended being one of the party. But how many—and who?

In the end it depended upon a grisly expedient. The uniforms worn by the Mechs who had manned the crawler were salvaged and cleaned and the fit of one of the tunics selected the man who would wear it. When one settled snugly across Kana's shoulders he knew he was in. And whether to be pleased or alarmed over that fact he had not yet quite decided before the Venturi vessels came in, to ride out a short storm and on the following day depart with the remainder of the Combatants, leaving Hansu and five men on the wharf. As the last conning tower vanished in the murk, the Blademaster reached for the reins of a waiting gu.

"We ought to make our first storm shelter before the next blow. Let's get going!"

The round dome at the improvised space field near the Landing came into view before the onset of the wind. But the protection offered by that one small building had none of the security they had known

behind the massive walls of the warehouses. Together
with their guen, the six Combatants crouched on the
floor, deafened by the howl of the wind, wondering
from one moment to the next whether that dome could
continue to stand under the frightful pressure. The
guen, flattening their bony carcasses as close to the
earth as they could, kept up a monotonous whimpering cry which rasped the nerves of the Terrans.

After what must have been hours—but seemed to
the dazed men days—later, they realized that the wind
was dropping.

"Up with you!" Hansu was on his feet, applying his
bat stick to the rump of his gu while the animal showed
its fangs in a snarl of rage.

Within five minutes they were on the road, urging
their mounts to that stiff-legged trot which left Terran
bodies aching and bruised, but which did cover the
ground at a good rate. They had been lucky—fabulously
lucky so far. But when the dark clouds gathering suggested that they must take cover again there was no
building to give them shelter.

Their only hope was a grove of trees, already showing splintered stumps where the wind had mangled
them. Into this the Blademaster headed, producing the
coils of tough cording which the Venturi had provided
against just such an emergency. Each man lashed first
his mount and then himself to the sturdiest trees. Since
the wind blew straight from the west, they had a thin
margin of safety against the eastern side of the trunks
and there they dug into the mold, protecting their
heads with their crossed arms, squeezing into the
ground.

If their stay in the small dome had seemed an
ordeal, this was indescribable. One fought to breathe,
the battle lasting from one suck of air to the next. Kana
lost all track of time, almost all knowledge of his own

identity in that dazed, half-conscious struggle for air.
Then hands pulled at him and he rolled limply over
on his back. A palm smacked against his cheek, rock-
ing his head on the ground.

"Come on—get up!" he was urged.

Stiffly he pulled his aching body into sitting position.
Three men stood about him, and one of them held his
bleeding head in his hands. Six Terrans had entered that
grove and four rode out, leading an extra gu. Of the
other two, they never saw one again, and the other they
had had to leave as they found him, buried except for
an outflung hand, under the tree he had chosen—the
tree which had not survived *this* storm.

Would any of them last to the end of this journey,
Kana speculated, as he clung to his mount by will
power alone? Could they even keep on riding at the
pace Hansu set?

But the rocky defiles of the coastline were cut by
a river before the time to take shelter arrived once
more. And in the cup of fertile land in the delta they
chanced upon a Llor village. Trading on the custom
of Fronn they knocked on the nearest door and asked
for protection of the guesting room.

Within, stretched on thin pads, the Combatants
dropped into a sodden slumber almost before they
gulped down their rations. And when they roused the
blow was over and the native household had come to
life. Hansu returned from an interview with their Llor
host and some of the shadow was gone from his eyes.

"That was the last of the big blows—anything after
this won't be any harder to face than something we
could weather on Terra. And we're heading right!
There's been two crawlers through here—bound for
Tharc."

"What"—Larsen was gingerly fitting his Mech helmet over his bandaged head—"do they think we're

doing here?" He pointed to the inner section of the house. "Any questions, sir?"

"They believe that we're from the ship. I told them that we were caught in a storm and our crawler wrecked—that we're trying to get back. To them all Terrans look alike, so they've accepted that. We only have to worry when we meet Mechs—if we do."

They were across the farm land in an hour, making their way around and through the debris of the storms. Before them now lay a stretch of twisted rocks, scoured clean by the wind, over which they traveled guided only by the compass in Hansu's hand (which might not be accurate at all) and the map the Venturi had given them. Gashed chasms which could not be descended led to detours and they camped that night in a crevice of bare rock while the wind screamed in their ears, much as it had in the badlands beyond the mountains. Only the threat of the Cos was missing.

And twice during the gray day following they were forced to take shelter to escape the buffeting of blasts which could have swept them to destruction among the towers of stone. A lengthy detour brought them on an arduous climb down to the sea strand where they beat a path through piles of slimy weeds thrust up in bales by the waves.

Hansu was almost thrown from his seat as the gu he was bestriding reared and screamed a shrill whistling defiance, lashing out with its clawed front feet at a shape floundering sluggishly in the shallows. Jaws, seemingly large enough to engulf both beast and rider, gaped. Kana, with one instinctive movement, raised the rifle he carried across his thighs and fired into that open gullet.

The creature's head snapped up and back as if it were turning over in a somersault, as the water boiled about its finned limbs. A horrible mixture of crocodile, snake, and whale was all the recruit could think of as Hansu sent another shot into the writhing monster.

Its struggles took it away from the shore, deeper into the sea, and the Terrans hurriedly backed up the slit of beach, putting as much space between them as possible, the nervous guen threatening to bolt at any moment.

It was Larsen who found the way through between two giant rocks which brought them away from that cove and out of sight of the struggling water dweller. Before them now was a wide space of open sand, matted with torn weed and other wreckage of the waves, including a battered metallic object which bore some resemblance to one of the small Venturi craft. A draggle of carrion birds hung about that and the Terrans did not halt to examine it. They fitted their pace to their Commander's, heading due south across the first good riding country they had found since the river delta.

The next gust of storm caught them in a narrow gorge. Sea water driven by the wind curled about the feet of the guen but Hansu kept doggedly to the trail and his persistence was rewarded with the discovery of a fragment of crushed stone marking the passing of a crawler. Heartened by this, he yielded and allowed them to hole up against the wind.

A steel gray sky had arched over them for most of the day and the coming of night only meant a general darkening of the gloom. But this time the dark served them better than light. It was almost as if the enemy had set a beacon to guide them. And that was no blue Llor flame which beckoned them, but the strong yellow of a Terran camp light.

Leaving the guen in Larsen's charge, Kosti, Kana and the Blademaster scouted ahead, dropping at intervals to crawl, alert for the slightest sign that those in the makeshift camp had posted sentries. At length the three lay on the rim of a small gorge staring at a splotch of light in which the tail fins of a small ship could be easily distinguished. No figures moved in the gleam and there was no sign of life there. It was Hansu who was ready with an order.

"Stay here!" Before they could object he had slithered away in the dark.

They shivered in the bite of the night wind, cringing from the salt-laden air. And below the sigh of that they could hear quite clearly the distant boom of surf. But nothing moved about the ship.

It seemed a very long time before Hansu rejoined them. And when he did it was only to order them back to where they had left Larsen and their mounts. There, as they huddled behind some rocks, he outlined his discoveries.

"—small ship—general outlines of a Patrol cruiser," he told them. "There're guards. Can't tell much more in the dark. We'll have to wait until daybreak and light before we make any plans."

Kana dozed off for broken snatches and he guessed that the others did too. Uncomfortable as they were, long service in the field had given them the power of taking sleep where and when they could find it. And dawn brought a lighter sky than they had seen since the beginning of the big blows.

The guen were secured by their head ropes in a side gully, though Hansu gave orders that they were not to be fastened tightly. And he did not need to advance his reasons. This was one venture from which the Terrans would not return. Either they would blast off in the ship—or they would no longer care about guen or anything else on Fronn.

They took the same way up the cliffs, working along

the broken rim to look down on the hidden camp. In the light of day the beams of the lamp had paled and the ship was distinguishable from the black and white stone of the walls. It had been set down with the skill of an expert pilot in the center of a small, almost flat-floored canyon. And as Hansu said, it looked like a fast cruiser such as were built for the use of the Galactic Patrol.

In fact the Combatants were not greatly surprised when the daylight revealed Patrol insignia etched on its space-scoured side. Needle slim, it would accommodate a crew of not more than a dozen. And if it had brought in a cargo of crawlers, the living quarters must have been even more reduced.

"That's what we want, all right." Larsen breathed hardly above a whisper. "Only, how do we take her?"

Under a slight overhang of the canyon wall across from them was the plasta-cloth bubble of a temporary camp. And now a man crawled out of its door vent to stand stretching at his ease. His uniform was that of a Mech, and, as far as they could see, he was a fellow Terran. But a moment later he was joined by another, who, though he wore the blue-gray of a Legion man, was physically an alien. Those too long, too thin legs, the curiously limber arms, as if the limbs possessed an extra joint—To Kana's trained eyes they betrayed his non-Sol origin at once, although the recruit could not, without a closer examination, have said which star he did claim as his native sun.

The Mech made way respectfully for the newcomer, who tripped forward into the open and stood gazing down the narrow mouth of the canyon as if waiting for something important to appear there. And he was not to be disappointed for the shrill squeal of a gu carried clearly to the ears of both the men in the canyon and the hidden Swordsmen on the cliff.

A mounted party shuffled into view. The Llor sagged as they rode and their guen paced very slowly, their bony heads drooping to knee level with the lag of overriding. Yet Kana judged none of the Fronnian natives were soldiers—they had more the appearance of backlands guen hunters the Terrans had encountered after their forced march over the mountains. Their leader had a rifle slung over his shoulder—the rest were armed only with swords, lances, and the thick coils of rope about their middles which served frontier hunters for both a weapon and a snare.

The Llor chief swung off his mount and immediately dropped cross-legged to the ground, while the alien in the Mech uniform sat on a small stool hurriedly brought from the bubble tent by a second Mech and placed to front the native. As the rest of the Llor slipped out of their saddles, one or two to lie full length on the ground, three more Terrans appeared, grouping themselves some distance away. It was plain that a conference was about to begin.

It was a discussion which grew heated at times. Once the Llor leader went so far as to get to his feet and jerk at the reins of his gu so that the animal ambled unhappily into a position in which it could be mounted. Yet a quick gesture and word from the alien apparently soothed the native commander and he seated himself once more.

To be a spectator but not an auditor at that meeting was wearing on the Blademaster. He shifted his position among the concealing rocks as if his first choice of hiding places had inadvertently harbored a nest of Vol fire ants. But unless he could develop the art of complete invisibility, he was not going to be able to hear that group below.

At length the meeting came to an end. The Llor chieftain gave some order to the lounging members of his escort. Four of them got up, without any display of alacrity, and as they trudged across the space dividing them from the Mech contingent, their reluctance could be read in every line of their woolly bodies. While their leader and the alien stood apart waiting, they slouched to the vent door of the bubble tent. The Mechs went inside and returned in a moment or two with large narrow boxes, one carried by each pair of men.

Hansu had gone so far as to rise to his knees and Kana wondered if he dared give a warning tug to the Blademaster's coat. But those below seemed so intent upon what they were doing that there was little chance of their looking aloft at that moment.

Two boxes had been passed on to the Llor who received them in charge with signs of open distaste, but did carry them to the foot of the ramp leading to the hatch of the ship. A second pair of boxes were man-handled out of the bubble, also to be transported. Kana tried to imagine what lay within them. Weapons of some sort? But why put weapons into the ship? It would be far more logical if those boxes had been drawn from the cargo hold of the spacer.

When six boxes were grouped about the ramp the alien and two of the Mechs worked on the covering of one.

"That—!" Hansu's face was oddly pale beneath its dark pigment. He was breathing in harsh, shallow gasps, as if he had been pounding up the slope. His eyes, glints of steel, deadly, measuring, were on the group. Alone of the Swordsmen he must have guessed at once the contents of those coffers.

Coffers—Kana's own skin crawled as he realized belatedly that the word was rightly "coffin." For the Mechs were taking out of the box what could only be the body of a dead man—a man who wore the white and black of the Patrol.

"But why—?" His muttered protest brought no answer except gasps from his two companions and an uninformative grunt from Hansu.

The boxes, now emptied, each of the same contents, were carried off by the Llor and piled against the wall of the canyon a good distance away from the ship. The alien was in command, directing the arrangement of the bodies in an uneven line.

Hansu hissed—there was no other way to name the sound he made with breath expelled between his teeth. To Kana the actions below did not make sense, but to the Blademaster the design must be growing clearer every moment.

Now the alien stood back, motioning the Mechs away, though the Llor still clustered about the ship as if examining the dead who had been so carefully placed there.

"He's making a record-pak!" The words came from Larsen and Kana saw that he was right. The alien, a sight scriber in his hands, was making a pictorial record of the scene—the ship—the tumbled bodies—the Llor moving among them. A record of what—to be shown to whom?

"A frame—a neat frame—" That was Hansu. "So that's their little game!"

The alien took several more shots and then nodded to the Llor chieftain who signaled his men. They scattered away from the ship with a speed which suggested that they were only too glad to be done with the odd duty their leader had demanded of them. And what followed was almost as mystifying to the spying Swordsmen.

Two of the Mechs struck the bubble tent, and the material, along with various bundles, was carried off. Shortly thereafter a crawler appeared from behind an outcrop but it did not approach the ship, only halted until the remaining Mechs and the alien hurried over and climbed through its hatch. Then it made off up the canyon eastward. The Llor waited as if to give the off-world men a good start and then mounted. But they did not follow the grinding passage of the crawler—instead they rode off down a side way.

The ship stood as they had left it, the bodies still lying at the ramp. And Hansu hardly waited until the last Llor was out of sight before he clambered down the side of the cliff, Kana and the others hurrying to follow him.

But the Blademaster easily outdistanced them and when they caught up he had already knelt to examine the nearest body. His face was bleak.

"This man has been shot," he said slowly, "with an Arch rifle."

15

If But One Of
Us Live—

"But were they Patrolmen?" Larsen demanded.

It was hard to believe—in spite of the evidence and the identification taken from the bodies—that such a massacre had occurred. The prestige of the Patrol was too well established.

There was no possible doubt that the men had been shot, and that those shots had not come from the lighter air rifles of the Llor, the blasters of the Mechs or the flamers of the Galactic Agents, but from those specialized weapons carried, or supposedly carried, by the Swordsmen of Terra alone.

"If they weren't, they'll serve as well as the real thing in those pictures," Kosti returned bitterly. "If that Agent was taking shots of this it wasn't just for amusement. Can't you see the force of those pictures in certain quarters—scene of Patrolmen ambushed by rebel Archs—"

Larsen kicked at a stone. "I still don't get it," he admitted. "Why stage all this?"

"Alibi for going after us." Kana broke the silence for the first time. "Isn't that it, sir? With a good story and those pictures the Agent could have us outlawed and we couldn't get a hearing anywhere—not even at Prime."

He wanted Hansu to protest that, to say that he was allowing an over-vivid imagination free rein. But instead the Blademaster nodded.

"That makes more sense than about fifty other explanations." The tall dark man got to his feet, his eyes fixed speculatively on the starship. "Yes, they've set the stage here for something nasty. And it would probably have worked if we hadn't come in time—"

"So they're trying to put us on the spot." Kosti was inclined to be belligerent. "Well, what can we do?"

"Spoil their plan!" There was decision in the Blademaster's answer. "Kosti, get on board and see whether this cruiser can be lifted out of here—"

The Swordsman hurried up the ramp and Hansu turned to the other two.

"Burial party—" He indicated the bodies.

They performed that distasteful task as they had for their comrades so many times in the last hard weeks, knowing that when their fire cartridges had done their work there would be no identifiable traces left. They were engaged in sorting the personal possessions they had taken from the dead for purposes of future identification, when Kosti appeared in the hatch of the spacer over their heads.

"First luck we've had, sir. She's ready and willing to lift!"

Hansu only nodded. It was as if, having made up

his mind to a certain course of action, he was now perfectly sure that fate would allow them to follow it to the proper end. Stowing away the Patrolmen's effects in a ration bag, he led the way up the ramp into the interior of the small ship.

The only starships Kana had known before were the ferry transports of the Combat Command. And narrow and cramped as those had seemed, this cruiser was even smaller and more confined. The ladder stair, curling in a breakneck fashion from level to level, looked too narrow to give any climber safe footing. But they went up it—beads on a string—with Kosti already disappearing through the first-level flooring and the Blademaster hard on his heels.

Smells assaulted their noses, oil, the taint of old air, or close living— They made their way up to the control cabin. Hansu pointed to the pilot's webbing before the controls.

"Can you take her up, Kosti?"

The Swordsman showed his teeth in a white grin. "It's a matter of have to, isn't it, sir?"

He buckled himself into position while Kana and Larsen explored the acceleration pads and Hansu moved toward the astrogator's position.

"Give you five minutes, ship time, to take a looksee around if you want, sir," Kosti suggested, perhaps because he himself desired a few moments' study of that puzzling board before he blasted them free of the doubtful safety of Fronn.

They made a quick inspection of the tiny personal quarters. The cubbys were in a state of wild disorder with clothing and supplies strewn about as if by looters. Kana picked up a tri-dee portrait someone had stepped upon. The oddly slanting eyes and triangular mouth of a Lydian woman could still be seen.

"Nice artistic job." Hansu surveyed the litter with

a professional eye. "Exhibit B or C—looting of quarters—done by the wicked Archs—"

"Do you suppose this was a real Patrol ship? That they actually killed Patrolmen so they could smear us with the job, sir?" Larsen demanded.

"Could be. Though it seems a mighty heavy argument to use against an outfit as small as Yorke's. We must be important—" Frowning, he turned back to the control cabin.

"Do you have a route tape for Terra in the file?" he asked of Kosti.

"Going to Prime, sir? I thought we were to make Secundus—" the new pilot protested.

"This may be a real Patrol cruiser. If they sacrificed that to get us I want to know why, and I want to start asking questions right at the top!"

"Real Patrol cruiser!" That sank in, and Kosti swung around to tap three keys in a case at his far left. There was an answering click and a small disc dropped into his cupped hand.

"Yes, sir, here're the co-ordinates for Terra."

He freed another disc from the apparatus before him and inserted the new one. "Strap down," he ordered.

Hansu stowed away in the second web while Kana and Larsen buckled down on the acceleration mats. A red light glowed on the board before Kosti as his fingers played over levers and keys.

"Let's hope we go up—and not off—" was his last observation as he pressed the crucial control.

A giant hand smashed down on Kana's chest, squeezing out air. Waves of red pain clotted into blackness. He had just time to know, before he lost consciousness, that they were lifting off-world—and not exploding.

Kosti was no experienced pilot and the thrust he had used to tear them loose from Fronn was greater than it need have been. Kana, coming back to life, found his face sticky with blood as he pulled groggily at his straps.

"The sleeper wakes!" Kosti looked back over his shoulder at the recruit. "Thought you had decided to make the trip in cold sleep, fella. Not necessary, we have plenty of room."

The ship was on Ro-pilot, to be guided through the warp by the tape Kosti had set in. They had nothing to do but eat and sleep, and live in the discomfort of return-to-Terra conditioning which would enable them to disembark on their own world without further adjustment.

"How long will we be in space?" Larsen asked.

All three looked to Kosti for an answer but he only shrugged. "I'd say maybe fourteen-fifteen days. These babies sure eat it up in warp. Patrol cruisers are built for speed."

Fifteen days. Kana, stretched in one of the inner cabin hammocks, had time to think without the pressure of immediate action or decision hanging over him. This mess was a nasty one—sinister. For some unknown reason that alien in a Mech uniform had set a scene, a scene which only their luck had spoiled. He was sure that the ship and its dead crew had been deliberately left to be discovered dramatically—for a purpose. Patrolmen shot with Arch rifles—on a planet where an Arch Horde was being hunted down. But why go to all this trouble? Why try to discredit as well as wipe out a Terran force, when the latter move was so easy and Combat might be led to dismiss it all as fortunes of war?

Such an elaborate frame meant that not only the renegade Mechs but the Agents wearing their uniforms had something to fear from Yorke's men. The story of the murder of Yorke and his officers? Hardly.

They had no real proof of that—not even a witness's account which would be accepted at a formal hearing. Why—why—such a deliberate and elaborate plan to blacken them?

Could it be possible—his hand went half-consciously to the hilt of his sword-knife—could it be that the age-old stalemate between Terra and C.C. was to be broken at last? That C.C. was working feverishly to not only whittle down the Terran forces by attrition, but also to discredit them among the stars as renegades and murderers? Perhaps this would be their chance for an open fight—to stand against that condition C.C. had imposed—to prove that Terrans had as much right to the star lanes in freedom as any other race or species! It was a hope, only a thin one, but in that hour Kana sensed that it was there and he swore to himself that the next time he went into space it would not be wearing that green-gray coat which had been forced upon him.

The ship came out of warp, but they were still two days from Prime port by Kosti's admittedly ignorant calculations when it happened. A faint "beep" drew the attention of Kana and Larsen to the screen above the control panel. The Blademaster and Kosti were asleep and there was no one to explain the meaning of the pin point of light moving across the dark surface. Kana went to rouse Kosti.

"We might just have company—seeing as how we are out of warp." The pilot pro-tem rubbed sleep from his eyes. But one look at the screen brought him fully awake.

"Get Hansu—" he ordered tersely.

When Kana returned with the Blademaster the plaintive "beep" of the signal had strengthened into a steady drone.

"You can establish contact?" Hansu asked.

"If you want to. But that's no between-planets trader

out there. We're on a cruiser course. Only another
Patrol ship would be likely to cross us."

On a planet, armed, they would have known what
to do when faced with a potential enemy. But in space,
they might even now be needlessly alarmed over a
routine happening.

"Shall I accept contact?" Kosti pressed.

The Blademaster ran his thumb along his lower lip,
staring at the light on the screen as if he would have
out of it "name, rank, and term of enlistment."

"Can that screen"—he jerked his thumb toward the
vision plate—"be used for receiving only, or do we
automatically broadcast when we switch it on?"

"It can be one way. But that would make them suspicious."

"Let them think what they want. We need a little
time and maybe some fast answers before they see our
faces. Cut out the tele-cast before you make contact."

Kosti adjusted some knobs. A bright wash of color
rippled across the screen and then they saw the narrow, high-cheek-boned face of a humanoid from
Rassam. The skull-tight cap of a Patrol officer covered
his hairless head and he wore the star-and-comet of
an upper-rank commander.

"What ship?" he demanded with the unconscious
arrogance of a Central Control official. He could not
see them, but he might almost have sensed he was
addressing Terrans. Kana bristled, noting by the set of
Hansu's jaw that he was not alone in that reaction.

"Give me the speaker." Hansu took the mike from
Kosti.

"This is a Patrol cruiser, name and registry
unknown." He spoke slowly, enunciating each word
flatly in basic trade speech, trying to keep his native
accent undistinguishable. "It was found by us deserted
and we are returning it to the proper authorities."

The Patrol Commander did not give them the lie openly, but his disbelief was plain to read on his face.

"You are not headed for a Patrol base," he pointed out crisply. "What is your destination?"

"As if he didn't know—or suspect!" whispered Kosti.

"We are reporting to our superior officers," Hansu continued, "according to law—"

That narrow face appeared to lengthen in a sinister fashion. "Terrans!" His lips shaped the word as if it were an incredibly filthy oath. "You will prepare to receive a boarding party—" His face vanished from the screen.

"Well," Kosti observed bleakly, "that's that. If we try to get away they'll burn us down with their big stuff."

"Come on!" Hansu was halfway through the door. And, revived by his confidence, the rest trailed him. Out of the artificial gravity of the living quarter they pulled themselves into the midsection of the ship where the Blademaster unfastened a hatch. Beyond was an escape bay complete with two boats. But they were so small—Kana eyed them doubtfully, battling his dislike for being confined in a limited space.

Hansu paused half inside the nearest. "Kosti, you take the other. That will give us a double chance of getting our report through. If but one of us lives he has to reach Prime! Failure to get through may—in a way—mean the end for Terra. This thing is bigger than all of us. Larsen, you team with Kosti. Set your tape for Terra—when you land make for Prime—if you have to beg, borrow, or steal transportation. Ask for Matthias—get to him if you have to kill to do it! Understand?"

Neither of the veterans displayed surprise at the drastic orders. Hansu lowered his body into the lifeboat and Kana climbed reluctantly after him. It required both of them to close the vent and seal it.

Then Hansu flung himself into the cushioned hollow of the pilot's section and Kana took the other padded couch.

The Blademaster set a pointer on a small dial before him, checking it three times before he cut in the power which blasted them free from the cruiser. The force of that blast was almost as hard to take as the acceleration which had torn them out of Fronn's gravity. Kana's ribs, still sore from that ordeal, were squeezed enough to bring a choked cry out of him. When he was able to turn his head once more he saw that Hansu lay at ease, his cupped hands supporting his chin, his eyes fixed on the dial, though his thoughts might have been elsewhere.

"Are we free—? Did—did we get away, sir?" Kana asked dazedly.

"We're still alive, aren't we?" Hansu's ironical humor quirked set lips. "If they had sighted our getaway we'd be cinders by now. Let's hope that they will continue to concentrate on the cruiser for a few seconds more—"

"What made them so quick on the trigger, sir? The Patrol usually doesn't flare up that way—or do they? And that officer said 'Terrans' as if we were Lombros muck worms—"

"It shouldn't surprise you, Karr, to discover that some of the more 'superior' races who make up the C.C. Councils at the present moment are inclined to rate us at just about that level—in private, naturally. One doesn't boast of caste openly—that's too close to shape and race prejudice. But I've seen an Ageratan leave an eating booth before he had finished his meal because a Terran was seated as his neighbor. It's illegal, unethical, violates all those pretty slogans and refined sentiments drilled into them from the cradle or the egg—but it persists."

"But the Zacathans aren't like that—and Rey and Mic were friendly with that Lupan on Secundus—"

"Certainly. I can cite you a thousand different shapes and races who accept Terrans as equals as easily as we accept them in return. But note two things, Karr, and they are important. The systems where we are persona non grata are dominated by humanoid races and they are systems which have had space travel for a very long time, who have pioneered in the Galaxy. Embedded deep in them is an emotion they refuse to admit—fear.

"Back on Terra in the ancient days before the nuclear wars we were divided into separate races, the difference in part depending on the color of skin, shape of features, and so forth. And in turn those races were subdivided into nations which arose to power, held in control large portions of the planet, sometimes for centuries. But as the years passed each in turn lost that power, the reins slipped from their hands. Why?

"Because the tough, sturdy fighters who had built those empires died, and their sons, or their sons' sons' sons were another breed. For a while, even after the fighting quality died out, an empire would still exist— as might a well-built piece of machinery set in motion. Then parts began to wear, or oiling was needed, and there was no one who remembered, or cared, or had the necessary will and strength to pull it together and make repairs. So another, younger and tougher nation took over—perhaps after a war. History progressed by a series of such empires—the old one yielding to the new.

"Now the races of the Galaxy with whom we have established the closest ties are, so far, not of our species. We like the Zacathans who are of reptile origin, we enjoy the Trystians, whose far-off ancestors were birds. The Yabanu—they're evolved felines. And most of these are also newcomers on the Galactic scene.

But—and this is important—they have different aims, backgrounds, desires, tastes. Why should a Zacathan fret over the passing of time, hurry to get something done the way we must do? His life span is close to a thousand years, he can afford to sit around and think things out. We feel that we can't. But we're not a threat to him or his way of life."

"But, sir, do you think we are to the others—the humanoids of Agerat and Rassam? Their civilizations are old but basically they are similar to ours—"

"And are showing signs of decay. Yes, we're a threat to them because of our young pushing energy, our will to struggle, all the things they openly deplore in us. For, old as Terra seems to us, she is very young in the Galaxy. So they've met us with a devious design. It is their purpose to wall us off—not openly and so provide us with a legitimate grievance which we may take before the Grand Council—but legally and finally. They struggle to dissipate our strength in needless warfare which in no way threatens their control, sapping our manpower and so rendering helpless a race which might just challenge them in the future. And because we have fought and dreamed of the stars we have been forced to accept their condition—for a time."

"A time, sir?" burst out Kana passionately. "For three hundred years we've played their game—"

"What is three hundred years on the Galactic chessboard?" Hansu returned calmly. "Yes, for three hundred years we have taken their orders. Only now they must be beginning to realize that their plan is not working. I'm not sure that their motives had been plain even to them. They have played omnipotence so long that they have come to believe in their godhead—that they can make no wrong moves. For they have always operated against us under cover—until now.

"From the first we have had friends, and we are

gaining more. And those worlds would ask questions if Terra were summarily condemned and restricted to its own system. Perhaps their own over-civilized minds shrink from such a practical solution, or have in the past. But where they could, they have cut us off. Terrans are not accepted in the Patrol—that is the service for 'superior' races. Traders do not allow us to join their companies. Even the war we play at is carefully denatured—though we still die— The most modern Mech equipment is years behind weapons the inhabitants of—say Garmir—already consider obsolete."

"But, sir, why this move with the cruiser?"

"Either some hot heads on the Council are going to push through ideas of their own, or they have begun to wake up to the fact that we Terrans are not exactly what we seem." Hansu turned his head and gave Kana a measuring glance which was sharp enough to reach into his mind.

"Why do you suppose that we have X-Tee training— that we make an AL man a necessary member of every Horde and Legion lifting off-world?"

"Why—you need liaison officers on other worlds, sir."

"That is the correct official explanation—and one which no Control Agent can successfully counter. But any Terran with the proper temperament for X-Tee is screened and classified from the moment of his first response to the tests. He is given, unobtrusively, all the instruction we can cram into him. He is urged to meet X-Tees on a friendly basis—under cover. And when he enlists he is given every opportunity by his commanding officers to widen his knowledge of other planets."

"So that was why you wanted me to contact Venturi, sir?"

"Yes. And that is why you went to Po'ult. We have long known that we must have all the AL men we can get. And the wider their acquaintance with other life forms the better for us. If we must challenge C.C. in the open, we cannot stand alone. And the more races friendly to us, or at least with a favorable knowledge of us, the better. Incidentally we may be preparing ourselves for another form of service entirely. What if Terra in the future was to provide not fighting men but exploring teams?"

"Exploring teams?"

"Groups of trained explorers to pioneer on newly discovered planets, to prepare for colonization those worlds where there may be no intelligent native life. Groups, the members of which are selected for their individual talents, going not as Patrol nor traders, not as police or merchants, but only to discover what lies in orbit around the next sun. Groups including not only our own kind, but combining in a working unit half a dozen different species of X-Tees—telepaths, techneers, some not even vaguely humanoid."

"Do you think that can be done, sir?" demanded Kana, finding in the idea an answer to his own half-formed dream.

"Why not? And the time may not be too far off. Let us reach Matthias with our report on Fronn and he'll have a concrete argument to use in Combat circles against C.C. Suppose that all the Hordes and Legions now scattered up and down the Galaxy received orders to rebel. Such a situation would upset C.C. and bring an end to their carefully supervised peace. It would be cheaper to let us go our way than to tackle rebellions and uprisings on some hundreds of planets at once."

"I've heard a lot of rumors, sir, but nothing about revolt—"

"I should hope not!" countered the Blademaster. "Most of Combat are conservative. And we of Terra have lived a specialized life for generations. Combatants haven't much interest beyond the affairs of their own Horde or Legion. At Prime they try to locate the records of those with promise, to steer the men into enlistments where they can serve the cause best. But this mess on Fronn is going to bring the latent danger of our position home—to even the most hidebound of the Big Brass. Once they see that Terran can be turned against Terran with the approval of Central Control, that Mech can be used to hunt down Arch—they will listen to what we have to say." Hansu balled his fist and thumped it on the edge of his pad. "Time—just give us time enough! We must reach Matthias and he'll touch off the powder!"

16

Road To Prime

But for the two inside the escape craft time moved leadenly. They could only sleep, cramped in the single position allowed them, swallow ration tablets, and talk. And talk Hansu did, spinning in an endless stream tales of far-off worlds on some of which their kind dared not venture, save in the protection of pressure suits, of weird native rites, and savage battles against stacked odds.

Kana forced himself to concentrate on every word, as if he were required to pass an examination on these lectures, for by doing so, he could forget the present, sealed in a minute ship which might or might not make a safe landing on his home world. And he also knew that his companion was now sharing freely with him the lore he himself had spent years in gathering. He was being crammed by a master in X-Tee, a man who was explaining the central passion of his own existence.

"—so they had a sacrifice on the night of the double moon and we hid out in the hills to watch. It wasn't at all what we had been led to expect—"

A sharp "ping" interrupted Hansu as a tiny bulb glowed red among the controls. They had entered atmosphere!

Kana tried to relax. The worst nightmare of all, that they would miss their home world and go traveling on forever into empty space, was behind them. There was still nothing to do—nothing they *could* do. Escape craft were entirely robot controlled—often those who rode in them were too injured or shocked to pilot any course. The tiny ships were designed to make the best landing possible for the passengers and they were to be trusted.

Where would they land? Kana stared blankly at the curve of metal roofing above him. A bad landing—say in the sea— But they did not have long to wait, that was a mercy.

"I hope we don't land too far from Prime, sir." He forced himself to deliver that in as even a voice as possible.

"We'd better not!"

When they did come in Kana discovered himself hanging head down in the straps and, panicked by that, he fought his fastenings, unable to loosen the buckles. Then the Blademaster came to the recruit's rescue and got him on his feet. The rear of the narrow cabin was now the floor, and the roof hatch through which they had entered was a side door the Blademaster turned to open. They wedged into the small air lock, to be met by a blaze of fire and billows of stifling white smoke. Hansu slammed the outer door, his face grim.

"The braking system—" he muttered. "It must have started a fire when we landed."

Fire—the ship must be surrounded by flames. But

the memory of one of Hansu's exploring tales flashed into Kana's mind.

"Aren't pressure suits part of the regular survival equipment stored on board these things, sir?"

"That's it!" Hansu edged back into the cabin.

The walls were solid, a few experimental raps told them there were no concealed cupboards. There remained the padded couches. Kana pulled at the surface of one, and the spongy mat came off in a sheet. He had been right! The base of each couch was a storage space and the suits were inside.

"They're going to be tight fits"—the Blademaster inspected the finds—"but we can stand them for at least an hour."

To climb into those bulky coverings in the limited space of the cabin demanded acrobatic agility from both of them. But they did it and the Blademaster set the temperature controls.

"Let us hope that the fire is merely local. When you leave—jump as far from the ship as you can."

Kana nodded as he screwed the bowl head covering into place.

Hansu went first, pausing only for an instant in the lock door and then vanishing. Kana followed as swiftly. He flashed through flames and smoke, and then he landed, went down on one knee, and regained his balance, to run clumsily straight ahead, away from the ship.

He blundered past trees whose crowns were masses of bursting flame, avoiding as best he could the pitfalls laid by roots and fallen logs. The smoke was a thick murk, concealing most of his surroundings. At first he had to nerve himself to stamp through fire, but as he remained unharmed, he grew more confident and did not try to avoid any blaze which crossed the path he had marked for himself.

Suddenly there were no more trees and he was out

in the open on the edge of a cliff. Below a road cut through and in the center of that stood a strange unearthly figure he recognized with difficulty as the Blademaster.

Kana edged along the drop hunting a way down but the man below waved his plated arms to attract his attention and then brought the claw gloved hands of his suit to the thick belt which marked its middle. Kana understood and fumbled for the button on his own belt. Then he walked over the rock rim and allowed his body to float to the road, making a good solid landing not too far from Hansu. Pity these things weren't equipped with rockets as well as antigravity, he thought regretfully. By the look of this stretch of wilderness about them, they were somewhere in the Wild Lands, and it would save a lot of time if they could just jet back to civilization.

Wisps of smoke still walled the road so they kept on the suits, not knowing when they might have to go through fire again. But the highway stayed in the cut where the bare soil and stone gave no foothold to the flames. Judging by the vegetation, they must be somewhere in the northeastern section of the ancient North American continent—which at least had them sharing the same land mass with Prime. This country for almost a thousand years had been deserted after the nuclear wars. There were tales of strange mutations which had developed here and even after the remnants of mankind came spreading back from the Pacific islands, Africa and portions of the southern continent, it still possessed wide uninhabited, almost unexplored areas.

Kana hoped that Hansu knew more of the country than he did and that they were not now just tramping farther into the wilderness. Maybe they should have stuck with the ship and waited for the firefighters who patrolled the wild areas.

It was proved that Hansu did know where he was going—or else had made a lucky guess as to direction. For the road sloped down to cross a wide river. And on the other side of the flood lay grain fields, yellow under the sun. The fugitives tramped over a bridge and then halted to pull off their suits with sighs of relief.

They drew deep breaths of rich Terran air with unspoken thanks. How rich it was Kana had never guessed until he had had to fill his lungs with the thin stuff of Fronn's atmosphere. Between the wine of the air and the warmth of the summer sun he was growing light-headed and light-hearted. He was home again, that was the most important thing right now.

"There ought to be a harvest station along somewhere soon now," Hansu said. "And we can find a vidphone there. It'll call us a 'copter to reach Prime—"

"How far do you suppose we are from Prime, sir?"

"Not too far would be my guess. There's a wilderness section such as this just north of the center."

They marched along the road between yellow-brown fields which stretched endlessly over the horizon. A daring rabbit hopped beside them for a while, its nose twitching curiously. And above birds flew in formation.

"This was all thickly settled country once," Kana mused.

"The Old Ones were lavish with everything—life as well as death. They bred faster than they killed in their wars. Ha—there's a station!"

The building ahead was sheltered by trees and there was the glint of a small lake, an oasis of coolness in the midst of all the dusty hot yellow. Kana felt almost as if he were coming home, remembering his own summer terms of land labor. Perhaps they were already there—the harvesters. This wheat was fully ripe.

But there was no one in the building. Its rooms and halls echoed to their steps with that resonance peculiar to an empty space. Kana went to the food storage place while Hansu hunted the vidphone. Beyond the back entrance was a strip of cool greenery spreading out toward the lake. Yellow and white lilies formed ranks along the stone set path which led down to the cupped coolness of the green waters and other flowers were banked in borders, the boldest of which had overtopped all boundaries to creep among the grass.

On impulse Kana went out. A breeze ruffled his ridge lock, thrusting fingers inside the collar of his tunic. Yet it was very quiet, quiet and peaceful.

Slowly he unfastened his tunic, shucking off the stale cloth with a feeling of relief. Then he groped inside his undershirt. He had come down to the water's edge by now. Long-legged insects skated jauntily across the quiet surface of the pond. Fish made swift, black, hardly seen shadows flitting in the depths. It was peace—it was home—it was quiet and forgetfulness. He poised his hand above it.

The Grace Knife, the sad dimness of its blade hidden by the sheath which had rubbed over his heart all those weeks, rested on his palm. His hand turned slowly. The knife slid, splashing into the dark murk, a swirl of disturbed mud marking its landing. But when Kana stared down he could see nothing of it. It must have buried itself, to be forever hidden from sight. As it should be!

He trailed his fingers in the water, and as his flesh tingled from the feel of the liquid, he knew a sense of relief—of peace. Maybe Hansu's dreams for their future would never know fruition—but he had made his own decision. If he went back to the stars he would not go as a Combatant—as a Swordsman of any class.

And being sure of that Kana rose briskly and strode back to the harvest house. When he opened the freezer and transferred food to the cooking unit he was whistling somewhat tunelessly, but with a very light heart. Luck was playing on their side, or at least had done so thus far. They had reached Terra, now they had only to contact Matthias at Prime. The rest of their mission might be very simple. He looked up smiling as the Blademaster came in. But Hansu met him with a frown.

"Could you get through, sir?" Kana poured stew out into soup plates.

"Yes. It was easy—too easy—"

"Too easy, sir?"

"Well, it was a little as if someone had been waiting for such a call. So we shan't wait for the 'copter—"

Kana put down the container of stew. "What—"

"What makes me think that? What made you suspect trouble just before that flood nearly trapped you in the Fronnian mountains? How did you guess the Ventur had a hiding place in the roof of the warehouse? Sixth sense—ESP warning? How do I know? But I know that it isn't going to be too healthy for us to stay here."

Kana got up from the table with a sigh. "But, sir, they can sight us easily in the open." He offered a last half-hearted protest.

"There may be a jopper in the depot here. They usually leave one or two at each station." Hansu tramped on into the machine storage room.

Again he was right. Two of the round-nosed, teardrop-shaped surface cars stood there, sealed with protective coating, but otherwise ready for use. It was the work of a very few minutes to slough off that film with clearing spray. And before Hansu got into the vehicle he caught up a dull green coverall from a hook on the wall and threw it at Kana, taking its counterpart for himself. Their Mech battledress was well hidden by those and they could pass for men from the general labor pools.

The jopper purred out to the road and began to eat miles. From above, if any 'copter was on their tail, there was nothing to distinguish their car from any other. And many of the transportation men favored the ridge-lock hairdress. The farm road soon brought them to a master highway where they found company. Giants of the heavy transport trucks boxed them in. Hansu cut speed, content to be lost in the procession which thickened as they drew nearer to the port of Prime. Most of the trucks Kana noted were carrying supplies—supplies to be sent off-world to the Hordes, the Legions, out in the lanes of space. For so long had Terra been geared to her task of supplying mercenaries and their needs—what would happen if a sudden change came, if the Hordes and Legions no longer had any reason for existence? How long would it take to re-gear this world, to turn the brimming energy of its inhabitants into other paths?

He found himself dozing now and again, and he was regretting that stew he had left untasted. Real Terrastyle food—fresh—hot— No rations!

"What's the matter?"

Kana's head jerked and his eyes opened. But Hansu's shout had not been directed at him. The inquiry was addressed to the driver in the bubble control seat on a transport which had come to a stop beside them. They were locked in a line of stalled transports and passenger joppers. The Blademaster got a garbled answer Kana could not hear. His face tensed.

"There's an inspection point ahead—not a regular one."

"Looking for us, d'you think, sir?"

"Might be. We'll hope that they're only after a hot runner."

A hot runner, one of the undercover dealers in illegal

foods and drugs, was the type of criminal at which most Terran police drives were aimed. And if the Combat Police were in search of a runner, every jopper and transport in that line would be inspected, every man would have to produce identification. One glimpse of their armlets, of the uniforms they wore under the coveralls and they would be scooped up at once. Then too, they might be the objects of this general hunt.

"Can we get out, sir, turn off somewhere?"

The Blademaster shook his head. "If we tried that now, we'd give ourselves away at once. Wish I knew who was in command at this post. It might just make a difference—"

If Deputy-Commander Matthias was part of some mysterious organization fighting for Terran freedom, as Hansu had hinted, there must be others of a like mind scattered through the whole system of Combat. And so the Blademaster might claim the assistance of such a one—if he were on duty here. But the chance was extremely slim.

There were men walking along the edge of the highway, moving up to see what was holding up the traffic. Hansu watched them and then stepped out of the jopper. When he joined the others he affected a heavy limp which quite cloaked the trained Swordsman's usual springy stride.

Kana ventured out into the neighboring field in an attempt to see what lay ahead. It was a temporary inspection post all right; the bright silver helmets of the police winked in the sun. But this was late afternoon. And with dark— If they did not have to pass that post until dusk— He turned to survey the fields, assessing the countryside for a promise of freedom.

Ahead they were setting up camp lights—stringing them along the road for about a quarter mile. But that illumination would not reach to where the jopper now stood. Then the steady beat of a machine brought his head around. So that was how they would keep them trapped in line until they had a chance to sort them out! A police coaster skimmed along the row of vehicles.

With eyes which had been trained from early childhood to evaluate such problems, Kana watched the three-man machine pass. He timed it with his watch. Yes, it looked as if they were on a regular beat. It was the most elaborate trap to catch a hot runner that he had ever seen. Which argued that either the runner was in the super class—which Kana did not believe, for those captains of undercover industry did not travel, they hired others to take the risks—or the police were after other game. What other game? Them?

Some of the drivers who had gone forward were now returning, loud in their complaints. Apparently none of them had had any satisfaction from the police. Hansu was with them.

"There's a coaster on patrol along the road, sir," Kana reported.

"Yes." The Blademaster motioned for him to climb back into the jopper. "We'll have to do some thinking and fast."

"Are they really after a hot runner, sir?"

"I believe that they are after us."

Kana was suddenly cold. "But why, sir?" he protested. "Terra police wouldn't pick us up on C.C. orders—not without a secondary warrant from Combat—and it would take them more time to get that."

"Don't ask me why or how!" Hansu's irritation spilled over in that bark. "But we're going to be kept from meeting Matthias—that's my bet!"

"And whoever is able to do that," Kana said, "has influence enough to call out the police. It's only a matter of time before they pick us up, sir. Unless in the dark—"

"Yes, it *is* getting dark. That's one point in our favor. They're searching every person to the skin up there."

And they were wearing Mech uniforms they had no means of discarding or destroying now.

Hansu snapped open a small compartment and pulled out the district map which was part of every jopper's equipment. He traced road markings with a finger tip and then leaned his head on the back of the seat and closed his eyes, a deep frown line between his brows. The sun was almost gone, but still the line of vehicles before them had not moved. More and more of the drivers were gathering in the fields and words of argument carried through the air. Now and then one of them went back to his jopper or transport, probably to ring in to his employer on a speecher and report his non-progress.

"Can we make it, sir, even in the dark?" Kana asked at last.

"Get away from here—yes—I'm sure of that. But reaching Prime—that's another matter. If they are searching for us they must have Prime sealed as tight as a lifting spacer. Karr, what did they teach you in ancient history about the pre-Blow-up cities?"

Though he couldn't see how ancient history was going to get them out of this, Kana obediently recited the few facts which had stuck in his mind for five years.

"The Old Ones built tower buildings—and they were open to the weather—no bubble domes. Wonder that the winds didn't wreck them—"

"What about underground?"

Underground? It was because the towers were unusual that he remembered them. During the nuclear wars most of the survivors had lived underground. There was nothing ancient about that mode of life. There had been one lecture during his training, delivered on a hot afternoon when he had wanted to be elsewhere with a Zacathan he admired more than the droning Terran instructor. Under the ground—

"They traveled under the ground sometimes, didn't they, sir? Through tubes running under their cities."

Hansu gave a curt nod. "What are those drivers doing?"

Kana surveyed the scene in the field from his side vision plate. "Building a fire, sir. I think they're going to open their emergency rations."

The Blademaster tore the map loose from its holder. "We'll join them, Karr. Keep your mouth shut and your ears open. And watch that police coaster. We want to know when to expect its passing."

Though some of the drivers still grumbled, most of them now looked upon the halt as an unexpected gift of free time. Having reported in on the speechers they no longer felt any sense of responsibility. There was a general air of relaxation about the fire as they opened their rations.

"Yeah, I'm driving a time job," announced a tall, red-haired man, "but if the C.P. says stop, I stop. And the boss can just argue it out with them. He said I should try to make time on the road if we ever get away from here."

One of his companions in misfortune shook his head. "Don't try the river cut-off, it's not too good at night. Since this new section of highway was opened, they don't run a breakdown crew along there and there've been cave-ins."

Hansu insinuated himself into this group, assuming a protective covering of manner so that he might have spent most of his adult life pushing one of the transports. Another example of a good AL man at work, Kana decided. On Fronn the Blademaster had met Venturi and Llor as an equal, here he was adapting to another clan with strange tribal customs of its own.

"This river road"—he addressed the red-head—"is it a short cut to Prime?"

"Yeah." The driver gave him a measuring look. "You new on this haul, fella?"

"Just been assigned to Prime. I'm driving a jopper from the west, don't know this country—"

"Well, the river road's not so good if you don't know it. It's an old one—parts of it pre-Blow-up—or so they say. Last summer there was a pack of fellas outta Prime digging around there, uncovered some old stuff, too. But it does save you twenty-thirty miles. Only it's posted as unsafe—"

"Unsafe!" echoed one of the others. "It's a trap, Lari. I don't care what the boss says, you'd better not run it in the dark. I've not forgotten that cave-in we saw. Big enough to pull a wheel out of the trans. That's what brought those digging fellas out—they had such a time filling it in they thought maybe there was a room or something underneath."

"Was there?" Hansu displayed just the proper amount of interest.

"Maybe. Fella from Prime thought it was part of a tunnel, but they couldn't clear it enough to be sure. But you'll be all right if you take it slow and beam your lights down. You have to turn off to the left about two miles from here—"

"Any more chance of a cave-in?"

"Could be. There's some ruins along it. I tell you, when we get past the barrier here, you cut your jopper in behind my trans and I'll guide you."

Hansu returned the proper thanks and in his own way faded into the general group where the talk now turned on the forest fire one driver had seen blazing that afternoon. A moment later the Blademaster's hand closed on Kana's arm.

17

Prisoners

"The coaster?"

"Passes at irregular intervals now, sir," Kana reported gloomily. "We can't depend on it being elsewhere—"

"Tough. If you knew this country we could split up and try to run for it separately."

"Do *you* know the country, sir?"

"Enough to believe that I have found a way for us to get into Prime unseen. Once we are away from here—that is."

"What we need, sir, is a diversion—"

"Hmm." The Blademaster might or might not have caught that, for their conference was interrupted by a shout from the barrier and the drivers scattered to the parked vehicles. Some move was indicated.

Kana climbed back into the jopper, unable to see any way out of their present impasse. Though it was dusk, the fire in the field lighted this area and if they moved far forward they would come into the section flooded by the camp lights.

"Hey!"

Hansu leaned out in answer to that shout.

"You fellas with the joppers are to pull out to the right—that's the new order. Wait 'til you get a space clear and then run out on the field."

Had the police narrowed their hunt to the point they knew their prey was in a jopper? Kana wished, not for the first time that long day, that he had one of the Mech blasters from the ship. Now he was without any weapons—even the Grace Knife.

But Hansu moved now. From within the breast of his coverall the Blademaster produced a three-inch tube of metal. Slowly he licked it all over with finicky care and then stuck it under the edge of the control panel. The transport just ahead of them pulled up several yards and Hansu nosed their jopper to the right, as he did so snapping an order to his companion:

"Pull up the rear seat pad and draw it over here!"

Kana obeyed as they bumped from the smooth surface of the road to the field. Other joppers were emerging from the packed traffic, before and after them.

"Ready!" Hansu set a dial on the controls and kicked open his own door. "Jump!"

Kana slammed back the door and flung himself out, hitting the ground with a bruising jar and rolling over, scraping skin raw in the process of his rough advance. Before he lost momentum he turned that roll into a forward crawl. And he was still making a worm's progress away from the road when the night split apart with a flash of fire and the sound of an explosion. The roar was succeeded by a confused shouting and the recruit cowered face down and motionless as the police coaster zoomed by on its way to the scene.

When that had gone he continued to crawl away from the light, making for a willow-lined watercourse he had noted earlier in the afternoon. And, though he expected any moment to be challenged, he made it safely, to tumble down the bank into a foot or so of cold water.

Reversing, he squirmed up once more so that his eyes were on a level with the road. Their jopper, ignited by the explosion Hansu had set, was burning briskly. The line of transports was jammed tight ahead and a crowd milled about the circle of light and heat. It was a very superior and successful diversion indeed. Only—had Hansu escaped as easily as he had?

Kana crawled eastward along the stream. Prime lay in this direction and if he found the Blademaster again it would be along this route. He became aware of movement ahead—stealthy but assured. Hansu? Or some policeman who had suspected what had really happened?

The recruit unbuckled the belt of his coverall and prepared to use it as he had the rifle sling on Fronn. The rustling stopped. Then came the faintest of whispers.

"Karr?"

"Yes, sir!"

"This way—"

Kana broke into a jog trot to keep up with his commander. They passed far to one side of the point of the police barrier where the glare of the lamps eclipsed that of the burning jopper. And now they crept half in the water until the illumination was behind. Hansu kept to their creek road until a rise in the ground and a turn in the sweep of the highway put both barrier and road out of sight.

"Where are we heading, sir?" Kana asked at last as they sloshed soggily up the bank behind a screen of trees and brush.

"To that river road the driver mentioned." The Blademaster walked at a slower pace now, and he carried his right arm across his body, supporting it with his left hand.

"Are you hurt, sir?"

"Just scorched a little. Had to put that pad up on the seat before I jumped."

Now Kana understood. Dimly seen by those who dared not venture too close to the flaming jopper, that seat pad might be mistaken for two occupants trapped within.

"Can't I see to your burn, sir?" he persisted.

"Later—" Hansu appeared intent only in putting distance between them and the police.

And "later" was a long time away. The Blademaster's sense of direction and his study of the map brought them out on a narrower road which cut away from the main highway southeast. Since there seemed to be little or no travel along it, they dared to walk in the open, making better time where the footing was sure.

The moon was up when Hansu slowed to a stop. He turned as if on a pivot until he had made a half circle. And Kana, imitating him, saw what his officer had been searching for—trenches cut into the earth just off the road.

"Your flash—" Hansu bit off the two words as if to say that much had cost him real effort.

Kana unlooped his hand torch, set it on low, and pointed the ray into the nearest of those gashes. There was broken masonry at the bottom of the excavation. These must be the ruins the driver had mentioned. Hansu counted the trenches audibly.

"—four—five—six. That's the one—the sixth on the left—"

Kana's beam flicked to number six and, as it picked out the stones and ancient brickwork at the bottom,

Hansu slid awkwardly down into it. The recruit jumped after the Blademaster, trying to keep his footing in the rubble of embedded blocks. Though he had no idea of what his companion was seeking, he knew better than to ask any questions just then.

This trench was longer than the others, running farther back from the road, but at last they came to a pile of loose dead brush and stones which marked the end of the excavation. Hansu pulled at the brush with his left hand and Kana sprang forward to help. Under their tugging the stuff came away, to display a dark hole.

"What—?" Kana began.

"Underground ways—running into Prime—from the old days—" Hansu's answer was broken by curious pauses and Kana swept the torch beam across the Blademaster's face. Sweat trickled down through the grime and dust and under that Hansu wore the look of a man forcing himself to go on nerve alone.

But Kana sensed that this was no time to offer help. He allowed the light to travel on, back into the hole. And then he stepped into what was clearly a manmade tunnel. Under his boots were two strips of rust which must have once been metal rails.

These ancient ways were often almost death traps. As the Swordsmen advanced they passed side corridors choked with cave-ins and twice they had to dig through piles of gravel and earth. However, surprisingly, the further they went from the entrance, the better the condition. Kana could not believe that these hidden ways had been abandoned ever since the days of the nuke wars. And his suspicion of that was confirmed as he caught sight—in a side tunnel—of some metal shoring, which reflected the beam of the torch, undimmed by the prevailing damp.

The main passage which they followed widened as

more and more side corridors emptied into it. This must have once been a main entrance to Prime, or rather to the now almost forgotten seaport upon the ruins of which Prime had been erected.

"How much farther—?"

"Don't know." Hansu walked mechanically. "I've heard about this. We should be able to contact the Reachers—maybe one of their cars will find us—"

That did not make sense to Kana, but he did not challenge it. Who Hansu's "Reachers" might be he was beginning to guess—the mysterious underground within Combat of which Matthias was the probable head. But why the Blademaster expected to encounter them here was a puzzle beyond his solving.

They rounded a turn, a wide sweep which now embraced not one set of tracks but four, and came out into a space which echoed hollowly to the sound of their boots and in which the torch beam was swallowed in the dark. Kana switched on its full power and pointed the beam at the walls, sweeping it from one dark arch of entrance to the next. They were in a vast circle, the center of a web the strands of which led out to every point of the compass. And which of those archways should they enter? As far as he could see they were all exactly alike.

The unease Kana had always felt when confined in a small space began to operate now—although the area of the crossing tracks was large. But beyond the limit of his torch the dark had a thickness to it which was almost tangible, as if they were truly buried far below the surface of the earth with no hope of winning to the open air again. The dank smell he thought born of the damp and earth carried other faint taints—nose-tickling reminders of the far past. And now that they had paused he was sure he could hear not too far away the gurgle of running water.

"Which way now?" His basic dislike of the dark, of being closed in by tons of earth, brought that query from him in an impatient demand.

Hansu grunted but made no other answer as Kana continued to mark the edges of the circle with his moving torch beam.

Their problem was given a sudden and dramatic solution. From one of the archways, Kana could not be sure of just which, there came a humming sound, which began as a drone and grew to the proportion of a siren as it moved toward them. He grabbed at Hansu's arm, striving to draw the Blademaster with him in retreat into one of the other passages, wanting to take cover until they had a chance to investigate.

But it was already too late. They were caught—pinned in a wide beam of light which blistered their eyes as if it had been blaster fire. And from beyond the source of that luminescence a voice snapped an order they dared not disregard:

"Up with your hands—and stand where you are!"

With a sinking heart Kana obeyed. They were helpless, unarmed prisoners.

And that capture had only one logical conclusion— as he might have foreseen, Kana thought bitterly some time later. The wall facing the bunk shelf where he sat was an even, solid gray without a single seam or crack to distract his eyes or give a slight root for his imagination and so relieve the monotony of a time which was no longer divided into minutes, hours, days, or even weeks.

Even the indirect lighting of his cell waxed or waned at intervals which had no regularity so that he could not gauge the passing of time by that. When he was hungry he opened the door of a tiny chute beside the bunk and took out the capsules and plastic water bubble he found there. How they were placed there, he had no knowledge.

The continual silence was the worst. It was a thick deadening blanket which he fought until his nerves were tense, pacing the floor, exercising in a frantic endeavor to wear himself out physically so that he could sleep away a small portion of the endless hours. He was caught in a trap from which there was no escape. And the worst was that he knew the time would come when he could erect no more barriers against the silence, when the demon which was his own particular fear would close in to inhabit his mind.

The whole world had narrowed to this windowless, doorless cell somewhere deep in the foundations of Prime. The functions of the room were entirely automatic. Kana could be forgotten by his human captors, left here for countless years, and still he would continue to receive rations, the light would go on and off according to some weird pattern set up on a machine. But he himself would cease to live—

It was when his thoughts centered in that groove that Kana had to fight for control, make himself think of something else. If he only had a record-pak or writing material— But for that matter, he might as well wish for freedom! He did not even know if he were already judged and condemned or was still awaiting trial.

Hansu had been wrong—so wrong—in believing that the underground ways of Prime were any secret to the Combat officials. There had been a C.C. Agent in the group to welcome them when they were herded from the rail truck at the brilliantly lighted station under the headquarters building.

They had been taken without a struggle. What had happened since to Hansu, he wondered dully. His last glimpse of the Blademaster had come when they were separated at the interrogation room, just before he had been turned over to the questioners.

Those specialists at Interrogation were not crude in their methods. The use of torture to loosen tongues of stubborn captives had vanished long ago. Now after he had been given certain drugs there was nothing a man could conceal. Kana knew that he must have babbled every secret of his life to any ears caring to listen. When he recovered consciousness he had been here, stripped to the shorts of a prisoner, and here he had remained ever since.

Now he began his self-allotted task for the period after each meal, the attempted recall of all X-Tee lore he had managed to absorb. Sometimes he could really lose himself in that mental labor for as much as several minutes.

"Zacan"—he spoke the word slowly, trying to give it the proper hissing accent—"is a planet of Terra type. The continental land masses are mainly archipelagoes of islands. The largest of these is Zorodal. The citadel of Zorodal was first founded in the semi-mythical reign of the Five Kings, now a period almost legendary. Archaeological excavations have verified some of the legends and have proved that there are the remains of at least ten civilizations on the same site, sometimes with a lapse of a thousand years between the downfall of one and the rise of the next. The Zacathans are a reptilian race, comparable to Terran lizard forms. Their life span is many times that of man. They are not aggressive, being contemplative with a well-developed interest in historical studies, producing many historians and philosophers of note—"

There was a click. A square space in the wall before him gaped like an opening mouth. Within rested a uniform case. For a moment Kana froze. Then his hands shot out and he snatched the case in desperate fear that it was there only to tantalize him and would disappear.

A uniform case, containing the complete new uniform of a Swordsman Third Class! His hands were still shaking as he began to dress. This must mean release, at least release from the cell. Was he on his way to trial—or to return to duty—or—? He was clumsy over buckles, awkward with the fastenings. But at last he was clothed. Only the sword was missing, the sheath at his new waist belt hung empty. And he had no Grace Knife.

He was latching the chin strap of his helmet when a second opening in the wall confronted him and he stepped through into a corridor. Base guards closed in, two before, two behind him. He wondered if he should be flattered by the size of that escort. But he fell into step with their pace, knowing it useless to ask any questions.

A lift took them up in a dizzy rise past level after level of headquarters' Administrative core. When they disembarked they were in a wide hallway on one of the staff floors. Murals of other world scenes where Hordes and Legions had made or unmade history alternated with windows which gave Kana his first sight of Terra since he had gone underground. It was midmorning as far as he could judge, and below, the bay gave on the sea. Tradition said that the ancient ruins which were the base of Prime were merely the outer fringes of a once great city which had covered an island in that bay, a city which the sea had licked over during the nuclear wars. 'Copters swung in heavy traffic between the buildings standing now along the shore. It was just the same sort of day on which he had first entered Prime to accept enlistment in Yorke's Horde—

But the guard allowed him no time to stare through windows or think philosophically of the past. He was speedily ushered into an audience chamber. There he found himself facing a Tribunal. High Brass—just about the highest! Three of Combat's four Councilors sat there and the fourth and fifth members of the court were a C.C. Agent and an officer of the Galactic Patrol, a sub-sector commander by his badges. Kana stiffened. What right had those aliens to be his judges? He was sure that he could protest that, and be backed by the Combat Code. But, biding his time until he was more certain, he came to attention and made the formal announcement expected of him.

"Kana Karr, Swordsman Third Class, under enlistment in Yorke's Horde, place of service, Fronn."

Hansu—where was Hansu? Why were they to be tried separately? More than anything else at that moment Kana wished that he could have a moment's conversation with the Blademaster. For he had just made another and more upsetting discovery—one of the Combat officers facing him was Matthias—the same Matthias that Hansu had been so sure would stand their protector, fight on their side if they could only reach him.

The faces of the combat officers were impassive, but the C.C. Agent, an Ageratan—the brilliant scarlet and gold of his cloak somewhat garish against the green-gray of the Terrans—shifted impatiently in his chair as if he wished to speed up the proceedings and did not quite dare, while his alien companion, the Patrol officer, affected in contrast a vast boredom.

Then Kana saw what lay before the senior of the Combat officers—an Arch sword. That answered one of his questions. He had been brought here for sentencing. They had condemned him without allowing him a chance to speak in his own defense. But—how could they? The interrogators had the exact truth out of him. These men must know of the massacre on

Fronn, of that strange scene by the plundered Patrol ship, of everything else which had happened, know it as if they had witnessed the events in his place. How could they then—?

"For unauthorized dealings with an X-Tee race against all regulations," began the Combat senior, "for desertion of your comrades on another world, for the theft of a cruiser belonging to the Galactic Patrol, you, Kana Karr, Swordsman Third Class, Arch rating, are hereby declared unfit for off-world service. You shall be stripped of all Combat rating and privileges and sent to the labor gangs for the rest of your natural life."

Long discipline kept him at attention. Labor gangs for the rest of his life—the closest thing to slavery. But—a fierce, blinding anger uncoiled within him—he was going to answer those frozen-faced devils with a few home truths before they shipped him off. And he was not in the gangs—not yet!

When he spoke it was not to his superior officers but directly to the C.C. Agent.

"I've learned to know you for what you are—you and your kind," he said slowly between set teeth. The ancient blood lust which had once sent his Malay ancestors into battle swinging a bolo might have been thinned by interbreeding with other and more peaceful races but it was still there and rising in him now. "You may be able now to force Terrans to obey your will. But someday you'll pay in kind—"

The Ageratan's white face did not change expression, only now he sat very quiet, his long eyes narrowed into slits, a bird of prey preparing to swoop.

"How long"—Kana's attention was now on his fellow Terrans—"do you think you can cover up such messes? You know from my testimony—whether I gave it drugged or not—what they are doing to us out there. I"—he paused until he was sure his voice was once more under full control—"I gave Grace to Deke Mills after I heard his story. You know—all of you—what he had to tell. We are supposed to be fighting men—if only mercenaries selling our skill to others. Isn't it time we began to fight—against murderers!" He hurled that charge straight at the Ageratan, at the Patrol officer.

Kana was trying hard to pick and choose the proper words, to keep his red rage battened down. Then his mood changed. Why should he stand there mouthing statements which made no impression on their impassivity when he wanted to leap that table between them, to feel the Ageratan's flesh pulp beneath his fist? What was the use in talking—nothing he said—could say—would break through to them—would ruffle the composure of that traitor Matthias.

He brought his hand up in salute and wheeled to fall in with his waiting guard. Would they take him back to the underground cell? Or try to—for it would be a case of trying. He was determined to escape somehow, somewhere along the route.

Hansu— If they had given him life in the labor gangs, they must have executed the Blademaster! How wrong Hansu had been in his belief in Matthias and the new day about to dawn. With Matthias ready to betray them the rebels had never had a ghost of a chance.

They marched back to the lift and whisked down, not to the cells. Instead Kana was escorted to a small room just off the main corridor near some entrance to the building—he was sure of that as he watched the constant stream of Combatants passing in the hall. Except for a sentry left at the door he was alone—to wait— To wait? No, to act!

18

No Guard On
The Stars!

Kana's mind raced as he assessed the situation. He was
in full uniform, except that he lacked arms. If it weren't
for the sentry he could simply walk out of this room, join
the crowd in the hall, and leave the building, before the
alarm was given. Once free in Prime he could find a way
out of the city itself. There remained the problem of the
sentry.

He watched the man narrowly. The fellow was in
the act of suppressing a yawn as Kana first studied
him. It was plain that he did not expect trouble from
the prisoner. And this was no proper detention room,
rather more like a waiting lounge for low-ranking
visitors. The bench Kana had been ordered to occupy
was cushioned and there was a visa-plate set in the
wall to his left, out of sight range of the doorway. The

guard's attention was often attracted by those passing without— Kana's eyes flickered to the visa-plate.
Was there some way of using that? A little
improvising— He waited until the guard's attention
was fixed upon something in the corridor and then
he jumped to his feet.

"Red alert!" he cried out as if startled.

The guard whirled, took one step in, glancing at the
visa-plate.

"I don't see anything—" he began, and then shot a
sour look at Kana as if angry at being tricked into
speaking to the captive against express orders.

"It was red alert!" Kana insisted, pointing to the
screen.

The guard came all the way in, uneasily. If the visa-
plate *had* flashed a red signal—then his duty was clear,
he must call back at once for instructions. And he
couldn't be sure that it had not.

"Keep me covered with your blaster," urged Kana.
"I tell you it was a red alert!"

The guard drew his blaster, aiming it at the recruit's
middle. And, with his back to the wall, his eyes on the
prisoner, he made a crabwise march along toward the
visa-plate.

"You sit down!" he snapped at Kana.

The recruit dropped down on the bench, but his
body was tense, his muscles ready—

There would come a single second when the guard
had to turn half away from him in order to push the
question button below the plate. And if he could move
then—

It came, the guard's head turned a fraction. Kana
flung himself forward almost at floor level. His shoulders struck just behind the other's knees and there was
a dull crack as the man's head struck against the screen,
slammed into it by the force of Kana's attack. The

recruit twisted on top, ready to carry on the fight. But the body beneath him was limp.

A little startled by such phenomenal luck—the fellow must have been knocked out when his head hit the screen—Kana got to his knees and hurriedly appropriated the guard's sword and blaster. But a moment later he reluctantly abandoned the gun. Only a base guardsman could go so armed and he would be picked up on the street if he were seen carrying that. He sheathed the sword—and hoped that luck would continue to ride with him.

The prostrate guard, bound with his own belts and gagged with a thick strip torn from his undershirt, was rolled back under the bench, well out of range of any casual glance from the door. Then Kana settled his clothing, donned the helmet he had lost during the brief struggle, and taking a deep breath, he stepped out into the corridor, closing the door of the waiting room behind him. He might have five minutes—perhaps more—before the hunt would be on. And now that he was again wearing a sword there was nothing to distinguish him from any other of the hundreds of Archs on the streets of Prime.

The streets of Prime—the sooner he got away from those same streets the better. This escape was all pure improvisation and it might work all the more effectively because of that, but he wanted to get away from Prime as quickly as he could. He covered the remainder of the corridor with the brisk strides of a man on an official errand and came out of the building on a 'copter landing some twenty floors above ground level. One of the dragonfly machines had just deposited a veteran and was about to rise when Kana waved. The pilot waited for him impatiently.

"Where to?"

It was a pity he did not know more of the geography

of the city. But he was sure that it would do little good
to approach the space port or any of the transcontinent
air ports—those were well guarded and the alarm
would be flashed to them the moment his escape was
detected. A little rattled by the pilot's demand he gave
as his destination the only place in the city where he
had been before.

"The Hiring Hall."

They arose and drifted west while Kana attempted
to identify points below. Would escape by water be
possible? There were only five surface roads out of
Prime and each passed a patrolled barrier where
vehicles were searched for smuggled goods.

"Here y'are."

The 'copter came to rest on a Hiring Hall staging.
Kana gave curt thanks and took the lift down, heading not to the hall itself nor to any of the levels where
the enlistment officers had their cubbys, but straight
to the one place he thought would offer not only
concealment for a space, but help in planning his next
move.

The record room was as quiet as it had been the
first time he had stepped within its sound-proof doors.
One booth near the entrance displayed the light which
signified occupancy, but the rest were dark. Kana
punched for four paks in rapid succession, and with
them retreated to the booth at the far end of the row.
Feeding his paks into the machine he settled back in
the reclining chair.

Three-quarters of an hour later the last pak had spun
to its conclusion. So—now he possessed two possible
answers to his dilemma. He removed the head piece
but did not leave the seat. Well, at least he was given
a choice. On impulse he went to the door of the booth
to survey the room. The light on the other booth had
gone out. But now there were three others in use. Was

that suspicious? Did it show an unusual amount of
study for one interval? Or was some big expedition
being planned?

He could not see any way that they might have
traced him here. The logical move for any escape would
be to get out of Prime with the least possible delay.
Certainly they would not expect to find him using
record-paks in the Hiring Hall archives.

Two ways—his mind returned to the problem as he
settled down in the booth to stare unseeingly at the
ceiling and try to plan. The sea way—he was able to
swim though he had not had much practice lately. And
the underground ways built by the Old Ones. Would
the Combat police believe that having been captured
down there he would be reluctant to try the maze of
passages for a second time?

He was hungry. The carefully balanced prison diet
had not been intended to build up any store of energy.
And he didn't quite dare to enter the transient mess
here, could not in fact without displaying the armlet which would betray him at once. First things
first—let him get out of Prime and then he could
worry about food. Out of Prime—the two choices
were still before him.

And sitting here was not speeding him on his way.
He had absorbed all the information the record-paks
held. It was time to go. And in a snap second Kana
made his decision.

The oldest building in modern Prime was the Histo-
laboratory Museum. Since history was not a subject
popular with the general public on Terra, the building
was never crowded. But, according to one of the paks
Kana had just consulted, it had been erected on the
foundations of a prewar structure. And so it might
provide an entrance to the ancient underground ways
said to feed all buildings of that era—a thousand-to-one

chance. But he had been trained to consider such chances.

Kana gathered up the paks and left the booth. Three others were still occupied and he hurried past their doors. He returned the paks and went out, concentrating on presenting an unhurried, casual demeanor. Luckily the building he sought was not more than three blocks away and his uniform would render him anonymous on the streets.

As he went down the four wide steps to the pavement he was aware of a clatter behind him. Someone in a hurry. He quickened his pace and caught his thumb in his belt not too far from the hilt of his sword. If he were cornered now he would fight. Better to be cooked at once in a blaster flame than live in a labor camp for life.

A hand clamped hard above his elbow, dragging his fingers away from his weapon before he could draw it. To the right and left grim-faced Archs had fallen into step with him.

"Keep marching—"

Kana did, mechanically, his eyes after one wild glance centered straight ahead. But they were not herding him toward headquarters. No 'copter settled down at their signal to collect guards and prisoners. They were still headed for the Museum.

Unable to guess what was going to happen now, Kana simply kept on between his silent companions. To anyone passing they might have been three friends on a sightseeing tour of Prime.

Just before they reached the entrance to the Museum the man who had kept that paralyzing grip on his arm spoke:

"In here—"

Completely bewildered, Kana turned in, the other two matching him step for step. They met no one in

the wide hall lined with cases containing prewar relics unearthed in the vicinity. And no one appeared as
they stepped on the down conveyor which lowered
them to the depths under the street.

That sudden pick-up when he had believed himself
safe had been a stunning blow, but now Kana was recovering, marshaling his energy to try another break at the
first opportunity. But why had he been brought here?
Could it be that they were under the impression that
he was a member of some secret organization—the one
Hansu had hinted about—and expected him to lead
them to his comrades? Curiosity replaced surprise and
he resigned himself to wait until they showed their hand
one way or another.

More hallways and exhibit cases, gloomy rooms with
displays or ranks of filing cabinets. Once or twice they
sighted a man at work at desk or file, but none looked
up or appeared aware of Kana and his escort—the
three might have been invisible.

They marched on until they reached the end of that
maze, a single large room crowded with machinery
which probably was a heating or air-conditioning unit.
Then the guard at his left took several paces ahead,
threading through the machinery to an inconspicuous
door which gave on a flight of stairs leading down into
a dimly lit area where several small track-running trucks
were pulled up at a platform.

There were men loading bulky packages on these,
but they, too, gave the three no heed.

"In." A pointing finger emphasized the order and
Kana climbed into an unloaded truck, hunkering down
on a small seat. One of his companions took his place
on an even smaller rest in front and the other crowded
in beside him. The vehicle started away from the platform, gathering speed as it spun along the rails, and then
whipped into the semi-darkness of a tunnel opening.

Were they on their way to Headquarters? But why travel underground when it would have been much easier to bundle him into a 'copter and make the short trip in the open? As the minutes of their swift journey began to pile up Kana guessed that now they were not only beyond Headquarters, but that they must be fast approaching the limits of Prime itself. He was completely confused over direction. They might have been out under the floor of the bay, or far inland, when the car came to a stop beside a second platform and his guards ordered him out of it.

This time they did not ascend but walked along a lighted side corridor into a place of regulated activity. Here, too, were series of file-filled rooms, and some laboratories with busy workers.

"In here—"

Again Kana obeyed that command, entered a room and—stopped short.

"Three hours, ten minutes." Hansu was consulting his watch. Now he turned to the man beside him, the man wearing a deputy-commander's uniform. "Pay me that half credit, Matt. I told you he could do it. Only a fraction slow—but entirely sure. I know my candidate!"

The other drew a coin from his belt pouch and solemnly passed it over. Kana shut his mouth. For the High Brass who had just dropped that metal token in the Blademaster's waiting palm had, not long before, sat granite-faced to sentence him to a labor camp for life.

Now Hansu's attention came back to him and Kana found himself measured with a critical stare.

"Rather lively for a dead man," was the Blademaster's strange comment. "You"—he pointed an accusing finger—"were blasted an hour ago when you tried to force your way on board a transport to the Islands."

For the second time Kana opened his mouth and this time he was able to get out words.

"Interesting—if true—sir—"

Hansu was grinning with an open light-heartedness Kana had never seen him display before.

"Amusing dramatics." Still his explanation made little sense. "Welcome to Prime—the real Prime. And meet its governor—Commander Matthias."

"You pick up your cues well, son." The Commander nodded at Kana approvingly. "Made that escape as smoothly as if you had had a chance to rehearse it."

"I told you," Hansu broke in. "He's good enough to make it worthwhile enlisting him."

Kana began to understand why he had been left in that corridor waiting room at Headquarters, how he had been able to trick the guard so easily.

"You set up that break for me," he said, half accusingly. "Did you have me tailed?"

"No. Your escape had to look natural. We just supplied the time, place, and opportunity—the raw materials as it were. The rest was up to you," Hansu replied.

"Then how did your men find me?"

"Through those paks you dialed out of the archives. That combination was a give-away—History of Prime, Ancient Remains in the Prime District, The Sea Coast, Map of Prime—all asked for at the same time by one person. So we just sent the boys along to pick you up."

Kana dropped down on a bench without having been invited to such relaxation. This was moving a little too fast for him. Easy—logical— But everything Hansu said spoke of a city-wide net of surveillance, of a tight and well-functioning organization. What kind and for what purpose?

"And the labor camp?" He asked the first question of the many in his mind at that moment.

"Oh, there are labor camps right enough—supposedly established for criminals and malcontents of all kinds," the Commander returned cheerfully. "Only we differ somewhat from the C.C. Agents in our definition of both 'labor camp' and 'crime against the Galactic peace.' And those Agents would be quite surprised if they visited any camps except the two or three we maintain for official display purposes. Right now you're in what might be termed 'Camp Number One.' And we can introduce you to a lot of hardened offenders against the status quo if you wish. So you're going to serve the sentence which was imposed on you this morning—there's no getting around that. However, I don't believe you will offer any objections to your fate. Hansu hasn't. Or do you harbor some deep, dark reservations, Trig?"

The Blademaster's grin grew even broader. "Not that you can see, Matt. I'll toil under your whips just as long as you'll persuade the powers that be to let me. I only wish that I had been let into the whole secret a lot earlier in life—there're a lot of things I could have done—" He ended on a wistful note.

"What about Kosti and Larsen, sir? And the rest of the Horde on Fronn?"

"Kosti and Larsen earthed in the far south and have been picked up by our men—the C.C. Agents won't ever know about them. As for the Horde—well, that will take some arranging here and there. For the present they're safe with the Venturi—and I think we can make a deal with those traders. They're the sort we want to contact. We'll lift the Horde out of that pinch before those renegades and the C.C. get to them. On the other hand we can't slap Device down or spill all we have discovered about his backers. But the Venturi will be allowed in on part of the secret so that they will know you have not gone back on your word.

Here in Prime Two we have a rather odd idea that promises should be kept—if it is humanly possible."

Kana felt as if he had been whirled through space without benefit of a ship. If someone would just explain everything from the beginning, carefully, and in words simple enough for his reeling mind to gather in, he would be happier.

"You'd like a few facts, wouldn't you?" Commander Matthias might have been reading his thoughts. "Well, this set-up isn't so simple that it can be explained in a couple of sentences. The whole project reaches back into our past—three hundred years back. You know—if you asked an Ageratan or a Rassami what he thought of a Terran, he'd paint you a mighty crude picture of a simple-minded barbarian. That has been our shield all along, and we have fostered the idea that we are rude savages of limited intelligence. It inflates the ego of the enemy and doesn't bother us at all.

"In reality Terra for at least two hundred and fifty years has been a double world—though that fact is known to a relatively small number of her inhabitants. One Terra and one Prime was fitted quickly and neatly into the pattern Central Control demanded and is a law-abiding member of their lesser confederacy, content with the role of third-class citizenship.

"But in the past hundred years one troop transport in every twenty which lifted from this planet was no troop transport at all, but a pioneer carrier. Men and women selected for certain qualities of mind and body—survivor types—went out in deep sleep to settle on planets our mercenaries had explored. On some of those worlds the native races had dwindled and retrogressed until civilization had faded almost to extinction, others were bare of intelligent life, or had dominant races, young, vigorous and humanoid with whom we could interbreed. There is even reason to believe that the latter may be descendents of the passengers of those legendary starships which left this world during the nuclear wars—though the people have long since forgotten their origin.

"So Terrans have been planted secretly on almost a thousand worlds now. On thirty our colonies could not take root, native diseases, adverse climatic changes, malignant life forms blotted them out. On six more they are still fighting a war for survival. On the rest they flourish and spread.

"Central Control has noted the decline in our planet birth rate, the fact that our race, which might have challenged the rule of the older groups, seems to be on the wane. They believe that this is due to their wise plans of the past, that as mercenaries we are bleeding our species out of existence. Only very recently have they had any hints as to what is really occurring. They may or may not have discovered that Terran Combatants, almost always hired to serve on backward, frontier planets, know of hidden colonies of their own kind—that our casualty lists often cover men who remain *on* the earth there and not *in* it when their Horde or Legion returns to base.

"We are leaving Terra for the stars just as we planned from our first Galactic flight. And now that Central Control suspects that, she is going to move against us. But she will discover that she is perhaps ten generations too late. One cannot move against colonies on almost a thousand different worlds, not and keep up the fiction of justice to all which must be maintained to preserve their carefully guarded balance of power."

"You are forgetting our allies," Hansu pointed out.

"The man in the field does right to correct the desk merchant at home," Matthias conceded. "Yes, several other young and vigorous races have fallen under the same ban against exploration and colonization which C.C. attempted to force upon us. And when these discriminated against X-Tees learned what we were doing—usually from our AL men sent to explain it in detail—they copied our methods all the way. There are about twenty of these worlds now following our pattern. This trouble on Fronn—the bald design of crediting a massacre of Patrolmen to an outlawed Horde, the betrayal of Yorke and his officers—is a blow back at us and may bring the whole scheme into the open. If so, we don't really care too much, we've been preparing lately for such an eventuality and we have our case far better organized for a general hearing than they suspect—too much of *their* planning won't bear the light of day. In the meantime—" He nodded to Hansu as if suggesting that it was now time for the Blademaster to take over.

"In the meantime operations shall continue as usual, both here and out in space. And as an AL man you're going to labor all right—just as you were sentenced to do."

Kana took it all in at last.

"I'll accept that sentence gladly, sir. When and where do I begin?"

Hansu crossed to the wall and pulled down the map hanging there—and the Galaxy was spread out for their viewing.

"They've tried to keep a guard on the stars and they have failed. No race or species has the power to do that, ever! You have a wide choice of operations, son. The whole of space is free!"

STAR
RANGERS

Prologue

There is an old legend concerning a Roman Emperor, who, to show his power, singled out the Tribune of a loyal legion and commanded that he march his men across Asia to the end of the world. And so a thousand men vanished into the hinterland of the largest continent, to be swallowed up forever. On some unknown battlefield the last handful of survivors must have formed a square which was overwhelmed by a barbarian charge. And their eagle may have stood lonely and tarnished in a horsehide tent for a generation thereafter. But it may be guessed, by those who know of the pride of these men in their corps and tradition, that they did march east as long as one still remained on his feet.

In 8054 A.D. history repeated itself—as it always does. The First Galactic Empire was breaking up. Dictators, Emperors, Consolidators wrested the rulership of their own or kindred solar systems from Central Control. Space pirates raised flags and recruited fleets to gorge on spoil plundered from this wreckage. It was a time in which only the ruthless could flourish.

Here and there a man, or a group of men, tried vainly to dam the flood of disaster and disunion. And, notable among these last-ditch fighters who refused to throw aside their belief in the impartial rule of Central Control were the remnants of the Stellar Patrol, a law enforcement body whose authority had existed unchallenged for almost a thousand years. Perhaps it was because there was no longer any security to be found outside their own ranks that these men clung the closer to what seemed in the new age to be an outworn code of ethics and morals. And their stubborn loyalty to a vanished ideal was both exasperating and pitiful to the new rulers.

Jorcam Dester, the last Control Agent of Perun, who was nursing certain ambitions of his own, solved in the Roman manner the problem of ridding his sector of the Patrol. He summoned the half dozen officers still commanding navigable ships and ordered them—under the seal of the Control—out into space, to locate (as he said) and re-map forgotten galactic border systems no one had visited in at least four generations. He offered a vague promise to establish new bases from which the Patrol might rise again, invigorated and revived, to fight for the Control ideals. And, faithful to their very ancient trust, they launched this mission, undermanned, poorly supplied, without real hope, but determined to carry out orders to the last.

One of these ships was the Scout—*Starfire*.

1

Last Port

The Patrol ship *Starfire* came into her last port at early morning. She made a bad landing, for two of her eroded tubes blew just as the pilot tried to set her down. She had bounced then, bounced and buckled, and now she lay on her meteor-scarred side.

Ranger Sergeant Kartr nursed his left wrist in his right hand and licked blood from bitten lips. The port wall of the pilot's cubby had become the floor and the latch of its door dug into one of his shaking knees.

Of his companions, Latimir had not survived the landing. One glance at the crazy twisted angle of the astrogator's black head told Kartr that. And Mirion, the pilot, hung limply in the torn shock webs before the control board. Blood rilled down his cheeks and dripped from his chin. Did dead men continue to bleed? Kartr didn't think so.

He drew a slow, experimental breath of his own and

knew relief when it was not followed by a stab of pain. Ribs were still intact then, in spite of the slam which had smashed him into his present position. He grinned mirthlessly as he stretched arms and legs with the same caution. Sometimes it paid to be a tough, uncivilized frontier barbarian.

The lights flickered and went off. It was then that Kartr almost panicked, in spite of his carefully nurtured veteran's calm. He grabbed at the door latch and pulled. Sharp stabs of agony shot from his injured wrist and jerked him back to sanity. He wasn't sealed in, the door *had* moved an inch or so. He could get out.

Must get out and find the medico to look at Mirion. The pilot should not be moved until they knew the extent of his injuries—

Then Kartr remembered. The medico wasn't around any more. Hadn't been with them since three—or was it four?—planets back. The ranger shook his aching head and frowned. That loss of memory was almost worse than the pain in his arm. He mustn't lose his grip!

Three planet landings back—that was it! When they had beaten off the Greenies' rush after the ship's nose blaster had gone dead on them, Medico Tork had gone down, a poison dart right through his throat.

Kartr shook his head again and began to work patiently, with one hand, at the door. It seemed a very long time before he was able to force it open far enough for a person to squeeze through. A blue beam suddenly shot up at him through the gap.

"Kartr! Latimir! Mirion!" The roll call followed the light.

Only one man on board carried a blue torch.

"Rolth!" Kartr identified him. Somehow it was encouraging that it should be one of his own squad of specialist-explorers waiting below. "Latimir got it, but Mirion is still living, I think. Can you come up? My wrist seems to be broken—"

He edged back to let the other squirm through. The thin blue spear of light swept across Latimir's body and centered on the pilot. Then the torch tube was thrust into Kartr's good hand as Rolth crawled over to untangle the webbing which held the unconscious man.

"How bad are we?" Kartr raised his voice to be heard over the moans now coming from the pilot.

"I do not know. Our ranger quarters came through all right, but the hatch to the drive section is jammed and when I beat on it there was no answer—"

Kartr tried to remember who had been on duty with the drive. They were so ruinously shorthanded that everyone was doing another's job. Even the rangers were pressed into the once jealously guarded Patrol duties. It had been that way ever since the Greenie attack.

"Kaatah—" A call more hiss than word came from the passage.

"Okay." The sergeant responded almost automatically. "Got a real light, Zinga? Rolth's up here, but you know how far his two-for-a-credit shiner goes—"

"Fylh is hunting out one of the big spots," the newcomer answered. "You have trouble?"

"Latimir is dead. Mirion's still breathing—but there's no telling how bad he is hurt. Rolth says that the drive room gang didn't answer at all. You all right?"

"Yes. Fylh and I and Smitt of the crew. We were bumped a little but nothing serious. Hah—"

A yellow-red beam of some brilliance silhouetted the speaker.

"Fylh brings a battle torch—"

Zinga climbed up and went to work with Rolth. They had Mirion free and flat on the plating before Kartr asked his next question.

"How about the Captain?"

Zinga turned his head slowly, almost as if he were unwilling to answer that. His agitation, as usual, was betrayed by the quiver in the pointed neck frill of skin, which would not lie flat on his shoulders when he was worried or excited.

"Smitt has gone to seek him. We do not know—"

"One spot of luck in the whole knock out." That was Rolth, his voice as usual unemotional. "This is an Arth type planet. Since we aren't going to lift off it again in a hurry we'd better thank the Spirit of Space for that!"

An Arth type planet—one on which the crew of this particular ship could breathe without helmets, walk without discomfort of alien gravity, probably eat and drink natural products without fear of sudden death. Kartr eased his wrist across his knee. That *was* pure luck. The *Starfire* might have blown anywhere within the past three months—she had been held together only with wire and hope. But to blow on an Arth type world was better fortune for her survivors than they would have dared pray for after the black disappointments of the past few years, years of too many missions and no refittings.

"It hasn't been burnt off either," he observed almost absently.

"Why should it have been?" inquired Fylh, his voice tinged with almost cheerful mockery—but mockery which also had a bite in it. "This system is far off our maps—very far removed from all the benefits of our civilization!"

The benefits of Central Control civilization, yes. Kartr blinked as that struck home. His own planet, Ylene, had been burnt off five years ago—during the Two-Sector Rebellion. And yet he sometimes still dreamed of taking the mail packet back, of wearing his ranger uniform, proud with the Five Sector Bars and the Far Roving Star, of going up into the forest country—to a little village by the north sea. Burnt off—! He had never been able to visualize boiled rock where that village had stood—or the dead cinder which was the present Ylene—a horrible monument to planetary war.

Zinga worked on his wrist and put it in a sling. Kartr was able to help himself as they angled Mirion through the door. By the time they had the pilot resting in the lounge the Patrolman, Smitt, came in, towing a figure so masked in head bandages as to be unrecognizable.

"Commander Vibor?" Kartr hazarded. He was on his feet, his shoulders squared, his heels brought smartly together so that the vlis hide of his boots rasped faintly.

The bandaged head swung toward him.

"Ranger Kartr?"

"Yes, sir!"

"Who else—?" The voice began with customary briskness but then it trailed off into a disconcerting silence.

Kartr frowned. The vlis skin gave off another whisper as he shifted his feet.

"Of the Patrol—Latimir is dead, sir. We have Mirion here—hurt. And Smitt is okay. The Rangers Fylh, Rolth, Zinga, and myself are all right. Rolth reports that the drive room hatch is jammed and that no one replied when he pounded on it. We will investigate that now, sir. Also the crew's quarters."

"Yes—yes— Carry on, Ranger."

Smitt jumped just in time to catch and ease that lank, limp body to the floor. Commander Vibor was in no shape to resume command.

Kartr knew again a touch of that panic which had gripped him when the lights had failed. Commander

Vibor—the man they had come to believe was a rock
of certainty and security in their chaotic world— He
sucked in the tainted air of the too old ship and
accepted the situation.

"Smitt." He turned first to the Patrol com-techneer,
who by all the rigid rules of the service certainly
outranked a mere ranger sergeant. "Can you take over
with the Commander and Mirion?"

Smitt did have some medico training, he had acted
as Tork's assistant once or twice.

"Right." The shorter man did not even look up as
he bent over the moaning pilot. "Go along and check
the rest of the wreckage, fly-boy—"

Fly-boy, eh? Well, the high and mighty senior service of the Patrol should be glad that the fly-boys
were with them during this tour of duty. Rangers were
trained to calculate and use the products of any
strange world. After a crack up they would certainly
be more at home in an alien wilderness than Patrol-
crewmen.

Holding his injured arm tightly to his chest Kartr
made his way back along the corridor, followed by the
begoggled Rolth, his eyes shaded against what was to
him the violent fire cast by the ordinary beam torch
the sergeant clutched in his good hand. Zinga and Fylh
brought up the rear, having armed themselves, as Kartr
noted, with a portable flamer to cut through jammed
bulkheads.

Even with that it took them a good ten minutes to
break the hatch of the drive room. And in spite of the
clamor they made during the process there came no
answer from within. Kartr steeled himself inwardly and
pushed through first. He looked only once at what was
caught in the full shaft of his beam and then backed
out, sick and shaking. The others, seeing his face, asked
no questions.

As he leaned against the edge of the battered door fighting nausea they all heard the pounding from the tail section.

"Who—?"

Fylh answered. "Armory and supplies—that would be Jaksan, Cott, Snyn, Dalgre." He counted them off on the tips of his claw-boned fingers. "They must be—"

"Yes." Kartr was already leading the rescue party toward the sound.

Again they had to apply the white-hot energy of the flamer to buckled metal. And then they must wait until the metal had cooled before three battered and blood-streaked men came crawling through.

Jaksan—yes, Kartr would have wagered a year's pay credits that the tough, very tough, Patrol arms officer would survive. And Snyn and Dalgre.

Jaksan began to speak even before he got to his feet again.

"How is it?"

"Smitt's okay. The Commander has some head injuries. Mirion's bad. The rest—" Kartr's hands swept out in a gesture from his childhood—one of those strange barbarian exuberances he had been so careful to suppress during his service years.

"The ship—"

"I'm a ranger, no Patrol techneer. Maybe Smitt could tell you better about that. He's the nearest to an expert that we have left."

Jaksan's fingernails rasped in the stubble on his unshaven chin. There was a long rip in his right sleeve, an oozing scratch under it. He stared at the three rangers absently. Already he was probably cutting losses. If the *Starfire* could function again it would be because of his drive and determination.

"The planet?"

"Arth type. Mirion was trying to set down in what

looked like open country when the tubes blew. No traces of civilization noted before landing." This information was Kartr's own territory and he answered with confidence.

If the rangers' sleds hadn't been too badly banged up they could break one out soon and begin exploring. There was, of course, the fuel problem. There might be enough in sled tanks for one trip—with a very even chance that the scouting party would walk home. Unless the *Starfire* was definitely done for and they could tap her supply— But that could all be gone into later. At least they could take a look now at their immediate surroundings.

"We'll sortie." Kartr's voice was crisp and assured and asked no permission from Jaksan—or any crewman. "Smitt is with the Commander and Mirion in the lounge—"

The Patrol officer nodded. This return to routine was correct, right. It seemed to steady them all, Kartr observed, as he found his way into the ranger's own domain. Fylh was there before him, freeing their packs from the general jumble the crash had made of their supplies. Kartr shook his head.

"Not full packs. We won't go more than a quarter mile. And, Rolth," he added over his shoulder to the begoggled Faltharian in the doorway, "you stay here. Arth sun is bad for your eyes. Your turn will come after nightfall."

Rolth nodded and went toward the lounge. Kartr picked up an explorer's belt with one hand but Zinga took it from him.

"This I do. Stand still." The other's scaled digits buckled and snapped the vlis hide band and its dangling accouterments about the sergeant's flat waist. He gave a wriggle to settle the weight in the familiar balance. No need to pick up a disrupter—he couldn't fire it with one hand. The short blaster would have to serve as his sole weapon.

Luckily they had not landed air-lock side down. To burn and burrow their way out was a job none of them would have cared for just then. But they only had to hammer loose the hatch and climb through, Kartr being boosted by his companions. Then they slid down the dull and scored metal to the still smoking ground, ran across that to the clean earth beyond the range of the blast. Once there they halted and wheeled to look back at the ship.

"Bad—" Fylh's chirp put all their dismay into words. "She will not lift from here again."

Well, Kartr was no mech-techneer, but he would endorse that. The wrenched and broken-backed ship before them would certainly never ride the space lanes again, even if they could get her to a refitting dock. And the nearest of those was, Space knew, how many suns away!

"Why should we worry about that?" asked Zinga mildly. "Since we first set out on this voyage we guessed that there would be for us no return—"

Yes, they had feared that, deep in their hearts, in the backs of their minds, with that flutter of terror and loneliness which plucked at a man's nerves as he rode between system and stars. But none of them had before admitted it openly to another. None—unless—

Maybe the humans had not admitted it, but the Bemmys might have. Loneliness had long since become a part of their lives—they were so often the only individuals of their respective species aboard a ship. If Kartr felt alien in Patrol crews because he was not only a specialized ranger but also a barbarian from a frontier system, what must Fylh or Zinga feel—they who could not even claim the kinship of a common species?

Kartr turned away from the broken ship to study

the sandy waste studded with rock outcrops. It must be close to midday and the sun beat down heavily upon them. Under this wave of heat Zinga thrived. His frill spread wide—making a fan behind his hairless head, pulsing a darker red with every passing moment, his slender tongue flickered in and out between his yellow lips. But Fylh moved to the protection of the shadow by the rocks.

This was desert land. Kartr's nostrils expanded, taking in and classifying strange scents. No life except—

His head snapped to the left. Life! But Zinga was before him, his big four-toed feet running lightly over sand, the thin webs between the toes keeping the reptilian ranger from sinking into the stuff through which the others slipped and slid. When Kartr joined him the tall Zacathan was squatting beside a rock on which curled a whiplash of scaled body. A narrow head swung up, a tongue flickered in and out.

Kartr stopped and tried mind touch. Yes, this was native life. Alien, of course. A mammal he might have made contact with. But this was reptile. Zinga might not have the same mind touch power that the sergeant possessed but this creature was distantly of his own kind—could he make friends? Kartr fought to catch and interpret those strange impressions which hovered just on the borderline of thought waves he could read. The creature had been alarmed at their coming, but now it was interested in Zinga. It had a high degree of self-confidence, a confidence which argued that it must have a natural weapon of potency.

"It has poison fangs—" Zinga answered that question for him. "And it does not like your scent. I think that you may suggest some natural enemy. But me it does not mind. It cannot tell us much—it is not a thinker—"

The Zacathan touched a horny fingertip to the creature's head. It permitted this liberty warily. And when Zinga rose to his feet its head lifted also, swinging higher above the coils of its body as if to watch him the better.

"It will be of little use to us, and to your kind it may be deadly. I shall send it away." Zinga stared down at the coiled creature. Its head began to sway in a short arc. Then it hissed and was gone, slipping into a crack between the rocks.

"Come here, leaden feet!" Fylh's voice drifted down from the sky.

The Trystian's feather-crested head with its large round eyes, unlidded, looked down from the tallest of the rock peaks. Kartr sighed. That climb might be nothing at all for the birdman with his light bones, but *he* certainly dreaded to try it—with only one hand in working order.

"What do you see?" he asked.

"There are growing things—over there—" The golden arms above his head swung eastward, the large thumb-claw out in added emphasis.

Zinga was already scuttling up the side of the sun-baked rock.

"How far?" Kartr demanded.

Fylh squinted and considered. "Perhaps two fals—"

"Space measure, please," Kartr pleaded patiently. In his aching head he simply could not translate the measures of Fylh's home planet into human terms.

Zinga answered. "Maybe a good mile. The growing things are green—"

"Green?" Well, that wasn't too strange. Yellow-green, and blue-green, and dull purple, red, yellow, even sickly white—he had seen all kinds and colors of vegetation since he had put on the comet insignia.

"But this is a different green—" The Zacathan's words floated down slowly, as if Zinga was now puzzled by the evidence before his eyes.

And Kartr knew that he must see too. As a ranger-explorer he had walked the soil of countless planets in myriad systems—nowadays he found it hard to reckon how many. There were some easy to remember, of course, because of their horror or their strange inhabitants. But the rest were only a maze of color and odd life in his mind. He had to refer to old reports and the ship's log to recall facts. The thrill he had once known, when he pushed for the first time through alien vegetation, or tried to catch the mind waves of things he could not see, had long since gone. But now, as he scrabbled for a hand hold and dug the toes of his boots into hollows in the gritty rock, he began to recapture a faint trace of that forgotten emotion.

Claw fingers and scaled digits reached down to hook in his shoulder harness and belt and heave him up to the narrow top of the spur. He flinched from the heat of the stone and shielded his eyes against the glare with his cupped hands.

What Fylh had discovered was easy to see. And that prick of excitement stirred again far inside him. For that ribbon of vegetation *was* green! But the green! It had no yellow tint, and none of the blue cast it would have held on his own vanished Ylene. It was a verdant green such as he had never set eyes upon before—running in a thin line across the desert country as if it followed some source of moisture. He blinked to clear his sight and then, knowing that his natural powers at that range were far inferior to Fylh's, he unhooked his visibility lenses. It was hard work to adjust them with only one hand but at last he was able to turn them on that distant ribbon.

Trees, bushes, leaped at him across the baked rock. He might almost touch one of those leaves, trembling in the passing of some faint breeze. And under that same cluster of leaves he caught a fleck of dancing light. He had been right, that was flowing water.

Slowly he turned, the lenses at his eyes, Zinga's hands closing on his hips to steady him as he moved, following that green streak north. Miles ahead it widened, spread into a vast splotch of the restful color. They must have crashed close to the edge of the desert. And that river could guide them north to life. Fylh stirred beside him and Kartr tipped the lenses skyward, having caught in his mind that far-away shimmer of life force. Wide wings wheeled and dipped. He saw the cruel curve of a hunter's beak and strong talons as the sky creature sailed proudly over them.

"I like this world—" Zinga's hissing speech broke the silence. "And I think for us it will be right. Here are those of my blood—even if far distant—and there, in the sky, is one akin to you, Fylh. Do you not wish sometimes that your ancestors had not shed their wings along the path they trod to wisdom?"

Fylh shrugged. "What of the tails and fighting claws your people dropped behind, my brave Zinga? And Kartr's race once went with fur upon them—maybe tailed too—many animals are. One cannot have everything." But he continued to watch the bird until it was out of even his range of sight.

"We might try getting one of the sleds loose. There ought to be enough fuel left to take us as far as that patch of green in the north. Where there is grass there should be food—"

Kartr heard a faint snicker from Zinga. "Can it be that our Bemmy-and-animal lover has turned hunter?"

Could he kill—kill to eat? But the supplies were low in the ship—if any had survived the crash. Sooner or later they would have to live off the land. And meat—meat would be necessary for life. The sergeant forced himself to think of that in what he hoped was a sensible fashion. But still he was not sure that he could align the sights of a blaster and pull the trigger—for the purpose of meat!

No need to think of that until the time came. He hooked the lenses back on his belt.

"Back to report?" Fylh began to lower himself over the edge of the pinnacle.

"Back to report," agreed Kartr soberly.

2

Green Hills

"—a stream bed with vegetation and indication of better land to the north. Request permission to break out one of the sleds and explore in that direction."

It was disconcerting to report to a blank mask of bandages, surprisingly difficult, Kartr found. He stood at attention, waiting for the Commander's response.

"And the ship?"

Sergeant Kartr might have shrugged, had etiquette permitted. Instead he answered with some caution.

"I'm no techneer, sir. But she looks done for."

There it was—straight enough. Again he wished he could see the expression on the face under that roll upon roll of white plasta-skin. The quiet in the lounge was broken only by the breath, whistling and labored, moving in and out of Mirion's torn lips. The pilot was still unconscious. Kartr's wrist ached viciously and, after the clean air outside, the smog in the ship seemed almost too thick to stomach.

"Permission granted. Return in ten hours—" But that answer sounded mechanical, as if Vibor were now only a recording machine repeating sounds set on the wire long ago. That was the correct official order to be given when the ship planeted and he gave it as he had so many countless times before.

Kartr saluted and detoured around Mirion to the door. He hoped that there was a sled ready to fly. Otherwise, they'd foot it as far as they could.

Zinga hovered outside, his pack on his shoulders, Kartr's dangling from one arm.

"The port sled is free. We've fueled it with cubes from the ship's supply—"

They had no right to do that ordinarily. But now it was sheer folly not to raid the stores when the *Starfire* would never use them again. Kartr crawled over the battered hatch to the now open berth of the sled. Fylh was already impatiently seated behind the windbreak, testing the controls.

"She'll fly?"

Fylh's head, the crest flat against the skull like some odd, stiff mane of hair, swiveled and his big reddish eyes met the sergeant's. The cynical mockery with which the Trystian met life was clear in his reply.

"We will hope so. There is, of course, a fair chance that within seconds after I set us off we will only be dust drifting through the air. Strap down, dear friends, strap down!"

Kartr folded his long legs under him beside Zinga, and the Zacathan fastened the small shock web across them both. Fylh's claws touched a button. The craft swept sidewise out of the hull of the *Starfire*, slowly, delicately until they were well away from the ship, then it arose swiftly with Fylh's usual disregard for the niceties of speed adjustment. Kartr merely swallowed and endured.

"To the river and then along it, hover twenty feet up—"

Not that Fylh needed any such order. This was the sort of thing they had done before. Kartr edged forward an inch or two to the spy-port on the right. Zinga was already at the similar post on the left.

It seemed only seconds before they were over water, looking down into the tangled mass of bright green which clothed its banks. Automatically Kartr classified and inventoried. It was not necessary this time to make detailed notes. Fylh had triggered the scanner and it should be recording as they flew. The motion of the sled sent air curving back against their sweating bodies. Kartr's nostrils caught scents—some old, some new. The life below was far down the scale of intelligence—reptile, bird, insect. He thought that this desert country supported little else. But they did have two bits of luck to cling to—that this was an Arth planet and that they had landed so close to the edge of the wasteland.

Zinga scratched his scaled cheek reflectively. He loved the heat, his frill spread to its greatest extent. And Kartr knew that the Zacathan would have much preferred to cross the burning sands on his own feet. He was radiating cheerful interest, almost, the sergeant thought a little resentfully, as if he were one of the sleek, foppish officers of a Control or Sector base being escorted on a carefully supervised sightseeing tour. But then Zinga always enjoyed living in the present, his long-yeared race had plenty of time to taste the best of everything.

The sled rode the air smoothly, purring gently. That last tune-up they had given her had done the trick after all. Even though they had had to work from instructions recorded on a ten-year-old repair manual tape. She had been given the last of the condensers. They had practically no spare parts left now—

"Zinga," Kartr demanded suddenly of his seat mate. "Were you ever in a real Control fitting and repair port?"

"No," replied the Zacathan cheerfully. "And I sometimes think that they are only stories invented for the amusement of the newly hatched. Since I was mustered into the service we have always done the best we could to make our own repairs—with what we could find or steal. Once we had a complete overhaul—it took us almost three months—we had two wrecked ships to strip for other parts. What a wealth of supplies! That was on Karbon, four—no, five space years ago. We still had a head mech-techneer in the crew then and he supervised the job. Fylh—what was his name?"

"Ratan. He was a robot from Perun. We lost him the next year in an acid lake on a blue star world. He was very good with engines—being one himself."

"What has been happening to Central Control—to us?" asked Kartr slowly. "Why don't we have proper equipment—supplies—new recruits?"

"Breakdown," replied Fylh crisply. "Maybe Central Control is too big, covers too many worlds, spreads its authority too thin and too far. Or perhaps it is too old so that it loses hold. Look at the sector wars, the pull for power between sector chiefs. Don't you think that Central Control would stop that—if it could?"

"But the Patrol—"

Fylh trilled laughter. "Ah, yes, the Patrol. We are the stubborn survivals, the wrongheaded ones. We maintain that we, the Stellar Patrol, crewmen and rangers, still keep the peace and uphold galactic law. We fly here and there in ships which fall to pieces under us because there are no longer those with the knowledge and skill to repair them properly. We fight pirates and search forgotten skies—for what, I wonder? We obey commands given to us over the signature of the two Cs. We are fast becoming an anachronism, antiques still alive but better dead. And one by one we vanish from space. We should all be rounded up and set in some museum for the planet-bound to gawk at, objects with no reasonable function—"

"What will happen to Central Control?" Kartr wondered and set his teeth as a lurch of the sled stabbed his arm against Zinga's tough ribs and jarred his wrist.

"The galactic empire—this galactic empire," pronounced the Zacathan with a grin which told of his total disinterest in the matter, "is falling apart. Within five years we've lost touch with as many sectors, haven't we? C.C. is just a name now as far as its power runs. In another generation it may not even be remembered. We've had a long run—about three thousand years—and the seams are beginning to gap. Sector wars now—the result—chaos. We'll slip back fast—probably far back, maybe even into planet-tied barbarianism with space flight forgotten. Then we'll start all over again—"

"Maybe," was Fylh's pessimistic reply. "But you and I, dear friend, will not be around to witness that new dawn—"

Zinga nodded agreement. "Not that our absence will matter. We have found us a world to make the best of right here and now. How far off civilized maps are we?" he asked the sergeant.

They had flashed maps on the viewing screen in the ship, maps noted on tapes so old that the dates on them seemed wildly preposterous, maps of suns and stars no voyager had visited in two, three, five generations, where Control had had no contact for half a thousand years. Kartr had studied those maps for weeks. And on none of them had he seen this system. They were too far out—too near the frontier of the galaxy. The map tape which had carried the record of this world—provided there had ever been one at all—must have rusted away past using, forgotten in some pigeonhole of Control archives generations ago.

"Completely." He took a sort of sour pleasure in that answer.

"Completely off and completely out," Zinga commented brightly. "Clear start for all of us. Fylh—this river—it's getting a bit bigger, isn't it?"

The expanse of water below them was widening out. For some time now they had been coasting above greenery—first over shrubs and patches of short vegetation, and then clumps of quite fair-sized trees which gathered and bunched into woodland. Animal life there—Kartr's mind snapped alert to the job on hand as the sled rose, climbing to follow the line of rise in the land beneath them.

There were strong scents carried now by the wind they breasted, good scents—earth and growing things—the tang of water. They still hovered over the stream bed and, below, the current was stronger, beating around and over rocks. Then the river curved around a point thick with trees and before them, perhaps half a mile away, was a falls, a spray veil splashing over the rocky lip of a plateau.

Fylh's claws played over the controls. The sled lost speed and altitude. He maneuvered it toward a scrap of sand which ran in a tongue from the rock and tree-lined shore. They dropped lightly, a perfect landing. Zinga leaned forward and clapped him on the shoulder.

"Consider yourself commended, Ranger. A beautiful landing—simply beautiful—" His voice cracked as he tried without much success to reach the high note which might be sounded by a gushing female tourist.

Kartr scrambled awkwardly out of the seat and stood, feet braced a little apart in the sand. The water purled and rippled toward him over green-covered rocks. He was aware of small life flickers, water creatures about their business below its surface. He dropped to his knees and thrust his hand into the cool wet. It lapped about his wrist, moistened the edge of his tunic sleeve. And it was chill enough and clear enough to offer temptation he could not resist.

"Going for a splash?" asked Zinga. "I am."

Kartr fumbled for the fastenings of his belt and slipped his arm carefully out of its sling. Fylh sat crosslegged in the sand and watched them both, disapproval plain on his thin delicate face as they pulled off harness and uniforms. Fylh had never willingly entered water and he never would.

The sergeant could not stifle an exclamation of pleasure as the water closed about him, rising from ankle to knee, to waist, as he waded out, feeling cautiously with exploring toes. Zinga kicked up waves, pushing on boldly until his feet were off bottom and he tried his strength against the deeper currents of midstream. Kartr longed for two good hands and to be able to join the Zacathan. The best he could do was duck and let the drops roll down him, washing away the mustiness of the ship, the taint of the too long voyage.

"If you are now finished with this newly hatched nonsense"—that was Fylh—"may I remind you that we are supposed to be doing a job?"

Kartr was almost tempted to deny that. He wanted to stay where he was. But the bonds of discipline brought him back to the sand spit where, with the Trystian's help, he pulled on the clothes he had taken a dislike to. Zinga had swum upstream and Kartr looked up just in time to see the yellow-gray body of the Zacathan leap through the mist below the falls. He sent a thought summons flying.

But then there was a flash of brilliant color, as a bird soared overheard, to distract him. Fylh stood with hands outstretched, a clear whistle swelling out of his throat. The bird changed course and wheeled about the two of them. Then it fluttered down to perch on the Trystian's great thumb claw, answering his trill with liquid notes of its own. Its blue feathers had an almost metallic sheen. For a long time it answered Fylh, and then it took wing again—out over the water. The Trystian's crest was raised proud and high. Kartr drew a full deep breath.

"That one is beautiful!" He paid tribute.

Fylh nodded, but there was a hint of sadness about his thin lips as he answered, "It did not really understand me."

Zinga dripped out of the water, hissing to himself as if he were about to go into battle. He transferred some object he had been holding in one hand to his mouth, chewed with an expression of rapture, and swallowed.

"The water creatures are excellent," he observed. "Best I've tasted since Vassor City when we had that broiled Katyer dinner! Pity they're so small."

"I only hope that your immunity shots are still working," Kartr returned scathingly. "If you—"

"Go all purple and die it will only be my own fault?" The Zacathan finished for him. "I agree. But fresh food is sometimes worth dying for. Formula 1A60 is *not* my idea of a proper meal. Well, and now where do we wend our way?"

Kartr studied the plateau from which the river fell. The thick green above looked promising. They dared not venture too far into the unknown with such a small fuel supply and the return journey to plan for. Maybe a flight to the top of that cliff would provide them with a vantage point from which to examine the country beyond. He suggested that.

"Up it is." Fylh got back in the sled. "But not more than a half mile—unless you are longing to walk back!"

This time Kartr felt the slight sluggishness of their break away, he strained forward in his seat as if by will power alone he could raise the sled out of the sand and up to the crest of the rock barrier. He knew that Fylh would be able to nurse the last gasp of energy from the machine, but he had no longing to foot it back to the *Starfire*.

At the top of the cliff there seemed to be no landing place for them. The trees grew close to the stream edge, thick enough to make a solid carpet of green. But a quarter of a mile from the falls they came upon an island—it was really a miniature mesa, smoothed off almost level—around which the stream cut some twenty feet below. Fylh set the sled down with not more than four feet on either side separating them from the edge. The stone was hot, sun baked, and Kartr stood up in the sled, unslinging visibility lenses.

On either side of the river the trees and brush grew in an almost impassable wall. But northward he sighted hills, green and rolling, and the river crossed a plain. He was restoring the lenses to their holder when he sensed alien life.

Down at the edge of the stream a brown-furred animal had emerged from the woods. It squatted by the water to lap and then dabbled its front paws in the current. There was a flicker of silver spinning in the air and the jaws of the beast snapped on the water creature it had flipped out of the river.

"Splendid!" Zinga paid tribute to the feat. "I

couldn't have done any better myself! Not a wasted motion—"

Delicately Kartr probed the mind behind that furry skull. There was intelligence of a sort and he thought that he might appeal to it if he wished. But the animal did not know man or anything like man. Was this planet a wilderness with no superior life form?

He asked that aloud and Fylh answered him.

"Did that bump you received when we landed entirely addle your thinking process? A slice of wilderness may be found on many planets. And because this creature below does not know of any superior to itself does not certify that such do not exist elsewhere—"

Zinga had propped his head on his two hands and was staring out toward the distant plain and hills.

"Green hills," he muttered. "Green hills and water full of very excellent food. The Spirit of Space is smiling on us this once. Do you wish to ask questions of our fishing friend below?"

"No. And it is not alone. Something grazes behind that clump of pointed trees and there are other lives. They fear each other—they live by claw and fang—"

"Primitive," catalogued Fylh, and then conceded generously, "Perhaps you are right, Kartr. Perhaps there is no human or Bemmy overlord in this world."

"I trust not," Zinga raised both his first and second eyelids to their fullest extent. "I long to pit my wits—daring adventurer style—against some fiendish, intelligent monster—"

Kartr grinned. For some reason he had always found the reptile-ancestored brain of the Zacathan more closely akin to his own thinking processes than he ever did Fylh's cool detachment. Zinga entered into life with zest, while the Trystian was, in spite of physical participation, always the onlooker.

"Maybe we can locate some settlement of your

fiendish monsters among those hills," he suggested.
"What about it, Fylh, dare we try to reach them?"

"No." Fylh was measuring with a claw tip the gage
on the control panel. "We've enough to get us back
to the ship from here and that is all."

"If we all hold our breath and push," murmured the
Zacathan. "All right. And if we have to set down, we'll
walk. There is nothing better than to feel good hot sand
ooze up between one's toes—" He sighed languorously.

The sled arose, startling the brown-coated fisherman.
It sat on its haunches, one dripping paw raised, to watch
them go. Kartr caught its mild astonishment—but it had
no fear of them. It had few enemies and did not expect
those to fly through the air. As they swung around Kartr
tried an experiment and sent a darting flash of good
will into that primitive brain. He looked back. The
animal had risen to its hind legs and stood, man fashion,
its front paws dangling loosely, staring after the sled.

They passed over the falls so low that the spray
beaded their skins. Kartr caught his lower lip between
his teeth and bit down on it. Was that only Fylh's flying
or did power failure drive them down? He had no
desire to ask that question openly.

"To follow the river back," Zinga pointed out, "is to
take the long way round. If we cut across country from
that peak we ought to hit the ship—"

Kartr saw and nodded. "How about it, Fylh? Stick
to the water or not?"

The Trystian hunched his shoulders in his equivalent of a shrug. "Quicker, yes." And he pointed the
sled's bow to the right.

They left the stream thread. A carpet of trees lay
beneath them and then a scrubby clearing in which a
group of five red-brown animals grazed. One tossed
its head skyward and Kartr saw the sun glint on long
cruel horns.

"I wonder," mused Zinga, "if they ever do any disputing with our river-bank friend. He had some pretty formidable claws—and those horns are not just for adornment. Or maybe they have some kind of treaty of nonaggression—"

"Then," observed Fylh, "they would be locked in deadly combat most of the time!"

"You know"—Zinga stared at the back of Fylh's crested head fondly—"you're a very useful Bemmy, my friend. With you along we never have to wear ourselves out expecting the worst—you have it all figured out for us. What would we ever do without your dark, dark eyes fixed upon the future?"

The trees and shrubs below were growing fewer. Rock and sections of baked, creviced earth and the queer, twisted plants which seemed native to the desert appeared in larger and larger patches.

"Wait!" Kartr's hand shot out to touch Fylh's arm. "To the right—there!"

The sled obediently swooped and came down on a patch of level earth. Kartr scrambled out, brushed through the fringe of stunted bush to come out upon the edge of what he had sighted from the air. The other two joined him.

Zinga dropped upon one knee and touched the white section almost gingerly. "Not natural," he gave his verdict.

Sand and earth had drifted and buried it. Only here had some freak of the scouring wind cleared that patch to betray it. Pavement—an artificial pavement!

Zinga went to the right, Fylh left, for perhaps forty feet. They squatted and, using their belt knives, dug into the soil. Within seconds each had uncovered a hard surface.

"A road!" Kartr kicked more sand away. "Surface transportation here at one time then. How long ago do you guess?"

Fylh shifted the loosened soil through his claws. "Here is heat and dryness, and, I think, not too many storms. Also the vegetation does spread as it would in jungle country. It may be ten years—ten hundred or—"

"Ten thousand!" Kartr ended for him. But the spark of excitement within him was being fanned into more vigorous life. So there *had* been superior life here! Man—or something—had built a road on which to travel. And roads usually led to—

The sergeant turned to Fylh. "Do you think we could pry enough fuel out of the main drive to bring the sled back here with the tailer mounted?"

Fylh considered. "We might—if we didn't need fuel for anything else."

Kartr's excitement faded. They would need it for other work. The Commander and Mirion would have to be transported on it when they left the ship—supplies carried—all that they would require to set up a camp in the more hospitable hill country. He kicked regretfully at the patch of pavement. Once it would have been his duty as well as his pleasure to follow that thin clue to its source. Now it was his duty to forget it. He walked heavily back to the sled and none of them spoke as they were again airborne.

3

Mutiny

They circled the crumpled length of the *Starfire* and saw
a figure waving from a point near her nose. When they
landed the sled Jaksan was waiting.

"Well?" he demanded harshly, almost before the sand
had fallen away from the keel of the sled.

"There's good, open, well-watered land to the north,"
Kartr reported. "Animal life in a wilderness—"

"Eatable water creatures!" Zinga broke in, licking his
lips at the memory.

"Any indications of civilization?"

"An old road, buried—nothing else. The animals know
no superior life form. We had the recorder on—I can
run the wire through for the Commander—"

"If he wants it—"

"What do you mean!" The tone in Jaksan's voice
brought Kartr up short, the reel of spy wire clutched
in his good hand.

"Commander Vibor," Jaksan's answer came cold and hard, "believes it our duty to remain with the ship—"

"But why?" asked the sergeant in honest bewilderment.

Nothing was ever going to raise the *Starfire* again. It was folly not to realize that at once and make plans on that basis. Kartr did now what he seldom dared to attempt, tried to read the surface mind of the arms officer. There was worry there, worry and something else—a surprising, puzzling resentment when Jaksan thought of him, Kartr, or of any of the rangers. Why? Did it stem back to the fact that the ranger sergeant was not a child of the Service, had not been reared of a Patrol family in the tight grip of tradition and duty, as had the other human members of the crew? Was it because he was termed a Bemmy lover and alien? He accepted that resentment as a fact, pigeonholed the memory of it to recall when he had to work with Jaksan in the future.

"Why?" The arms officer repeated Kartr's question. "A commander has responsibilities—even a ranger should realize that. Responsibilities—"

"Which doom him to starve to death in a broken ship?" cut in Zinga. "Come now, Jaksan. Commander Vibor is an intelligent life form—"

Kartr's fingers moved in the old warning signal. The Zacathan caught it and fell silent while the sergeant cut in quickly on the heels of the other's last word.

"He will undoubtedly wish to see the record tape before making any plans anyway."

"The Commander is blind!"

Kartr stopped short. "You are sure?"

"Smitt is. Tork might have been able to help him. We don't have the skill—the wounds go beyond the help of the medic-first-aid."

"Well, I'll report." Kartr started toward the ship,

feeling as if he carried several pounds of lead in the sole of each boot and some vast and undefinable burden had settled down upon his shoulders.

Why, he asked himself dispiritedly as he climbed through the lock of the port, did he have this depression? Certainly leadership now in no way fell upon him. Both Jaksan and Smitt outranked a sergeant—as a warrant officer of rangers he was just barely within the borderline of the Service as it was. But even knowing that did nothing to free him from this unease.

"Kartr reporting, sir!" He came to attention before the masked man propped up against two bedrolls in the lounge.

"Your report—" The request was mechanical. Kartr began to wonder if the other really heard him, or, hearing, understood a word he said.

"We have crashed near the edge of a desert. By sled the scouting party traveled north along a river to a well-watered, forested tract. Because of the limited supply of fuel our cruising range was curtailed. But there is a section to the north which looks promising as a base for a camp—"

"Life indications?"

"Many animals of different types and breeds—on a low scale of intelligence. Only trace of civilization is a portion of roadway so covered as to argue long disuse. Animals have no memory of contact with superior life forms."

"Dismissed."

But Kartr did not go. "Pardon, sir, but have I your permission to break out what is left of the main drive energy supply to use when we arrange for transportation—"

"The ship's supply? Are you completely mad? Certainly not! Report to Jaksan for repair party duty—"

Repair party? Did Vibor honestly believe that there

was the slightest chance of repairing the *Starfire*? Surely— The ranger hesitated at the door of the lounge and half turned to go back. But, guessing the uselessness of any further appeal made to Vibor, he went on to the rangers' quarters where he found the others gathered. A smaller figure just within the doorway turned out to be Smitt, who got up to face Kartr as he came in.

"Any luck, Kartr?"

"He told me to report for repair party duty. Great Winds of Space, what does he mean?"

"You may not believe it," answered the com-techneer, "but he means just what he says. We are supposed to be repairing this hulk for a take-off—"

"But can't he see—?" began Kartr and then bit his lip, remembering. That was just it—the Commander could not see the present condition of the wrecked ship. But that was no excuse for Jaksan or Smitt not making it plain to him—

As if he was able to pick that thought out of the air the com-techneer answered:

"He won't listen to us. I was ordered to my quarters when I tried to tell him. And Jaksan's only agreed with every order he's issued!"

"But why would he do that? Jaksan's no fool, he knows that we aren't going to lift again. The *Starfire's* done for."

Smitt leaned back against the wall. He was a small man, thin and tough and almost black with space tan. And now he appeared to share a portion of Fylh's almost malicious detachment. The only things he had ever really loved were his communicators. Kartr had seen him once furtively stroking the smooth plastic of their sides with a loving hand. Because of the old division of the ship's personnel—Patrol crew and rangers—Kartr did not know him very well.

"You can easily accept the idea that we're through," the com-techneer was saying now. "You've never been tied to this hunk of metal the way we are. Your duty is on planets—not in space. The *Starfire* is a part of Vibor—he can't just walk into the wide blue now and forget all about her— Neither can Jaksan."

"All right. I can believe that the ship might mean more to you, her regular crew, than she does to us," agreed Kartr almost wearily. "But she's a dead ship now and nothing any of us or all of us can do will make her ready to lift again. We'd best leave her—try to establish a base somewhere near food and water—"

"Cut clean from the past and begin again? Maybe. I can agree with you—intellectually. Only in suggesting that you'll come up against emotions, too, my young friends. And you'll find that another matter altogether!"

"And why," asked Kartr slowly, "is it up to *me* to deal with anything?"

"Process of elimination elects you. If we're grounded past hope of escape, who is the best able to understand our problems—someone who has spent his life in space almost since childhood—or a ranger? What *are* you going to do?"

But Kartr refused to answer that. The longer Smitt needled him in that fashion the more uneasy he became. He had never been treated with such frankness by a crew officer.

"The Commander will decide," he began.

Then Smitt laughed, a short harsh sound which lacked any thread of mirth. "So you're afraid to face up to it, fly-boy? I thought you rangers could never be rattled— that the fearless, untamed explorers would—"

Kartr's good hand closed on the tunic folds just below Smitt's throat.

"What kind of trouble are you trying to start, Smitt?" he asked, omitting the respect due an officer.

But the com-techneer made no move to strike away the sergeant's hand or twist free from the hold. Instead his eyes lifted to meet Kartr's steadily, soberly. Kartr's fingers loosened and his hand dropped. Smitt believed in what he was trying to say, believed in it very much even though he had been jeering. Smitt had come to him for help. Now for the first time Kartr was glad he possessed that strange gift of his—to sense the emotions of his fellows.

"Let's have it," he said and sat down on a bedroll. He was aware that the tension which had held them all for a second or two was relaxing. And he knew that the rangers would follow his lead—they would wait for his decision.

"Vibor is no longer with us—he's—he's cracked." Smitt fumbled for words. And Kartr read in him a rising fear and desolation.

"Is it because of his loss of sight? If that is so, the condition may be only temporary. When he becomes resigned to that—"

"No. He has been heading for a breakdown for a long time. The responsibility of command under present conditions—that fight with the Greenies—he was good friends with Tork, remember? The ship falling to pieces bit by bit and no chance for repairs— It's added up to drive him under. Now he's just refusing to accept a present he doesn't dare believe in. He's retired into a world of his own where things go right instead of wrong. And he wants us in there with him."

Kartr nodded. There was the ring of truth in every word Smitt said. Of course, he himself had never had much personal contact with Vibor. The rangers were not admitted to the inner circle of the Patrol—they were only tolerated. He was not a graduate of a sector academy, or even a product of the ranks. His father had not been Patrol before him. So he had always been aloof from the crew. The discipline of the Service, always strict, had been tightening more and more into a rigid caste system, even during the few years he had worn the Comet—perhaps because the Service itself had been cut off from the regular life of the average citizens. But Kartr could at this moment understand the odd incidents of the past months, certain inconsistencies in Vibor's orders—one or two remarks he had overheard.

"You think that there is no chance of his recovering?"

"No. The crash pushed him over the edge. The orders he's given during the past hour or so—I tell you—he's finished!"

"All right." Rolth's low voice cut through the thick air. "Then what do we do—or rather, what do *you* want us to do, Smitt?"

The com-techneer's hands spread out in a gesture of hopelessness.

"I don't really know. Only we're down—permanently—on an unknown world. Exploration—that's your department. And somebody's got to take the lead in getting us out of here. Jaksan—well, he might follow the Commander even if Vibor says blast us and the ship. They went through the battle of the Five Suns together and Jaksan—" His voice trailed off.

"What about Mirion?"

"He isn't conscious. I don't think he's going to pull through. We can't even tell how badly he's injured. He can be counted out."

Counted out of what, wondered Kartr, and his green eyes narrowed. Smitt was hinting now of some kind of conflict to come.

"Dalgre and Snyn?" asked Zinga.

"They're both Jaksan's squadmen. Who knows how they'll stand if he starts giving orders?" returned the com-techneer.

"There is one thing I find puzzling." Fylh broke in for the first time. "Why do you come to us, Smitt? We're not crew—"

There was the question which had been in all their minds—at last brought into the open. Kartr waited for the answer to it.

"Why—well, because I think that you're the best equipped for the future. It's your job. I'm dead weight now anyway—the crash did for the coms. The crew's dead weight without a ship to raise. So, all right—we should be ready to learn what it takes to keep on living—"

"A recruit, is it?" Zinga's chuckle was more hiss. "But a very green one. Well, Kartr, do you sign him?" The Zacathan's grotesque head turned to the sergeant.

"He's speaking the truth," Kartr returned very soberly. "I call council!" He gave the order which alerted them all. "Rolth?"

That white-skinned face, more than half masked by the dark goggles, was hard to read.

"The land is good?"

"Very promising," Zinga replied promptly.

"It's plain we can't keep on squatting here forever," mused the ranger from dusky Falthar. "I'd vote to strip the ship, take everything we can possibly use, and establish a base. Then look around a bit—"

"Fylh?"

The Trystian's claws beat a tattoo on his broad belt. "I agree with that wholly. But it's probably too sensible." His half-sneered ending appeared to be directed at Smitt. Fylh was not going to forget in a hurry the old division between ranger and Patrol crewman.

"Zinga?"

"Establish a base, yes. I would say close to that river which houses those delectable creatures. A fine mess of them right now—" His eyelids dropped in mock ecstasy.

Kartr looked at Smitt. "My vote goes with theirs. We have one usable sled left. On it we could ferry the Commander, Mirion and the supplies. If we plunder the main drive we should be able to fuel it for a number of trips. The rest of us can walk out, and pack stuff on our backs besides. The land is good, there's food and water to be found—and it seems to be deserted—no evidence of anything like the Greenies to fight us for it. If I were the Commander—"

"But you aren't—you Bemmy ranger—you aren't!"

Kartr's hand had fallen to the grip of his hand blaster even before he saw the man who was edging through the door. The wave of menace which he emitted was like a physical blow to the ranger's sensitive perception.

Knowing that any answer he might make verbally would only feed the other's rage, Kartr hesitated, and in the moment of silence Smitt took up the challenge.

"Shut up, Snyn!"

Light glinted from the small weapon almost completely concealed in the armsman's hand as he turned it toward the com-techneer. The waves of fear-based hatred were so thick that Kartr marveled that the others could not feel them too. Without attempting to gain his feet the sergeant hurled himself sideways, his shoulder catching Snyn at knee height. A bolt of searing green flame cut high through the air as the armsman's trigger finger tightened convulsively. He staggered forward as Kartr tried in vain to use his one good hand to pull him off balance.

A second or two later and it was over. Snyn still rolled and screamed muffled curses under Zinga but Fylh was methodically forcing his arms behind him so that a "safe" bar might be locked across his wrists. That done he was pushed over on his back and settled into

position for questioning, with jerks which were anything but gentle.

"He's crazy!" Smitt stated with honest conviction.
"Using a hand blaster like that. What in Black
Heaven—!"

"I should have burned you all—" mouthed the
captive. "Always knew you ranger devils couldn't be
trusted. Bemmys—all of you!"

But his stark hatred was more than three-quarters
fear. Kartr sank down on the bedroll and regarded the
twisting man with startled concern. He had known that
the rangers were not accepted as full members of the
Patrol, he also knew that there was a growing prejudice against nonhuman races—the "Bemmys"—but this
raw and frightening rage directed by a crewman against
his own shipmates was worse than anything he had ever
dreamed possible.

"We've done nothing against you, Snyn—"

The armsman spat. And Kartr guessed that he could
not reach him with any reasoning. There was only one
thing left to do. But it was something he had sworn
to himself long ago never to try—not against any of
his own kind. And would the others allow him if he
wished to? He stared across the writhing body of the
armsman at Smitt.

"He's dangerous—"

Smitt glanced up at the ragged tear in the wall, still
glowing cherry red.

"You don't have to underline that!" Then the com-
techneer shifted his feet uneasily. "What are you going
to do with him?"

Long afterward Kartr realized that that had been
the turning point. For, instead of appealing to Smitt
or to his own men for backing, he made his own
decision. Lightning swift and compelling he launched
his will against the guard of the man before him. Snyn's

contorted face was a dusky red, his twisted mouth
flecked with foam. But he had no control, no mind
barrier which could hold against the sergeant's trained
power. His eyes glazed, fixed. He ceased to struggle,
his mouth fell slackly open.

Smitt half drew his own blaster.

"What are you doing to him?"

Snyn was relaxed and very still now, his eyes on the
metal above him.

Smitt reached out to clutch at Kartr's shoulder.
"What did you do to him?"

"Quieted him down. He'll sleep it off."

But Smitt was edging toward the door, backing out.
"Let me alone!" His voice rose shakily. "Let me
alone—you—you blasted Bemmy!" He scrambled for
the opening in panicky haste but Rolth reached it
before him to block his exit. Smitt turned and faced
them, breathing hard—a hunted animal.

"We're not going to touch you." Kartr did not move
from his seat or raise his voice. Rolth caught the hand
signal he made. The Faltharian hesitated a second and
then he obeyed, stepping out of the doorway. But even
seeing a clear exit now Smitt did not move. Instead
he continued to watch Kartr and asked shakily:

"Can you do—do that to any of us?"

"Probably. You've never cultivated a high mind
block—any of you."

Smitt's blaster went back into its holster. He rubbed
his sweating face with trembling hands.

"Then why didn't you—just now—?"

"Why didn't I use the mind power on you? Why
should I? You weren't planning to burn us—you were
entirely sane—"

Smitt was steadying. The panic which had ridden him
was almost gone. Reason controlled emotion. He came
forward and peered down at the sleeping armsman.

"How long will he be like this?"

"I have no way of knowing. I have never used this on a human being before."

Awe overrode the other's personal fear.

"And you can knock us all out like that?"

"With a man of greater self-control or strong will, it would be a harder task. Then they have to be tricked into dropping their mind guards. But Snyn had no guards up at all."

"That," Zinga said smoothly, "is not going to be your way out of this, Smitt. If you are planning to have the sergeant go around and drop all the opposition in their tracks you can just forget it. We will either reason it out with them or—"

But Smitt was already aware of the next point. "We fight?" he asked almost grimly. "But that will be—"

"Mutiny? Of course, my dear sir. However, if you had not had that in your mind all along you would not have come to us, would you?" Fylh demanded.

Mutiny! Kartr made himself consider it calmly. In space or on planet Vibor was the Commander of the *Starfire*. And every man aboard had once sworn an oath to obey his orders and uphold the authority of the Service. Tork, realizing the officer's condition, might have removed Vibor. But Tork was gone and not one man aboard the ship now had the legal right to set aside the Commander's orders. The sergeant got to his feet.

"Can you get Jaksan and Dalgre—"

He looked about the rangers' quarters. No, it would be wiser to hold a meeting in some more neutral place. Outside, he decided swiftly, where the psychological effect of the ruined ship right before their eyes all during the discussion might well be the deciding point.

"Outside?" he ended.

"All right," agreed Smitt, but there was a note of reluctance in that. He went out.

"Now," Zinga asked, after watching the com-
techneer safely out of hearing range, "what are we
in for?"

"This would have come sooner or later anyway—it
was inevitable after the crash." That was Rolth's soft
voice answering. "When we were space borne, they had
a reason for life—they could close their eyes and minds
to things, drugging themselves with a round of familiar duties. Now that has been swept away from them.
We are the ones who have a purpose—a job. And
because we are—different—we have always been
slightly suspect—"

"So," Kartr put into words the thought which had
been growing in his own mind, "unless we act and give
them something to work for, *we* may become the target
for their fear and resentment? I agree."

"We could cut loose," Fylh suggested. "When the ship
crashed our ties with her were broken. Records—who's
ever going to see any of our records now? We're able
to live off the land—"

"But they might not be able to," Kartr pointed out.
"And it is just because that is true that we can't cut
loose and go. Not now anyway. We shall have to try
and help them—"

Zinga laughed. "Always the idealist, Kartr. I'm a
Bemmy, Fylh's a Bemmy, Rolth's half Bemmy and
you're a Bemmy lover and we're all rangers, which in
no way endears any of us to these so-called human
Patrolmen. All right, we'll try to make them see the
light. But I'll do my arguing with a blaster near my
hand."

Kartr did not demur. After the resentment with
which Jaksan had greeted him when they returned from
the trip and the insane attack of Snyn, he knew enough
to understand that such preparedness on their part was
necessary.

"Do we count on Smitt, I wonder," Zinga mused. "He never before impressed me as a ranger recruit."

"No, but he does have brains," Rolth pointed out. "Kartr"—he turned to the sergeant—"it will be your play—we'll let you do the talking now."

The other two nodded. Kartr smiled. Inside him was a good warm feeling. He had known it before—the rangers stood together. Come what might, they were going to present a united front to danger.

4

Beacon

Together the four rangers crossed the ground burnt off by the ship's drive to stand partially in the shadow of a tall rock outcrop. The sun was far down now—sending red and yellow spears of light up the western sky. But its day heat still radiated from both sand and stone.

Jaksan, Dalgre and Smitt awaited them, eyes narrowed against the light reflected from the metal of the *Starfire*—standing close together as if they were expecting—what? Attack? There were grim lines about the mouth of the arms officer. He was middle-aged, but always before there had been an elasticity in his movements, an alertness in his voice and manner which had given the lie to the broad sweeps of gray hair showing on his temples. In the golden days of the Service, Kartr realized with a slight shock of surprise, Jaksan would not have been in space at all. Long since, regulations would have retired him to some administrative post in one of the fleet ports. Did the Patrol still have any such ports? Kartr himself had not earthed in one for at least five years now.

"Well, what do you want with us?" Jaksan took the initiative.

But Kartr refused to be in any way impressed or intimidated. "It is necessary"—by instinct he fell back into the formal speech he had heard in his childhood—"for us to consider now the future. Look at the ship—" He did not need to wave his hand toward that shattered bulk. They had, none of them, been able to keep their eyes away from it. "Can you truly think that it shall ever lift again? We began this last flight undersupplied. And those supplies we have drawn upon now for months— they must be almost gone. There remains but one thing for us to do—we must strip the ship and establish a camp on the land—"

"That is just the sort of yap we expected to hear out of you!" snapped Dalgre. "You are still under orders—whether we have crashed or not!"

But it wasn't Jaksan who had made the hot retort. Jaksan was steeped, buried in the Patrol, in orders, in tradition—but he was not blinded or deafened by it.

"Whose orders?" asked Kartr now. "The Commander is incapacitated. Are you in command now, sir?" He addressed Jaksan directly.

The arms officer's space-burned skin could not pale, but his face was drawn and old. His lips drew back from his teeth in an animal's snarl of rage, pain and frustration. Before he answered he stared again at the broken ship.

"This will kill Vibor—" He bit out the words one by one.

Kartr braced himself as the wild emotion of the other tore at his perceptive sense. He could still Jaksan's pain by joining the other—by refusing to believe that the old life was ended and gone. Perhaps the Service had warped them all, the rangers as well as the crew, perhaps they needed the reassurance of orders, of routine—even going through the forms might be an anchor now.

The sergeant saluted. "Have I your permission to prepare to abandon ship, sir?"

For a moment he tensed as Jaksan whirled upon him. But the arms officer did not reach for a blaster. Instead his shoulders hunched, the lines in his face deepened into gashes of pain.

"Do as you please!" Then he strode away from them, behind the rocks and no one moved to follow him.

Kartr took command. "Zinga, Rolth, get out the sled and two days' supplies. Raid the main drive for fuel. Then go up and establish a base below the falls. You bring the sled back, Rolth, and we'll send along the Commander and Mirion—"

They ate an unpalatable meal of rations, and went to work. Some time later Jaksan was back among them to labor doggedly without speech. Kartr thankfully surrendered to him the responsibility of gathering the arms and the crew's supplies. The rangers kept away from the crewmen—there was plenty to do in stripping their own quarters and breaking out all the exploring gear the *Starfire* had ever carried. Piloted by Rolth, to whom the darkness was as bright as day, the sled made three trips during the night, taking the injured and the still unconscious Snyn as well as supplies of salvage.

A moon, a single one, rose to hang in the night sky. They were glad of its light to eke out the short line of their small portable lamps. They worked, with brief periods of rest, until the gray of dawn made a rim about the desert. It was in that last hour of labor that Jaksan made the most promising find. He had crawled alone into the crushed drive room and then shouted loud enough to bring them, numb with fatigue, hurrying to him.

Fuel—a whole extra tube of cubes! They stared round-eyed as the arms officer dragged it out into the passageway.

"Save it," Jaksan panted. "We may need the use of the sled badly later—"

Kartr, remembering the height of the falls cliffs, nodded.

So it was, that in spite of their find, when Rolth came back the next time they loaded the tube on the sled but gave him orders not to return. They would eat, sleep away the heat of the coming day, and make the trip on foot, packing their personal possessions on their backs.

The sun was shining when they gathered together in a little group by the rocks. And a blue-black shadow cast by the wrecked ship fell on three mounds in the sand. Jaksan read with parched lips and a stumbling tongue the old words of the Service farewell. They would erect no monument—until the years wore her remains into red dust the *Starfire* would mount guard above her crewmen.

After that they slept soddenly, for the last time, in the stripped ship. Fylh shook Kartr awake after what seemed only a moment's rest—but it was close to sunset. The sergeant choked down dry scraps of ration with the others. Then together, without much talk, they settled their packs and set out across the wedge of desert, steering by rock formations Kartr had noted the day before.

It was soon night again, lighted by a full moon, and they did not turn on the hand lamps. Which was just as well, thought the sergeant grimly, as there was no hope of ever renewing the fire units in those. Since they were not trying to follow the river, but cutting cross country by the route the sled had followed on its first return, they came out on that smooth section of roadway. Kartr called it to Jaksan's attention.

"Road!" For the first time the arms officer was lifted out of his depression. He went down on his knees to pass his hands over the ancient blocks, snapping on his torch to see the better. "Not much of it showing. It must have been here a long, long time. Could you trace it—?"

"With the tailer on the sled, yes. But with fuel so low—would it be worth it?"

Jaksan got wearily to his feet again. "I don't know. We can keep that in mind. It could be a lead, but I don't know—" He lapsed into a deep study as they moved on but at the next halt he spoke with some of his old fire. "Dalgre, what was that process you told me about—the one for adapting disruptor shells for power?"

His assistant armsman looked up eagerly.

"It is—" Within three words he had plunged into a flood of technicalities which left the rangers as far behind as if he were speaking some tongue from another galaxy. The *Starfire* might have lacked a mechtechneer, but Jaksan was an expert in his field and he had seen that his juniors knew more than just the bare essentials of their craft. Dalgre was still pouring out his explanation when they moved on and the arms officer walked beside him listening, now and then shooting a question which set the younger man's tongue to racing again.

They did not make the lift up the cliff to the plains country at once. Mirion died three days later, to be buried in a small clearing between two of the tall pointed trees. Fylh and Zinga rolled a sizable boulder from the river's edge and Rolth used a palm disrupter as lightly as a color brush to etch into its side the name, home world, and the rank of that thin wasted body they had laid to rest there.

Vibor never spoke. He ate mechanically, or rather chewed and swallowed what Jaksan or Smitt put into his mouth. He slept most of the time and showed no interest in what went on about him. The old division between rangers and crew, between the regulars and the less strictly disciplined specialists, was slowly closing as they worked together, hunted together, ate of unfamiliar flesh, nuts and berries. So far their immunity shots continued to work—or else they had not sampled anything poisonous.

The morning after Mirion's burial Kartr suggested that they go up into the more hospitable country behind the falls. Jaksan raised no objection and they lifted their supplies via the sled to a point about a mile up and farther ahead of their first base. From there Fylh took the sled with Vibor and Jaksan as passengers toward the promise of open country, while the others cached such equipment as they could not pack and started to follow overland.

Zinga splashed first through the flood pools along the rocky shore of the river—the leader because he had two hands to Kartr's one. The sergeant followed behind with Dalgre, Snyn, and Smitt strung out in his wake and Rolth bringing up the rear to discourage straggling. There was a sweetness in the morning air. It was chill enough to prickle the flesh, but it bore with it scents which promised and pleased. Kartr lifted his head to the touch of the wind, drawing it deeply into his lungs. The smog of the *Starfire* was very far in the past. He discovered that he had few regrets for its loss. What if they *were* exiled here for life—just to find such a world was luck enough!

He sent out his sense of perception, blanking out the

touches of those about him—trying to make contact with a native life. A reddish animal with a pouf of tail escorted them for a space, traveling high in tree limbs, making a chattering noise. It was only curious—curious and totally unafraid.

A bird—or maybe it was some form of insect—sailed through the air, coasting on wings which were brilliant patches of color. Then another animal trotted out of concealment perhaps a hundred feet ahead of their line of march. It was large—almost as formidable in size as the brown-coated fisher they had seen on their first day. But this one's fur was a tawny yellow-brown and it moved shadow-silent, slipping across the rocks with surety and arrogance. It crouched, belly close to the gray stone, and watched them through slitted eyes. The tip of its tail twitched. Zinga stopped to allow Kartr to join him.

Arrogance—arrogance and curiosity—and the faint stirrings of hunger, no thread of fear or wariness. The beast was beginning to consider them as food—

Kartr studied it, saw the muscles ripple under the thick fur as it moved slowly forward. It was beautiful— so wonderful in its wild freedom that he wanted to know more of it. He made contact, felt his way into that alien brain.

The hunger was there, but at his touch it began to submerge—the curiosity was stronger. It sat up, front limbs straight, haunches tucked in. Only the twitching tail tip betrayed its slight unease.

Without turning his head Kartr gave an order. "March to the left a bit—angle around the rock there. It will not attack us now—"

"Why don't you just blast it?" demanded Snyn querulously. "All this stupid 'don't kill this—don't kill that'! That thing's only an animal after all—"

"Shut up!" Smitt gave the crewman a slight push to

set him going. "Don't try to teach a ranger his business. Remember, if they hadn't made contact with those purple jelly flying things we wouldn't have come through the Greenie attack—those devils would have wiped us out without warning."

Snyn grunted, but he turned to the left. Smitt, Dalgre and Rolth followed—Zinga went last of all. Kartr remained until the last of the party had passed the forest beast. It yawned abruptly, displaying wicked fangs. Then, almost sleepy-eyed, it sat there, statue still, to watch them out of sight. Kartr brought up the rear. The creature was in two minds about following them. Curiosity pulled it after the travelers, hunger suggested the more immediate employment of hunting. And, at last, hunger won, the sergeant's contact faded as the animal slipped back into the woodland, away from their path.

But the meeting left Kartr both puzzled and faintly disturbed. He had made contact easily enough—had been able to impress the animal properly with the idea that they were not food and that they meant no harm. But he had been totally unsuccessful in his attempt to establish any closer relationship. Here was certainly nothing like the purple jelly thing, nothing which could be counted upon to render aid to man. The forest animal had a wild and fierce independence which refused the command of his will. If all the natives of this world were so conditioned it would leave the handful of shipwrecked survivors just that much more isolated and alone.

Man, or at least some type of superior life form had once lived here. They had been here a long time and in some numbers—or that road would not run through the edge of wastelands. And yet no living creature he had so far encountered had any memory, or even an instinctive fear, of man. How long had the race who built that road been gone—where had they gone—and why? He longed to take off with the sled and the tailer and run along the road which could never be buried so deeply that the pointer could not betray it—run along it to the city which must lie somewhere near its end or beginning.

Cities—cities were mostly found along the edges of continental land masses where there were opportunities of sea travel—or in strategic points by river beds. There were seas on this planet—he mourned again in silence the crushing of the pilot's recorder which had rendered useless the notations made as they had come in to that fatal landing. Maybe if they struck due east now—or west—they would come out upon the sea coast. Only which way—east or west? He had had only one fleeting glimpse at the ship's viewplate and it had appeared that the land mass they had set down upon had been a very large one. They might be hundreds of planet miles from either coast. Would even that road be the right guide?

Once they had a good base established he was going, Kartr promised himself, to get to the bottom of the fuel source Dalgre and Jaksan had been talking about. With the sled repowered they could explore much farther than they could hope to do on foot. And with the road as a beginning—

Rolth had come to a full stop and was looking back. "You are happy?"

Kartr realized that he had been humming.

"I was thinking about that road—of following it—"

"Yes—it sticks in one's mind—that road. But what good would it be to us? Do you honestly believe that we shall find man—or even man's distant kindred—at the end of it?"

"I don't know—"

"That, of course"—Rolth wriggled his shoulders to

settle his pack the better—"is my true answer. What we do not know, we must find out— It is that urge to go and see what lies beyond the hills which brought us into the rangers. We are conditioned to such searching. I must admit that I would relish such an expedition much more than I do this crawling from place to place through a wilderness, bending under burdens as if I were a draft pfph from the outer islands of Falthar!"

It took them almost two full days of tramping to reach the camp Fylh and Jaksan had made. But once there they found waiting them shelters constructed from tree branches, a fire going to light them in through the dusk of evening, and the savor of roasting meat to turn their tired shuffle into strides again.

A shelf of rock ran down smoothly into the shallows of the stream, offering a natural landing place for the sled. At the back of this was piled the material ferried up the river. Jaksan had located some wild grain, fully ripe, and some sourish fruit from trees growing at the edge of the woods. A man would have no difficulty living off the land here, Kartr decided. He wondered about the seasons—whether there was any great change between them during the years. Not to know—not to have any guides! Seasons had not mattered when they were only visitors in a strange world—but now— There was so much they should know—and would have to learn by the hard way of experience.

He stretched out by the fire, trying to list all that should be done—so deep in his thought that he was honestly startled when Rolth touched his shoulder. The night world was Rolth's and he was alive with it as were the beasts now prowling beyond the circle of the firelight.

"Come!" The urgency in that one whispered word got Kartr to his feet. He gave a quick glance about the

fire. The rest were in their bedrolls, asleep, or putting on a good show of being so. The sergeant crept
out of the light, not setting his full foot to the ground
until he reached the shadows.

"What—?" But he did not get to complete that
question. Rolth's hand was on his arm and the fingers
pressed into his flesh as a warning.

Then those fingers slipped down until they tightened about his and Rolth drew him on into the full
dark.

They were going up a slope which steepened as they
advanced. The trees thinned out and vanished, leaving
them in the moonlit open. On the crown of the hill the
Faltharian pulled the sergeant around to face north.

"Wait!" Rolth ordered tersely. "Watch the sky!"

Kartr blinked into the curtain of the night. It was
a clear one, stars made familiar and unfamiliar patterns
across the sky. He remembered other suns and the
myriad worlds they nourished.

Across the horizon from left to right swept a yellow-
white beam, reaching from some point on the earth
ahead far into the heavens. It took three seconds for
it to complete the full sweep. Kartr counted. Sixty
seconds later it leaped into sight once more, moving
in the same course. A beacon!

"How long—?"

"I saw it first an hour ago. It is very regular."

"It must be a beacon, a marker—but for whom—run
by whom—?"

"Must it be run by anyone?" asked Rolth thoughtfully. "Remember Tantor—"

Tantor, the sealed city. Its inhabitants had been overwhelmed by a ghastly plague two centuries ago. Yes,
he recalled Tantor well. Once he had flown above the
vast bubble which enclosed it in an eternal prison for
the safety of the galaxy, and had watched the ancient

machines going about their business below, running a city in which no living thing walked or ever would walk again. Tantor had had its beacons too, and its appeals for help streaming into the skies mechanically long after the hands which had set them going had been dust. Behind those hills ahead might well rest another Tantor—it would explain the puzzle of a fair but deserted world.

"Ask Jaksan to come," Kartr said at last. "But do not arouse the others."

Rolth disappeared and the sergeant stood alone, watching the light sweep across the sky in its timed sequence. Was the machine which cast that tended or untended? Was that some signal for help, a help long since unneeded? Was it a guide set for a ship from the stars which had never arrived?

He heard the roll of loose gravel started by an impatient foot. The arms officer was on his way.

"What is it?" Jaksan demanded impatiently a moment later.

Kartr did not turn around. "Look due north," he ordered. "See that!"

The beam made the arc across the horizon. Kartr heard a gasp which was almost a cry.

"It must be a signal of some sort," the sergeant continued. "And I would judge mechanically broadcast—"

"From a city!" Jaksan added eagerly.

"Or a landing port. But—remember Tantor?"

The other's silence was his answer.

"What do you propose to do?" Jaksan asked after a long moment.

"This process you were discussing with Dalgre—can you use disruptor charges in the sled? We must keep the extra fuel for emergencies."

"We can try to do it. It was done once and Dalgre read the report. Suppose we can—what then?"

"I'll take the sled and investigate that."

"Alone?"

Kartr shrugged. "With not more than one other. If that is a dead monument, another Tantor, we dare not be too precipitant in exploration. And the fewer to risk their necks the better."

The arms officer chewed on that. Again the touch of resentment he could not altogether keep under reached Kartr. He guessed what the other must be feeling now. That signal ahead might mean at the very best a star port, a chance to find another still navigable ship, to return to the safe familiar life the Patrol officer had always known. At the very least it promised remains of a civilization of sorts, if only a pile of ruins which could be used to shelter men against the raw life of a wilderness world.

It was up to the rangers to be patient with such men as Jaksan. What to them was a promise of a free and proper way of life was to these unwilling companions of theirs a slipping back into utter darkness. If Jaksan would give way entirely to his emotions now he would rush madly for the sled, and ride it toward the beacon. But he kept that desire under stiff curb, he was no Snyn.

"We go to work on the sled at dawn," the arms officer promised. As Kartr started down the hill, he did not move to follow, "I shall stay here a little while longer."

Well, Rolth was making the rounds as night guard. He would see that Jaksan came to no harm. Kartr went back to the fire alone. Crawling into his bedroll he closed his eyes and willed himself to sleep. But in his dreams a thrust of yellow-white light both threatened and beckoned.

Jaksan was as good as his word. The next morning Dalgre, Snyn and the arms officer dismantled the largest of the disruptors and gingerly worked loose its power unit. Because they were handling sudden and violent death they worked slowly, testing each relay and installation over and over again. It took a full day of painful work on the sled before they were through, and even then they could not be sure it would really rise.

Just before sunset Fylh took the pilot's seat, getting in as if he didn't altogether care for his place just over those tinkered-with power units. But he had insisted upon playing test pilot.

The sled went up with a lurch, too strong a surge. Then it straightened out neatly, as Fylh learned how to make adjustments, and sped across the river, to circle and return, alighting with unusual care considering who had the controls. Fylh spoke to Jaksan before he was off his seat.

"She has a lot more power than she had before. How long is it going to last?"

Jaksan rubbed a grimy hand across his forehead. "We have no way of telling. What did that report say, Dalgre?"

"That kind of hook-up brought a cruiser in three light years to base. Then they dug it out. They never learned how long it might have lasted."

Fylh nodded and turned to Kartr.

"Well, she's ready and waiting. When do we take off, sergeant?"

5

The City

In the end the rangers drew lots for the pilot's place and
the choice fell, not to Fylh, but to Rolth. Secretly Kartr
was pleased. To fly with Rolth at the controls would mean
going by night—but that would be the wiser thing to do
when covering a strange city. And, after all, Rolth had been
the one to discover the beacon.

They set off at dusk, rations and bedrolls strapped
under the single seat remaining in the stripped-down
sled. And with the bedrolls was the single disruptor
they had left. Jaksan had insisted upon their taking that.

Rolth sang softly as they sped through the chill of
the dusk—one of the minor wailing airs of his own
twilight world. Without his protective goggles his dark
eyes were alive in his pallid face.

Kartr leaned back against the seat pad and watched
the ground darken from green to dusky blue. Just on
chance he triggered the tailer. Now if they did pass

above any large man-made object they would be warned.

There was life abroad in the hills below—animal hunters on the prowl. And once a wild screech reached them. Kartr read in that sound the rage and the disgust of a hunter that had missed its spring and must stalk again. But no man walked below them—nothing even close to human.

The tailer clicked. Kartr leaned forward and consulted the dial. One point only. And a small one. But—man-made. A single building perhaps—maybe long buried. Not the site of the beacon.

Even as he thought of it the beam swept across the dusk-darkened sky. No, whatever lay below had no connection with that.

There were hills and more hills. Rolth applied power which raised them over, sometimes hardly skimming above rocks which crowned the peaks. Then they began to drop away again, making steps for a giant down into another low land.

And now they could see what lay in the heart of that. A blaze of light, not all yellow-white, but emerald, ruby, sapphire too! A handful of gigantic gems spilled out to pulse and glow in the night.

Kartr had visited the elfin ruins of lost Calinn—needle towers and iridescent domes—a city no man living in the days of human civilization could duplicate. He had seen sealed Tantor, and the famous City of the Sea, built of stone-encased living organisms beneath the waters of Parth. But this—it was strangely familiar as well as alien. He was drawn and repelled by it at the same time.

He put a hand to the controls to give Rolth a chance to resume his goggles. What was bright light for the sergeant was blinding to the Faltharian.

"Do we just fly in—or scout first?" asked Rolth.

Kartr frowned, sending his perceptive sense ahead—

a surgeon's delicate probe, prying into the source of the lights.

He touched what he sought, touched and recoiled in the same instant, fleeing the awareness of the mind he had contacted. But what he had found was so astounding that he was too startled to answer that question at once. When he did it was decisively.

"We scout—!"

Rolth cut down the speed of the sled. He swung it out in an arc to encircle the splotch of light.

"I wouldn't have believed it!" Kartr gave voice at last to his bewilderment.

"There are inhabitants?"

"One at least—I contacted an Ageratan mind!"

"Pirates?" suggested Rolth.

"In an open city—with all that light to betray them? Though, you may be right at that, that is just where they might feel safe. But be careful, we don't want to walk straight into a blast beam. And that kind fire before they ask your name and planet—especially if they see our Comets!"

"Did he catch your mind touch?"

"Who knows what an Ageratan gets or doesn't get? No one has been able to examine them unless they are either completely unaware or deliberately open. He could have been either then."

"More than one?"

"I got out—fast—when I tapped him. Didn't stay to see."

The tailer was clicking madly. Kartr should have switched on the recorder, too. But without a machine to read the wire that was useless. From now on scouting reports would be oral. The sled glided slowly over a section where the buildings stood some distance apart, vegetation thick between them.

"Look—" Rolth pointed to the left. "That's a landing

stage there—if I ever saw one. How about setting down
on the next one and going ahead on foot—"

"Get in closer to the main part of the city first. No
use in walking several miles after we go down."

They found what they wanted, a small landing stage
on the top of a tower, a tower which seemed short
when compared to the buildings around it, though they
must have landed forty floors above street level. But
it was a good place from which to spy out the land.

They dropped on it. Then Kartr whirled, his blaster
out—aimed for the middle of the black thing scuttling
toward him from the roof shadows. He tried in the
same instant for mind contact—to recoil with an instant
of real panic. And Rolth put his discovery into words.

"Robot—guard—maybe—"

Kartr was back in the sled as Rolth brought it up
above the head of the figure.

Robot, guard or attendant, the thing stopped short
when the sled left the stage surface. As they went on
up it turned squarely and trundled away into the dark.
Kartr relaxed. The metal guardian could have beamed
them both before they had even had a chance to sight
it. Of course, it might only have been an attendant—
but there was no sense in taking the risk.

"No more landing stages," he said and Rolth agreed
with him fervently.

"Those creatures might be conditioned to a voice
or a key word—give them the wrong answer and they
take you apart quick—"

"Wait a minute." Kartr put his blaster back in its
holster. "We're judging this city by what we know of
our own civilization." He squinted against the brilliance
of a wave of green light and recited the instructions
of their manual. "There is always something new for
the finder, go out with an open mind—"

"And," Rolth added, "a ready blaster! Yes, I know

all that. But human nature remains the same and I'd rather be wary than dead. Look down there—see those squares of pavement between the buildings? How about setting down on one of those? No landing stage alarms or controls we could trigger—"

"Promising. Can you get in behind that big block? Its shadow should hide us well—"

Rolth might not get as much speed out of the sled as Fylh did, but his caution on such a mission as this was more to be desired than the Trystian's reckless disregard for the laws of gravity. Earthing required of him a good five minutes of painful maneuvering, but he brought them down in the middle of the pool of shadow Kartr had indicated.

They did not stir from their seats at once, but sat watching for robots, for any moving thing which might promise menace.

"A city"—Rolth stated the obvious—"is not the place to play hide and seek in. I'm sure that I'm being watched—maybe from up there—" He jerked a thumb at the lines of blank windows overlooking the court in which they had landed.

That eerie sensation—that myriad eyes were peering hostilely from the blank expanses—Kartr knew it too. But his sense told him it was a lie.

"Nothing lives here," he assured the Faltharian. "Not even a robot."

They moved away from the sled, skirting the side of the nearest building, staying in the shadows, racing across lighted open spaces. Rolth ran his fingers along the wall at his shoulder. "Old, very old. I can feel the scars of erosion."

"But the lights? How long could those keep running?" wondered Kartr.

"Ask your friend from Agerat. Maybe he put them in working order when he arrived. Who knows?"

There was little ornamentation on the buildings they passed, the walls were smoothly functional, yet the very way the towers and blocks were fitted into a harmonious whole argued that they were the product of a civilization so advanced in architecture as to present a city as a unit, instead of a collection of buildings and dwellings of individual tastes and periods. So far Kartr had seen no inscriptions on any of the structures.

Rolth's blue torch flashed on and off regularly as they went, pin-dotting their trail through this new kind of wilderness. When they wanted to retrace their way he need only touch his light again on these walls and the tiny blue circles would glow in return for a second.

The rangers made a half circle around one of the three buildings hedging in the court and crept along a street into the surface of which their feet sank almost ankle deep. The old pavement was covered with a thick growth of short tough grass. Half a block ahead, from a recess between two buildings, a rainbow of light played. They approached it cautiously—to come upon a fountain, a fountain of plumed light as well as tinkling water. The flood it raised sank back into a round basin, the rim of which was broken on the side near them so that a small stream was free to cut a channel through the sod until it reached a hole in the ancient pavement.

"No one around," Kartr whispered. Why he whispered he could not have explained. But the feeling of being watched, of being followed, persisted. Beneath the shadow of these dead towers he felt it necessary to creep and crawl silently—unless he awaken—what?

They dared to leave the protection of the dark and come out to the edge of the fountain. Now, through the spray of water and light, they could see its center column. There was a statue on it—more than life size, unless the builders of the city had been giants.

It was not of any stone they could recognize but some white, gleaming stuff upon which time had left no marks. And, at the full sight of it, both Kartr and Rolth stopped almost in midstride.

The figure was a girl, her arms above her head, with a mane of unbound hair flowing free below her slender waist. In her upheld hands she grasped a symbol they both knew—a star of five points. And it was from the tips of those points that the water gushed. But the girl—she was no Bemmy—she was as human as they.

"It's Ionate—the Spirit of the Spring Rain—" Kartr reached far into his mind and drew forth a legend of his blasted home.

"No—it's Xyti of the Frosts!" Rolth had memories, too, stemming from his own dusky world of cold and shadow.

For a second they stared at each other almost angrily and then both smiled.

"She is both—and neither—" Rolth suggested. "These men had their spirits of beauty, too. But it is plain by her eyes and hair she is not of Falthar. And by her ears—she is no kin of yours—"

"But why—" Kartr stared at the fountain in puzzlement. "Why does she seem as if I have known her always? And that star—"

"A common symbol—you have seen it a hundred times on a hundred different worlds. No, it is as I have said. She is the ideal of beauty and so we see her, even as he who fashioned her dreamed her into being."

They left the court of the fountain reluctantly and came into a wide avenue which stretched its green length straight toward the center of the city. Now and again colored lights formed untranslatable signs in the air or across the fronts of the buildings. They passed by what must have been shops and saw the cobwebs of ancient wares spread inside the windows. Then Kartr caught Rolth's arm and pulled him quickly into the shelter of a doorway.

"Robot!" The sergeant's lips were close to his companion's ear. "I think it is patrolling!"

"Can we circuit it?"

"Depends upon its type."

They had only their past experience to guide them. Robot patrols, they knew, were deadly danger. Those they had seen elsewhere could not be turned from duty except by the delicate and dangerous act of short-circuiting their controls. Otherwise the robot would either blast without question anything or anyone not natural to that place—or who could not answer it with the prescribed code. It was what the rangers had feared on the landing stage, and it would be even worse to face it now when they had no sled for a quick getaway.

"It will depend upon whether this is a native or—"

"Or introduced by the Ageratan?" Rolth interrupted. "Yes, if he brought it, we know how to handle it. A native—"

He stopped whispering at the faint sound of metal clinking against stone. Kartr straightened and flashed his torch above their heads. The doorway in which they crouched was not too high and a small projection overhung it. Just over that was the dark break of a window. Seeing that he began to plan.

"Inside—" he said to Rolth. "Try to reach the second floor and get out of that window upon the ledge. Then I'll attract the robot's attention and you can burn its brain case from above—"

Rolth was gone, slipping into the darkness which was no barrier to him. Kartr leaned against the side of the doorway. It would be a race, he thought, with a little sick twinge in the pit of his stomach. If the robot got here before Rolth reached that ledge—! If he, Kartr, couldn't manage to avoid the first attack of the patroller—! Luckily he didn't have too long to wait and catalogue all those dismal possibilities.

He could see the patroller now. It was at the far end of the block. The flashing lights on the buildings played across its metal body. But the sergeant was almost sure that it was unlike the ones known to galactic cities. The rounded dome of the head casing, the spider-like slenderness of the limbs, the almost graceful smoothness of its progress, were akin more to the architecture of this place.

Its pace was steady and unhurried. It paused before each doorway and shot a spy beam from its head into the entrance. Manifestly it was going about its appointed task of checking the security of each portal.

Then the sergeant sighed with relief. Rolth had crawled into place and crouched now well above the line of the robot's vision. If only this patroller was constructed on the same general pattern they knew and *could* be short-circuited through the head!

But when it reached the next doorway it hesitated. Kartr tensed. This might be worse than he had thought. The thing had some sense perception. He was sure that it suspected his presence. No spy beam flashed. Instead it stood there unmoving—as if it were puzzled, making up its mind.

Was it relaying back to some dust-covered headquarters an alarm?

But its arms were moving—

"Kartr!"

Night sight or no night sight, Kartr had not needed that shout from Rolth to warn him. He had already seen what the patroller held ready. He hurled himself backward, falling flat on the floor of the hall, letting momentum carry him in a slide some distance along it. Behind him was a burst of eye-searing flame, filling the whole entrance with an inferno. Only his trained muscles and sixth sense of preservation had saved him from cooking in the midst of that!

Shakily he crawled on his belly away from the fury. Was the robot going to follow him in and complete its mission?

Hollow sounds of feet pounding—

"Kartr! Kartr!"

He had levered himself to a sitting position when Rolth plunged around an angle in the hallway and almost fell over him.

"Are you hurt? Did he get you?"

Kartr grinned lopsidedly. To just be alive—he winced as Rolth's examining hands touched skin scraped raw.

"What about—?"

"The bag of bolts? I scragged him all right—a blast hole right through his head casing and he went down. He didn't reach you?"

"No. And at least he's told us something about the civilization they had here." The sergeant surveyed the blaze behind him with critical distaste. "Blow a hole in a city block to get someone. Wonder what they would have thought of a stun gun." With Rolth's hand under his arm Kartr got to his feet. He hoped that he had not rebroken his wrist and that the red agony in it was only from the jar of his fall.

"I have a feeling," he began and then was glad that Rolth had retained a grip on him because the hallway appeared to sway under his feet, "that we'd better get away from here—fast—"

The thought which plagued him was the memory of that momentary pause before the robot had attacked. Kartr was sure that then a message had been flashed from the patroller—where? If the timeless machine had only been performing rounds set him generations before the city had been deserted by its builder—then such a report would be no menace—unless it activated other machines in turn. On the other hand, if the mysterious Ageratan controlled the robots, then the rangers might have successfully met a first attack, only to face other and perhaps worse ones.

Rolth agreed with this when he suggested it aloud.

"We can't go back that way anyhow." The Faltharian pointed to the blazing pit of radiation which had once been the door. "And they may just be combing the streets for us, too. Listen, this city reminds me in some ways of Stiltu—"

Kartr shook his head. "Heard of it, but have never been there."

"Capital of Lydias." Rolth identified it impatiently. "They're old-fashioned there—still live in big cities. Well, they have an underground system of links—ways of traveling under the surface—"

"Hm." Kartr's mind jumped to the next point easily. "Then we might try going down and see what we can find? All right. And if that patroller did rouse out the guard before you burned him, it will be some time before they can even get in here to see if their tame hunter bagged us. Let's look for a way down."

But to their bafflement there seemed to be no way down at all. They threaded rooms and halls, pushing past the remains of furnishings and strange machinery which at other times would have set them speculating for hours, hunting some means of descent. None appeared to exist—only two stairways leading up.

In the end they discovered what they wanted in the center of a room. It was a dark well, a black hole in which the beam of Kartr's flash found no end. Although the light did not reveal much it helped them in another way because its owner dropped it. He gave an exclamation and made a futile grab—much too late. Rolth supplied an excited comment, reverting in this stress to his native dialect and only making sense when Kartr demanded harshly that he translate.

"It did not fall! It is floating down—floating!"

The sergeant sat back on his heels. "Inverse descent! Still working!" He could hardly believe that. Small articles might possibly be upborne by the gravity-dispelling rays—but something heavier—a man—say—

Before he could protest Rolth edged over the rim, to dangle by his hands.

"It's working all right! I'm treading air. Here goes!"

His hands disappeared and he was gone. But his voice came up the shaft.

"Still walking on air! Come on in, the swimming's fine!"

Fine for Rolth maybe who could see where he was going. To lower oneself into that black maw and hope that the anti-gravity was *not* going to fail—! Not for the first time in his career with the rangers Kartr silently cursed his overvivid imagination as he allowed his boots to drop into the thin air of the well. He involuntarily closed his eyes and muttered a half-plea to the Spirit of Space as he let go.

But he was floating! The air closed about his body with almost tangible support. He was descending, of course, but at the rate of a feather on a light breeze. Far below he saw the blue light of Rolth's torch. The other had reached bottom. Kartr drew his feet together and tried to aim his body toward the pinprick of light.

"Happy planeting!" Rolth greeted the sergeant as he landed lightly, his knees slightly bent, and with no shock at all. "Come and see what I have found."

What Rolth had found was a platform edging on a tunnel. Anchored to this stand by a slender chain was a small car, pointed at both ends, a single padded seat in its center. It had no drive Kartr could discern and it did not touch the floor of the tunnel, hovering about a foot above that.

A keyboard was just before the seat—controls, Kartr deduced. But how could they aim it to any place? And to go shooting off blindly into the dark, liable to crash against some cave in— The sergeant began to reconsider that—too risky by far. To face a battalion of robot patrollers was less dangerous than to be trapped underground in the dark.

"Here!"

Kartr jumped at Rolth's call. The other ranger had gone to the back of the platform and was holding his dim torch on the wall there. The sergeant could just barely see by the blue light. Rolth had found something all right! A map of black lines crossing and recrossing—it could only be of the tunnel system. Having solved much more complicated puzzles in the past they set to work—to discover that this was apparently a way leading directly into the heart of the city.

Ten minutes later they crowded together on the narrow seat. Rolth pressed two buttons as Kartr threw off the restraining chain. There was a faint puff of sound—they swept forward and the dank air of the tunnel filled their nostrils.

6

The City People

"This should be it," Rolth half whispered.

The car was slowing down, drawing to the right side of the tunnel. Ahead a dim light glowed. They must be approaching another platform. Kartr glanced at the dial on his wrist band. It had taken them exactly five minutes planet time to reach this place. Whether or not it was the one they wanted—that was another question. They had aimed at a point they thought would be directly under what seemed to be a large public building in the very center of the city. If any human or Bemmy force had taken over here that would be the logical place to find them.

"Anyone ahead?" asked Rolth, trusting as usual to Kartr's perception.

The sergeant sent a mind probe on and then shook his head. "Not a trace. Either they don't know about these ways or they have no interest in them."

"I'm inclined to believe that they don't know." The Faltharian grabbed at a mooring ring as the car came along the platform.

Kartr climbed out and stood looking about him. This place was at least three times the size of the one from which they had embarked. And other tunnels ran from it in several directions. It was lighted after a fashion. But not brightly enough to make Rolth don his goggles again.

"Now"—the Faltharian stood with his hands resting on his hips, surveying their port—"how do we get out—or rather up—from here?"

There were those other tunnels, but, on their first inspection, no other sign of an exit. Yet Kartr was sure that this platform must have one. It was air which betrayed it—a puff of warmer, less dank breeze which touched him. Rolth must have felt it too for he turned in the direction from which it had come.

They followed that tenuous guide to a flat round plate at the foot of another well. Kartr crooked his neck until his throat strained. Far above he was sure he could see a faint haze of light. But they certainly couldn't climb— He turned to Rolth bitterly disappointed.

"That's that! We might as well go back—"

But the Faltharian was engrossed by a panel of buttons on the wall.

"I don't think we need do that. Let's just see if this works!" He pressed the top button in the row. Then he jumped back to clutch his companion in a tight hold as the plate came to life under them and they zoomed up.

Both rangers instinctively dropped and huddled together. Kartr swallowed to clear the pressure in his buzzing ears. At least, he thought thankfully, the shaft was not closed at the top. They were not being borne upward to be crushed against an unyielding surface overhead.

Twice they flashed by other landing places abutting the shaft. After they passed the second Kartr squeezed his eyes shut. The sensation of being on a sideless elevator moving at some speed was one he believed he would never choose to experience again. It was infinitely worse—though akin to—the one attack of space fear he had had when he lost his mooring rope and had floated away from the ship while making repairs on the hull during flight.

"We're here—"

Kartr opened his eyes, very glad to hear a quaver in Rolth's voice. So the Faltharian had not enjoyed the voyage any more than he had!

Where was "here"? The sergeant scrambled off the plate, almost on all fours, and looked around him. The room in which they appeared was well lighted. Above him, rising to a dizzy height, reached floor after floor, all with galleries ringing upon the center. But he did not have long to examine that for a cry from Rolth brought him around.

"It's—it's gone!" The Faltharian was staring with wide eyes at the floor.

And he was entirely right. The plate-elevator on which they had just made that too swift ascent had vanished and the floor where it had entered was, as far as Kartr could see, now a smooth, unbroken stretch of pavement.

"It sank back"—Rolth's voice was under better control now—"and then a block came out from one side and sealed it."

"Which may account for the under ways not being discovered," suggested Kartr. "Suppose this shaft only opened when our car pulled up at the platform in the tunnel, or, because we started some other automatic control—it may be set to operate in that fashion—"

"I," Rolth stated firmly, "am going to stay away from

the middle of rooms in here until we leave this blasted place. What if you were on the trapdoor and some-body stepped on the proper spot below? Regular trap!" He scowled at the floor and walked carefully, testing each step, to the nearest of the doorways. Kartr was almost inclined to follow his example. As the Faltharian had pointed out there was no way of knowing what other machinery their mere presence in the ancient buildings might activate. And then he wondered if it had been their sled's landing which had set the patroller to its work and so brought the robot upon them.

But a potential menace greater than machines which might or might not exist alerted him a few seconds later. There was an unknown and living creature ahead. The Ageratan? No. The strange mind he touched was not that strong. Whoever was before them now lacked the perception sense. Kartr need not fear betrayal until they were actually seen. Rolth caught the signal he made. And, while the Faltharian did not draw his blaster, his hand hovered just above its grip.

But the hall beyond the first door was empty. It was square and furnished with benches of an opaline sub-stance. Under the subdued lighting, which came out of the walls themselves, sparks of rich color caught fire in the milky surface of the simply wrought pieces. This must be an ante-room of some sort. For in the opposite wall were set a pair of doors, twice Kartr's height, bearing the first relief sculpture he had seen in the city—conventionalized and symbolic representation of leaves. It was behind those doors that the other awaited them.

The sergeant began the tedious task of blocking out his own impressions, of concentrating only on that spark of life force hidden ahead. He was lucky in that the unknown was not a sensitive, that he could contact, could insert the mind touch, without betraying his own identity.

Human, yes. A point three—no more. A four would have been dimly aware of his spying—uneasy under it—a point five would have sensed him at once. But all this stranger knew was a discouragement, a mental fatigue. And—he was no pirate—or a prisoner of pirates—all feeling of violence past or present was lacking.

But—Kartr had already set his hand on the wide fastening of the door. Someone else had just joined the man in there. And from a first tentative contact the sergeant recoiled instantly. The Ageratan! In the same second he identified that mind, he knew that all hope of concealment was now over—that the Ageratan knew where they were as well as if his eyes could pierce stone and metal to see them. It was, Kartr's lip caught between his teeth, almost as if the Ageratan had dropped his own mind shield to bait them into showing themselves. And if that were so—! The ranger's green eyes were centered with a spark of dangerous yellow fire. He made a sign to Rolth.

Reluctantly the other's hand moved away from his blaster. Kartr studied him almost critically and then glanced down along the length of his own body. Their vlis hide boots and belts had survived without a scratch in spite of the rough life in the bush. And those blazing Comet badges were still gleaming on breast and helmet. Even if that Comet was modified by the crossed dart and leaf of a ranger it was the insignia of the Patrol. And he who wore it had authority to appear anywhere in the galaxy without question—in fact by rights the questions were his to ask.

Kartr bore down on the fastening of the doors. They parted in the center, withdrawing in halves into the walls, leaving an opening wide enough for six men instead of just the two standing in it.

Here the light radiating from the walls was brighter

and much of it was focused on an oval table in the exact center of the room—a table so long that the entire crew of a cruiser might have been accommodated around it. It was of the opaline stone and there were benches curved to follow its line.

Two men sat there, quietly enough, though, Kartr noted, a blaster lay close to the hand of the taller one—the Ageratan. But when *he* saw the badge of the Patrol his face was a mirror of amazement and he was on his feet in one swift movement. His slighter companion stared, licked his lips—and Kartr knew when his utter surprise turned into incredulous joy.

"The Patrol!" That was the Ageratan and there was certainly no pleasure to be read in his identifying exclamation. But his mind block was tightly in place and Kartr could not know what lay behind those black, hooded eyes.

They were not pirates—those two. Both were dressed in the fantastically cut and colored tunics favored by the civilians of the decadent inner systems. And the blaster on the table was apparently their only weapon. Kartr strode forward.

"You are?" he demanded crisply, molding his stance and voice on Jaksan's. He had never before assumed the duties of a Patrolman, but as long as he wore the Comet no civilian would be allowed to guess that.

"Joyd Cummi, Vice-Sector Lord of Agerat," the tall man answered almost sneeringly. He had the usual overbearing arrogance of his race. "This is my secretary, Fortus Kan. We were passengers on the Nyorai *X451*. She was attacked by pirates and went into overdrive when in a damaged condition. When we came out we discovered that her computer had failed and we were in a totally unfamiliar section of the galaxy. We had fuel enough to cruise for two weeks and then it gave out and we were forced to land near here. We have been trying to communicate with some point of civilization but we had no idea that we were so successful! You are from—?"

A Vice-Sector Lord, eh? And an Ageratan into the bargain. Kartr was treading on dangerous ground now. But, he decided, he was not going to let this Joyd Cummi know that the Patrol had not arrived to rescue castaways—but as fellow refugees. There was a suggestion of something wrong here. His perception was alert, trying to measure words where he could not tap minds.

"We are Ranger Rolth and Ranger Sergeant Kartr, attached to the *Starfire*. We shall report your presence here to our commander."

"Then you did not come in answer to our signals?" burst out Fortus Kan. His round boyish face sagged with disappointment.

"We are engaged in a routine scouting mission," returned Kartr as coldly as he dared. The uneasiness in the atmosphere was growing stronger every moment. The Ageratan's shield might be strong but he could not altogether control all emotions. And he might not be trying to.

An Ageratan was a five point nine on the sensitive scale, yes. But unless Cummi had met one of Kartr's little-known race before—which was hardly likely since so few of them had ever volunteered for off-planet duty—he could not guess he was now facing a six point six!

"Then—" Fortus Kan's voice became close to a wail. "You can't get us away from here. But at least you can bring help—"

Kartr shook his head. "I will report your presence to my commanding officer. How many of you are here?"

"One hundred and fifty passengers and twenty-five

crew members," Joyd Cummi returned crisply. "May I ask how you reached this building without our notice? We activated for our protection the patrol robots we found here—"

He was interrupted, much to his evident annoyance by Fortus Kan.

"Did you destroy that patroller?" he demanded eagerly. "The one on Cummi Way?"

Cummi Way! Kartr caught the significance of that. So the Vice-Sector Lord ruled here—enough to give his name arbitrarily to the main thoroughfare of the city.

"We deactivated a robot in what we thought a deserted city," he returned. "Since your being here is of importance we shall end our exploration and return immediately to our camp."

"Of course." Cummi was now the efficient executive. "We have been able to restore to running order several of the ground transportation vehicles we discovered here. Let one of them drive you back—"

"We flew in," Kartr countered swiftly. "And we shall return the same way. Long life, Vice-Sector Lord!" He raised his hand in the conventional salute. But he wasn't to escape so easily.

"At least you can be driven to where you left your flyer, Ranger Sergeant. There are other robot patrollers in use and it will be safer if one who knows their code accompanies you. We cannot afford to risk you of the Patrol—"

Kartr dared not refuse what so smoothly appeared to be a sensible suggestion. Yet—he knew that there was trouble here. He felt along his spine the cold prickle of fear which had warned him so many times in his life before. If he could only probe Fortus Kan! But he dared not try it when the Ageratan was there.

"I think it is best not to over-excite the people with

the report of your arrival at just this moment," the Lord continued as he escorted the rangers back across the ante-room. "It will, of course, be encouraging for them to know that we have been contacted by the Patrol. Especially when, after five months of broadcasting from here on a feeble com, we had begun to believe that we were exiled for life. But I would prefer to discuss matters with your commander before allowing their hopes to arise. You probably noted Kan's response to your appearance. He saw in it the promise of an immediate return to the comforts of civilization. And since a Patrol ship could not possibly transport all of us we must make other arrangements—"

Twice during that speech the Ageratan had made assaults at Kartr's mind, trying to learn—or—trying to win control? But the sergeant had his shield up and he knew that Cummi would only receive carefully planted impressions of a Patrol ship set down in a far district, a ship under the command of an alert and forceful officer, a difficult man for a civilian adminis-trator to overawe.

"I think you are wise, Vice-Sector Lord," Kartr inserted into the first oral pause. "You have been here for five months then—within this city?"

"Not at first, no. We made an emergency landing some miles from here. But the city had registered on our photoscreens when we came down and we were able to locate it without undue difficulty. Its functions are in an amazing state of preservation—we must con-sider that we have been unusually favored by fortune. Of course, having Trestor Vink and two of his assistants among our number was an additional aid. He is the mech-techneer for the Nyorai line. And he has become quite absorbed in the mechanics here. He believes that originally its inhabitants were in some ways more advanced than we are. Yes, we have been very lucky."

They crossed the room of the hidden elevator shaft
and came out on a vast balcony overhanging a hall so
large that Kartr felt swallowed up in space. There was
a stairway from the balcony to the lower floor of the
hall—a flight of steps so wide that it might have been
fashioned to accommodate a race of giants. And the
lower hall opened through a series of tree-like pillars
into the street.

"Coombs!"

The figure lounging against one of the pillars
snapped to attention.

"You will take the road vehicle and drive these
Patrolmen to their ship. I do not say good-bye, Sergeant." The Lord turned to Kartr with the gracious-
ness of a great man addressing an admitted inferior.
"We shall meet again soon. You have done a very good
night's work and we are exceedingly grateful to you.
Please inform your commanding officer that we shall
be eagerly waiting to hear from him."

Kartr saluted. At least the Ageratan was not insist-
ing upon going with them to the sled. But he did stand
there until they had taken their places in the small car
and the driver put it into motion.

As they moved away from the building Kartr turned
his attention to the driver. That bristling shock of black
hair with its odd brindling of brown showed up clearly
as they swept beneath one of the banners of city
light—the long jaws, too. So—that was why Cummi
let them go off alone! No wonder he had not thought
it necessary to accompany them himself. He would be
with them in one way if not bodily. Their driver was
a Can-hound, the perfect servant whose mind was only
a receiving set used for the benefit of his master.

Kartr's skin roughened as if something slimy trailed
across him. He had the sensitive's inborn horror for
the creature before him—a thing he would not dignify

as either human or Bemmy. And now he would have to—have to—! The very thought made him so sick that his empty stomach twisted. This was the worst, the lowest task he had ever had forced upon him. He would have to go into that mind, skillfully enough not to be detected by the distant master, and there implant some false memories—

"Which way?" Even that voice rasped sickeningly along his nerves.

"Along this wide street here," he ordered with stiff lips. His hand closed over Rolth's. The Faltharian did not move but he answered with a light return pressure.

Kartr began, while his mouth twisted into a tortured ring of disgust and his mind and body alike fought wildly against the will which forced him to do this thing. It was worse than he had expected, he was degraded, soiled unspeakably by that contact. But he went on. Suddenly the car pulled to the side of the street, wavered into an open space between buildings, came to a stop in a courtyard. They remained in it while Kartr fought the miserable battle to the end. That came when the Can-hound's head fell forward and he slumped limply in the driver's seat.

Rolth got out. But Kartr had to steady himself with his hands as he followed. He reeled across the court and hung retching on a window sill. Then Rolth reached him and steadied his shaking body. With the Faltharian's arm still around him, the sergeant wavered out on the street.

"Just ahead—" Kartr got out the words painfully between spasms of sickness.

"Yes, I have seen."

The faint gleam of radiation was undoubtedly clearer to Rolth's light-sensitive eyes than it was to his own. They were about four blocks now from the point where the robot had fired at the doorway. And from there they could easily find their marked trail back to the sled.

Rolth asked no questions. He was there, a hand ready to support, a vast comforting glow of clean friendship. Clean—! Kartr wondered if he would ever feel clean again. How could a sensitive—even an Ageratan—deal with and through a creature such as that? But he mustn't think of the Can-hound now.

He was walking steadily again by the time they detoured around the nuclear fire in the doorway. And he turned the walk into a ground-covering lope as the Faltharian retraced the trail he had earlier marked. When they got to the sled Kartr made a single suggestion.

"Lay a crossed course out of here—they may have some sort of scanner on us—"

Rolth grunted an assent. The sled took to the air. A cold wind, heralding the dawn, cut into them. Kartr wanted to wash in it, wash away the filth of the encounter with the Can-hound.

"You do not want them to know about us?" That was half question, half statement.

"It isn't up to me—that's Jaksan's problem," returned Kartr, out of a vast and overwhelming weariness. The drain of that mind battle had almost meant a drain of life force too. He wanted to lie down and sleep, just sleep. But he couldn't. And he forced himself to give Rolth an explanation of what they had been pitted against—what they might have to fear in the future.

"That driver was a Can-hound. And there is something very wrong—completely wrong back there."

Rolth might not be a sensitive but as a ranger he knew a lot. He snapped out a biting word or two in his own tongue.

"I had to get into his mind—to make him a set of false memories. He will report back that he took us to the sled, certain things we were supposed to have said during the trip—the direction in which we departed—"

"So that was what you were doing!" Rolth's dark eyes lifted from the course indicator long enough to favor his companion with a look in which respect and awe were mingled.

Kartr relaxed, his head drooped to rest on the back of the seat. Now that they were out of the glare of the city the stars shone palely overhead. How was Jaksan going to handle this? Would he order them in to unite with the castaways in the city? If so—what about Cummi? What was he doing—planning right now?

"You distrust the Ageratan?" Rolth demanded as they streaked north on the evasive path Kartr had suggested.

"He is an Ageratan—you know them. He is a Vice-Sector Lord, there is no doubt he is in complete command in the city. And—he would not take kindly to having his rule disputed—"

"So he might not be in favor of the Patrol?"

"Maybe. Sector Lords are uneasy enough nowadays—there is a pull and tug of power. I would like very much to know why he was making a trip on an ordinary passenger ship anyway. If he—"

"Were getting away from some local hot spot he would be only too glad to found a new kingdom here? Yes, that I can well understand," said Rolth. "Now we go home—"

The sled made a long curve to the right. Rolth shut off the propulsion rockets, kept on only the hover screens. They drifted slowly on the new course. It would take time, add an extra hour or so to their return journey. But unless the city had something new in scanners they were now off every spy screen.

They did very little talking for the rest of the trip. Kartr dozed off once and awoke with a start from a black dream. The need for complete rest drugged his mind when he tried to flog his weary brain into making plans. He would report the situation to Jaksan. The arms officer was hostile to the impressions of a sensitive—he might not welcome Kartr's description of the unease in the city. And the sergeant had no proof to back his belief that the farther they stayed away from Cummi the better. Why did he fear Cummi? Was it because he was an Ageratan, another sensitive? Or was it because of the Can-hound? Why was he so sure that the Vice-Sector Lord was a dangerous enemy?

7

The Rangers
Stand Together

"You must admit that his account was plausible enough—"

Kartr faced Jaksan across the flat rock which served the camp as a table.

"And the city," persisted the arms officer mercilessly, "is in an excellent state of preservation. Not only that, but this party from the *X451* includes mech-techneers who have been able to start it functioning again—"

The sergeant nodded wearily. He should have brought to this contest of will a clear mind and a rested body. Instead he ached with both mental and physical fatigue. It was an effort to hold his stand against the hammering disapproval of the other.

"If all this *is* true"—Jaksan reached what he certainly believed to be a logical and sensible conclusion—for the third time—"I cannot understand this reluctance of yours, Kartr. Unless—" he was radiating hostility again but the sergeant was almost too tired to care— "unless you have taken a dislike to this Ageratan for personal reasons." Then he paused and his hostility was broken for an instant by an emotion close to sympathy. "Wasn't it an Ageratan who gave the order to burn off Ylene?"

"It might have been for all I know. But that is not the reason why I distrust this Joyd Cummi," began Kartr with such remnants of patience as he could muster.

There was no use in making an issue of Cummi's use of the Can-hound. Only another sensitive could understand the true horror of that. Jaksan had settled on an explanation for Kartr's attitude which was reasonable to him and he would hold to it. The sergeant had learned long ago that those who were not sensitives had a deep distrust of perception and the mind touch and some refused to even admit its existence as a fact. Jaksan was almost of that group—he would believe in Kartr's ability to meet and deal with animals and strange non-humans, but he inwardly repudiated the sergeant's being able to contact or read his fellow men. There was no arguing with him on that point. Kartr sighed. He had done what he could to prevent what he knew would be Jaksan's next move. Now he could only wait for the menace he believed was in the city to show itself.

So they made the journey to join the *X451*'s survivors, and they admitted, against all Kartr's pleas, their own shipwrecked condition. Joyd Cummi greeted them with urbane and welcoming ease. There was a ship's medico to attend to Vibor—there were luxurious quarters in, as Kartr noted with suspicion, corridors adjacent to the Vice-Sector Lord's own, for the crewmen and the officers.

The welcome granted the rangers was, however, somewhat cooler. Kartr and Rolth were accepted, given subtly to understand that, as humans, they would stand equal with the commoners of Cummi's kingdom. But the Ageratan had given Zinga and Fylh no more than a nod and made no suggestions for their lodging. Kartr gathered his small command together in the center of a large bare room where no eavesdropper could possibly listen in.

"If," Zinga said as they settled themselves cross-legged on the floor, "you still maintain that the odor issuing through these halls is far from flower-like, I shall agree with you! How long"—he turned to Kartr—"are you going to let some ragged tails of loyalty pull you into situations such as this?"

Fylh's claws rasped along the hard scales on the other's forearm.

"Rangers should only speak when spoken to. And Bemmy rangers must let their superiors decide what is best for them. Such must be dutiful and humble and keep their places—"

The close guard which Kartr had kept upon his temper ever since his warning had been so quickly disregarded vanished at Zinga's remark.

"I've heard enough of that!"

"Zinga has a point," Rolth paid no attention to Kartr's outbreak. "We either accept the prevailing conditions here—or we leave—if we can. And maybe we can't wait too long or be halfway about it."

" 'If we can,' " repeated, Zinga with a grin displaying no humor but many sharp teeth. "That is a most interesting suggestion, Rolth. I wonder if there were—or are—any Bemmys numbered in the crew or among the passengers of the *X451*. You notice that I am inclined to use the past tense when I refer to them. Indications would make that seem proper."

Kartr studied his two brown hands, one protruding from the dirty sling, the other resting on his knee. They were scratched and calloused, the nails worn down. But though he was examining each one of those scratches with minute attention he was really absorbed in the nasty implications of Zinga's words. No—he didn't have to accept matters as they were. He should make a few preparations of his own.

"Where are our packs?" he asked Zinga.

Both eyelids closed in a slow wink. "Those creatures are under our eye. If we have to leave in a hurry we'll be able to do so with full tramping equipment."

"I shall suggest to Jaksan that the rangers take quarters on their own—together—" Kartr said slowly.

"There is a three-story tower on the west corner of this building," cut in Fylh. "Should we withdraw to that lofty perch—well, it may be that they will be so glad to be rid of us that they will permit it."

"Let ourselves be bottled up?" asked Zinga with some sting in his hissing voice.

Fylh clicked his claws with an irritated snap. "No one is going to be bottled up. Please remember we are dealing with highly civilized city dwellers, not explorers. To them all possible passages in and out of a building are accounted for by windows and doors only."

"Then this tower of yours boasts some feature not included in that catalogue which would serve us in a pinch?" There was a little smile curving Rolth's pale lips.

"Naturally. Or I would not have seen its possibilities as our stronghold. There are a series of bands projecting in a pattern down the outer walls. As good as a staircase to someone who knows how to use fingers and toes—"

"And keep his eyes closed while he does it," groaned

Zinga. "Sometimes I wish *I* were civilized and could lead a sane and peaceful life."

"We could allow"—Fylh had talked himself back into his best humor again—"these people to believe that we are safely out of mischief. They can put a guard at the single stairway leading up in that tower if they wish."

Kartr nodded. "I'll see Jaksan. After all, we may be rangers, but we are also Patrol. And if we want to stick together no civilian has any right to question us—Vice-Sector Lord or not! Stay out of trouble now."

He got up and the three nodded. They might not be sensitives—though he suspected that Zinga had some power akin to his, but they knew that they were only four in a potentially dangerous environment. If they could just get themselves exiled into Fylh's tower!

But he had to wait a long time to see Jaksan. The arms officer had accompanied Vibor to the medico. And when he at last returned to his quarters and found Kartr waiting for him, he was anything but cordial.

"What do you want now? The Vice-Sector Lord has been asking for you. He had some orders—"

"Since when," Kartr interrupted, "has even a Vice-Sector Lord had orders for one of the Patrol? He may advise and request—he does not order any wearer of the Comet, patrolman or ranger!"

Jaksan had crossed to the window and now he stood there, tapping his nails against the casing, his shoulders and back stubbornly presented to the sergeant. He did not turn when he answered:

"I do not believe that you take our position now into proper consideration, Sergeant. We do not have a ship. We—"

"And since when has a ship been necessary?" But maybe that was the exact truth, right there. Maybe to Jaksan and the crew the ship *was* necessary—without it they were naked, at a loss. "It is because I feared this very thing," he continued more quietly, "that I was against our coming here." Whether it was politic or not he had to say that.

"Under the circumstances we had very little choice in the matter!" Jaksan showed some of his old fire in that burst. "Great Space, man, would you have us fight the wilderness for food and shelter when there was this to come to? What of the Commander? He had to have medical attention. Only a—" He stopped in mid-sentence.

"Why not finish that, sir? Only a barbarian ranger would argue against it. Is that what you want to say? Well, I maintain, barbarian that I am, that it is better to be free in the wilderness than to come here. But let me have this clear—am I to understand that you have surrendered the authority of the Patrol to Joyd Cummi?"

"Divided authority is bad." But Jaksan refused to turn and face him. "It is necessary that each man contribute his skills to help the community. Joyd Cummi has discovered evidence that there is a severe cold season coming. It is our duty to help prepare for that. I think he wishes to send out hunting parties as food may be a problem. There are women and children to provide for—"

"I see. And the rangers are to take over the hunting? Well, we shall make a few plans. In the meantime we will take quarters for ourselves. And it might be well to arrange those with an eye to the future—unless there is also a butcher to be found among these city men."

"You and Rolth were assigned rooms here—"

"The rangers prefer to remain as a unit. As you know, that is only Patrol policy. Or has the Patrol totally ceased to exist?" If Kartr had not been needled by increasing uneasiness he might not have added that.

"See here, Kartr." Jaksan turned away from the

window. "Isn't it about time that you looked straight at some hard facts? We're going to be here for the rest of our lives. We are seven men against almost two hundred—and they have a well-organized community going—"

"Seven men?" queried Kartr. "We number nine if you count the Commander."

"Men." Jaksan stressed the word.

There it was—out in the open. Kartr had feared to hear it for a long time now.

"There are four qualified Patrol rangers and five of you," he returned stubbornly. "And the rangers stick together."

"Don't be a fool!"

"Why shouldn't I have that privilege?" Kartr's rage was ice cold now. "All the rest of you seem to enjoy it."

"You're a human being! You belong with your kind. These aliens—they—"

"Jaksan"—Kartr repudiated once and for all the leadership of the arms officer—"I know all those threadbare, stock arguments. There is no need to run through them again. I have had them dinned into me by your kind ever since I joined the Service and asked for ranger detail—"

"You young idiot! Since you joined the Service, eh? And how long ago was that? Eight years? Ten? You're no more than a cub now. Since you joined the Service! You don't know anything at all about it—this Bemmy problem. Only a barbarian—"

"We'll admit that I'm a barbarian and that I have odd tastes in friends, shall we? Admit it and leave it out of this conversation!" Kartr was gaining control of his temper.

It was plain that Jaksan was attempting to justify some stand he had taken or been forced into agreement with, not only to Kartr but to himself.

"Suppose you allow me to go to perdition my own way. Is this 'All humans stand together' a rule of Cummi's?"

Jaksan refused to meet the sergeant's demanding gaze. "He is very prejudiced. Don't forget he is an Ageratan. They had an internal problem in that system when they had to deal with a race of alien non-humans—"

"And they solved that problem neatly and expediently by the cold-blooded massacre of the aliens!"

"I forgot—your feeling against Ageratans—"

"My feeling for Ageratans, which, I might say, is different from the one you deem it to be, has nothing to do with this case. I simply refuse now or ever to hold any such views against any stranger, human or Bemmy. If the Vice-Sector Lord wants the rangers to do his hunting—all right. But we shall stick together as a unit. And if to continue to do so means trouble—then we might oblige in that direction also!"

"Look here." Jaksan kicked moodily at the bedroll which lay on the floor. "Don't stop thinking about it, Kartr. We'll have to live the rest of our lives here. We're really lucky beyond our dreams—Cummi believes that this city can be almost entirely restored. We can start all over. I know that you don't care for Cummi, but he is able enough to organize a shipload of hysterical passengers into a going settlement. Seven men can't fight him. All I ask of you for the present is don't repeat to Cummi what you just said to me. Think it over first."

"I shall. In the meantime the rangers will take quarters together."

"Oh, all right." Jaksan shrugged. "Do it—wherever you please."

"Maybe he should have said where Cummi pleases," thought Kartr as he left the room.

He found the rangers waiting for him and gave his own orders.

"Rolth, you and Fylh get up to that tower. If anyone tries to stop you pull Patrol rank on him. It may still carry some weight with the underlings here. Zinga, where did you leave our packs?"

Five minutes later Kartr and the Zacathan gathered the four pioneer packs. "Slip an anti-gravity disc under them," said Kartr, "and come on."

With the packs floating just off the floor and easy to tow, they made their way toward the rear of the building. But, as they approached the narrow flight of stairs Zinga said led to the roof, they were met by Fortus Kan. He edged back against the wall to let them pass, since Kartr did not halt. But he asked as they went by:

"Where are you going?"

"Settling in ranger quarters," the sergeant returned briefly.

"That one is still watching us," Zinga whispered as they mounted. "He is none too stout of heart. A good loud shout of wrath aimed at him would send him scuttling—"

"But don't try it," Kartr returned. "There is enough trouble before us now without stirring up any more."

"Ho! So you learned that, did you? Well, a short life and a merry one, as my egg brother often said while we were still shipmates. I wonder where Ziff is now—rolling in silk and eating brofids three times a day if I know that black-hearted despoiler! Not that it wouldn't be good to see his ugly face awaiting us above when we have finished this climb. His infighting is excellent, a very handy man with a force blade. Zippp—and there's an enemy down with half his insides gone—"

They could do, thought Kartr bitterly, with about fifty good infighters right now—or even with only ten.

"Welcome home, travelers!" That was Rolth, his goggled eyes lending his face an insect-like outline as he looked down at them. "For once the old pepper bird has found us a real perch. Come in and relax, my brave boys!"

"Flame bats and octopods!" Even Zinga seemed truly amazed as he stared about the room they entered.

The walls were a murky translucent green. And behind them came and went shapes of vivid color, water creatures swimming! Then Kartr saw that it was an illusion born of light and some sort of automatic picture projection. Zinga sat down on the packs, bearing them under his weight to the floor.

"Luscious! Luscious! Enough to tempt the most fastidious palate. The being who planned this room was a gourmand. I would be proud to shake his hand, fin or tentacle. Magnificent! That red one—does it not resemble almost to the last scale the succulent brofid? What a wonderful, wonderful room!"

"What about rations?" Kartr inquired of Rolth over Zinga's head.

The Faltharian's eyebrows raised until they could be seen over the rim of his goggles. "Are you contemplating our sitting out a siege? We have a few basic supply tins still unopened—about five days of full meals—twice that if we have to draw in our belts."

"Do you mean to tell me," Zinga broke out, "that you have brought me into this place of culinary promise and now propose to feed me extract of nourishing—bah—what a word, nourishing! As if nourishment and *food* are ever the same—to feed me extract of fungus and the rest of that unexciting goo we have to absorb when we are climbing over bare rock with no chance of hunting! This is a torture which cannot be refined upon. I insist upon my rights as a freeborn citizen—"

"A freeborn citizen?" queried Fylh. "Second class—third class twice removed, would be much more apt. And you have no rights at all—"

But Rolth had been watching Kartr's expression and now he broke in.

"Is that the way of it—honestly?"

"Just about, I'm afraid." Kartr sat down on the room's single piece of furniture—an opaline bench. "I went to Jaksan. He said Cummi had orders for me—"

"Orders?" Again the Faltharian's eyebrows betrayed his surprise. "A civilian giving orders to the Patrol? We may be rangers, but we are also still Patrol!"

"Are we?" Fylh wondered. "A Patrolman has ships, force to back him up. We're just survivors now, and we can't ring in the fleet if we get in a tight place—"

"Jaksan agrees with that. I gathered that he has more or less abdicated in Cummi's favor. The idea is that the Vice-Sector Lord has a running concern here—"

"And that we are more or less lucky to be included in?" demanded Rolth. "Yes, I can see that argument being advanced. But Jaksan—he's veteran Patrol to the core. Somehow his standing aside this way—it doesn't fit!"

Fylh made a gesture of brushing aside nonessentials. "Jaksan's psychological response need not concern us as much as something else. Do I gather that here Bemmys *are* second class citizens?"

"Yes." That answer was bald but Kartr saw no need to temper it.

"I take it that you were urged to—er—withdraw from contagion," Zinga drawled, leaning back and hooking his taloned fingers over his knees.

"That was part of it."

"How stupid can they get?" Rolth wanted to know. "If they want us to do their hunting, they must need food. And a bunch of these soft inner system men are not going to get much game by running out and beating the bushes. Instead of antagonizing us they ought to be making concessions."

"When did you ever know prejudice to act logically? And Jaksan seems to have agreed to this down-with-the-Bemmys plan, hasn't he?" Fylh's red eyes had gleams in them not very pleasant to see.

"I don't know what's happened to Jaksan," Kartr exploded. "And I don't care! It's what is going to happen to us which is more important right now—"

"You and Rolth," Fylh pointed out, "need not worry—"

Kartr jumped to his feet and took two strides across the room so that his green eyes were on a level and boring into those round red ones.

"That is the last time I ever want to hear anything like that! I told Jaksan and I shall tell Cummi—if it becomes necessary—that the rangers stand together."

Fylh's thin lips shut. Then the hard points of fire in his eyes softened. He made a small soothing gesture with his claws and when he spoke his voice was even again.

"What was Jaksan's reaction to your speech?"

"Just a lot of words. But it gave me an excellent chance of putting through our coming here together."

Zinga had arisen and was prowling around the room. "Done any more exploring, you two?" he asked Rolth. "What's the layout?"

"One more room beyond that archway on this floor. It has two windows both of which overhang Fylh's outside stairway. There is one large room immediately above this one and a third over that with a bathroom off. Believe it or not—the water is running in that!"

Kartr disregarded Zinga's exclamation of approval. "Only the one way in—unless someone climbs up the wall? Sure of that?"

"Yes. Of course they might descend upon us from the sky. But I hardly think we need fear that. And this door can be locked—watch—"

Rolth trod on a dull red block set in the floor. A door moved silently out of the right wall and sealed the entrance. On it was a metal plate and the Faltharian set his hand on it for an instant.

"Now try to get that open," he urged the sergeant.

But, even when Zinga and Fylh added their strength to his, Kartr was unable to force the door. Then Rolth stepped again on the stone and it opened easily.

"Fylh locked me out when we were exploring and we had a time finding out how to open it again. Tricky, the fellows who built that. It would take a full size disruptor to breach that."

"Which leads me to wonder if they do have one of those." Zinga put Kartr's thought into words.

But then that worry was blocked out for he sensed someone coming up the stairs. At the sergeant's signal the rangers melted away. Zinga was now flat against the wall beside the door where he could be at the back of anyone who entered before the stranger would know of his presence. Fylh lay belly down behind the pile of packs, and Rolth had drawn his blaster, standing a little behind the sergeant who waited, his good hand empty.

"Kartr!"

They knew the voice but they did not relax.

"Come in."

Smitt obeyed. He gave a start as Zinga materialized behind him. But there was a worried frown on his face and Kartr knew that he was no danger to them. For the second time the com-techneer had come to them because he was in trouble and not because he was an enemy.

"What is it?" asked the sergeant with very little

welcome. After all Smitt was to be normally reckoned with Jaksan's forces.

"They're talking—a lot. They've said you rangers are too alien to be trusted."

"Well"—Kartr's lips curled back in what was not even a shadow of a smile—"I've heard that a good many times before and I can't see that we're any the worse for it."

"Maybe you weren't—before. But this Ageratan—he's—the man must be mad!" Smitt exploded. "I tell you"—his voice slid up the scale a little—"he must be raving mad!"

"Suppose," hissed Zinga, "you just sit down—over there where we can keep an eye on you—and tell us all about it."

8

Palace Revolution

"That's it— I've practically nothing concrete to tell. It's just a kind of feeling—the way he persists in keeping us away from all but his own men. He has a guard—that Can-hound, a couple of jetmen from the *X451*, one of the officers, two intal planters, and three professional mercenaries. They're all armed—Control issue blasters and force blades. But I haven't heard of or seen any of the other officers from the *X451*. And Cummi's taken over—gives commands to *us*! Dalgre and Snyn were sent to join his techneers and help run the city. Ordered to do so, mind you—and they Patrolmen! And Jaksan didn't make any objection."

"And what about you—has he drafted you yet?" asked Rolth.

"Luckily I wasn't there when they came hunting techneer recruits. Look here—how does he dare give orders to the Patrol?" There was honest bewilderment in Smitt's voice.

For the second time Kartr explained. "Better get it into your head, Smitt, that as far as you, and Cummi, and the rest of us are concerned, the Patrol has ceased to exist. We've nothing to back up any show of authority—he has. That is just why—"

"You argued against our coming here?" Smitt's lips thinned. Kartr felt the other's rage. "Well, you were right! I know you rangers don't feel the same about the Service as we crewmen do. You've always been independent cusses. But my father died on the barricades at the Altra air locks—one of the rear guard who held their posts long enough for the survivors' ships to leave. And my grandfather was second officer of the Promixa dreadnaught when she tried to reach Andromeda. We've served five generations in the Patrol. And may I be Space-burned if I ever take orders from a Cummi while I still wear this!" His hand went to his Comet badge.

"A very fine sentiment which will not help you any if Cummi's private police force comes a-hunting," Zinga remarked. "But was it just this disinclination to take orders from a mere civilian which drove you to us?"

"You," Smitt snapped at the Zacathan, "needn't be so cocky. I overheard enough to learn that Cummi is death on fraternization with Bemmys and that goes for rangers, too," he aimed in Kartr's direction. "There's a rumor, it came in the form of a secondhand warning from one of the intal planters, that Cummi's had a couple burned already—"

"A couple of what?" That was Fylh, and his crest was rising. "Bemmys? Of what species?"

Smitt shook his head. "I don't know, the planter was vague. Only, you're not going to get a fair deal from Cummi, that's plain. And I'm not going to take his orders. Maybe we haven't always run the same course before, but we have a common problem before us now."

"So?" Fylh's claws preened his crest. "But the best of the bargain seems to be yours under the circumstances. What do you have to offer us in return?"

"He has something we might need," Kartr broke in.

The appeal of the com-techneer was an honest one. He did want to throw in with them.

"It will depend upon you, Smitt. Can you swallow your pride enough to co-operate with Cummi's party—co-operate until you can learn something of their set-up—how much power Cummi really has, whether there are any rebels among the passengers, what are some of his future plans? We're not"—he spoke now to the rangers—"going to strike out blindly. You two, Fylh and Zinga, will have to lie low until we do know how we stand. No use attracting any attention. As for me, since my talk with Jaksan, I am doubtless down in their black books with a double star. Rolth is handicapped for daytime work. So, Smitt, if you are really willing to join up with us, keep that wish under mind block—and I mean *under* block. The Ageratan is a sensitive and what he can't scrape out of an unsuspecting mind the Can-hound may be able to get for him. It'll be a tough assignment, Smitt. You've got to join the anti-Bemmy, pro-Cummi crowd—at least with lukewarm attachment. A little initial rebellion is all right, they would expect that from a Patrolman with your background. But can you play a double game, Smitt—and do you want to?"

The com-techneer had listened quietly and now he raised his head and nodded.

"I can try. I don't know about this mind block business." He hesitated. "I'm no sensitive. How much can Cummi do with me?"

"He's a five point nine. He can't take you over, if

that is what you're afraid of. You're from Luga—or your family was Lugan stock originally, weren't they?"

"My father was Lugan. My mother came from Desart."

"Lugan—Desart—" Kartr looked to Zinga.

"High resistance core," the Zacathan informed him promptly. "Imaginative, but excellent control. Resistance is above eight. No, no Ageratan could take him over. And you do have a mind block, Smitt, whether you've ever tried to use it or not. Just think about some com-machine when you're around a sensitive. Concentrate on some phase of your old job—"

"Like this?" demanded Smitt eagerly.

It was as if he had snapped off some switch. Where Smitt sat there was now a mental blank. Kartr bit off an exclamation and then said:

"Keep that up, Smitt! Zinga—!"

His own power went out toward the com-techneer, and then he felt a second stream of energy unite with it, driving into that blankness with him like the tip of a blaster beam. So, he had been right! Zinga was a sensitive, too, and to a degree he could not even measure. Together their wills smashed at Smitt, smashed on a barrier which held as staunchly as the hull of a space ship.

There were beads of moisture on Kartr's forehead, gathering under the edge of his helmet to trickle down his cheeks and chin. Then his free hand moved in a gesture of defeat and he relaxed.

"You need not worry about mind invasion, Smitt. Unless you get careless."

The com-techneer was on his feet. "Then we are allied?" He asked that almost shyly, as if he had come there expecting to be turned away.

"We are. Just stir around some and see what you can find out. But don't, if possible, get sent off from here where we can't reach you. We may have to move fast if trouble comes."

"I won't let you down." Smitt crossed to the door. Now he hesitated and turned. And before he went out his hand moved in a gesture which included all of them—human and Bemmy alike—the full salute of a Patrolman to his equals.

"Now—just in case—" Fylh flitted across the room and stamped on the door-controlling block, locking the portal with the heat of his claws.

"Yes," Zinga agreed, "one does feel more relaxed when it isn't necessary to think about guarding one's back. Shall we settle in?"

Kartr slipped his left wrist out of the sling and rubbed it thoughtfully.

"They have a medico here. I wonder—"

Rolth moved up beside him. "Are you thinking of venturing into the slith's cave alone?"

"A well-equipped ship's hospital should include a renewer ray. And I'd like to go into battle—if I have to—with two good hands instead of one. Also it gives me a legitimate excuse for wandering around below. I can ask questions—"

"All right. But you don't go alone," Rolth agreed. "Somehow I don't fancy any of us prancing about alone in this building. Two's pretty good company—and two blasters can clear a wider path than one."

"None of that! I'm a sufferer in search of a medico, remember?" But Kartr's lips stretched in what had come during these past days to be an unfamiliar curve, a genuine smile. "Have you two enough to amuse yourselves with while we are gone?"

"Don't worry about us." Zinga grinned and his inch fangs shone in the greenish light to ghoulish advantage. "We shall set up housekeeping. We do, I take it, lock the door behind you?"

"Yes. And you open it only when you pick up our mind patterns."

Zinga didn't even blink at that. Of course, he had revealed the extent of his power when he had aided Kartr in attacking Smitt's block. But, with his usual disregard for human emotions, he apparently saw no reason for discussing his long concealment now.

Fylh opened the door and they started down the stairs. It was quiet below and they were almost into the corridor before Kartr's perception warned him of a stranger's approach. It was a young man, in the rather ornate uniform of a passenger ship's officer, who strode confidently toward them.

"You are Sergeant Kartr?"

"I am."

"The Vice-Sector Lord wishes to see you."

Kartr stopped and gazed with mild interest at the newcomer. Perhaps the sergeant was even a year or so younger than this assured Flight Spacer—allowing for planetary and racial difference—but suddenly he felt almost grandfatherly.

"I have not received any orders from my superior officer delegating me to be attached to the service of the Central Control Civil Section."

And for a wonder that pomposity actually disconcerted the other. Maybe the old magic of the Patrol still held a small power. Kartr and Rolth started on, passed the officer, and were several feet down the hall before he caught up with them again.

"See here!" He tried to project the sting of an order into his voice, but it faded when both rangers wheeled to give him grave and courteous attention. "The Lord Cummi—he is in charge here, you know," he ended lamely.

"Section six, paragraph eight, general orders," answered Rolth. " 'The Patrol is the guardian of the law under Central Control. It may assist the civil branch if and when requested to do so. But at no time and in no manner does it surrender its authority to any planetary or sectional advisor or ruler, except under the direct seal and order of Central Control.' "

The youngster stood with his mouth slightly open. The last thing he had expected, thought Kartr with a relieving chuckle of real humor which he was able to suppress, was to have general orders spouted in his face. Zinga would have loved to hear this. Kartr hoped that the Zacathan had followed them mentally and *was* enjoying it.

"But—" whatever protest the Spacer was about to make died away as the rangers' expressions of polite but impatient attention did not alter.

"Now," Kartr said when the officer added nothing to that forlorn "but," "perhaps you can direct me to your medico's quarters. I require attention for this." He indicated his wrist.

The officer was eager to oblige. "Down two flights of stairs at the end of this corridor and turn to your right. Medico Tre has the first four rooms in that hall."

He remained where he was, still staring after them as they moved on.

"What do you suppose he is going to report to the great Cummi?" Rolth wondered as they followed directions. "I don't think that I would care to be in his boots. "Do you believe—"

"That I was wise to stand up and resist at this point? Maybe I wasn't, but they must have discovered from Jaksan that I am hostile. And"—Kartr's face was entirely expressionless—"that was something I had to do. He set the Can-hound on us!"

And Rolth, having seen that fighting face before and knowing what its mask covered, decided to say no more.

They met no one else on those two flights of stairs. Apparently this portion of Cummi's stronghold was more or less deserted. And they were approaching the first door along the medico's corridor when a thin whisper of sound caught their attention. Here the tall windows were set in deep recesses and it was from one of those that the summons came.

"A woman—"

But Kartr already knew that, having met the block which always prevented a sensitive from interpreting the emotions of one of the opposite sex. She was leaning forward, daring to beckon with one hand. Rolth edged toward that side of the hall and Kartr nodded. The Faltharian would contact the woman while the sergeant kept on to their destination. If any one except Zinga had a mind watch on them at present such a move might be confusing.

Rolth stepped into the embrasure and drew back against the window, taking the woman with him. To anyone not directly before the recess they were not visible. Kartr went on a yard and glanced back. Rolth had made the right move—from where he was now they could not be seen.

The sergeant turned into the next open door. Medico's quarters all right from the equipment in sight. Almost at the same instant a tall man came from an inner room. Kartr tried mind contact and then lost some of his tension. This was no Ageratan, and no enemy either. He could scan nothing but good will in the other's mind.

"You have a renewer ray?" he asked, drawing his arm out of the sling.

"We have. How long it will continue to function locked to these city currents is another question. We cannot be sure of anything. I am Medico Lasilo Tre. A break?" His fingers were already busy about Kartr's wrist, unfastening the bandages Zinga had put on that morning.

"I don't know. Ah—" Kartr sucked in his breath as Tre began probing the bruised and purple flesh.

Then the ranger was pushed down on a stool at the edge of the renewer beam, his throbbing arm stretched out under the concentrated ray, feeling again the draw of those invisible healing motes. Twice Tre snapped off the current and came to examine the hurt with delicate finger tips—only to turn it on again after shaking his head. The third time he was satisfied. Kartr lifted his arm gingerly and flexed first his fingers and then his wrist. Although he had once before been under the ray—to renew a leg almost chewed to pieces—the wonder of the restoration was as great as ever. He pulled off his sling and grinned happily at the medico.

"Better than new," Tre commented. "Only wish that your officer could be as easily put to rights, Sergeant—"

Vibor! Kartr had almost forgotten the Commander. "How is he?"

Tre frowned. "The physical wounds—those we were able to heal. But the other— I'm no psycho-sensitive. He needs the type of care and treatment he'll never be able to get now—unless a miracle occurs and we are rescued—"

"Which you do not believe will ever happen," suggested Kartr.

"How can any sensible man believe that we will?" countered the medico. But there was something else, another emotion hidden beneath that answer. "This planet—this solar system—does not even exist on any map the X451 carried."

"But those who built this city were at a high level of civilization," Kartr pointed out. "Where did they go?"

"They were and they weren't. Mechanically they

were far advanced, yes. But there are odd gaps. I understand you rangers are trained to assess strange civilizations. I shall be eager to have your reaction to the ruins of this one after you have had the time to study it. The one thing I *have* noticed is that there is no space port here and there never was. Maybe the men of this world never knew space flight—"

"But what happened to them?"

Tre shrugged. "At least this is no second Tantor. We made sure of that before we entered the city. And we have found no human remains here. It seems almost as if they all walked away one day, leaving their city ready and waiting, all geared to go again when they wished to return. There are signs of time—some erosion. The machinery, though, had all been left protected, oiled, laid up in such a way as to set our mech-techneers running around begging people to come and look at an excellent preservation job."

"They must have planned on returning, then." Kartr digested that. Was there, on some other land mass of this unknown world, a remnant of civilization?

"If they did they were prevented. It has been a long time since they left. Wrist okay, Sergeant?"

Kartr did not start at the abrupt change in the other's speech. He knew that Rolth was at the door behind him.

"Medico Tre, Ranger Rolth." He was careful to glance around before making the introductions. No need to tip off Tre that he was a sensitive.

The medico acknowledged the Faltharian's salute. "Pleased to see you, ranger. Any aches or pains to report? Goggles holding up? Need any skin burn cream? You *are* a Faltharian?"

The lips below Rolth's goggle mask curved into a smile which expanded under the medico's friendliness. "You know all about my problems then, Medico?"

"Had a Faltharian patient once—bad skin burn. That's what started me messing around with creams. Found one which did help a lot. Wait a minute—"

He hurried to a medicine case in the corner and began checking over the assortment of plaso-tubes it held. "Try this." He brought one out. "Spread it on before you go into direct daylight. I think you'll find it will stop irritation."

"Thanks, Medico." Rolth put the tube into his belt pouch. "So far I've been okay. Only the sergeant here had work for you."

Kartr flipped his left hand up and down from the restored wrist. "And this is as good as new. What's your fee?"

Tre laughed. "Credit slips wouldn't have much value here, would they? If you come across anything interesting in my line when you go exploring, just let me know. That will be good enough for me. Glad to be of service to the Patrol at any time, anyway. You boys deserve the best we civilians can give you. I hear that you may be hunting—any chance of going along some time on one of your trips?"

Kartr was surprised. There was an urgency in that question and the medico's eyes locked with his as if Tre were trying desperately to tell him something—a message vitally important to both of them.

"I don't see why not," the sergeant returned. "If we do go. I've had no orders as yet. Thanks again, Medico—"

"Not at all. Only too glad to be able to help. See you around—"

But still underneath that urgent appeal. Then Kartr's eyes widened. The fingers of the medico's right hand—they had moved—were moving again—to shape a figure he knew well. But how—how and when had Tre learned that? Automatically he made the prescribed answer with his forefinger, even as he said loudly:

"If and when we go out, we'll let you know. Clear skies—"

"Clear skies." The other returned the spaceman's good-bye.

Outside the door Kartr's hand closed for a moment only on Rolth's. The Faltharian at once began talking about hunting.

"Those horned beasts we saw in the clearing," he said as they mounted the stairs again, "they should make excellent eating. There may be some way of salting down the flesh—if we could locate salt deposits. And the same for those river creatures Zinga is always talking about. We needn't send him to bring in those." The Faltharian laughed as light-heartedly as if he had not caught the message and was speaking now for other ears. "He'd eat more than he'd bring back."

"We'd better not use the blasters," Kartr cut in as if he were giving some serious thought to the questions. "Spoils too much of the meat. Force blades—"

"Have to get in close to use them, wouldn't you?" asked Rolth dubiously.

Both of them were climbing faster. There was someone behind them now. Kartr's mind touched and then recoiled, sickened. The Can-hound was trailing them. But they did not run, though they were breathing hard when they reached the top of the last flight and saw the door to the tower open just enough for them to squeeze through. Zinga slammed it shut on their heels with an open-jawed snarl of rage.

"So that's after you!"

"As a trailer only, I think. Let him stew around outside. Now, Rolth, what about that woman. What did she want?"

"She thought we were brave heroes come to the rescue. Cummi's kept it dark—our arrival—but word got around—our uniforms are too well known. She came to ask for help. The situation here is just about what you thought it was. Cummi's set himself up as a pocket-sized Central Control. You do just as he says or you don't eat. And if you protest too loudly you disappear—"

"How many have disappeared?" Fylh wanted to know.

"The Captain of the *X451* and three or four others. Then there were four Bemmy passengers—they disappeared too. But not in the same way. I gather that they saw which way the stars were showing right after the landing and went off into the blue by themselves—"

"Bemmys! What species?" Zinga's frill made a fan behind his head. He still stood by the door as if listening to something on the other side of the portal.

"I couldn't get that out of her. She didn't see them until after the ship came down—it was a two-class liner. Anyway there is now a Cummi party, small but armed and dangerous, and an anti-Cummi party badly organized and just milling around—taking it out in talk where they can't be overheard by the lord and master. Cummi himself keeps holed up here and has his men patrolling. Those who know anything—the techneers, the medico—he keeps right under his eyes. That Can-hound is one of his big threats."

"Are we invited to join the anti-Cummi party?" Fylh asked.

"I don't think it has gone that far yet. They had an idea that the Patrol had moved in to take over. And do you know—I think that that is just what we might have done if we had handled this the way you wanted to, Kartr—allowed them to think we had an undamaged ship and were on duty. I had to tell the woman that we were not in charge. But I also informed her that the rangers were sticking together."

"They may plan a palace revolution," Kartr mused. "Very well. I say we stick tight here until we know more."

"Where did that medico learn ranger hand talk?" Rolth wondered.

"A question I'll ask him if I ever get the chance. He's another who suggested the waiting game and to keep our eyes open and our mouths shut."

"Our eyes and other things open—" Zinga's head was pressed against the surface of the door. "The Can-hound is about to do a little prying. Think sweet thoughts for him—quick!"

9

Showdown

"Then you press this little knob and— Neat, isn't it?"

Kartr had to agree with the Zacathan that the results of pressing the little knob were neat. Water, clear, honest, fresh water splashed out of a spout disguised as a monster's head and fell into a basin set in the floor, a basin large enough to accommodate with ease even Kartr's inches.

"Go on—try it!" urged Zinga. "I did—twice! And you don't see me any the worse for it, do you?" He turned slowly around flexing his muscles and grinning toothily.

Rolth leaned back against the edge of the doorway and watched the flood suspiciously.

"What about the water supply? Could our friends down below shut it off if they wanted to?"

Kartr had unbuckled and thrown aside belt and tunic. Now he paused uncertainly. It might be wiser to conserve water instead of wasting it on baths. But the Zacathan shook his head.

"The pipes carrying this run up through the walls. If they shut us off they will probably have to shut off their own supply also. Anyway—if a siege is included in their future plans we'd be fools to allow ourselves to get bottled up here any longer than it would take us to climb down that outer wall. Don't be a spoilsport," he ended. "Or do you *like* to go dirty?"

Kartr peeled off the rest of his clothing and kicked it across the floor. He had one clean outfit in his bag and he reveled in the thought of using it.

"I wonder what they looked like—" He tried the temperature of the pool with his toes and found it to be pleasantly warm—much more comfortable than the mountain stream.

"Who—? Oh, you mean the builders of this delightful spot? Well"—Zinga indicated the mirrored walls—"they were not ashamed to look themselves in the face. Wonder if those ever before reflected any bathers as ugly as you two—"

Kartr laughed and splashed water at the Zacathan. "Speak for yourself, Zinga. I'll have you know that my face is not considered suitable for frightening children—"

Or did that still hold true, he wondered suddenly, and for the first time surveyed his reflection critically as it appeared in the mirror which ran the full length of the wall behind the basin.

The deep brown skin which proclaimed his space-borne occupation had only a few lines as yet. Of course, above that dark expanse the color of his hair did look rather odd. But its soft cream and red brown in waving strips was perfectly natural for a son of Ylene. He had two eyes, green, set slightly aslant—a straight nose—a mouth centrally placed—all proper for a human.

"Teeth too small—"

Kartr flushed and watched the dark crimson creep up along his sharply defined cheek bones.

"Freeze and blast you, Zinga! Can't you leave a man's thoughts alone?"

"Admiring himself, was he? But I don't agree about the teeth—large ones aren't marks of beauty among our kind, you know—"

Zinga was standing open-jawed just before his own section of mirror. "And why not? Useful and beautiful both. I'd like to see either of you two puny humans take part in one of our warrior duels—no talons—no proper teeth—you wouldn't last a minute!"

"Beauty is in the eye of the beholder and conditioned by upbringing," announced the Faltharian. "Now Kartr's people have two-shaded hair—so does their ideal of beauty. My race"—he had been shedding helmet and tunic as he talked—"have white hair, white skin—pale eyes. So—for us those attributes are necessary to be considered handsome."

"Oh, you are all answers to the sighs of maidens." Fylh's voice deflated from the doorway. "Why not finish up that absurd splashing about in liquid and come and eat. Such a stupid waste of time—"

But Kartr refused to be hurried and Rolth was as leisurely in enjoying Zinga's discovery. When they were again clad and followed Fylh into the outer room they found the Trystian curled up on the ledge of an open window exchanging trills with several large birds.

"Gossiping again," commented Zinga. "And where is this food that it was so important that we eat? I'll wager two credits that he's passed it out to those feathered friends of his!"

"Serve you right if I had. But you'll find it just beyond your noses."

The concentrated rations were twice as tasteless to

anyone who had recently dined on roasted meat and the fresh fruits of the wilderness. Kartr chewed and swallowed conscientiously and longed to return to the past.

"I'll take it back." Zinga gagged realistically after he downed the last cube. "Fylh wouldn't pass this offal on—it would kill the birds and he likes birds—"

"What are we doing here anyway?" There was the whir of wings as the birds went and Fylh dropped to the floor, closing the window. "We should have stayed out there. This is a dead place and there is no sense in trying to bring it to life!"

"Don't worry. We'll probably be outside again sooner than we bargain for. Let's go down and agree to go hunting like good little rangers and then go—and never come back!"

Kartr looked up. He could understand that plea of Zinga's, and part of him wanted to do just what the Zacathan suggested. And he could participate in Fylh's feeling that this was a dead place returned to an unnatural life. But—there were women and children below in the city and there was a cold season approaching—unless Cummi had lied about that also. Maybe the intal planters, and some of the other passengers had hunted, but could their efforts supply all the needs of the community? And that woman today, she had appealed to Rolth, believed in their help just because they wore the Comets.

"It is like this," the sergeant began slowly, trying to put all these tangled feelings into the right words, to spread out before the others both sides of the question. "Do we have any right to walk out when we may be needed? On the other hand, if Cummi's anti-Bemmy talk puts you two in danger, you must go—"

"Why—?"

Zinga interrupted Fylh. "We don't go yet. But I see

your point. Only, let me warn you, Kartr, there are times when a man—or a Bemmy—has to harden his heart. We needn't make any decisions tonight. A good rest—"

"Locked door or not, I'm suggesting a watch," Fylh stated.

"They won't try to reach us—that way." Kartr shook his head.

"You mean—mind touch!" Rolth whistled. "Then Fylh and I won't be much help."

"True. So Zinga and I will divide the night."

There followed uneasy hours. Three rolled in bed-rolls, one on guard, slipping on unbooted feet from room to room, up and down, listening with both ears and mind. They did it in two-hour watches and Kartr had taken to his bed for the second time when Zinga hailed him with a low hiss. The sergeant pulled out with a sigh to join the Zacathan at an open window.

"Smitt is coming—across that other roof—"

The Zacathan was right; the mind pattern of the com-techneer identified him. And only a trained ranger could have sighted him. His dodging from shadow to shadow, his use of every bit of cover was Patrol work at its best.

"I'll go down to meet him." Before Zinga could protest Kartr was through the window and on that ladder of block design. Fortunately it was a cloudy night and he thought that unless someone were watching him through vision lenses he could not be seen, his uniform being almost the same shade as the stone.

As the sergeant came within a foot or two of the roof over which Smitt was advancing he gave a soft whistle of Patrol recognition. There was a moment of silence and then he was answered and the com-techneer came running to join him.

"Kartr here—"

"Thank the Spirit of Space! I've been trying to reach you for hours!"

"What's up?"

"The men—those against Cummi. They've taken our appearance here as a signal to fight him. The idiotic fools! He has a disruptor mounted in every main corridor, they can't get anywhere near him. And that Can-hound has knocked out two of the leaders—put them to sleep the same way you did Snyn back in the ship. It'll be nothing but raw murder if they try to storm Cummi's quarters! He had Jaksan locked up with the medico—and the techneers are under guard. He'll wipe out all opposition—"

"He's planted a force bomb at the foot of your tower stairs. If you try to come down—finish! And he and the Can-hound are cooking up something special to smoke you out—"

Something special! If the Ageratan believed that he was only dealing with a sensitive of equal powers there were many things he could try. But against a six point six *and* Zinga such attacks might backfire.

"I've got to get back." Smitt nursed his blaster in one hand. "I've got to keep those fools from attacking head on. Is there anything you can do?"

"I don't know. But we'll try. Hold off your men as long as you can. Maybe we can turn the tables—"

Smitt melted away into the night. If he kept his mental guard he was going to be a formidable addition to the rebel forces. Neither the Ageratan nor the Can-hound could get to him that way. Kartr climbed back up to the tower window to discover all the rangers waiting for him.

"That was Smitt." As usual darkness had not confused Rolth. "What did he want?"

"There's a rebellion against Cummi. The other side took our arrival for the signal to break loose."

"And Cummi, of course, has not been slumbering peacefully meanwhile. What have his merry men prepared for us?"

"Yes"—Rolth added his question to Fylh's—"what is ready and waiting for us?"

"Smitt said a force bomb at the foot of the stairs, ready to go off as we go down—"

"Play rough, don't they? Do you know, I think that somebody should put the old healthy fear of the Patrol into these gentlemen—"

"Where's Zinga?" Kartr interrupted the Faltharian.

"Gone below to do what he calls 'listening.' " Fylh laid a torch on the floor, pulled the edge of his bedroll partially over it and by the shielded light began to count out the extra clips for their blasters. It did not, unfortunately, take him very long to finish the task.

"That all we have?" Kartr asked grimly.

"You have the charges now in your weapons and the extras in your belt loops—if you've followed regulations. These are the rest."

"All right. It comes to three apiece and the one over for Rolth. If this is to be a night fight we might as well give the advantage to the one who can make the best use of it."

The Faltharian was busy at a task of his own, securing their packs. If they did not have to make a run for it, they might be able to bring off their equipment too.

"They've moved our sled into the hallway down there and it is probably under guard now. If we win through—"

"If we win," Fylh broke in, "we can march right in and take it. We might just do that anyway. What's keeping the old lizard?"

Kartr had wondered about that, too, enough to send a questing thought which was answered instantly with a strong impression of danger. The sergeant scooped up his share of the blaster clips and tucked them into his belt before he crossed the room and went down to the green fish chamber. Zinga stood pressed against the door as if he wished to melt into its surface. Kartr joined him to "listen."

There were movements—not too far away—maybe just beyond the foot of the staircase. Two living things withdrew, a third remained—that was the Can-hound. But why did they leave that one on guard unless—

Unless, Zinga's thought answered him in a second's flash, they suspect that you—or I—are not what we seem. But they cannot know the full truth or they would not leave the Can-hound. Not after the way you handled him before. They must have discovered that—

Or is he—bait? Kartr thought back to Zinga, reveling in the freedom of this exchange which he had always longed to experience but had never found before.

That we shall see. This time the task is mine—brother!

Kartr withdrew mind touch and concentrated only on trying to sense the approach of any other who might break Zinga's control. He felt the Zacathan's body grow tense and guessed the agony Zinga was feeling.

It was as if they had stepped out of time—planet time. Kartr never knew how long they fought their soundless battle before he had to give a warning.

"One comes." He said that aloud, not daring to break in by thought.

Zinga hissed a long sigh. "He *was* bait of a sort," he answered in words, as if his thought power was almost exhausted. "But not as we had feared. He has been under observation all the time—if he withdrew against orders then they could assume that we were powerful enough to control him. So they suspect—but they do not know."

"You say—they—we face more than Cummi and the Can-hound?"

"Cummi has learned to tap the mind energy of some others—how many I do not know. If a five point nine can do that—"

"What will he be able to raise himself to?" A great deal of Kartr's confidence was wiped out by the thought of that. Even with Zinga could he face down a Cummi so reinforced?

"I suggest," Zinga said a little dryly as if he were shaken also, "that we continue to stick to blasters as offensive weapons for a while. That way the odds are easier to assess."

"And we'll have to get out of here to be able to use those. If we leave, that thing below will know it at once."

"Which leaves us only one answer—we'll have to split up for now. You and Rolth take the outside route down and see what you can do in the general melee. Fylh and I shall hold the fort and try to make two think as four."

Kartr could see the wisdom in that. As humans Rolth and he would have a better chance of getting co-operation from the rebels. At the same time the Bemmy scouts would be safe from ruthless shooting.

The climb down to the roof top across which Smitt had come was ridiculously easy. They paused there long enough to pull on their boots, and then snaked over it from shadow to shadow. When they reached the parapet Rolth looked over. Then he dropped back and put his lips close to Kartr's ear.

"One floor below there is a ledge. It leads to a lighted window. The drop is sheer, I do not think that anyone who may be in that room would expect company to arrive through the window—"

"And how do you reach the ledge?"

"Our belts hooked together and passed around this—here—" The Faltharian put his hand on a tooth-shaped projection ornamenting the parapet.

If Kartr had an instant picture of what it meant to dangle so precariously over the edge of a sheer drop he did not betray himself.

"It is good that we are both tall." Rolth buckled his belt to the one the sergeant reluctantly passed over. "A short man could not make it."

The Faltharian slipped the loop in one end of his improvised rope over the projection and climbed over the parapet. Holding his body at an angle he half slid, half walked down the stone. Kartr huddled against the edge and forced himself to watch. Then Rolth stopped and the belt swung loosely in the sergeant's fingers.

Not so skillfully as Rolth, Kartr made the same trip, keeping his eyes fast on the stone before him, trying not to think of the darkness below. He inched downward for an eternity and then Rolth's hand pulled him straight and his boots touched the path of the ledge. He found that it was wider than it appeared from above, he could get all but a small scrap of heel onto it.

"Anyone in the room?" Rolth demanded as they crept toward the window.

Kartr sent out the probe. "Not in the room—near though—"

The Faltharian answered that with a ghost of laughter. "We're almost as good as some of Fylh's feathered friends. Here goes!" He caught at the window frame and pulled himself against it, jamming open the casement with his knee. It gave a faint squeak of protest and Rolth landed lightly on his feet within where Kartr joined him a second later.

They were in a chamber where someone was at home. A pile of bedding lay on a bunk bed which had been obviously torn out of ship's fittings. Two expensive Valcunite luggage bags stood against the wall and a table, also ship use, was piled almost to the sagging point with personal belongings.

Rolth's nostrils wrinkled. "What a stink!" he commented under his breath.

Kartr tried to remember where he had smelled that too-sweet cura blossom fragrance before.

"Fortus Kan!" When they had run against the secretary in the corridor that morning he had certainly carried cura lily with him.

And as if that identification had been either a summons or an entrance cue, the Vice-Sector Lord's man was coming toward them now. Kartr had warning enough to plaster himself back against the wall by the door, and Rolth, seeing his move, did the same on the other side of the portal.

There was apprehension to be read in the mind of the man who was fumbling with the intricate ancient fastening. Fortus Kan was afraid. The fastening was defying him, too, so that exasperation began to drown out the fear. He lost command enough to kick the panel as it gave. With such a medley of emotions uncovered it would be easy for Kartr to—

The sergeant allowed him four steps into the room before he put the flat of his hand against the door and sent it shut again. Fortus Kan spun around—to face the small and deadly mouths of two Patrol blasters. And at the sight all his resistance crumbled at once.

"Please!" His hands went up to his working mouth. He retreated backward, without looking where he was going, until the cot caught him behind the knees and he plumped down upon it as if he were as boneless as a Lydian gelisar.

As Kartr walked toward him the little man cringed as if he wanted to burrow into the tangle of bedding.

"One would begin to think, Kartr, that this gentleman has a guilty conscience—"

Rolth's words might have been the lash of a Tullan slaver's whip the way Fortus Kan reacted. He stopped trying to pull himself under the covers and sat stone still, his mouth trembling, his eyes glassy with—Kartr recognized—pure fear.

"Please—" The secretary had to work to get that one word out, but it was a stopper which had held up the flood. "Please—I had nothing to do with it—nothing! I advised him not to antagonize the Patrol. I know the law— Why, I have a second cousin who is the clerk in your administration office on Sexti. I wouldn't go against the Patrol—never. I had nothing, absolutely nothing to do with it!"

His fear was so rank that it was almost an odor in the room. But what was he afraid of—the planting of the force bomb, that trick with the Can-hound? There was only one way to get at the full truth. And for the second time in his life Kartr ruthlessly invaded a fellow human's mind, breaking down the feeble block, exploring, learning what he wanted—in part. Fortus Kan whimpered, was quiet. He would be quiet for a while now. Kartr turned away. There was a lot to do. A pity that Cummi had not trusted the little man more, there were such big gaps in his information—gaps which might be fatal if the rangers were not careful.

The sergeant came back to Rolth. "There's a force bomb under the tower stairs, all right. And the Can-hound is set to trick us out and blow it up. Everyone is being moved out of the top floors here before it goes off. Kan came back for some precious personal possessions. The stairs are under guard—"

"We could blast through—rather noisy though."

"Yes. One thing I'm wondering about—why all these

staircases when they had gravity wells, too. Odd—maybe important."

"This was a state building," Rolth reminded him. "Might use stairs for reasons of ceremony. Like those Opolti who fly everywhere except in the Affid's quarter. No evidence of any other way down from here. What about the boys? If that Can-hound gets tired of waiting for them to come out he may just set the bomb off anyway and trust to luck to bag the game."

"Yes—"

Kartr stood stiffly. He was blacking out, first the corridors, then this room, his awareness of Rolth, of Fortus Kan, of his own person. He did it! His mind touched Zinga's! He gave the warning. Then he was back in the frowzy room, shaking his head dazedly, to see Rolth crouched by the door listening. Men—two—three of them were coming along the hall outside—straight for this room!

10

Battle

A sharp rap on the door froze both rangers.

"Kan! We're moving out now. Come along!"

But Fortus Kan was deep in a world of his own.

"Kan! You fool, come on!"

Kartr made mind contact. Out there was the young ship's officer he had met early in the day, two others—human, non-sensitive. They were impatient, impatient because of fear. And the fear won out. After some garbled conversation, which came through the door only as a murmur, they went on. Rolth glided to the window and studied what lay below.

"I take it that we have to move fast?" he asked without turning around.

"They were afraid—too afraid to linger very long. What's below?"

"Another roof outcrop, but so far down we couldn't hope to make it without a climber's sucker pads."

"We have a substitute for sucker pads." Kartr rolled Fortus Kan off the bed and set to work tearing its coverings into strips which Rolth caught up and knotted together. Working against time, but testing each knot, they produced a rough rope.

"You first," ordered the sergeant. "Then this." He touched Kan with the toe of his boot. "I'll come last. Over now—time must be running out fast or they wouldn't have been in such a hurry to clear out."

Rolth was gone almost before he finished speaking. Kartr hung over the window sill to watch but the Faltharian was so quickly hidden in the dark that only the movements of the rope told when he stopped climbing down and signaled a safe landing. Kartr pulled the clumsy line back into the room, his palms wet against the torn cloth. There was a terrible urgency goading him. He tied the cloth loop under Kan's arms and manhandled the secretary's limp body over the sill, lowering it as slowly as he could until a sharp jerk told him Rolth was in charge. Kartr did not even wait until Kan was untied before he was descending hand over hand.

And as his feet hit the surface of the roof below it happened. There was no sound at first. But the support under him danced. He fell flat and buried his head in his arms, not daring to watch what was happening above. Force bomb all right. He had once before been caught in the backwash of one. Had Zinga and Fylh escaped in time? Resolutely he shut that fear out of his mind. There was a faint moan from Kan. Rolth—?

But on the edge of that thought came the Faltharian's voice.

"Quite a display! Cummi likes to play rough, doesn't he?"

The sergeant sat up. He was trembling—perhaps with reaction from that frenzied descent—but, he decided, mostly from the black rage which possessed him now whenever he thought of the Ageratan. A rage he must best or that other sensitive could turn it into a weapon against him.

"How do we get away from here?" He must depend on Rolth's ability to pierce the gloom. For it was real gloom which walled them in now. The dancing lights of the city were gone—they were crouched in the middle of a black blot.

"Window over there—not too high to reach. What about this prize package? Do we have to lug him along?"

"He'll wake by morning. Get him inside a room and leave him. I don't think they'll try another bomb."

"Not unless they want to bring the whole place down around their heads. Let's go. If you'll take Kan's legs, I'll heave his head."

Kartr stumbled along, trusting to Rolth to guide them. They reached a window, beat open the casement and crawled through with their unconscious burden.

"Aren't we in the wrong building now?" the sergeant wanted to know. "I thought we climbed down over there—"

"You're right. We're in a different one. But this was the easiest and quickest route out. Did the boys get away?"

For the second time Kartr tried to reach Zinga—sent out those shafts of thought. Once—for a single joyful second he thought he had made contact—then it was gone. He dared not try too long, the Can-hound—if that creature still lived—or even Cummi might be able to pick up his signal.

"No use," he told Rolth. "I can't make contact. But that doesn't mean we have to worry. They may be too far away—we've never been able to discover what governs mental reception or how far we can beam a

call. And they may be lying low because the Ageratan
is too near. But I did reach Zinga before the blast
and they had several minutes more than we did to
escape."

That was not much to pin any hope to, Kartr knew
that. But with such veterans as Fylh and Zinga it was
almost enough.

"Do we try to locate Smitt?"

"I think so. Or at least we can make contact with
his rebels."

Kartr hooked his fingers in Rolth's belt and allowed
the Faltharian to tow him through dark rooms and
darker hallways, while he tried to keep some sense of
direction.

"Street level," came the welcome whisper at last.

"I believe that we are facing the street which runs
along the front of Cummi's headquarters—"

But, before Rolth could affirm or deny that, a brilliant bolt of fire snapped across the dark and both of
them involuntarily ducked.

A blaster shot! And that was another from down the
street. A third beam brought a choked, horrible scream
in answer.

"The war's on!" Rolth pointed out unnecessarily.
"And which is our side?"

"Neither, just yet. I don't want to guess wrong and
be fried," returned Kartr grimly. "There's one to our
left—about five feet away— He's crawling past us at
an angle. I'll try contact as he goes by and see who
he is—"

The lashes of fire continued to light up the sod-
grown street at intervals. There were no more cries
so either the aim continued to be poor, or very, very
good.

The sniper crawled across their vantage point.

"No uniform," Rolth reported. "Looks like a civilian

to me. But he knows blasters. Maybe the veteran of
a sector war—"

"He's not a Cummi man but—" Kartr had no time
for a warning.

No, the man out there was not one of Cummi's
followers, but he had caught that tentative mind touch
in an instant—something which had never happened
to Kartr before. And his blaster swung around at the
rangers.

"Patrol!" Rolth yelled.

The blaster aim wavered, and then held steady at
them.

"Come out—with your hands up!" ordered a harsh
voice. "I've set this on 'spray' and I'll use it that way,
too!"

Kartr and Rolth obeyed, hunking forward at a half
stoop for there were other blasters busy farther down.

"Who in Space are you?" demanded their captor.

"Patrol rangers. We're trying to contact Smitt, our
com-techneer—"

"Yeah?" There was deep suspicion in that voice.
"Well, you're going to contact him now. Get going down
in that direction and I'm right behind you if you try
to run—"

They followed orders which brought them to a dark
doorway some distance away.

"Stairs here," Rolth informed his companion.

"Sure," agreed the man behind them. "Go down
them, and shut up!"

But five steps down brought them to a barrier.

"Knock on that four times quick, wait a second and
knock again!" came the order of their guard.

Rolth obeyed and the portal moved aside. They
blundered through a thick curtain and found themselves
in a dimly lighted hall where two men eyed them with
no pretense of friendship and blasters were pointed at

their middles. But when the light touched their comets there came recognition and relaxation. One of the guardians stepped closer.

"Take off your helmets," he commanded.

The rangers obeyed and then blinked as a torch beam centered on them.

"It's okay. They're not Cummi's—they must be Patrol. Take them in to Krowli. How is it going topside?"

"We lie on our bellies and shoot—they do the same. At least we knocked out the robots' signal cables so they can't turn those against us again. Far as I can see it's stalemate," their late captor replied. "Okay. Let the old man out, boys—back to the firing line!"

"Get one of them for me, Pol!"

"I'll do that little thing. Fry him on a platter. Good landing!"

"And clear skies!" One of the guards closed the door and rearranged the folds of the improvised blackout curtain. The other jerked a thumb at the rangers.

"Down this way."

They went down the length of the hallway into a large room which was the scene of some activity. Several men squatted around some boxes digging machinery parts out of packing. Two others sat at a box table and three more were making a scratch meal at the far end of the room. The newcomers were waved toward the two at the table. One of them raised his head and then jumped to his feet. It was Smitt.

"It is stalemate all right." The com-techneer ran his fingers through his hair.

Kartr and Rolth studied the crude map which lay on the table top.

"We have them bottled up in the headquarters building. By the way, did they blow the tower? We felt some sort of a shock—"

The sergeant nodded without replying aloud. "If Cummi has disruptors," he said, "I don't see why he lets a handful of snipers pen him in. He could blow himself a path out any time he wants to."

"Well." The slim, middle-aged man who shared Smitt's table when the rangers had been brought in, stretched and grinned. "Cummi doesn't want to blow big holes in his nice city, not if he can help it. And snipers are hard to locate."

"Not for a sensitive," Kartr pointed out. "Give me five minutes out there and I can tag every one of your men. Cummi need only send out the Can-hound and—"

Krowli's grin vanished as if wiped off by a brutal hand. "You have a point there, Sergeant," he admitted in a voice of mild tone, but the emotions seething below it were anything but mild.

"Could it be," Rolth struck in, "that disruptor shells are not too many in Lord Cummi's armory?"

"That thought has also occurred to us," Krowli answered. "Only it is a little difficult to prove. Cummi has had all the arms under his control since the second day we landed. We have only personal side arms which he could not logically take from us. This whole rotten mess came about just because he was able to think faster than the rest of us. And be sure that he didn't overlook the point of holding all the guns he could! We might storm Cummi's headquarters, sure, but if the disruptors do work—that would be the end of the stormers. And he has two sensitives—we have—"

"Two also, if I can contact Zinga. Any more among your people?"

Krowli shook his head. "We are—were—about as ordinary a crowd of average citizens as you could find anywhere in Control territory. Cummi grabbed all those of use to him, along with the arms."

Rolth had been studying the map and now he dug

a fingernail into the center of the square representing Cummi's hold.

"I notice you don't have the tube-tunnel marked—"

"What tube-tunnel?" Krowli wanted to know.

Smitt smashed his fist down on the box and swore at the pain. "I'm three kinds of a Domanti idiot," he shouted. And then Kartr's explanation interrupted him.

"It depends now upon whether Cummi has discovered those underground routes," the sergeant concluded.

"He doesn't know of them—I'm almost certain of that! None of us heard of them before—unless the techneers have discovered them and kept the secret."

Rolth looked up. "If they did just that we may be leading a forlorn hope right into a stinger's nest."

"And if they don't know"—Smitt was almost exultant—"we'll be in their midst before they are aware of it!"

"You've got to pick the right men for this," Kartr warned without any of Smitt's enthusiasm. "You're the right type, Smitt. They can't crack your mind shield. But the rest—we'll have to have men with whom the Can-hound and Cummi can't tamper. Now take that fellow who brought us in—he isn't a sensitive, at least he doesn't seem to be, yet he caught my thought beam and jumped us at once."

"That must have been Norgot. He has had good reason to learn how to protect himself against mind invasion. He was one of the Satsati hostages—"

"So!" Rolth paid tribute. "No wonder he was edgy when you tried to probe him, Kartr. He ought to be a perfect choice for the boarding party."

"Boarding party!" thought Kartr fleetingly. Odd how the space terms stuck in their speech even now when they were permanently earthed.

"Yes," he said aloud. "Any more of his caliber around?"

Krowli beckoned to one of the men who had just finished eating. "You're a sensitive, Sergeant. We'll leave the selection up to you."

In the end they assembled eight men with mind shields tight enough to make them possibilities. Kartr longed for Zinga and Fylh, but so far nothing had been heard from the Bemmy rangers, although the rebel patrols had been alerted to keep watch for them.

Together the party of ten descended one by one in the gravity well the rangers had first discovered. There was a single car at the platform and three was a very tight fit for the voyage. But they made it that way, with Rolth at the controls each trip forward and back. And at last they stood near the plate elevator under Cummi's headquarters. Kartr could see no indication that there had been any visitors there since the time he and the Faltharian had passed that way before.

It was those two other stops along the way, the ones they had sped by then, which interested him now. If there was any welcoming party waiting for them at the top of the shaft it might be well to make an earlier stop. So he pushed the lowest button on the wall. The five of them who had managed to crowd on the plate clung together as they were whisked up.

Their support came to a stop in darkness and Kartr marshaled his four companions off to let the elevator sink back. Then he dared to flash his beam about.

They were on a ledge from which a ramp ran up into the darkness. Underfoot was a coating of fine, gritty dust which Kartr believed had not been disturbed for centuries. And there was no indication of life other than their own, his perception assured him of that. Cummi must be ignorant of this breach in his defenses.

The swish of displaced air heralded the arrival of

the plate again and then Smitt, Rolth and the other three rebels joined them. Rolth hung out over the well and surveyed the space overhead.

"Okay. It closed up when the plate hit bottom. Unless someone was up there watching at just this moment they'll never know."

Kartr switched off his torch and Rolth took the lead, each man grasping hold of the belt of the one before him, forming a chain to negotiate the dark through which only Rolth could pass freely. At first the angle of the ramp was a steep one, but it began to level off until they found themselves in a large room, coming around the base of a partition into a lighted space filled with the buzz of running machinery. The partition from this side seemed solid wall and Kartr did not wonder that the ramp and the shaft it led to had not been discovered. At the same instant he not only became aware of a man ahead but was able to identify him.

"Dalgre!"

The sergeant beckoned to Smitt. "Dalgre's ahead— with another—maybe a guard, unless he has joined Cummi. You might have better luck contacting him than I would. And I can cover you—"

The com-techneer replied with a short nod and signaled to his rebel followers to stay where they were. Then, together with Kartr, he ran from the shadow of one giant machine to another, until they were able to see into a pool of brighter light where Dalgre sat before the board of controls and a man in the rumpled uniform of a jetman lounged several feet away, a force beam projector cradled in his arm.

Kartr touched Smitt's shoulder and pointed to himself and then to the left, a path which would, with continued luck, bring him near the guard. He took it, moving like a gray wisp of fog around machines whose purpose he could not guess, until he came up behind the jetman. From where he crouched he could see the tip of Smitt's helmet ridge crest.

Then the com-techneer stepped boldly out and in that same instant Kartr sprang, bringing the butt of his blaster down on the guard's right arm. The man screamed and doubled up against the side of the control board, dropping the projector which flew across the floor. In a second Dalgre had scooped it up and was in a half crouch ready to fire. But Smitt's familiar grays were in his sights and he did not squeeze the trigger.

"Very neat," commented the com-techneer. "One would think you had practiced it. I take it that you are *not* a convert to Cummi, Dalgre?"

The Patrolman showed his teeth. "Is that likely? They needed me—so I'm still alive. But they blasted Snyn and the Commander—maybe Jaksan also for all I know—"

"What?" all three of the Patrol demanded almost with a single voice.

"Did it an hour ago. Last I heard Jaksan and the medico were barricaded in the west wing. This is a madhouse. About time we put some fear for the Comet back into these space-blasted fools! If it weren't for the Can-hound being able to find out where everyone is and what he's doing, I'd have tried to make a break before this—"

The jetman guard was tied with his own belt to the legs of the bench before the control board. Kartr looked over the array of dials there.

"Anything you can do to this that might put the odds in our favor?"

Dalgre grinned ruefully. "I'm afraid to chance it. I'm no real mech-techneer. And they gave me only a half hour's briefing before they put me here. If I pull the wrong lever I might blow us up. Too bad—because we might be able to shake them right out of the building if we only knew what all those gadgets mean."

"How do you get out of here?" one of the rebels wanted to know.

"Anti-gravity lift." Dalgre guided them to an alcove beyond the control board. "Only trouble is that they may have a guard on the upper level who will become suspicious if we rise before my shift is up."

"And how long will that be?"

Dalgre consulted his wrist dial. "A full half hour, planet time."

"Can't wait that long," Kartr decided. "Any other stops on this rise beside the one you are supposed to use?"

"No."

"But there is something else—" Rolth had been examining the walls of the shaft. "Here are holds for hands and feet—perhaps to be used in times of emergency. We can climb out—"

And climb they did. Kartr caught the message of a stranger ahead—the guard Dalgre had predicted. It was also Dalgre who had the answer.

"Let me hail him—"

The sergeant pulled back against the side of the well and kept only a single handhold on the climbing bars as the other Patrolman squeezed by him. A moment later they heard Dalgre hail whoever was at the top.

"Give us a hand—"

"What's the matter?"

"I'm no mech-techneer—send for one of your fellows—one of these blasted machines down here is running wild. It may blow us up or something!"

Dalgre climbed the last few feet out of the shaft and moved away from its mouth.

"Where's Taleng? Why didn't he come up with the message?" The guard was openly suspicious.

"Because—" Kartr heard Dalgre start to answer and then came sounds of a struggle.

The sergeant swarmed up the last rungs and out of the hole. Dalgre was fighting with the guard for the possession of a hand force-beam. Kartr did not try to reach his feet but sent his body plunging forward to bring down both men. They fell on him with force enough to drive the air out of his lungs in an agonized grunt.

Minutes later the foggy scene began to clear again. The guard lay bound and gagged close to the wall and Rolth knelt beside the sergeant kneading Kartr's ribs to force the air back into him again. Smitt, Dalgre and the rebels had vanished. Rolth replied to the question the sergeant did not yet have breath enough to ask.

"I couldn't hold them back."

"But—" Kartr's words came between painful gasps, "Cummi—the Can-hound—"

"They don't honestly believe very much in danger from a sensitive's power," Rolth reminded him. "Even if they have seen a demonstration—they simply refuse to believe the evidence presented by their eyes. It's the way most humans are made—"

"How very true. Luckily for us—"

Kartr froze and did not finish his sentence. Instead he turned on Rolth and sent the Faltharian sprawling forward into a doorway beyond. "Get out there quick and see if you can stop those fools making targets of themselves. I know that there's trouble waiting for them ahead—"

He watched Rolth pick himself up and go. Because the trouble wasn't ahead he hoped that the Faltharian would not stop to ask questions. There was trouble, right enough, but it lay behind, coming closer every second.

Cummi was coming—and this time Kartr knew that it was to be battle between them, an all-out battle without quarter on either side—a battle fought on no visible field and for an untellable victory.

11

Outcast

Kartr was lying on his back, staring up into a leaden sky, and fine needles of rain stung eyes and skin. The cold was numbing and from somewhere nearby came a whimpering. After long minutes he knew that he was the whimperer. But he could not stop the sound, any more than he could control the shudders which shook his whole aching body. He willed his hands to move and they dragged heavily across torn clothing and patches of raw flesh.

Then he tried to sit up. His head swam sickeningly and the gray world whirled around. But he could see rocks, scrubby bushes ringing him in. His mind sorted the evidence of his eyes, as he watched blood ooze sluggishly from a cut along his ribs. He accepted the reality of the pain in his body, the stone ledge on which he lay, and the bushes— All were a part of this world—

This world? What world?

That question brought to life a white-hot fire in his mind. He cringed and tried not to think as the rain washed the blood away from his chest. He was almost content as long as he did not think. There was a second thrust of agony through his head as he became aware of other life near. A tawny muzzle broke through the bushes, round yellow animal eyes regarded him unwaveringly, a cold curiosity touched his mind. He sent a silent appeal to it for aid—and the head vanished.

Then he moaned and his clumsy hands caught his spinning head. For he knew now that for him there was no help. Behind him lay a barrier which cut him off from the past. He shrank from the torture that edge of memory brought him.

But deeper than memory lay some hard core of resistance. It flogged him into effort. Panting, whimpering, he dragged his feet under him, and, clawing at the stone, got to his knees and then to his feet.

He lost his balance and fell down a steep slope into a stream. Pulling himself out of the flood, he huddled beside a tall rock and fought for memory.

It came clear and sharp as a video-print—too clear, too vivid.

He was in a strange building, surrounded by high walls, and he was waiting, waiting for a danger beyond all dangers. It came toward him, unhurried, purposeful. He could feel the beat of power which enveloped it. He must fight. And yet he already knew every move of the coming battle, knew that it was a lost one—

There was a clash of wills, the pouring out of mind force against mind force. There was a sudden leap of confidence at his own strength.

Another mind snaked in to aid his enemy, a devious, evil one which left in its wake an unclean trail. But the two together were not able to force his barrier.

He held to the defensive for a while and then struck.
Under that blow the evil mind quivered—shrank. But
he dared not follow its slight retreat for its partner
fought. And now that first mind began to plead—to
promise—

"Come in with us. We are of your own kind. Let
us unite to rule these stupid cattle—nothing can withstand us then!"

He seemed to listen, but under cover he planned.
There was one very dangerous move he had not yet
tried. But it was all that was left him.

So he dropped his barrier, only for an instant. With
a purr of triumph the evil fighter surged in and he
allowed it. Once it had come too far to retreat he
turned on it, surrounded and utterly crushed it. There
was a scream which was only mental. And the evil was
snuffed out as if it had never existed.

But the other, the one who had beckoned and promised, was still waiting. And at the very moment of his
victory it struck, not only with its own force, but with
added power it had kept cunningly in reserve. And he
had known that this would happen—

He fought, desperately, vainly, knowing that the end
was already decided. And he broke, so that that other,
exultant, wild with victory, swept in. That which was
his will was imprisoned, held in bonds, while his body
obeyed the enemy.

Down that blank-walled corridor he marched stiffly,
purposefully, a blaster in his hand, his finger on the
firing button. But within he was shrieking silently
because he knew what he would be compelled to do.

Stabbing flashes of blaster fire cut back and forth
across a wide open space. And at the opposite edge
of that area was what he had been sent to find—the
ranger sled. Against his will he crouched and crept
from protection to protection.

He saw men fall and the one who shared this weird journey with him snarled in rage as they went down. The opposition was being overcome—and those who brought them down were his own friends.

One more short rush would take him to the sled. And even as he was wondering why the other who commanded him wanted that so terribly he made the spring. But two who crouched behind its shadow stared up at him in stunned surprise. He knew them—but still his arm and hand were forced down and he fired. The startled croak from the fanged jaws of the nearer rang in his ears as he scrambled into the seat and grabbed at the controls.

With his mind sick and cowering, he only half relaxed under the take-off which slammed him breathless against the padding of the seat. And that other inside his mind set the course, one which sent the slight aircraft spiraling up into the dusky dome, up and up, until it touched a balcony high above the heads of the fighters and another leaped into the sled.

And that other's will goaded them away, speeding out of the hall and away at top speed over the city, heading toward a horizon where a faint rim of gray proclaimed daybreak. Although he was obeying that order he still struggled. It was a noiseless, motionless duel, carried on high above the ancient city, will against will, power against power. And it seemed to Kartr that now the other was not quite so confident—that he was on the defensive, content to hold what he had rather than to attempt to strengthen his control.

How did it end—that fight in the sky? Kartr pillowed his aching head on the stone beside the stream and tried vainly to remember. But that was gone. He could only recall that he had—had blasted Zinga! That he had brought Cummi safely out of the city. That he had betrayed in his over-confidence and recklessness those who had most reason to depend upon him. And realizing all that— He closed his eyes and tried to blank out everything—everything!

Exhausted, he must have slept again. For he opened his eyes to be dazed by sun reflected from the water. He was hungry—and that hunger triggered the same instinct of self-preservation which had brought him earlier to the water. His hands were still slow and clumsy but he managed to catch a creature which came out from under an overturned stone. And there were others like it.

Toward evening he got to his feet again and stumbled along beside the water. He fell at last and did not try to struggle up. Maybe he dreamed, but he snapped to full wakefulness from a haze in which Zinga had called him. Awake, desolation closed in. Zinga was gone. Almost viciously he dug his hands into his eyes—but he could not wipe from memory the sight of the Zacathan's face as he had gone down under the beam from Kartr's blaster.

It would be best not to try to go on. To just stay here until he went into a world where memory could not follow— He was so tired!

But his body refused to accept that; it was getting up to stagger on. And in time the stream led him out on a wide plain where tall yellow grass tangled about his legs and small nameless things ran squeaking from his path. In time the stream joined a river, broad and shallow so that rocks in some parts of its bed showed dry tops under the sun.

Bluffs began to rise beside the water. He climbed, and slipped, and slid painfully over obstructions and he lost all count of time. But he dared not leave the water, it was too good a source of food and drink.

He was lying full length on a rock by a pool, trying to scoop out one of the water creatures when he started and cried out. Someone—something—had touched his mind—had made contact for an instant! His hands went to his head as if to protect himself from a second calling.

But that came. And he was unable to shut out the alien presence which flooded into him, asking questions—demanding—Cummi! It was Cummi trying to get at him again—to use him—

Kartr threw himself off his perch, skinning his arm raw, and began to run without taking thought. Get away! Away from Cummi—away—!

But the mind followed him and there was no escaping its contact. He found a narrow crevice leading away from the water, half choked with briars and the water-worn drift of storm floods. Unheeding scratches he plunged into the tangle.

It was a very small pocket ending in a hollow under the overhang of the bluff. And into this he crawled blindly, a child taking refuge from a monster of the dark. He curled up, his hands still pressed to his head, trying to blank out his mind, to erect a barrier through which the hunter could not pierce.

At first he was aware only of the desperate pounding of his own heart, and then there was another sound—the swish of an air-borne craft. The contacting mind was closing in. What frightened him so much he could not have explained—unless it was the memory of how the other's dominion had made him kill his own men. What Cummi had done once, he might well do again.

And that fear of his was the other's strongest ally. Fear weakened control. Fear—

With his face buried between his arms, his mouth resting on the gritty soil under the overhang, Kartr stopped fighting the pursuer and tried to subdue his own fear.

Faintly he heard the sound of a shout, the crackling of brush. Cummi was coming down the notch!

The ranger's lips set in a snarl and he inched out of the pocket of earth. His hands chose, almost without help from eye or brain, a jagged rock. He had been tracked like a beast—but this beast would fight! And the Ageratan might not be expecting physical attack, he might well believe his prey to be cowering helplessly, waiting for the master's coming!

Cautiously Kartr pulled himself up so that his back was against the welcome solidity of the gully rocks. His stone weapon was a good one, he thought, balancing it in one hand—just the right size and weight and it had several promising projections.

"Kartr!"

The sound he made in answer to that call was the growl of a baited animal.

His name—Cummi daring to use his name! And the Ageratan had even disguised his voice. Clever, clever devil! Illusions—how well that warped brain could create them!

Two figures burst through the brush to face him. The stone dropped from nerveless fingers.

Was Cummi controlling his sight too? Could the Ageratan make him see this—?

"Kartr!"

He shrank back against the stone. Run—run away—but there was no escape—

"Cummi—?" He almost wanted to believe that this was a trick of the Ageratan's, that he was not honestly seeing the two coming toward him, the smiling two in ranger gray.

"Kartr! We've found you at last!"

They had found him right enough. Why didn't they just draw and blast him where he stood? What were they waiting for?

"Shoot!" He thought he screamed that. But their faces did not change as they came in to get him. And he believed that if they touched him he would not be able to bear it.

"Kartr?" another voice questioned from down the gully.

He jerked at the sound as if a force blade had ripped his flesh.

A third figure in ranger uniform beat through the brush. And at the sight of *his* face the sergeant gave a wild cry. Something burst in Kartr's skull, he was falling down into the dark—a welcoming, sheltering dark where dead men did not walk or greet one smilingly. He hid in that darkness thankfully.

"Kartr?"

The dead called him, but he was safe in the dark and if he did not answer no one could drag him out again to face madness.

"What is the matter with him?" demanded someone.

He lay very quiet in the dark, safe and quiet.

"—have to find out. We must get him back to camp. Look out, Smitt. Use binders on him before you put him aboard, he could twist right over the edge—"

"Kartr!" He was being shaken, prodded. But with infinite effort he locked his lips, made his body limp and heavy. And his stubbornness gave him a defense at last. He was left alone in his dark safety.

Then slowly he became aware of a warmth, a soothing warmth. And, as he had at his first awaking in the wilderness, he lay still and felt his body come back to life. There were hands moving over him, passing over half-healed wounds and leaving behind them a refreshing coolness and ease.

"You mean he is insane?"

Those were words spoken through his dark. He had no desire to see who spoke them.

"No. This is something else. What that devil did to him we can only guess—planted a false memory, perhaps. You saw how he acted when we caught up with him. There are all sorts of tricks you can play—or rather someone without scruples can play—with the mind, your own and others'—when you are a sensitive. In some ways we are far more vulnerable than you who do not try to go beyond human limits—"

"Where's Cummi? I'd like to—" There was a cold and deadly promise in that and something in Kartr leaped to agree with it. And that act of emotion pushed him away from the safety of the dark.

"Wouldn't we all? But we shall—sooner or later!"

A hard edge was pushed against his lips, liquid trickled into his mouth and he was forced to swallow. It burned in his throat and settled into a pleasant fire in his stomach.

"Well, so you have found him?" A new speaker broke through the mists about him.

"Greetings, Haga Zicti! We have been waiting for you, sir. Maybe you can suggest treatment—"

"So—and what is the matter with the rescued? I see no wounds of importance—"

"The trouble is here." Fingers touched Kartr's forehead. And he shrank away from that touch. It threatened him in some odd fashion.

"That is the way of it, eh? Well, we might have deduced as much. A false memory or—"

He was running away, running through the dark. But that other was behind him, trying to compel him—and, with a moan of desolate pain, Kartr found himself again in the hallway, facing Cummi and the Can-hound, made to relive for the third time that shameful and degrading defeat and murderous attack upon his own comrades.

"So Cummi took him over! He must have used other minds to build up such power—!"

Cummi! There was a hot rage deep inside Kartr, burning through the shame and despair—Cummi— The Ageratan must be faced—faced and conquered. If he did not do that he would never feel clean again. But would he even if he vanquished Cummi? There would remain that moment of horror when he had fired straight into Zinga's astonished face.

"He took over." Was he actually saying those words or were they only ringing in his head. "I killed—killed Zinga—"

"Kartr! Great Space, what *is* he talking about? You killed—!"

"Describe the killing!" And he could not disobey that sharp command.

He began to talk slowly, painfully, and then with a spate of words which seemed to release some healing in their flow. The fight for the sled, the escape, his awaking in the wilderness, he told it all.

"But—that's perfectly crazy! He didn't do that at all!" someone protested. "I saw him—so did you, and you! He walked right through the whole fight as if he didn't see any of us—took the sled and went. Maybe he did pick up Cummi as he said—but the rest—it's crazy!"

"False memories," stated the authoritative voice. "Cummi supplied them—guilty ones so that he would want to keep away from us even if Cummi couldn't control him fully. Simple—"

"Simple! But Kartr's a sensitive—he does that sort of thing himself. How could he be taken in—?"

"Just because he is a sensitive he could be that much more vulnerable. Anyway—now that we know what is wrong—"

"You can cure him?"

"We shall try. It may leave some scars. And it will depend upon how adept Cummi has been."

"Cummi!" That was spat out as if the name were an obscene oath.

"Yes, Cummi. If we can turn Kartr's will to meeting— Well, we shall see."

Again a hand was laid on his forehead, soothingly.

"Sleep—you are asleep—sleep—"

And he *was* drowsily content now—it was as if some weight had been shrugged away. He slept.

Waking was as sudden. He was staring up at a sloping roof of entwined branches and leaves—he must be lying in a lean-to such as the rangers built when in temporary camp. There was a cover over his body, one of the blankets of Uzakian spider silk from their packs. He turned his head to see a fire. There was a dankness in the air, a mist or fog dulled the outlines of the trees that ringed in the clearing.

Someone came out of the mist and flung down an armload of wood.

"Zinga!"

"In the flesh and snapping!" returned the Zacathan genially, bringing his jaws together smartly to prove it.

"Then it *was* a false memory—" Kartr drew a deep breath of wonder and infinite relief.

"That was the biggest lie you ever dreamed, my friend. And how do you feel now?"

Kartr stretched luxuriously. "Wonderful. But I have a lot of questions to ask—"

"Which can all be answered later." Zinga went back to the fire and picked up a cup which had been resting on a stone close to the flames. "Suppose you get this inside you first."

Kartr drank. It was hot broth and well flavored. He glanced up with a smile which seemed to stretch muscles that had not been used for a long, long time. "Good. I think I detect Fylh's delicate talent in cooking—"

"Oh, he stirred it up now and then right enough, and added some of his messy leaves. Down every drop of it now—"

But Kartr was still holding the cup and sipping at intervals when another stepped out into the firelight. And the sergeant stopped in mid-gulp to stare. But Zinga was right here, beside him. Then who, in the name of Tarnusian devils, was that?

Zinga followed Kartr's eyes and then grinned. "No. I haven't twinned," he assured the sergeant. "This is Zicti—of Zacan to be sure—but a Hist-techneer, not a ranger."

The other reptile man strolled up to the lean-to. "You are awake then, my young friend?"

"Awake and"—Kartr smiled at them both—"in my right mind again—I think. But it may take some time for me to sort them out—the real and fake memories, I mean—they are rather mixed—"

Zinga shook his head. "Do not work too hard at that sorting until you are stronger. Weak as you are it might set you twirling about like a Tlalt dust demon."

"But where—?"

"Oh, I was a passenger on the *X451*, along with my family. We joined your force yesterday—or rather the rangers found us in the early morning—"

"What happened in the city after I—er—left?"

Zinga's taloned finger moved with a faint scraping sound along his jaw. "We decided to come away—after the fight was over."

"Hunting for me?"

"Hunting for you, yes, and for a couple of other reasons. Smitt and Dalgre came across a ship the city people built. It brought us this far before it gave out. They are still working on it under the delusion that they may be able to put it back together again if they can just solve a few of its internal mysteries."

"Smitt and Dalgre?"

"Yes, the Patrol withdrew as a unit. It seemed best at the time."

"Hmm." Kartr considered all that statement might imply. There *had* been changes. He was suddenly eager to know how many.

12

Kartr Takes
The Trail

Three in the uniform of the Patrol squatted on their heels by the fire. Kartr sat up, his back braced against bedrolls, watching them.

"You never said"—he broke the silence at last—"why you left the city—"

None of the three seemed to wish to meet his gaze. Finally it was Smitt who answered, an almost defiant ring in his tired voice.

"They were grateful to have Cummi and his men removed—"

Kartr continued to wait but that appeared to be all the answer the com-techneer was going to give.

"Big of them," Dalgre added after a long pause, a dry rasp under-running his words.

"They decided," Zinga took up the explanation,

"that they did not want to exchange one official ruler out of the past for another—at least the impression they conveyed was that the Patrol had better not plan to take over in Cummi's place. So we weren't welcome—especially the rangers."

"Yes, they made it clear." Smitt was bleakly cold. " 'Now that the war is over, let the troops depart'—the usual civilian attitude. We tended to be a disturbing element as far as they were concerned. So we took one of the city aircraft and left—"

"Jaksan?"

"He went after the jetman who had burned down the Commander. When we found them later they were both dead. We're the last of the Patrol—except for Rolth and Fylh—they're out scouting—"

The three did not enlarge on that story and Kartr accepted their reticence. Perhaps to the city castaways who had tasted Cummi's grab for power the Patrol had become too much a symbol of the old way of things. And so the Patrol had to go, after the ruler had been deposed. But one thing had come of that—there were no longer crewmen or rangers—there was only Patrol—their second exile had cemented tight the bonds of the survivors.

"Ah, our fishing party returns!" Zicti, who had been napping in the warmth of the flames, rolled over and got to his feet to greet the three coming through the screen of the trees. "And what luck did you have, my dears?"

"We put Rolth's blue torch down at the water's edge and the creatures were attracted by its light, so we return heavily laden," the thinner voice of a Zacathan female answered. "This is indeed a very rich world. Zor, show your father the armored creature you found under the rock—"

The shortest of the three ran into the firelight,

holding in one hand a kicking thing of many legs and thick claws. Zicti accepted the captive, being careful not to encounter the claws, and examined it critically.

"But how strange! This might almost be a distant cousin of a Poltorian. But it is not intelligent—"

"None of the water dwellers appear to be," agreed his wife. "However, we should be glad of that, for they are excellent eating!"

Kartr had seen few Zacathan women, but his long companionship with Zinga had accustomed him to the difference between human and Zacathan features and he could understand that both Zacita and her young daughter, Zora, would be considered attractive by others of their race. As for young Zor—like an impish young male of any species, he was enjoying every minute of this wilderness life.

Zacita made a graceful gesture to suggest that the company seat themselves again. Kartr noted that Smitt and Dalgre had been as quick to rise to greet the Zacathan ladies as the others. Their feelings concerning Bemmys had certainly undergone a change.

Kartr awoke early the next morning and lay still for a long moment frowning up at the slant roof of the lean-to. There was something— Then his mouth straightened into a thin hard line. He knew now what it was he had to do and soon. Meanwhile, he crawled out of his bedroll. Above the drowsy quiet of the sleeping camp he could hear the murmur of the river not too far away.

A little unsteadily at first and then firmly as he gained balance he made his way down to its edge. The water was chill enough to bring a gasp out of him as he waded in. Then he lost touch with the sands of its bed and began to swim.

"Ah—the supreme energy and recuperative powers of the young!"

The booming voice was drowned out by a splash. Kartr raised his head just in time to receive a face full of water as Zor passed him at full swimming speed. And Zicti was sliding cautiously down over a flat rock, allowing the stream to engulf him by inches.

The dignified Zacathan blinked in mild benevolence over the wavelets at the ranger sergeant. With two lazy strokes Kartr joined him.

"Pretty primitive, I'm afraid, sir—"

The former hist-techneer of the Galactic University of Zovanta gave a realistic shudder but answered calmly:

"It does one good at times to be shaken out of the comfortable round of civilized life. And we Zacathans are not so physically breakable as you humans. The general idea now held by my family is that this is a most delightful holiday, showing much more imagination on my part than they had believed possible. Zor, for one, has never been so happy—" He grinned as he watched that small scaled body shoot across the current of the stream in pursuit of a water creature.

"But this is not a holiday, sir."

Zicti's large grave eyes met Kartr's. "Yes, there is that to take into consideration. Permanent exile—"

He looked away, over the tumbled rocks, the bluffs beyond the river, the massed greenery of the wilderness. "Well, this is a rich world, and a wide empty one—plenty of room—"

"There is the city, partly in working order," Kartr reminded him.

And in that instant he felt a warmth of reassurance close about him, a mental security he had not known for a long, long time. Zicti was not replying with actual mind speech, but answering the ranger in his own way.

"I believe that those in the city must be left to work out their own destiny," the hist-techneer said at last. "In a manner of thinking that choice is now a retreat. They wish life to remain as it always has been. But that is just what life never does. It goes up—one advances—or it goes down—one retreats. And if one tried to stand still—that is retreat. We are now following the path our whole empire is taking. We have been slowly slipping back for the past century—"

"Decadence?"

"Just so. For example—this spread of dislike for those who are not human. That is increasing. Luckily we Zacathans are sensitives—we are ready to meet situations such as that which ensued after the *X451* set down—"

"What *did* you do then?" asked Kartr, momentarily distracted.

Zicti chuckled. "We landed, too—on a lifeboat. There was a promising tract of wilderness not too far away. Before they got over the surprise of seeing us pop out of the escape port we were safely beyond their reach. But—had we not been able to sense Cummi's attitude—it might have ended differently—

"We came in this direction and established a camp. And I must tell you, sergeant, I was the most amazed being in this solar system when I accidentally contacted Zinga. Another Zacathan here! It was as if I had met a sootacl face to face when I was not wearing a wrist blaster! After we joined forces with your party everything was, of course, satisfactorily explained. They were hunting you—you are very well regarded by your men, Kartr—"

Again that warmth of security and reassurance flooded the sergeant's mind. He colored. "Then, when they found me—"

"Yes, when they found you—well, they loaded you on the lifeboat and brought you here. And your adventure has taught all of us an important lesson—not to

underrate an opponent. I would never have believed
Cummi capable of such an attack. But, in turn, he was
not as strong as he thought himself to be, or you would
not have been able to escape from his control after you
left the city—"

"But did I?" Kartr's frown was black. "In spite of
your therapy I can't remember what happened between
leaving the city and waking up alone in the wilderness."

"I believe that you did break free from him," Zicti
said soberly. "Which is why I have laid the compul-
sion on you— But, let us examine the facts, you men
of Ylene are six point six on the sensitive scale, are you
not?"

"Yes. But Ageratans are supposed to be only five
point nine—"

"True. But there is always the chance lately that one
may be dealing with a chance mutant. And this is the
proper time in the wave of history for mutants to
appear. A pity we do not know more of Cummi's
background. If he *is* a mutant that would explain a
great deal."

"Would you mind," Kartr asked humbly, "telling me
just where on the sensitive scale Zacathans place themselves?"

The big eyes twinkled at him. "We have purposely
never submitted to classification, young man. It is
always best and wisest to keep some secrets—especially
when dealing with non-sensitives. But I would rate us
somewhere between eight and nine. We have produced
several persons who are combination telepaths and
teleports, and more only a step or two below them,
during the past three generations. So I am sure that
while such mutation is on the increase among my
people, it must be working in other races also."

"Mutants!" Kartr repeated and he shivered. "I was on
Kablo when Pertavar started the Mutant Rebellion—"

"Then you know what can come of such an upcurve in mutant births. There are good and bad results from all changes. Tell me, when you were a small child, were you aware of being a sensitive?"

Kartr shook his head. "No. In fact I was never aware of my powers until I entered the ranger cadet school. Then an instructor discovered my gift and I was given special training."

"You were a latent sensitive. Ylene was a frontier planet, its people too close to barbarism to know their full strength. Ah—to have such a vigorous world thrown away! The foul sins of war! It is just because things such as the destruction of Ylene are happening too often now that I am convinced our civilization is nearing its end. Now in this camp we are a strange mixture." He pulled himself out of the water and applied a towel with vigor. "Zor, it is time to come!" he called after his son.

"Yes, we are a strange mixture—a collection of odds and ends of the empire. You and Rolth, Smitt and Dalgre, are human, but you are all of different races and widely separated stock. Fylh, Zinga and my family are non-human. Those back in the city are human and highly civilized. And, who knows yet, there may also be natives in this world. One might almost believe that Someone or Something was about to conduct an experiment here." He chuckled and sniffed the air. "Ah, food, and I am indeed empty. Shall we go to see what lies in the cooking pots?"

But before they came up to the fire Zicti touched Kartr's arm.

"There is only one thought I wish to leave with you, my boy. I know little of your race—you may not be a mystic, although most sensitives tend to look beyond the flesh and seek the spirit—and you may have no religious beliefs. But if we *have* been chosen to work out some purpose here, it is up to us to prove worthy of being so selected!"

"I agree," Kartr returned shortly but he knew that the other recognized his sincerity.

The Zacathan nodded. "Fine, fine. I am going to enjoy my declining years. And to think I have been given this just when I thought that life was totally devoid of excitement. My dear"—he raised his voice to address Zacita—"the aroma of that stew is delightful. My hunger increases with every step I draw nearer to the fire!"

But Kartr spooned up the soup mechanically. It was very well for Zicti to paint the future in such bold strokes. A hist-techneer by his training was always taught to look at the whole situation, not to study details. Now ranger instruction worked in just the opposite fashion, it was the small details which mattered most, the careful study of a new planet, the long hours of patient spying upon strange peoples or animals, the rebuilding by speculation from a few bricks of a whole vanished civilization. And here and now they were faced with a detail which he and he alone must handle.

He must render Cummi harmless!

That was the thought which had held over from sleep that morning, had been part of his dreams, and was now crystallized into a driving urge. Living or dead—he must and would find the Ageratan. If Joyd Cummi were still alive he was a menace to all of them.

Odd—Kartr shook his head as if to clear it—he was so haunted by that thought. Cummi was a danger, and Cummi was *his* business. Luckily the Ageratan was no trained explorer-woodsman, he must leave a trail so plain it would be child's play for a ranger to follow. They had been together when they left the city. Somewhere that night they had parted company. Had

Cummi pushed him off the sled in the dark, intending the fall to kill him? If that were so it would be a much more difficult task to locate the Ageratan—he would leave no footprints on clouds. The thing for Kartr to do was to return to that ledge where he had first gained consciousness.

"That's ten—maybe fifteen miles north—"

The sergeant started to hear the words come from Zinga's thin lips—picked out of his own thoughts.

"And—Kartr—you do not go alone, not on that trail!"

He stiffened. But Zinga must know his protest without his putting it into words.

"That job is mine," the sergeant returned, his teeth set hard.

"Granted. But still I say you do not take such a trail alone. We have the lifeboat—it will cover ground with time-saving speed. And with it we can better prospect for any traces of Cummi's passing."

That was good common sense, but it was no sweeter to swallow because it was logical. Kartr would rather have left camp alone and on his two feet. It burned inside him that Cummi was his alone, and that he would not feel whole and well again until he had fronted the Ageratan and won.

"Take one more day of rest," Zinga advised, "and then, I promise, we shall go. This matter of Cummi—it is one of importance."

"Others might not think so. He is alone in a wilderness he can know very little about. The wilds may already have done our job for us."

"But he is Cummi, and so will continue to linger as a threat until we are sure of him. Did Zicti tell you that he believes him a mutant? Remember Pertavar and what that one was able to do. And Cummi is not going to win next time you face him!"

Kartr smiled at the Zacathan, a smile which was hardly more than ten percent humor. "D'you know, my friend, there I think you are right! And this time I do not believe that I am being too confident—the mistake I made before. He has no Can-hound—and surely no other brains to tap!"

"Very well." Zinga arose. "Now let me go and pick Dalgre's store of mechanical knowledge. It might be wise to know just how much ranging power the lifeboat unit has left."

They took off the next morning and no one asked questions although Kartr was sure they all knew his mission. The lifeboat did not have the springy lift of the sled and its pace was slower. Zinga, at the controls, held it steady over the winding reaches of the river until they found the stream which had served to guide Kartr's wanderings.

From time to time the Zacathan glanced anxiously at the heavy clouds bulging over the horizon. Storm was indicated and they had best take shelter when the wind which was driving those clouds struck. To be tossed about the sky in a light-weight lifeboat was no experience to be desired.

"Anything below look familiar?"

"Yes. I'm sure I crossed this open field. I remember pushing through the tall grass. And those trees ahead are promising. Think we'd better land in their shelter?"

Zinga measured the cloud spread again. "I'd like more to reach that ledge where you came to. Flame bats! It's getting dark. Wish I had Rolth's night eyes."

It was darkening fast and the rising wind swept under the boat so that it lurched as it might on pounding sea waves. Kartr clung to the edge of his seat, his nails biting into its cover.

"Wait!" He got the word out at the risk of a bitten

tongue as the lifeboat bucked. Through the dusk he had caught a glimpse of a recent rock slide down the side of a hill beside the stream. "This looks like where I fell!"

They were already past the point but Zinga circled back, as Kartr squinted through the storm dusk and tried to imagine how that same section would look to a man lying flat on the ledge near the top of the rise.

The aircraft snapped out of the circle and veered suddenly to the right, across the crest of the hill. Kartr's protest was forgotten as he sighted what had drawn Zinga's attention. The top of a tree had been shorn off, the newly splintered wood of the trunk gleaming whitely. With the pressure of expert fingers on the controls the Zacathan set the lifeboat down on the slope of the rise, a piece of maneuvering which might have at another time brought honest praise from the sergeant. But now Kartr was too intent upon what might lie just beyond the broken tree.

He found a mass of crushed branches and the remains of the sled. No one, not even a master mech-techneer, could ever reassemble what lay there now. The wreckage was jammed almost bow down in tight wrappings of withered leaves and broken wood and it was empty.

Zinga sniffed deeply as his torch revealed the bareness of that crumpled seat.

"No blood even. The question is—were either or both of you aboard when she hit?"

Kartr shook his head, a little awed by the completeness of the crack-up.

"I don't think either of us could have been. Maybe he threw me out and—"

"Yes—and if you fought back that could have made him lose control so this would happen. But then where is Cummi—or his remains. No mess at all—something would remain if he had been collected by a wandering meat eater—"

"He could have jumped just before she hit," suggested the sergeant. "If he had an anti-grav on his belt he could have made it on such a short fall without smashing himself."

"So we look for a few tracks now?" Zinga's long jaw jutted out as he glanced up at the sky. "Rain is going to spoil that—"

For the clouds were emptying their weight of water at last. Together the rangers stumbled through a beating downpour to the lee of a rock outcrop which gave a faint hint of shelter. The trees might have kept off more of that smothering blast but, Kartr decided as he saw branches whiplash under the wind, that might be more dangerous an asylum than the corner where they huddled gasping, the rain stinging their skin and finding its way through every crevice of their tunics and breeches.

"It can't keep on like this forever—there isn't that much water," Kartr said and then realized that the drum of rain drowned out any but a parade ground pitch of voice.

He sneezed and shivered and thought bitterly that Zinga was going to be proved right. This deluge would mask any trail Cummi might have left hereabouts.

Then, in an instant, he snapped erect and felt Zinga's answering jerk. The Zacathan was as startled as he had been.

They had caught a faint, very faint plea for help. From Cummi? Somehow he believed not. But it had come from a human—or rather from an intelligent mind. Someone or something which was alive, and reasoning, was in trouble. The sergeant turned slowly, trying to center the source. The pain and terror in that plea must be answered!

13

Cummi's Kingdom

"Due north—" Zinga's gutturals reached him, and the Zacathan's keener perception was right.

"Can the lifeboat ride this?" Kartr's own experience with small air craft had been limited to those of the Patrol and the stability of their exploring sleds was proved—they had been designed for rough going under strange weather conditions. But the machine they had to use now did not arouse any confidence in him.

Zinga shrugged. "Well, it isn't the sled. But the force of the wind is lessening and we certainly can't start out on foot—"

They sprinted through the wall of falling water. And a moment later gained the cramped cabin of the lifeboat. It was a relief to be out of the pounding rain. But, even as they settled into their seats, the light craft rocked under them. Get this up into the full force of

the wind—they would be riding a leaf whirled around
in a vortex—!

But, with that thought in both their minds, neither
hesitated. Zinga started the propeller beams and Kartr
sent out a mind probe, trying to touch the one who
had asked for their help.

They were lucky in some things, the dusk of the
storm clouds was clearing. And Zinga had been correct, the wind was dying. The light craft bucked,
swerved, dipped and soared as the Zacathan fought at
the controls to hold her on course. But they were
airborne and high enough above the tree tops to escape
the fate of the wrecked sled.

"Should we circle—?" Zinga thought instead of
spoke.

"Enough fuel?" Kartr asked in answer to that as he
leaned forward to read the gage on the instrument
board.

"You're right—can't afford that," Zinga agreed. "A
quarter of a tal of bucking these winds and we'll be
walking anyway—"

Kartr did not try to translate "tal" into his own terms
of measurement. He had a suggestion to make.

"Pick out some good landmarks ahead and set us
down—"

"Then we take to our feet? It might work. It will—
if this deluge slackens. And there is your landmark—
agreed? Put us in the middle of that—"

"That" lay about a mile before them, a wide circle
of bare and blackened ground covered with the charred
stumps of trees among which the thin green heads of
saplings were beginning to show. Sometime not too far
in the past this section had been burnt over. Zinga
brought them down where the stumps were fewer.

And just as they left the lifeboat that plea for help
reached them again, the terror in it plainer. Kartr

caught something else. They were not the only living things to answer that call. There was a hunter on the trail ahead, a four-footed hunter, hungry—one who had not fed that day or the night before.

The slot of an old game trail led across the burnt land. Years of pressing hooves and pads had worn it so deep that it could be followed by touch as well as by sight. Kartr's boots slipped into it easily and he trotted on through the slackening rain toward a sharp rise of bare rock. The rock wall which had once kept the fire from advancing was broken in one place by a narrow gap through which the game trail led. And then it went down slope into the heart of a real forest.

Not too far ahead was the hunter, very close to its prey. Kartr caught the mind of the one who was trapped. It was human—but not Cummi. A stranger, hurt, alone, and very much afraid. A different mind—

Now the hunter knew it was being followed. It hesitated—and Kartr heard a cry which was hardly more than a moan. There was a screen of bushes through which he beat his way and then he stood looking down at broken tree limbs and at a small, pitifully thin body pinned to the ground by one shattered branch. A distorted face was turned up to him—and he saw that the captive was no straggler from the city.

Kartr threw himself down in the soft muck and tried to lift the weight of the limb. But he could not shift it far enough for the other to escape. And now the hunter waited—just beyond a neighboring clump of bushes.

"Yahhhhh—" That rising, horrible bellow was the battle cry of a Zacathan warrior. A blaster cracked above Kartr's head.

The tawny-furred body had been met in mid-spring by a searing shaft of flame. And the power of the beam bore it back, already terribly dead, into the very nest of leaves from which it had just sprung. A thick stench of singed hair and flesh curled about them.

Kartr went back to work. He was scooping the soft earth from under the branch when a shriek of pure, unreasoning terror whipped him around.

The captive's face was a mask of naked fear, distorted out of human shape.

But there was nothing there to fear—the giant cat was dead. Only Zinga stood there, slipping his blaster back into its holster.

Only Zinga—but it was the Zacathan who aroused that fear!

Kartr did not need to give warning, the other ranger had sensed what was happening and disappeared, melting back into the bushes instantly. Kartr saw the captive was limp now, eyes closed—unconscious! Well, if he would stay that way for a while it would simplify the task.

As silently as he had vanished Zinga came back and together they worked until they had that slim body free and straightened out between them on the ground. Kartr's hands made quick and skilled examination.

"No bones broken. The worst damage is this." There was a deep and ugly gash across the ribs where a fold of the stranger's flesh had been pinned by a sharp stub.

The body was thin, outlines of ribs showed beneath the sun-browned skin. And the stranger was small and slight—very small to be full grown or close to that, as Kartr judged the boy to be. His head was covered with a tangled, mud-and-briar-filled mass of yellow hair and there were downy sproutings along the lines of his jaw and across his upper lip. His torn garments consisted of a sleeveless, open jerkin made of the hide of some animal and a pair of leggings of the same material, while there were strange bag-like coverings on his feet.

"Very primitive—a native?" Zinga wondered.

"Or a survivor of another wreck—"

The Zacathan bit at one talon. "Might be. But then—"

"Yes—if the stranger was the survivor of another galactic shipwreck why his terror at the sight of you?"

The Zacathans were widely known, and they did not arouse fear—they had never been raiders. But—Kartr studied his companion objectively for the first time— suppose one had never seen a Zacathan before? Suppose one's world was only inhabited by beings more or less like one's self? Then the first glimpse of those pointed, fanged jaws, of that scaled skin, of the frill depending about a hairless head and neck—yes, it would be enough to frighten a primitive mind.

Zinga nodded; he had followed that reasoning. Now he had an answer ready.

"I'll go back to the lifeboat and keep out of sight. You can try to discover where he came from and all the rest. If you move him, I'll follow. Natives here! What if Cummi finds them?"

But Kartr did not need that implied warning. "Get going now— I think he's coming around!"

Eyelids flickered. The eyes they had shielded were light blue, almost faded. First there was terror mirrored in them, but when they saw only Kartr's human features the fear went and a sort of wary curiosity took its place. The sergeant probed lightly and found what he had suspicioned. This was no survivor of a space shipwreck, or, if the lad was descended from galactic rovers, their landing on this forsaken world was many generations back.

To make entirely sure of that Kartr asked his first question in the speech so common to all travelers of the stellar routes.

"Who are you?"

The boy was puzzled and his surprise deepened into

fear once more. He was not accustomed to hearing a strange tongue, apparently, and galactic speech meant nothing to him. Kartr sighed and returned to the easiest methods of communication. He jabbed a thumb at himself.

"Kartr—" he said slowly and distinctly.

The wariness remained, but the curiosity was stronger. And after a moment of hesitation the boy repeated the ranger's gesture and said:

"Ord."

Ord. That might be the native term for man, but Kartr thought it more likely a personal designation. Again, and with infinite caution, the sergeant tried mind contact. He expected some shrinking, fear— But, to his surprise and interest, the boy appeared familiar with such an exchange. Yet—surely—he was not a sensitive! Kartr went deeper and knew that the stranger was not.

Which meant only one thing—he had had in the past some dealings with a sensitive—enough not to fear the mind touch. Cummi! The sergeant's own signal went out to Zinga. The Zacathan was in the lifeboat ready and waiting.

Kartr turned to Ord. Making the boy comfortable on a bed of boughs under the drooping branches of a neighboring tree where the rain could not drench them so completely, he went to work. Sometime later, with mind touch and a fast-growing vocabulary, he learned that Ord was one of a tribe who lived a roving life in the wilderness. Any mention of the city sent him into shivering evasion—it was in some manner taboo. Those "shining places" had once been the homes of the "sky gods."

"But now the gods return—" Ord was continuing. Kartr's attention snapped to "alert."

"The gods return?"

"Even so. One has come to us, seeking out our clan—that we may serve him as is right—"

"What is the appearance of this sky god?" asked the sergeant, keeping his voice carefully casual as if it mattered very little.

"He is like unto you. But—" Ord's eyes widened— "but then are you also of the sky gods!" And he made a gesture with crossed fingers pointed at the ranger.

Kartr took the plunge. "After your way of speaking— yes, I come out of the sky. And I am trying to find the god who is now among your people, Ord."

The boy moved uncomfortably, inching away from the sergeant. His hand fell on his bandaged side and he looked up with the old wary suspicion.

"He said that there were those who might come hunting him—night demons and doers of evil. And"— terror colored his voice again—"when first you came upon me I thought I saw with you such a one—a demon!" His voice slid up scale until it was almost a scream.

"Do you see him now, Ord? I, alone, am here with you. And you say that I look like the sky god who is with your people—"

"You must be truly a god—or a demon. You killed the silent hunter with fire. But if the god who came to us is your friend, why did he say that those who came after him were his enemies?"

"The ways of the gods," Kartr answered loftily, "are not always the ways of men. Had I been a demon, Ord, would I have brought you out from under that tree, bandaged your hurt, and treated you well? I think that a doer of evil would not have done that for you."

The other responded to this simple logic almost eagerly. "That is right. And when you come with me to the clan we shall have a great feast and later we shall go together to the Meeting Place of the Gods where you can be as you were in the very ancient days—"

"I want very much to go with you to your clan, Ord. How may we reach them?"

The boy's hand pressed his injured side and he frowned. "It lies one day's travel away—does the camp. I will not be able to walk swiftly—"

"We shall manage, Ord. Now this 'Meeting Place of the Gods'—that is where your people live?"

"No—it is much farther away. Ten days of travel from here—maybe more. We go once a year, all the clans together, and there is trading and warriors are raised up at the Man Fire, and the maidens make their choices of mates. There is fine singing and the Dance of Spears—" His words trailed off.

Kartr smoothed the matted hair back from the boy's eyes.

"Now you will sleep," he ordered. The pale blue eyes closed and the boy's breathing came even and unhurried. Kartr waited for a few minutes and then slipped into the fringe of trees where seconds later Zinga joined him.

"This 'sky god' he speaks of must be Cummi—" the sergeant began.

"Cummi, yes, and with him at large time is of importance. This Ord is a member of a primitive, superstitious culture—just the type Cummi could wish for—"

"He can start a fire in such tinder which would spread with ease," Kartr agreed. "We've got to get to him!"

His fingernails drummed on his belt. "We'll have to take the boy," he continued. "And he says that the camp is at least a day's journey away. I can't carry him that distance—"

"No. We'll take the lifeboat."

"But, Zinga, he thinks you are a demon. He couldn't be dragged aboard that with you in it—"

"No? But there is going to be no trouble. Use your wits, Kartr. You are a sensitive but you have no idea even yet of how much power you have to draw on at will. Ord will see and hear just what I want him to when we go and he will guide us to just the right spot, too. But we shall not land at his camp—I cannot control any number of minds—especially where Cummi has been tampering. So you will carry him in to his people and he will have no memory of the flight or of there being a second ranger."

It went just as Zinga had promised. Ord seemed but half awake, lying between them in dreamy content. He answered the Zacathan's questions readily. The visibility was better than it had been all day and they were flying out of the rain.

"Smoke!" Kartr pointed to the right.

"That must be their campsite. Now for a landing place—not too far away. You take him in—"

Ten minutes later Kartr grunted as he paused, the boy's limp body in his arms. He was on the edge of an open park-like expanse in which were set up, in no particular order, a cluster of skin tents. He could sense some twenty individuals within range of mind touch. But not Cummi.

"Ord!"

A girl was running toward the ranger, long braids of the same yellow hair as the boy's swinging over her shoulders.

"Ord?" She stopped short, staring with a hint of terror at the sergeant.

To his relief the boy roused at her cry and turned his head.

"Quetta!"

There were others coming from the tents now. Three men, hardly taller than the boy, moved warily along, their hands not far from the hafts of the long knives at their belts. Their cheeks and chins were covered with thick mats of hair—they were furred almost like animals.

"What you do?" The demand came from the tallest of the three.

"Your boy—hurt—I bring him—" Kartr shaped the unfamiliar words slowly and as clearly as he could.

"Father—this is a sky god—he seeks his brother—" Ord added.

"The sky god is away. He hunts."

Kartr gave silent thanks for the chance to learn the ground before Cummi's return. "I will wait—"

They did not dispute that. Ord was taken from him and established on a pile of furs in the largest of the tents. And the ranger was given a mat by the fire and offered a steaming bowl of stew. He ate hungrily but it was not appetizing stuff.

"How long ago did—did the sky god leave?" he asked at last.

Wulf, the hairy chieftain and Ord's father, squinted and sucked upon a tightly rolled stick of dried leaves which he had lit with a blazing splinter and moved contentedly between his bearded lips, puffing out a gray, acrid smoke.

"With the first light. He is very clever. With his magic he holds fast the beasts until the young men can spear them. We feast in plenty since he came to us. He will go to the Meeting Place of the Gods and there call upon his people and they shall come to us. Our maidens shall marry with them and we shall be great and rule this land—"

"Your people have lived here always?"

"Yes. This land is ours. There was a time of burning

fire and the gods departed into the sky—then we were left behind. But we knew that they would come again and bring a good life with them. And so it has come to pass. First came Koomee"—he had trouble with the name—"now you are here. There will be others—as the old ones promised."

He puffed silently for a moment or two and then added, "Koomee has enemies. He said that the demons fear that he may make us great again."

Kartr nodded. He gave every appearance of listening closely to what the chieftain was saying, but he was listening with more than ears alone. They were expert woodsmen, these natives. For the past five minutes they had been creeping into position in the dark behind him. They planned a sudden rush—a neat enough idea—it might have worked with a non-sensitive caught in the trap. As it was he could turn and put hand on every one of them. And he must make some move before that rush came.

"You are a great and clever chieftain, Wulf. And you have many strong warriors, but why do they lurk in the dark like frightened children? Why does he with a split lip crouch there"—the sergeant pointed to his left—"and the one with the two knives there?" His hand moved from side pocket to the fire as Wulf's head jerked around. A tongue of greenish flame shot up to bring light to the faces of the men who had believed themselves completely hidden.

There was a wild animal howl of fear as they threw themselves back out of that betraying light. They scattered. But to give full credit to the chieftain's courage he did not move. Only the roll of leaves dropped from his mouth to singe the hide legging on his right knee.

"If I *were* a demon," Kartr continued in his ordinary voice, "those would now be dead men, for I could have slain them as they hid. But I have no hatred for you or your people in my heart, Wulf."

"You are Koomee's enemy," returned the other flatly.

"Has Cummi said so? Or do you only guess that? Let us wait until he returns—"

"He has returned." The chieftain did not turn his head but there was a subtle alteration in his voice, a quickening of intelligence in his eyes as if another personality now inhabited the squat body.

Kartr got to his feet. But he did not draw his blaster. He could only use that weapon for a last defense. Surely the Ageratan wouldn't hurl these poor fools at him—!

"That I shall believe when I face him. Gods do not fight from behind others—"

"So say the noble Patrol! The fearless rangers!" Wulf's lips twisted as he shaped words entirely alien to his own tongue. "You are still bound by those out-moded codes? The worse for you. But I am glad you have come back to me, Sergeant Kartr, you are a better tool than these brainless woodsrunners."

And before Wulf had half finished that speech a bolt of mental force struck Kartr. If Cummi had not betrayed himself by words he might have had a better chance. But the ranger was armed and prepared. And into him flowed Zinga's support, so that he stood smiling faintly in the firelight as he parried and thrust in the silent motionless duel.

Cummi did not try heavy assaults, instead he used quick rapier stings of attack which one must guard against constantly. But Kartr's confidence grew. And he was doing all the work, he realized with mounting exultation—Zinga was only in watchful support. Let Cummi be a mutant of unknown powers, he was going to meet his match now in a frontier barbarian from a vanquished planet. The ranger had a second's flicker of new knowledge—Ylene had been burnt off because an Ageratan had realized the threat of that world.

His confidence grew. Perhaps Ylene had been the check upon the growing Ageratan ambition. Very well, a man from Ylene was about to avenge both his people and his world!

14

Plague

But that confidence was to be suddenly shaken. The pressure exerted by Cummi stopped as quickly as if some force blade had cut it. And in place of that darting attack there was a confused boiling of unrelated thoughts and impressions. Was that to lure him from behind his block, to set him up for some more subtle attack? But Kartr remained wary, ready to meet what came—and it came with a wild blast of desperation as if the Ageratan must win at once.

That ebbed and still the sergeant was on guard, believing that the other had withdrawn to gather his forces for another assault. And by thinking that he almost died.

For the attack which came was not mental but physical—a lance of blaster fire.

With a choked cry of pain Kartr dropped. He lay flaccid in the glow of the flames.

The chieftain shook his head and stared almost stupidly at the limp body of the ranger. He was still in the process of getting to his feet when another came out of the shadows and approached the fire, a gleaming blaster in his hand.

"Got—got him!" There was an odd hesitation in those words of triumph. And before he reached the body the newcomer stopped and half raised his hand to his head. Then his face twisted and he cried out. The blaster fell to the ground, bounced, and landed close to the body of his victim. And a second later he, too, had crumpled up.

Kartr raised himself. His hand went to his left shoulder. The vlis hide jerkin had taken some of the force of the blast, and it had not been well aimed. He had a nasty burn, but he was still alive, scooping up Cummi's blaster as he got to his feet.

That blaster—why had Cummi tried to burn him down? The sergeant was sure that the Ageratan relied on mental power—the weapon was entirely out of character—Cummi was too civilized, too self-confident. And how in the world had he been able to knock the Ageratan out so easily just a minute ago? Why—Cummi had reacted to his bolt as if he had had no mind blocks up at all!

As the ranger bent over him Cummi stirred and moaned faintly. The Ageratan's breath came in painful gasps, his chest laboring as if he were fighting hard for every lungful of air. But that was not natural—what *was* wrong with the man?

"Koomee? What does—?"

Wulf hovered timidly by the two. Kartr shook his head.

"Turn him over," he ordered briefly.

The chieftain obeyed gingerly, as if he dreaded touching the man on the ground. Kartr went down on one knee, setting his teeth against the sharp twinge of pain that motion cost him. In the firelight the Ageratan's sharp features were plain to see, his mouth was open and he was gasping. There was a faint, dark shadow pinching in above his beaked nose and about his lips—Kartr stiffened.

"Emphire fever!" he broke out though Wulf could not understand.

It was a common enough disease, he had had a bout with it once himself. The remedy was galdine. But before the medicos had discovered that drug, emphire had been serious all right. A man who caught it strangled to death because muscles locked against breathing. Galdine! But where could one find galdine here? Did they carry it in their packs of ranger equipment? He tried to remember if it were included. It might not be—their immunity shots were supposed to leave them free from the necessity of carrying such supplies.

In the meantime Cummi was going to die unless he could get air. And he, Kartr, couldn't apply artificial respiration with a blast-burned shoulder.

"You"—he turned to Wulf—"put your hands here. Then push hard and let go, like this—one, two, one, two—"

With visible reluctance the chieftain obeyed orders. Kartr contacted Zinga.

"Okay," came the calm response. "Will try for galdine in camp if you can hold on. Give me two hours—maybe three—"

Kartr bit hard on his lower lip; little hot waves of pain spread from the burn.

"Get going!" he flashed back.

Wulf glowered at him from under the tangle of his thick hair.

"Why must I do this to Koomee?"

"If you fail to do it he will die."

For a moment the rhythm ceased as the chieftain looked at the ranger in open surprise.

"But there is no wound upon him. And he is a sky god—one of those of all knowledge. Have you laid a spell upon him—being his enemy?"

"There is no spell." Hurriedly Kartr discarded two possible explanations and gave a third which this clansman might not only understand but accept. "Cummi has swallowed certain demons which cannot be seen. They do not wish to come forth, but they must be forced to do so—or they will slay him as surely as if your knife had torn him open—"

Wulf considered this and went back to his task. The manpower—and womanpower—of the camp ringed them in. And, as Wulf began to tire, Kartr arbitrarily chose the nearest and strongest of the men and set him to work in the chieftain's place. The sergeant watched Cummi's face narrowly. He could not be sure but he was almost certain that some of the strain was passing.

It might be that the first attack would be over before Zinga returned. Emphire came in cycles, he recalled. If the first disastrous paralysis of the disease did not kill, there was a period of relief before the second attack began. For that second crisis only galdine was the answer. If not treated with it the patient generally succumbed. The fever, which had faded in four generations to light attacks of mild discomfort, had once been a plague which had devastated whole planets.

Yes, Cummi was definitely breathing easier. At a sign from the ranger the man now working over the Ageratan stopped, but the Vice-Lord continued to draw shallow breaths. Kartr touched the dank skin of the sick man's face; the characteristic cold sweat was beading on forehead and upper lip.

"Bring robes to cover him," he told them.

Wulf pulled at his sleeve. "Are the demons out?"

"They have withdrawn; they may yet return."

A woman squirmed by the line of men and tossed a tanned skin in the general direction of Cummi. But she came no closer to draw it over the unconscious man. Kartr pulled it awkwardly into place himself. The natives were edging away. Wulf had retreated to the other side of the fire where he hovered nervously as if in two minds about whether to follow his people into the tight group of whisperers by the tents.

Two hours, Zinga had said, maybe three. And perhaps no galdine after all. Kartr didn't like to see the natives gathering that way, to hear the whispers hissing in the dark. They couldn't start any trouble without his knowledge. But he was one man against twenty or more of them. He had two blasters—which he could only use as a very last resort. The years-long conditioning of the rangers would not permit him to fire until it was absolutely necessary in order to save his life.

"You—"

That weak thread of voice came from beside him. Cummi was awake.

"What—?" The Ageratan began with a question.

Kartr answered with one word: "Emphire."

"Beaten—by—by a virus!" There was self-contempt in that. "Galdine?"

"Maybe. I have sent someone to see if it is among our supplies."

"So? Then there *were* two of you!" Cummi's voice was gaining strength. "But you are alone now—"

"I am alone."

The Ageratan's eyes closed wearily. He was holding a complete mind block. Perhaps behind it he was planning. But emphire affected the mental powers as well as the muscles. He could do little to start trouble now.

"You are going to have difficulties with the clan, you know." He was continuing in a conversational tone, a sort of malicious amusement just below the surface. "I've had time to indoctrinate them pretty thoroughly. They are not going to take kindly to my collapse—they'll believe that you've tried to murder me."

Kartr did not answer and his silence appeared to sting Cummi to another effort.

"You won't win this bout, Ranger, any more than you won the last. If I die you'll go down under their knives and spears—a fitting end for a barbarian."

The sergeant shrugged although that motion almost wrung a cry of pain from him. Cummi's half-open eyes narrowed and a grin drew back his lips in an animal snarl.

"So I did mark you! Well, that will make you easier meat for Wulf and his men when the time comes."

"You have it arranged very neatly, I suppose." Kartr dared to yawn. He might not be able to read what was going on behind the Ageratan's block, but he could guess how he himself would answer such an impasse and he gave Cummi credit for devising something as easy. "I will be taken care of and then you will lay an ambush for whoever comes with the galdine. It will be simpler to get it from a dead man."

But Cummi's eyes were closed again and he gave no sign that the other might have scored. Kartr looked to Wulf. The chieftain was sitting cross-legged again, staring into the fire. Was Cummi busy now making mind contact with that hunched figure? The sergeant sighed. During the past few days he had discovered that there were vast unexplored possibilities tied up with this gift of his. Why, the adept who had schooled him had known practically nothing—he knew that after meeting with Zicti, discovering communication with

Zinga. If he had *their* ability now he might well be able to intercept any orders or suggestions the Ageratan was trying to plant in Wulf's mind. He had no idea of the extent of Cummi's power—if he were a mutant, anything was possible.

The rest of the clan were still bunched in the dark by the tents. But they were squatting down, there was no immediate danger of attack. He had only to be alert and ready—

Time passed leadenly. Now and again someone crept up to feed the fire. Wulf drowsed and awakened with a jerk of the head. To all appearances Cummi either slept or was unconscious. But Kartr stayed on guard. Fortunately the pain in his shoulder would not let him rest.

At last the sound he had been straining to hear came—the faint swish of the lifeboat's air passage. He drew a deep breath of relief and straightened. Then he glanced down. Cummi's eyes were open, dark holes of evil malevolence. What was the Ageratan going to try?

Wulf stirred and Kartr's hand reached for the blaster Cummi had dropped. The chieftain arose stiffly to his feet. Three more men came out of the shadows to join him.

"Kartr!" That mental call was imperative and it came from Zicti not Zinga. "There is no galdine!"

Even as the message reached the ranger Cummi uncoiled, his legs flailing out in a move which might have brought Kartr down had he not sprung backward at the same instant. The Ageratan was crazy if he thought he could ever surprise a sensitive. But by his maneuver the Vice-Lord had been able to get to his hands and knees.

This was it! Kartr lurched to the left, keeping the fire between him and the clansmen who were moving to come up to him. They had their knives out. And he couldn't turn his blaster on the poor fools, he couldn't!

He lashed a kick at Cummi, who, reflexes weakened by the fever, could not dodge the blow. As the Ageratan sprawled flat on his face, the ranger hurdled his body and began to back toward the woods in the general direction of the hidden aircraft.

Seconds later he heard a welcome voice behind him.

"I have them covered, Kartr—"

"Cummi controls them—"

"Okay. I've got him, too. Fall back to the trees, Zicti is waiting for us." Rolth spoke calmly as he stepped out of the shadows to stand shoulder to shoulder with the sergeant.

Cummi caught at Wulf as the chieftain passed him. Using the native as a support he pulled himself up on his feet.

"So you don't have galdine," he spat at them. His face was no longer malevolent. It was twisted and white with pure fear.

"I may be a dead man," he went on softly, "but I still have time to finish you, too." He released Wulf suddenly and pushed him at the rangers. "Kill—!" he screamed.

"We'll do what we can for you—" Kartr said slowly.

The Ageratan was holding himself erect with an effort which was draining the last resources of his strength. "Still living by the code, fool! I shall live to see your blood—barbarian!"

"Ahhhhhhhh!" The scream was shrill and it bit rawly at the nerves. It could only have been torn from a woman's throat.

Wulf and his men half turned just as a second scream broke. There was a frenzied gabble of words which Kartr did not catch. But Zicti's thought translated for them.

"One of this tribe—a maiden—has fallen ill. They

believe that the demons of Cummi have entered into her—"

Wulf had gone to the source of the screaming; now he came back into the firelight walking heavily.

"The demons"—he spoke directly to the Ageratan—"are in Quetta. If you are truly a sky god— bring them forth."

Cummi swayed, conquering the weakness of his body by sheer power of will.

"It is their doing." He pointed to the rangers. "Ask them."

But Wulf's attention did not waver.

"Koomee is a sky god, he has sworn it. These have not sworn it. Koomee brought the devils hither in his body. They are the devils of Koomee, not the devils of my people. Now let Koomee summon them forth out of the body of my daughter!"

Cummi's ravaged face, gaunt and hollowed, was a mask of pain in the flickering light. His black eyes held on the rangers.

"Galdine." Kartr saw the Ageratan's lips form the word. Then slowly, as if he were fighting to the last, he lost control and toppled forward into the trampled dirt and ashes on the very edge of the fire.

Wulf stooped and twisted his fingers in the Ageratan's cropped hair, fumbling for a hold, and then he jerked up the head. But Cummi had not lost consciousness. And, before either of the horrified rangers could move, the chieftain drew his knife in a quick stroke across the stretched throat of the Vice-Lord.

"Here is an open door for the devils to enter," he remarked, "and also much blood for them to drink. May they speedily find it." He wiped the knife on Cummi's tunic. "Sometimes it takes very much blood to satisfy the thirst of a strong demon," he ended as he looked up at the rangers.

Rolth's blaster was ready but Kartr shook his head. Together they backed into the darkness under the trees.

"They will follow—" suggested the Faltharian.

"Not yet," came Zicti's reassurance. "I think that they are still a little daunted by their chieftain's act. After all, it is not every day that one slays a god—or ex-god. Now, let us make haste to the lifeboat."

It was morning again and there was a sun bright and hot across Kartr's knees but his thoughts were dull and gray.

"We couldn't do anything to help them." Smitt was making his report. "If we had had the galdine— maybe—if they would let us near them. But we have tried during these last three days. When Dalgre and I went there two hours ago one of them crawled out just to throw a knife at us. Most of them must be already dead." He spread out his hands in a gesture of defeat. "I do not think any will be alive by nightfall."

"Twenty people—maybe more—murdered. It was murder," Kartr returned bleakly.

"We don't catch it," Dalgre wondered.

"Immunity shots—and the Zacathans have never come down with emphire. But this is the way it used to hit—when it was a plague. It hasn't been like this for years—"

"We've had galdine. And we've known emphire a long time, remember. It struck us just after the Ciran worlds were explored. Through generations," Rolth pointed out, "we may have built up some natural immunity to it, also. Man does, by natural selection. But how do we know how many other germs we may carry with us—harmless to us but devastating to this world. The best thing we can do from now on is to stay away from the natives."

"And that move may not be altogether altruistic," added Zinga. "Suppose they have bred some pleasant little viruses of their own. Let us pray that our immunity shots continue to work."

"It is a tragedy, but one we can do nothing to end." Zicti pulled off his traveling cloak and let the sun beat warmly on his shoulders. "From now on we shall keep away from these people. I gather that they are not a numerous race—?"

"I believe not," answered Kartr. "From the little I was able to learn there are only a few small family clans—but they unite once a year at—"

"The Meeting Place of the Gods, yes, that is a most interesting point. These 'gods' who departed into the sky—who were they, some galactic colony later withdrawn? That would account for the city left in order to wait a return. Pardon me, gentlemen, I am being swept away again by my own subject." The hist-techneer smiled.

"But there was no space ship landing field near the city," protested Dalgre.

"That was only one city. There may be others," Fylh pointed out. "Suppose they had only one or two space ports on the whole planet. That could be true of a colonial outpost."

"The Meeting Place of the Gods," mused Zicti. "What does that suggest?"

"We've got to go there!" Dalgre sat up eagerly. "The city machinery, what I saw of it, was in an amazing state of preservation. If we find a space port we might even find a ship we can use!"

A ship to use. Kartr frowned. And then he could only be surprised at the instant protest those words had sparked in him. Didn't he want to leave this world?

Zacita and her daughter came out of the makeshift tent that was their own domain and joined the group by the fire. Kartr noted with an inner tickle of amusement how quick Zinga was to heap up the grass intended for seating.

"You have news of importance?" Zacita asked.

"There may be an ancient space port near here. The native boy told Kartr of a 'Meeting Place of the Gods' which suggests possibilities," replied her husband.

"So—" Zacita considered that. But Kartr caught a fleeting impressing that she was not altogether pleased with that news. Why? A Zacathan lady of the highest rank—for the gold forehead paint she wore proclaimed her an Issitti, one of the fabulously wealthy and noble Seven Families—certainly would rejoice at the chance to return to galactic civilization as quickly as possible.

"Techneer Dalgre believes that if we find one of the old ships we might be able to activate it again—since the machinery in the city was in such an excellent state of preservation. They used a city form of aircraft to come here, remember—"

"I hope that any spaceship we might discover would last longer than that did," Dalgre stuck in ruefully. "It did bring us this far but then it went to pieces."

"An important point to consider." Kartr met Zacita's eyes and it was almost as if he read in them some subtle encouragement. "I have no desire to blast off in a ship which will go powerless after we hit deep space. I can think of many more effective and less painful ways of committing suicide—"

"But we can visit this Meeting Place of the Gods." Dalgre was almost pleading.

"I would say yes, if we can keep free of the natives. It is time for their annual pilgrimage there. And we can't mingle with them. Cummi infected and killed that clan just as truly as if he had taken a disruptor to their camp! We can't be walking death to a whole nation!"

"Very true," Zicti agreed. "Let us do this—send out a scouting party to make mind contact with some clan bound for this assembly. But our men must keep out of sight. The natives thus discovered will serve us as unconscious guides. Once contact is established we can follow with our supplies— Will the lifeboat be of any more service?"

"It can go twenty—maybe twenty-five miles." Dalgre answered that with authority.

"Well, walking is good for the figure," Zicti continued good-humoredly. "What do you think, Sergeant Kartr?"

"You have the best solution," Kartr returned.

Zinga got up, crooking a taloned finger in Rolth's direction. "Let us go out by night—owl eyes here can watch and I can think us into contact. Should we find what we seek, you shall speedily know of it."

15

The Meeting Place
Of The Gods

Before midnight they received the message they had been waiting for, Zinga and Rolth had found a clan of natives camped for the night and had made sure that they were en route to the Meeting Place of the Gods. In the late afternoon of the next day the rangers abandoned their own camp and set out on the trail blazed by their unknowing guides.

On the eighth morning both Kartr and the Zacathans caught the warning of a multitude gathered not far ahead—they must be approaching their goal. And, picking a well-sheltered and secluded thicket, they made camp, sleeping uneasily by turns until nightfall when Zinga, Kartr and Rolth set out to learn the general lay of the land before them.

It was not the lights of a city which lit a glow in

the northern sky to beckon them, but the rising flames of at least a hundred campfires. The three rangers moved gingerly about the rim of the wide, shallow cup which held the clan rendezvous, avoiding any near contact with the few stragglers still coming in.

"This *is* a space port!"

"How can you be sure?" demanded Kartr, striving to see what had made Rolth declare that with such firmness.

"The ground—all over this depression—it has been blasted time and time again by take-off back-flares! But it's old—no new scars showing."

"All right. So we've located an old space port." Zinga sounded irritated, almost disappointed. "But a port isn't a ship. See any of those, bright eyes?"

"No," Rolth returned calmly. "But there is a building on the other side—there. See—that fire lights it just a little—"

Kartr, now that his attention had been directed, sighted it, an expanse of massive blocks only barely perceptible in the poor light.

"It's large—"

Rolth cupped his hands around his eyes to cut some of the fire glare. "Let's have the visibility lenses, Kartr." And when he used those he added with a faint trace of excitement:

"Its huge—bigger than anything we saw in the city! And—did you ever visit Central City?"

Kartr laughed bitterly. "I saw visigraphs of it. Do you think we outer barbarians ever came so close to the fount of all knowledge as to see it in reality?"

"And what has Central City got to do with this?" Zinga wanted to know. "Were you ever there yourself?"

"No. But one can get a pretty good idea of the place from the visigraphs. And that building over there is an exact duplicate of the Place of Free Planets—or I'll eat it stone by stone!"

"What!" Kartr snatched the lenses out of his companion's hands. But, although the fires and the figures of the natives moving about them leaped up to meet his eyes, the building beyond remained only a shadowy blurred shape shrouded in the night.

"But that is impossible!" Zinga cried almost triumphantly. "Even the newly hatched know that the Place of Free Planets is archaic, designed by architects who lived so far in the past we don't even know their names or home worlds. And it has never been copied!"

"Except that it has—right here," Rolth returned stubbornly. "I tell you, there is something odd about this world. Those tales you heard, Kartr, of the 'gods' who took to space—that city left waiting, ready for its owners to return, this place where the natives have a tradition that they must gather at regular intervals to await such a homecoming—it all adds up—if we only knew how to add—"

"Yes," agreed Kartr, "there is some mystery here, a bigger one maybe than we have ever tried to solve before—in spite of our system ranging—"

"Mysteries!" Zinga scoffed. "And now, my friends, we had better withdraw in a hurry unless you wish to be trampled by a select party from below—"

But Kartr had received the same sense warning and was already creeping on his hands and knees back from the rim of the ancient space port.

"If we made a wide circle to the west," Rolth pointed out, "we might be able to come out behind that building and see more of it."

So the Faltharian wanted to see more of it. Kartr shared his impatience. A solitary building which resembled the sacred Place of Free Planets! He must get to the bottom of the mystery; he had to! A world not included on even the most ancient routing tapes which he had seen—in a solar system so near the rim of the galaxy that it had been overlooked—or forgotten—centuries before he was born. Yet here beside an age-old space port stood a replica of the oldest and most revered public building ever built by human beings! He must find out why—and who—and what—

During the next few hours they made the western circle Rolth had suggested, and when, just before dawn, they were joined by the other rangers and Patrolmen, they were behind the building. Kartr's eyes were grainy from lack of sleep but excitement would not let him go back to their camp. He had to see what Rolth had described.

They moved from cover to cover, at last crawling snakewise to reach a point from which they could see clearly.

"Rolth was right!" Dalgre's voice rose to a squeak in his amazement as he looked down at the white mass. "My father was stationed at Headquarters one year—we lived in Central City. I tell you that's the Place of Free Planets down there!"

Kartr's hand pushed him flat. "All right, we'll take your word for it. But keep your voice and your head down. Those men below are trained hunters—they could easily spot you."

"But how did it get here?" Dalgre turned an honestly bewildered face to the sergeant.

"Maybe"—Kartr brought out the thought which had been born in him during the night—"this came first—"

"Came first!" Smitt wriggled up and screwed the lenses tight to his eyes. "Came first—but how?"

"You mean it could be that old?" breathed Rolth.

"You've the lenses, Smitt. Take a good look at the

edge of the roof and the steps leading up to the portico—"

"Yes," the com-techneer agreed a moment later. "Erosion—that place is very old."

"Older than the city even—" he added. "Unless being set out alone in the open had hastened decay. I'd like to have a closer look—"

"Wouldn't we all?" Zinga interrupted him. "How long do you suppose our friends down there are going to sit around?"

"Some days at least. We'll just have to button up our curiosity until they do leave," Kartr answered. "It'll probably keep us busy to just elude parties coming in and going out. We had better stay some distance away from now on."

Smitt uttered a slight groan of protest and Kartr could sympathize with him. To be so near and yet have to refrain from covering that last quarter mile which kept them from the mystery was enough to irritate anyone. But they did withdraw and there was no argument over the wisdom of keeping aloof from the natives.

Their account of the building intrigued Zicti and the next morning he calmly appropriated the services of Zinga, saying:

"Since I am unfortunately not acquainted with the proper methods of lurking, crawling, and dodging, I shall require the aid of an expert to teach this old one new tricks. Alas, even when removed, perhaps permanently, from my lecture halls, I cannot suppress my desire to collect knowledge. The customs of these natives are certainly of great interest and with your permission, Sergeant, we shall lurk and crawl to watch them—"

Kartr grinned. "With my permission, or without it, sir. Who am I to interfere with the gathering of knowledge? Though—"

"Though"—Zicti caught his thought smoothly—"it may be the first time in many years that one of my rank has gathered source material personally in the field? Well, perhaps that is one of the ills of our civilization. A little personal attention can often stop leaking seams, and a fact learned from a fragment of one culture can be applied to salve the ills of another."

Kartr ran his hands through his hair. "They are a good people—primitive—but we could help them. I wish—"

"If we only had the medical skill and learning we could mingle with them in safety. Or *you* could. Whether they would ever accept a Bemmy"—Zicti stabbed a talon at his own arched breast—"is another question. Among primitives, what is the general attitude toward the unknown? They fear it."

"Yes—that poor boy thought that Zinga was a demon," Kartr replied reluctantly. "But in time—when they learned that we meant them no harm—"

Zicti shook his head regretfully. "What a pity that we do not have a medico among us. That is one of the few limitations of our present situation which bothers me."

"You are ready to march, Haga Zicti?" Zinga came up to them, bowing his head and addressing the elder Zacathan with one of the Four Titles of Respect, which confirmed Kartr's suspicions that the hist-techneer was a noble on his own world.

"Coming, my boy, coming. There is one thing which I and my household may thank the First Mother for," he added, "and that is that we have such companions in misfortune!"

Kartr, warm with pleasure, watched the two Zacathans out of sight. He realized that Zicti, much as he withheld from giving any opinion until asked, or from intruding upon the ranger councils, was a leader. Even Smitt and Dalgre, for all their inborn suspicion

not only of unhumans but also of sensitives, had fallen
under the spell of the urbane charm and serene good
nature of the hist-techneer and his family. The Patrolmen fetched and carried cheerfully and readily for
Zacita and Zora, and preserved a lordly, big-brother-
plagued-by-small-tag-along attitude toward Zor. Just as
the difference between ranger and crewman had vanished, so had that between human and Bemmy.

"And what are you thinking of when you stand there
smiling at nothing at all?" Fylh dropped a bundle of
firewood and stretched. "You should come and haul in
some of these logs—if you have nothing better to do."

"I was thinking that there have been a lot of
changes," began the sergeant.

But for once he found Fylh as intuitive as Zinga.
"No more Bemmys, no more crew and rangers, you
mean? It just happened—somehow." He sat down on
the woodpile. "It may be that when we got out of
the city they"—he jerked his head in the direction
Smitt and Dalgre had taken a few minutes previ-
ously—"had to make a choice, once and for all. They
made it, and they aren't looking back. Now they don't
think about differences—any more than you and Rolth
ever did—"

"We were almost Bemmy ourselves, Rolth with his
night sight, and I a sensitive. And I was a barbarian
into the bargain. Those two are both inner-system men,
more conventional in their conditioning. We must give
them credit for conquering some heavy prejudices."

"They just started to use their brains." Fylh's crest
lifted. He raised his face to the sky and poured out a
liquid run of notes, so pure and heart tearing a melody
that Kartr held his breath in wonder. Was this Fylh's
form of happy release from emotion?

Then came the birds, wheeling and fluttering. Kartr
stiffened into statue stillness, afraid to break the spell.

As Fylh's carol rose, died, and rose again, more and more of the flyers gathered, with flashes of red feathers, blue, yellow, white, green. They hopped before the Trystian's feet, perched on his shoulders, his arms, circled about his head.

Kartr had seen Fylh entice winged things to him before but never just this way. It appeared to his bewildered eyes that the whole campsite was a maze of fluttering wings and rainbow feathers.

The trills of song died away and the birds arose, a flock of color. Three times they circled Fylh, hiding his head and shoulders from sight with the tapestry of tints they wove in flight. Then they were gone—up into the morning. Kartr could not yet move, his eyes remained fixed on Fylh. For the Trystian was on his feet, his arms outstretched, straining upward as if he would have followed the others up and out. And for the first time, dimly, the sergeant sensed what longings must be born in Fylh's people since they had lost their wings. Had that loss been good—should they have traded wings for intelligence? Did Fylh wonder about that?

Someone beside him sighed and he glanced around. The three Zacathans—Zacita, Zora, and Zor—stood there. Then the boy stooped to pick up a brilliant red feather and the spell was broken. Fylh dropped his arms, his feather crest folded neatly down upon his head. He was again a ranger of the Patrol and not a purveyor of winged magic.

"So many different kinds—" That was Zacita, with her usual tact. "I would not have dreamed that these trees give harborage to so many. Yes, Zor, that is indeed an unusual color for a sky creature. But every world has its own wonders."

Fylh joined the Zacathan boy who was smoothing the scarlet feather delicately between two talons. "If you wish," he said with a friendliness he had not often displayed before, "I can also show you those who fly by night—"

Zor's yellow lips stretched in a wide smile. "Tonight, please! And can you bring them here in the same way?"

"If you remain quiet and do not alarm them. They are more timid than those who live by the sun. There is a giant white one who skims through the dark like a Corrob mist ghost—"

Zor gave an exaggerated shiver. "This," he announced loudly, "is the best holiday we have ever had. I hope that it is never going to end—never!"

The eyes of the four adults met above his head. And Kartr knew they shared the same thought. This exile would probably never end for them. But—did any of them care? Kartr wanted to ask—but he couldn't—not just yet.

The rangers spent the day overhauling their equipment and making minor repairs. Clothing was a problem—unless they followed the example of the natives and took animal skins to cover them. Kartr speculated about the coming cold season. Should they tramp south to escape its rigor? For the sake of the Zacathans perhaps they should. He knew that exposure to extremes of cold rendered the reptile people torpid until they lapsed into complete hibernation.

They spied upon the natives, going out in pairs to do so, turning in all information to Zicti who compiled it as if he fully intended to give a documented lecture on the subject.

"There are several different physical types among them," he commented one evening when Fylh and Smitt, who had drawn that day's watch, had given their report. "Your yellow-haired, white-skinned people, Kartr, are only one. Now Fylh has seen this clan of very dark-skinned, black-haired men—"

"By their light clothing and strange equipment they are from a warmer country," added the Trystian.

"Odd. Such dissimilar races on the same world. But that is a humanoid characteristic, I believe," continued the hist-techneer. "I should have had more grounding in humanoid physiology."

"But they are all very primitive. That is what I can't understand." Smitt wore a puzzled frown as he spooned up the last of his stew. "That city was built—and left all ready to run again—by men who were at a high state of technological advancement. Yet all the natives we have discovered so far live in tents made of animal hide, wear skins on their backs, and are afraid of the city. And I'll swear that that pottery I saw them trading today was made out of rough clay by hand!"

"We don't understand that any better than you do, my boy," answered Zicti. "We never shall unless we can penetrate the fog of their history. Some powerful memory—or threat—has kept them out of the city. If they ever possessed any technical skill they forgot it long ago—maybe by deliberately suppressing such knowledge because it was sacred to the 'gods,' perhaps because of a general drop in a certain type of intelligence—there could be many explanations."

"Could they be the remains of a slave population, left behind when their masters emigrated?" ventured Rolth.

"That, too, would be an answer. But slavery does not usually accompany a highly mechanized civilization. The slaves would be machine tenders—and the city people had robots which would serve them better in that capacity."

"It seems to me," began Fylh, "that on this world there was once a decision to be made. And some men made it one way, and some another. Some went out"—his claws indicated the sky—"while others chose

to remain—to live close to the earth and allow little
to come between them and the wilds—"

Kartr straightened. That—that seemed right! Men
choosing between the stars and the earth! Yes, it could
have happened just like that. Maybe because he, himself, was a barbarian born on a frontier world where
man had not long taken to space, he could see the truth
in that. And perhaps because Fylh's people had made
just such a choice long ago and sometimes regretted
it, the Trystian had been the first to sense the answer
to the riddle here.

"Decadence—degeneracy—" broke in Smitt.

But Zacita shook her head. "If one lives by machines,
by the quest for power, for movement, yes. But perhaps to these it was only a moving on to what they
thought a better way of life."

A moving on! Kartr's mind fastened on that eagerly.
Maybe the time had come for his own people to make
a choice which would either guide them utterly away
from old paths—or would set them falling back—

Time continued to drag for the watchers until the
last of the natives departed. They even waited another
five hours after the last small clan left, making sure
that there would be no chance of being sighted by
lingerers. And then, in the middle of an afternoon, they
came down the slope at last, picking their way through
the debris of the campsite and around still smolder-
ing fires.

At the foot of the stairs which led to the portico
of the building they left their packs and bundles. There
were twelve broad steps, scored and pitted by winds
of time, with the tracks of hide sandals outlined in
dried mud where the natives had wandered in and out.
Up these steps they climbed and passed through lines
of towering pillars into the interior.

It would have been dark inside but the builders had

roofed the center section with a transparent material so that they could almost believe they still stood in the open.

Slowly, still in a compact group, they came down an aisle into the very middle of the huge hall. Around them on three sides were sections of seats, divided by narrow aisles, each ending at the floor level in one massive chair on the back of which was carved, in such high relief that time had not worn it away, a symbol. On the fourth side of the chamber was a dais supporting three more of the high-backed chairs of state, the center one raised another step above the other two.

"Some type of legislative building, do you think?" asked Zicti. "The presiding officer would sit there." He pointed to the dais.

But Kartr's torch beam fastened on the sign carved on the nearest of the side chairs. As he read it he stood incredulous. Then he flashed the light to illuminate the marking on the next seat and the next. He began to run, reading the symbols he knew—knew so well!"

"Deneb, Sirius, Rigel, Capella, Procyon." He did not realize it, but his voice was rising to a shout as if he were calling a roll—calling such a roll as had not sounded in that chamber for four thousand years or more. "Betelgeuse, Aldebaran, Pollux—"

"Regulus." Smitt was answering him from the other side of the hall, the same wild excitement in his voice. "Spica, Vega, Arcturus, Altair, Antares—"

Now Rolth and Dalgre began to understand in turn.

"Fomalhaut, Alphard, Castor, Algol—"

They added star to star, system to system, in that roll call. In the end they met before the dais. And they fell silent while Kartr, with a reverence and awe he had never known before, raised his torch to give more light to the last of those symbols. That bright one which should gleam in this place was there!

"Terra of Sol." He read it aloud and the three words seemed to echo more loudly down the hall than any of the shouted names of the kindred stars. "Terra of Sol—man's beginning!"

16

Terra Calling

"I don't believe it." Smitt's voice sounded thin; his attention was fixed on that high seat and the incredible sign it bore. "This can't be the Hall of Leave-Taking. That was just a legend—"

"Was it?" asked Kartr. "But legends are not always fables."

"And out there"—Dalgre pointed toward the doorway without turning his head from the dais—"is the Field of Flight!"

"How long—?" Rolth's question dwindled off into silence, but his words continued to echo down the hall.

Kartr wheeled to face those rows of chairs and the section of seats each one headed. There—why, right there had sat the commanders, and behind them crews and colonists! And so they must have gathered, shipful after shipful for years—maybe centuries. Gathered, spoke together for the last time, received their last orders and

instructions—then went out to the field and the waiting ships and blasted off into the unknown—never to
return. Some—a few—had won through to their goals.
They, Smitt, Dalgre, Rolth and he, were living proof of
that. Others—others had reached an end in the cold of
outer space or on planets which could not support
human life. How long had it gone on, that gathering,
that leave-taking? With no return. Long enough to drain
Terra's veins of life—until only those were left who were
temperamentally unfitted to try for the stars? Was that
the answer to the riddle of this half-and-half world?

"No return—" Rolth had picked that out of his
thoughts somehow. "No return. So the cities died and
even the memory of why this exists is gone. Terra!"

"But *we* remember," Kartr answered softly. "For
we have made the full circle. The green—that is the
green of Terra's hills. It has been a legend, an ancient
song, a dim folk memory, but it has always been ours,
going with us from world to world across the galaxy.
For *we* are the sons of Terra—inner system, outer system, barbarian and civilized—we are all the sons of
Terra!"

"And now," Smitt observed with wistful simplicity,
"we have come home."

It was a home which bore no resemblance to the
dark mountains and chill valleys of Rolth's half-frozen
Falthar, to his own tall forests and stone cities now
forever dust, to the highly civilized planets which had
been the birthplaces of Smitt and Dalgre. It was a
planet of wilderness and dead cities, of primitive natives
and forgotten powers. But it was Terra and, as different
as their races might be today, they were all originally
of the stock which had walked this earth.

Once more he surveyed that assembly of empty
seats. Almost he could people it. But those he summoned to sit there could not be the ones who had

once done so. The men of Terra had been gone too long—were scattered too far—

He walked slowly down the center of the hall. The Zacathans and Fylh had drawn apart. They must have watched with amazement the actions of the humans. Now Kartr tried to explain.

"This is Terra—"

But Zicti knew what that meant. "The ancient home of your species! But what an amazing discovery!"

What else he might have added was drowned out in a shout which drew all their attention to the dais again. Dalgre stood at the left of it beckoning to them. Rolth and Smitt had disappeared. In a body they hurried to join Dalgre.

The new discovery was behind the dais, hidden by a tall partition—and it covered most of the wall. A giant screen of some dark glass on which pin points of light made patterns.

Below it was a table top of which was inlaid with a paneling of switches and buttons. Smitt crouched on the bench before it, his face intent.

"A communication device?" asked Kartr.

"Either that or some kind of a course plotter," Dalgre answered. Smitt merely grunted impatiently.

"Could it still be in working order?" Zacita marveled.

Dalgre shook his head. "We can't tell yet. The city functioned again after they pulled the right switches. But this"—he indicated the giant star map and the intricate controls on the table—"will have to be studied before *we* can push the right levers. Why, we don't understand any of their wiring methods—"

The techneer, any techneer, might possibly put the machine into working order again. But, Kartr knew, such a feat was totally beyond the rangers. He studied the star map slowly, identifying the points he could recognize. Yes, here was the galaxy as it appeared from this ancient planet close to its rim. He noted the brilliance of Sarmak, moved on to Altair and the others. Had this board once plotted the course on which man went out to those far-off suns and the worlds they nourished?

It was growing darker as the evening closed down. But even as the light faded from overhead, a soft glow outlined the star map and illumined the table—although the rest of the hall remained shrouded with shadows.

Kartr moved. "Shall we camp outside or return to the hills?" he asked Zicti.

"I see no reason for returning," the Zacathan replied. "If all the natives have withdrawn, as they apparently have, surely there can be no objection to our staying—"

Behind him Zinga laughed and pointed a talon at Smitt. "If you think that you can drag him away from here even by force, you are sadly in error, Sergeant."

Which, of course, was true. The com-techneer, confronted by a mysterious device in his own field, refused to leave even for food, preferring to gulp down a cup of water and chew on a piece of tough meat absently while his eyes were busy with the marvels before him.

They chose to drag their bedrolls into the hall when the full night fell, putting out their cooking fire and lying closely together below the empty seats of the vanished colonists.

"There are"—Zicti's voice boomed through the emptiness—"no ghosts in this place. Those who gathered here once were already voyaging on in spirit, even as they sat here, eager to be gone. They have left nothing of themselves behind."

"In a way," Rolth agreed, "that was also true of the city. It was—"

"Discarded." Kartr produced the right word as the

Faltharian hesitated. "Discarded as might be a garment grown too small for its wearer. But you are right, sir, we shall meet no ghosts here. Unless Smitt can awaken some with his tinkering. Is he going to stay there all night?"

"Naturally," Zinga replied. "And let us hope that he will *not* raise any voices out of the past—even out of your human past, friend. I have an odd desire to spend this night in slumber."

Kartr awakened twice during the night. And by the faint glow which crept around the edges of the partition he saw that Smitt's bedroll was still unoccupied. The com-techneer must be hypnotized by his discovery. But there was a limit to everything. So, at his second awakening, Kartr pulled himself out of the warmth of his bed with an impatient sigh, shivered in the chill, and padded on bare feet across the cold stone. Either Smitt would come willingly or he would be dragged to bed now.

The com-techneer was still on the seat, his head thrown back, his gaze fixed on the star map. In the reflection of the light his eyes appeared sunken and there were dark shadows like bruises along his cheek bones.

Kartr followed the direction of the other's set stare. He saw what held Smitt fascinated, blinked, and gave a gasp.

There was a red dot on the black glass surface, a dot which moved in a steady curve.

"What is it—"

Smitt replied without taking his eyes from the traveling dot.

"I'm not sure—I'm not sure!" He passed his hands across his face. "You *do* see it, too?"

"I see a red dot moving. But what is it?"

"Well, I've guessed—"

And Kartr knew the nature of that guess. A ship—
moving through space—headed in their general
direction!

"Coming here?"

"It's on a course—but—how can we tell? Look!"

Another dot had sprung into being on the screen.
But this moved with a purpose. It was on the track
of the first, a hunter on the trail. Kartr pushed down
beside Smitt on the bench. His heart was thumping
so that he could feel the sullen beat of blood in his
temples. It was very important—that flight and
pursuit—somewhere within him he knew that—so
important he feared to watch.

The first dot was moving in a series of zigzags now.

"Evasive action." Smitt mouthed the words. He had
served on a battle cruiser, Kartr knew.

"What kind of ships are they?"

"If I understood this"—Smitt swept his hand over
the controls before him—"maybe I could answer that.
Wait—!"

The first dot engaged in a complicated maneuver
which had no meaning as far as the sergeant could see
but which flipped it back on a level with its pursuer.

"That's a Patrol ship! It's offered battle—but why—"

They were even, those two dots. And then—a third
appeared on the board! It was slightly larger and moved
more slowly, avoiding the two which would shortly be
locked in combat. And, in making the arc to avoid the
fight, it headed straight toward Sol's system.

"Covering action," Smitt translated. "The Patrol is
covering for this other ship! A suicide mission, I think.
Look—their battle screens are up now!"

A faint, very faint orange haze encircled the two dots
near the outer verge of Sol's system. Kartr had never
been in space action, but he had heard enough tales,
seen enough visigraphs, to be able to create in his mind

a picture of the struggle now beginning. The larger dot had no part in the struggle. Instead it crept at its snail's pace on and on, away from the dead-locked fighters.

Pressure—pressure of screen against screen. And when one of those screens failed—flaming and instant death! That was a Patrol ship out there holding the enemy at bay while a defenseless prey escaped.

"If I could only read this!" Smitt smashed his fists against the edge of the table.

On the board a tiny bubble of light blazed suddenly to light.

"Set off by the ship coming this way?"

Smitt nodded. "Could be." He leaned forward with quick decision and pressed his finger on the button set under that pinprick of light. There followed sound—a vast roar as of rushing winds. They stared at the map almost deafened. And then through the roar came the chatter of something else, a sharp clicking which formed a pattern. Smitt jumped to his feet.

"Patrol summons, Patrol summons—TARZ—TARZ—"

Kartr's hand reached for a blaster he was not wearing. The old call to action for the Service! He heard amazed cries behind him. The others were up, crowding around the partition to see and hear what was happening.

The beat of the summons echoed hollowly through the building. It might go on until the end of that battle or until there was some answer. But no answer came. The haze about the dots thickened until they were completely hidden in it and each spot was a stationary fire.

"Top pitch—!" that was Dalgre breathing the words down Kartr's back. "Reaching overload fast. They can't take that much longer—they can't!"

"Tar—"

One spot swept from orange to yellow—to incandescent white. It was an instant of splendor and then it was gone. They blinked blinded eyes and looked again. But there was nothing—nothing at all of the two fiery spots. The dark glass of the screen where they had been was as bare and cold as the wastes of outer space it represented.

"Both—out!" Dalgre was the first to speak. "Overload and it blasted them both. One ship took the other with it."

"But the third—it is still intact—" Zicti pointed out.

That was true. The battle had wiped out two ships, but the third dot still moved—the one which the Patrol ship had died to save. It was on course—toward Sol and Terra!

The clicking sound changed, made another series of coded calls. Smitt listened and read them aloud for his companions.

"Patrol—auxiliary—personnel ship—2210—calling nearest Patrol ship or station. Come in, please—come in. Survivors of Patrol Base CC4—calling nearest Patrol ship or station—off known courses—need guide call—come in please—"

"Survivors of Patrol Base CC4," Rolth repeated. "But that was a Ranger Station! What in the name of Space—!"

"Pirate raid, maybe—" suggested Zinga.

"Pirates don't tangle with the Patrol—" began Dalgre.

"You mean—pirates didn't! We've been out of circulation and off the maps for some time. A coalition of pirate forces can do a lot of damage," Zinga observed.

"Note also," Zicti added to that, "this ship now flies from the more populated sections of the galaxy. It heads out toward the unknown which it would not do if there were not some barrier between it and more familiar routes."

"Personnel survivor ship—families of Patrolmen." Dalgre was visibly shaken. "Why, the base must be utterly gone!"

The clicking of the code still filled the musty air of the hall. And on the map the dot moved, on the board before Smitt the tiny bulb still blazed. Then, as suddenly, it snapped off and a second went on in turn in the block next to it. Kartr glanced from that new light to the screen. Yes, the dot was appreciably closer to the system of Sol.

Smitt's fingers hovered over the board. He licked his lips as if his mouth was dry.

"Is there any chance of guiding her in here?" Kartr asked the question he knew was tormenting the other.

"I don't know—" Smitt snarled like a tortured animal.

His finger went down and pressed the button below the second light. And then he jumped back, as did Kartr, for out of the edge of the table sprang a thin black stalk ending in a round bulb. The com-techneer laughed almost wildly and clutched at the thing.

Then he began to speak into it, not in code but in the common tongue of Central Control.

"Terra calling! Terra calling! Terra calling!"

They were frozen, silent, listening to the chatter of the code filling the air. Kartr sagged. It hadn't worked after all. And then came a break in the ship's broadcast. He had forgotten about the time lag.

"Terra calling." Smitt was cool, calm again. To that statement he began to add a series of code words and clicks. Three times he repeated the message and then leaned back to await reply.

Again the wait seemed too long—tearing at their

ragged nerves. But at last an answer came. Smitt translated it for them all.

"Do not entirely understand. But think can ride in on message beam—keep talking if you have no signal. What—where is Terra?"

So they talked. First Smitt, until his voice was but a husky whisper issuing from a raw throat, and then Kartr, using ordinary speech and the old formula, Terra calling—then Dalgre and Rolth—

There was sunshine lighting the space around them and then it grew dark again and still they crouched in turn on the bench before the sky map and talked. And the red dot crept on, now on a straight course for Terra. It was when it had drawn almost even with the outermost planet of Sol's system that Zor pointed out to the half-dazed Kartr on duty, the newcomer. Another dot—already past the point where the battle had been fought—and on a line after the personnel ship! Enemy or friend?

Kartr shook Zor's shoulder and pushed him toward the outer hall with the message to bring Smitt. The com-techneer, rubbing sleep-heavy eyes, half reeled in. But when Kartr showed him the dot he was thoroughly awake. He shoved the sergeant away from the microphone and took over with a sharp question in code.

After lagging minutes it was answered:

"Undoubtedly enemy ship. Pirate signals have been picked up during last quarter hour—"

To Kartr's sick eyes the enemy ship was darting across space. It was now a race, a race in which the Patrol ship might already be the loser. And, even as he thought that, there was a flash of light on the control board. The enemy was now within hailing distance. Smitt turned a grim face to him.

"Get one of the Zacathans and Fylh. If they can talk in their own language it will be better than using control speech or the code as a guide. There are few Bemmys in pirate crews. All the ship needs is a steady sound to center her finder on—"

But he spoke his last words to empty air. Kartr was already on his way to rout out the others. Seconds later Zinga slipped into Smitt's place, hooked his talons around the stem of the phone and unloosed a series of hissed sounds which certainly bore no resemblance to human speech. When he tired, Fylh was ready and then twittering and fluting broke across space to talk the ship in. But ever relentlessly behind it came that other dot, seeming to leap across great expanses of space as if such stretches were nothing.

Zora brought in a canteen of water and they all drank feverishly. They ate after a fashion, too, of whatever was thrust into their hands, unknowing and untasting.

The Patrol ship passed more planets. Then a third light snapped on the board. Zor came running in.

"There is a big light—reaching into the sky!" he shouted shrilly.

Kartr jumped to his feet to see that for himself when a sound of ship's code stopped him.

"Pulse beam picked up. We can ride it in. If we still have time—"

Zinga let go of the phone and as one they hurried out into the open. Zor was right. From the end of the roof directly over the control table a beam of light speared into the evening sky.

"How did that—?" Kartr began.

"Who knows?" Dalgre replied. "They were master techneers in their day. That must pulse strongly enough to be picked up by a ship approaching this planet within a certain distance. At least we can now stop talking."

In the end they drifted back to the map—to watch the ship and its pursuer. The gap between those two

was narrowing—too quickly. A last light flashed on the
control board—it was warning red.

"Ship's entered the atmosphere," Smitt guessed. "Get
everybody inside here. It may not land on the field and
the power wash will be brutal—"

So they waited inside the ancient Hall of Leave-
Taking and they heard rather than saw a ship land on
a field which had not felt the bite of spaceship's fire
for at least a thousand years. But it was a good landing.

Smitt remained at the board. "The other is still
coming—" His warning rang out to hasten the others.

Still coming! They might lose even now, Kartr
thought, as he watched the exit bridge swing out from
the side of the rusty old tub perched in the field. All
the enemy would have to do would be to hover and
blast them with missiles. He wouldn't have to land, but
when he pulled out again he would leave nothing
behind but a blackened and lifeless waste.

If they could get the refugees into the hall they
might have a chance to survive that—a very thin one.
The sergeant ran to the edge of the smoking landing
area and waved at the figure who had appeared on the
bridge.

"Get your people off and into the hall!" he shouted.
"The pirate's coming and he can try for a burn-off!"

He saw the jerk of an assenting nod and heard
orders. The passengers filed down the bridge at the
double quick. They were mostly women, some carrying or leading children. The rangers and the Zacathans
stood ready to act as guides. Kartr half hauled, half
carried the strangers to the precarious safety of the old
building. Then when the flow of refugees ceased he
hurried back to the bridge.

"All out?"

"All out," the officer replied. "And what course is
the pirate on—can you tell—?"

Zinga came running toward them. "Pirate coming in on the same course—"

The officer turned and went inside the ship. Kartr drummed nervous fingers on the guard rail of the bridge. What in the name of Space was the fellow waiting for?

Then the sergeant was almost bowled over as five men flung themselves out of the hatchway and ran for the hall, taking both rangers with them. They had just reached the protection of the doorway when the Patrol ship took off.

Blinded by the sweep of flame Kartr clung to one of the pillars to keep his footing.

"What—?" he gasped.

And a babble of question joined and drowned out his.

17

The End Is Not Yet

The hard surface of the partition ground into Kartr's back as the pressure of the crowd jammed him against that barrier. All the refugees were there in the narrow space behind the control table, tense, expectant, with no attention for anything but the sky map on the wall. Beside the sergeant a tall girl in the battle-stained tunic of a civilian supply assistant muttered half aloud to herself.

"There's only one of them—by the Grace of the Three—there is only one for him to face!"

Her "one" was that ominous red dot of the pirate ship still on course to Terra—headed without doubt for the very point on that planet where they now stood. But, even as they watched that advance helplessly, a second dot appeared on the screen—the Patrol ship moving out to meet the enemy.

"Time to try evasive!" Kartr caught the urgency in

459

that man's voice rising from the mass of watchers. "Evade, Corris!"

And, as if that half-order half-plea had actually reached across space, the course of the Patrol ship changed. It seemed now as if it were attempting to make a futile run for safety, trying to elude the pirate. Out there a single brave man swung before a control panel, enmeshed in a pilot's web, prepared to fight a last battle to save his fellows. One lone Patrolman!

He continued to evade skillfully, altering his course just enough each time to draw the enemy after him, to persuade the other ship into pursuit and away from Terra. He had his screen up as the haze testified. That should act as a flaunting challenge to the pirate. The impulse of the pursuer would be to follow, to beat down the weak barrier, to put on a traction beam and warp in the Patrol ship. Only, what Captain Corris flew was no longer a ship, it was a single deadly weapon! And the enemy who strove to overtake and capture it would only trigger his own death in the same instant that he drew it in!

Kartr heard sobs, subdued, and little angry mutters from those about him.

"He has the war head ready." That was the girl. She was talking as if to reassure herself, not to inform anyone else of what lay behind that silent battle out in the dark between worlds. "We were going to blow it if we were taken. He'll trigger it when they beam him in—" Her voice was hoarse, almost fierce.

The red dots moved as fighters sparring for an opening, making patterns on the screen. Kartr, though he was ignorant of space maneuvers, guessed that he was now watching the last fight of an inspired pilot. And yet to the pirate it must appear that a weak ship was trying desperately to escape.

"If only they don't suspect!" The girl's tone was that

of a prayer. "Spirit of Space, keep them from suspecting—"

The end came as the Patrol pilot had planned it. A glow of battle screens hazed both ships—and then the one surrounding the Patrol ship disappeared. The dots moved toward each other—the pirate had clamped a pincher beam on its prey, was dragging the helpless ship to where they could lock air-locks for boarding. At last the dots touched.

A flower of fire burst on the screen. It glowed for only a second and then died, to leave nothing behind it—nothing at all. The map was as blank as it had been when first they found it. Only the specks which were stars sparkled with aloof chill in the void.

No one in the crowd moved. It was as if they did not believe in the truth of what they had just witnessed, that they did not wish to believe. Then there was a single sigh and the tight mass broke apart. People drifted, with eyes which seemed to see nothing, out into the hall. Except for the shuffle of feet over the stone it was very quiet.

Overhead the gray light of another dawn gave a pale radiance. Kartr stepped up on the dais. He rested one hand on the back of the chair which was Terra's and looked closely for the first time at these new companions in misfortune.

They were a mixed lot, both as to race and species, as might be expected from a Patrol Ranger base. There were two more Zacathans, a pale-faced woman and two children with the goggles of the Faltharians hanging from their belts, and he was sure he had seen a feather crest which could only have graced the head of a Trystian.

"You are in command here?"

Kartr's attention flickered from the refugees to a girl—the same girl who had stood beside him to watch the battle—and two men standing together at the foot of the dais. Automatically Kartr's hand arose to touch a helmet he no longer wore.

"Ranger Sergeant Kartr of the *Starfire*. We crashed here some time ago. Our party consists of three other rangers, a com-techneer and an arms-techneer—"

"Medico-techneer Veelson," the shorter of the two men responded in a low and surprisingly musical voice. "This is Third Officer Moxan of our Base Ship, and Acting Sergeant Adrana of the Headquarters section. We are entirely at your service, Sergeant."

"Your party—"

"Our party," Veelson answered quickly, "numbers thirty-eight. Twenty women and six children are ranger dependents. Five crewmen under Moxan, and six supply corpswomen with Sergeant Adrana—and myself. As far as we know we are the only survivors of Base CC4."

"Zinga—Fylh—Rolth—" Kartr gave the order which came naturally to him. "Firewood detail and get some fires going—" He turned back to the medico-techneer. "I take it, sir, that you haven't much in the way of supplies?"

Veelson shrugged. "We have only what we could carry. It certainly isn't too much."

"A hunting party out, too, Zinga. Smitt, take over the communication board again. We don't want to be caught napping if there is another ship on its way. Any of your men know com, sir?" he asked Moxan.

Instead of answering directly the third officer turned on his heel and called down the length of the hall. "Havre!"

One of the men in crew uniform came running.

"Com work," his officer grunted. "Under this techneer."

"I take it that we can live off the country, since you mentioned hunting," Veelson asked.

"This is an Arth type planet. We've found it hospitable. In fact—this *is* Terra, you know."

Kartr watched the medico-techneer closely to see if that registered. It took a second or two, but it did.

"Terra." Veelson repeated the word blankly and then his eyes widened. "The home of the Lords of Space! But that is a legend—a fable!"

Kartr stamped on the dais. "Fairly substantial fable, don't you think? You are in the Hall of Leave-Taking now—look at the seats of the first star rangers, if you wish." He pointed to the chairs. "Read what is carved on the back of this one. Yes, this is Terra of Sol!"

"Terra!" Veelson was still shaking his head wonderingly when Kartr spoke to the girl.

"You have your corpswomen. Can you take charge of the women and children?" he asked abruptly. This sort of duty was beyond his experience. He had established field camps, led expeditions, fought his way back and forth across many weird worlds in the past, but never before had he been responsible for such a group as this.

She started to nod, flushed, and raised her hand in salute. A moment later she was back circulating among the tired women and the fretful children—aided by the Zacathan family.

"Any chance of there being another pirate after you? What *did* happen at the base?" Already forgetting the women, Kartr began to question the medico-techneer.

"The base was wiped out. But things had begun to go wrong before that. There has been a breakdown somewhere along the supply and communication route. Our yearly supply ship was three months overdue even before the attack. We'd received no messages from Central Control for two weeks. We sent out a cruiser and it never returned.

"Then the pirate fleet came in. It was a *fleet* and

the whole raid had been carefully planned. We had five ships on the field. Two raised and accounted for three of the pirates before they were blasted out. We manned the perimeter guns as long as we could and cleared the air for the survivors to take off.

"What caught us napping was that they came in under false colors and we accepted them as friendly until too late. They were Central Control ships! Either some section of the Fleet has mutinied or—or something terrible has happened to the whole empire. They acted as if the *Patrol* had been outlawed—their attack was vicious. And because they had come in with all the proper signals we weren't expecting it. It was as if *they* were the law—"

"Perhaps they are now," Kartr suggested grimly. "Maybe there has been a rebellion in this sector. The winner may be systematically mopping up all Patrol bases. That would leave him free to rule the space lanes as he pleases. A very practical and necessary move if there has been a change of government."

"That idea did occur to us. I can't say that we welcomed it." Veelson's voice was bleak. "Well, we did manage to crowd aboard a supply ship and one of the Patrol scouts. After that it was a running fight across space. They were between us and the regular routes so we had to head out this way. We lost the scout—"

Kartr nodded. "We saw that on the screen before we were able to contact you."

"It rammed a flagship—a flagship of the Fleet, mind you!"

"But effectively," the sergeant reminded him. "There were only the two ships following you—are you sure?"

"Only two registered on our screens. And—now if neither returns— Do you think that they will send another to track us down?"

"I don't know. They would accept the idea that the

Patrol would be desperate enough to go out fighting. And so they may be willing to write off their ships as a case of blasting each other. But Smitt and your man can keep at their posts. They'll be able to give us warning in time if another heads this way."

"And if one does come?"

"Large portions of this world are wilderness. It will be easy to take cover in plenty of time and they could never find us."

By the end of the day the new camp was well established. The hunting party had been successful enough so that everyone was fed. Under the leadership of the corpswomen a party had spread out on the hill, hacked off branches, and fashioned beds. And there had been no warning—the screen in the hall remained blank.

It was night now. Kartr stood at the top of the stairs gazing down abstractedly at the landing field. A gleaning party had worked under his direction most of the afternoon, shifting the debris of the natives' encampment. And they had salvaged two spears and a handful of metal arrow points, treasures to be guarded against that day when the last blaster charge would be expended—when weapons which were the products of civilized skill would be useless.

Tomorrow they must hunt again and—

"A pleasant night, is it not, lady? There is, of course, only one moon instead of three. But it is a very bright one."

Kartr started and turned his head. Zicti was walking toward him accompanied by the girl, Adrana.

"Three moons? Is that the number which shine down on Zacan? Now I would consider two to be a more normal number." And she laughed.

Two moons. Kartr tried to remember all the two-mooned worlds he had known and wondered which had been her native one. But there were at least ten—and probably more which he had never heard of. No man, even if he had at least four lifetimes, could learn all that lay within the galaxy. Two moons was too faint a clue.

"Ha, the sergeant! So the night draws you also, my boy? One might believe that you were a Faltharian, this interest you show in a dark, sleeping world."

"Only doing some planning for the future," Kartr replied. "And I'm no Faltharian, only a barbarian," he added recklessly. "You know what they said of us of Ylene—that we eat raw meat and worship strange gods!"

"And you, lady," Zicti asked the girl, "upon which world did your two moons beam?"

She lifted her head with close to a defiant gesture, and stared out over the launching field as she answered.

"I was space born—a half-breed. My mother was of Krift. My father came from one of the outer system worlds, I don't know which. My two moon world I knew only for a short time when I was a small child. But I have seen many worlds for I am Service bred."

"We have all seen many worlds," Kartr observed, "and now I think we are going to learn one thoroughly."

Zicti inhaled the night air with gusto. "But such a pleasant world, my children. I must say that I have great hopes for our future here."

"It is good to know that someone has," Kartr said somberly.

But it was Adrana who rose to the Zacathan's challenge. "You are right!" She laid her fingers on the hist-techneer's scaled arm. "This *is* a good world! When I was up on the hill today, the air was like wine in my throat. It is free—alive! And we are very lucky. For the first time in my life"—she paused as if she were surprised at her own words—"I feel at home!"

"Because this is Terra—racial memory—" suggested Kartr.

"I don't know. After so long a time—that couldn't be possible, could it?"

"Perhaps." He added a confession of his own. "The first day we landed here—when I saw the green of this vegetation—it seemed then that I, too, remembered."

"Well, children, I do *not* remember Terra, nor can any of my race. But still I say that we have landed on a good world—a pleasant one to make our own. We have only to do that—"

"What of the city and the clans?" inquired the sergeant. "Are they going to sit passive and allow us such usurpation?"

"This is a wide world. And that problem we shall face when it arises. Now, moon gazers, not being a Faltharian, I shall seek my bedroll. You must pardon my withdrawal." Chuckling he padded away.

"What did you mean—the city and the clans? Are there natives here?" questioned the girl.

"Yes." Briefly Kartr gave her the facts. "So you see," he ended, "this world is not altogether ours for the taking. And since we cannot remain at this point on it indefinitely we shall have decisions to make soon."

She nodded. "Tell the others tomorrow. Tell them all you have told me."

"You mean—leave the decision up to them? All right." He shrugged.

What if they chose the comfort of the city? Such a decision would only be natural. But, he was very sure, he would not go back there nor would the others who had followed him out of that monument to a too-ancient past.

Because he agreed that each must decide for him- or herself, he stood again the next morning in the pool of hot sunlight which crossed the dais. His throat was dry. He had been talking steadily. And now he was tired, as tired as if he had spent half the day cutting through heavy brush. Those faces all turned to him, so impassive, so controlled.

Had any of them really heard what he had been saying, or having heard, did they understand? Was this indifference the result of their immediate past, were they sure that the worst had already happened and that nothing could shake them again?

"And that is the situation we now face—"

But there was no response from the seated refugees. Then he heard the scrape of bootsoles across the pavement, sounding louder because of the silence in the hall. Veelson jumped up on the dais to join him.

"We have the report of the ranger sergeant. He gives us two courses which may be followed. First—we may try to contact this civilian party now occupying a city not too far distant, a city with part of its functions restored. But they have the problem of limited food supply and in addition"—the medico-techneer paused, and then he added without any change of tone or expression—"that party is an entirely human one."

Again there was no response from the listeners. Had they met with anti-Bemmy feeling before? They must have! It had been growing so powerful. But if they had it made no difference. In the wide seat marked Deneb was the Faltharian woman and she cradled in her arms a tiny Trystian girl whose mother had not survived the base raid. And Zor sat between two inner system boys of his own age. There was no drawing apart in this company—Bemmy to Bemmy, human to human. These were the rangers!

"So we may go to the city," Veelson repeated, "or we may choose the second solution which could mean a much greater measure of hardship. Though we of the rangers, by training and tradition, are better able to face what it may demand of us. And that is to live on the land after the fashion of the natives.

"Sergeant Kartr has spoken of a cold season reported to be approaching now. He has also pointed out that we cannot remain here—due to lack of supplies. We can travel south—as the majority of the natives did when they left here a few days ago. Contact with the natives, while impossible now—judging by the sergeant's unfortunate experience—may be allowed later as we have some medical supplies and knowledge. But it might be years before we dare attempt such fraternization.

"These are the two choices we are now assembled to vote upon—"

"Medico Veelson!" One of the crewmen was on his feet. "Do you rule out the possibility of rescue then? Couldn't we remain near here and try to use that communicator to summon help? Any Patrol ship—"

"Any *Patrol* ship!" Again the lack of expression in the medico-techneer's voice underlined his words. "A communication attempt might just as well bring down roving pirates upon us. There is no way of identifying until too late any ship we might be able to beam in. And remember, Terra is off every known chart—so forgotten that its name is now only a legend."

A murmur ran from seat to seat.

"So we must accept exile?" That was a woman.

"I believe that we must." Veelson's answer came clear and firm.

Another silence followed. They were facing truth now. And—Kartr thought proudly—they were accepting it quietly.

"I believe that we wish to remain together—" Veelson continued slowly.

"Yes!" That answer was so loud it woke a faint echo from the roof. The Patrol would stand together, that creed which had been theirs for generations still held them.

"We will abide by the will of the majority. Those who wish to seek shelter in the city may take their places against that wall. Those who would remain apart—on the land—stand here—"

Veelson had not even finished speaking before he himself moved with two distance-eating strides to the left of the dais. And Kartr joined him. Only for a moment were they alone. Adrana and her six co-workers arose from their seats in the group and marched to stand beside the medico-techneer. But then there was a pause—the other women did not move.

It was the Faltharian woman who broke the spell. Still carrying the Trystian infant and pushing her own two children ahead, she walked quickly to the left. But she did not reach the others before Zicti and his family.

Now there was a steady shuffling of feet and when it was quiet again there was no need to count heads. Not one stood on the city side. They had made their decision, weighing the evidence and the chances of the future. And, Kartr knew, seeing their serene faces, they would stand by it. Suddenly he was vaguely sorry for those in the city. They would struggle there to keep up a measure of mechanical civilization. Perhaps they would live in greater ease for this generation. But in a way they had turned their backs upon the future and they might not be allowed a second choice.

But the Patrol were eager to be gone, once their minds were made up. And the dawn of the second day saw them in marching order, their scanty belongings in packs, their faces set toward the unknown lands of the south.

Kartr watched Fylh and Zinga lead that line of women and children, crewmen and officers, all one now under an alien sun, going into the future.

He glanced back into the deserted hall. The sun caught and held on the symbols in the captains' seats along one side. Old Terra— And down there—heading into the wilderness was the NEW!

"Shall we rise again to be the lords of space and the rangers of the star lanes?" he wondered. "Do we begin this day a second cycle leading to another empire?"

He was a little startled when Zicti's thought answered his. "It is just history, my boy, history. We fashion that whether or no. But there is a very old saying known to my people—'When a man comes to the end of any road let him remember that the end is not yet and a new way shall open for him.' "

Kartr turned his back upon the Hall of Leave-Taking and ran lightly down the eroded steps. The wind was chill but the sun was warm. Dust puffed up from beneath the marching feet.

"Yes, the end is not yet! Let us go!"

THE SHIP WHO SANG IS NOT ALONE!

Anne McCaffrey, with Mercedes Lackey, S.M. Stirling, and Jody Lynn Nye, explores the universe she created with her ground-breaking novel, The Ship Who Sang.

THE SHIP WHO SEARCHED
by Anne McCaffrey & Mercedes Lackey

Tia, a bright and spunky seven-year-old accompanying her exo-archaeologist parents on a dig, is afflicted by a paralyzing alien virus. Tia won't be satisfied to glide through life like a ghost in a machine. Like her predecessor Helva, *The Ship Who Sang*, she would rather strap on a spaceship!

THE CITY WHO FOUGHT
by Anne McCaffrey & S.M. Stirling

Simeon was the "brain" running a peaceful space station—but when the invaders arrived, his only hope of protecting his crew and himself was to become *The City Who Fought*.

THE SHIP WHO WON
by Anne McCaffrey & Jody Lynn Nye

"The brainship Carialle and her brawn, Keff, find a habitable planet inhabited by an apparent mix of races and cultures and dominated by an elite of apparent magicians. Appearances are deceiving, however... a brisk, well-told often amusing tale.... Fans of either author, or both, will have fun with this book."
                                                    —*Booklist*

Got questions? We've got answers at

BAEN'S BAR!

Here's what some of our members have to say:

"Ever wanted to get involved in a newsgroup but were frightened off by rude know-it-alls? Stop by Baen's Bar. Our know-it-alls are the friendly, helpful type—and some write the hottest SF around."
> **—Melody L** *melodyl@ccnmail.com*

"Baen's Bar . . . where you just might find people who understand what you are talking about!"
> **—Tom Perry** *perry@airswitch.net*

"Lots of gentle teasing and numerous puns, mixed with various recipes for food and fun."
> **—Ginger Tansey** *makautz@prodigy.net*

"Join the fun at Baen's Bar, where you can discuss the latest in books, Treecat Sign Language, ramifications of cloning, how military uniforms have changed, help an author do research, fuss about differences between American and European measurements—and top it off with being able to talk to the people who write and publish what you love."
> **—Sun Shadow** *sun2shadow@hotmail.com*

"Thanks for a lovely first year at the Bar, where the only thing that's been intoxicating is conversation."
> **—Al Jorgensen** *awjorgen@wolf.co.net*

 Join BAEN'S BAR at
WWW.BAEN.COM
"Bring your brain!"